Entangled

In Paradise Series

Book 1

LEILA LOVE

Published by Lovestruck Publishing
leilalovebooks.com

ISBN: 9781737743903 (paperback)
ISBN: 9781737743910 (digital)
First Edition: December 2021

Printed in the United States of America
Cover illustration by Jacqueline Bisset
Cover design by Najla Qamber Designs
Book design by Jennifer Stimson

CHAPTER ONE

Riley

Gazing across the Potomac River dividing and connecting two cities, she observed its steady current leading to and from something, depending on the perspective. At nearly half past 7:00 p.m., the sun's dissent on the Southwest waterfront of Washington, D.C., was nearly complete, revealing an evening canvas of pale pink, golden yellow, and soft orange filtering through voluminous white clouds against a light blue sky. From the hotel's floor to ceiling windows, Riley St. James watched reflections of cherry blossom trees dance along the river's edge, while small clusters of people absorbed the last bit of daylight, snapping photos, or just walking beneath the canopy of floral glory.

The somber rhythms of a jazz tune in the background soothed her somewhat frantic nerves. She took a deep inhale, letting the magic of the evening wash over her. When she released it, any remnants of doubt and insecurity evaporated, mostly, and she counted her blessings. Her mother and father were with her—and actually being cordial with one another—along with her extended family and closest friends, all present to celebrate her big day. This solitary moment, basking in the life she'd built for herself and culminating in this occasion, was pure perfection. Whoever said perfection was an illusion lied. She had expected it, orchestrated it, and was now living it.

She adjusted the waist of her dress and turned just as the jazz track transitioned to Coltrane's *Equinox*.

Jonathan S. Jasper, III, entered as if on cue.

Her eyes drank in her betrothed with both lust and love. His satin-textured black-on-black dinner jacket clung to perfectly formed arms and broad shoulders, while black slim fit, tailored pants contoured to his lean muscular thighs. But it was the collared black shirt that did it for Riley. Unrestrained by a tie, the top two open buttons exposed his deep bronze skin and distracted her with thoughts of spreading kisses across his neck. His designer shoes shined and he walked with an air of confidence, a swagger, that she never tired of watching—coming or going. His dark hair was neatly trimmed and his clean-shaven face was smooth to the touch. As he approached, she caught the scent of his cologne as it lingered in the air, subtle but definitely present.

He was a real-live, walking, talking, breathing one-percenter all around, down to his magnetic grey eyes—possessed only by one percent of the world's population. The youngest partner in his grandfather's law firm, just one of his family's many business enterprises, Riley's wayward mother had proclaimed him a catch. While her more cynical father predicted the relationship would be more like a catch and release scenario. Rarely did she side with her mother; but on this point, they agreed.

"Well, hello, gorgeous," he said, a dazzling white smile spreading across his face. "You look ready for your last night as Miss Riley St. James."

"Hi, yourself, handsome," she said through a school girl grin.

He slid one hand around her waist and pulled her closer. With his warm palm resting on her hip, he whispered in her ear, "I can't wait to make you my wife and this body legally mine."

A warmth rose in her and a soft moan escaped as she fought back the temptation to press her body further into his, enticing him, teasing him, daring him. But she let reason win.

Not wanting to ruin her make-up or sheer sleek white dress, she eased back, smiled, and let her eyes search his face. She had memorized the curve of his lips, the shape of his eyebrows, the texture of his facial hair, and the pool of grey that swirled in his eyes. And yet, something about him always seemed to elude her, like an unsolved mystery or closely guarded secret. It frightened and thrilled her.

He returned her smile as his hand firmly traced the spine of her back.

"Control yourself, Mr. Jasper," she whispered in his ear as his hand reached the nape of her neck. "The night is young and our guests will be arriving momentarily."

She slid herself gently from his embrace, and he made a show of adjusting his collar and jacket. When he was done, she placed her arm through his and they headed to the ballroom.

Riley and Jonathan stood at the entryway of the event space like urban royalty, personally greeting their guests as they arrived. They had chosen to ditch the standard rehearsal dinner format, opting instead to have a reunion of sorts with her sorority sisters and Jonathan's fraternity brothers, alongside their wedding party. When they had all started arriving with their plus one's, she knew they had nailed it.

The Rehearsal Soiree was a red-carpet affair, with everyone dressed in semi-formal attire parading down a candlelit hall where they greeted and were photographed with the guests of honor. It was a scene plucked straight out of the *Great Gatsby* movie, minus Leonardo DiCaprio. Their guests, dripping glamour and achievement, caused such a spectacle that complete strangers snapped random photos as they exited the stretch Hummers hired for the night.

Riley watched endearingly as Jonathan exchanged secret greetings with his fraternity brothers, masculinity oozing from his pores. And while she knew it was against the night-before-the-wedding rules—she couldn't help thinking that she just might demonstrate her appreciation tonight. That's something he'd never expect from his "Catholic good girl."

He had started referring to Riley as a good girl in college when he realized that matching wits to win the heart of a girl who was saving herself for marriage meant that he had to be all in or all out. True to form, he went all in.

Tonight, he had held Riley close, his hand rested on the small of her back with his thumb gently massaging the small dip at the base of her spine. The sensation of that slight touch pulsed through her body and kept her right at the edge of her sanity.

Surrounded by their families and closest college friends, it was a night she knew they would always remember.

And yet, surrounded by all that perfection, there was one small anomaly in the evening. A bothersome suspicion that assaulted Riley's wall of confidence.

One of her sorority sisters, Sierra Charles, had brought as her plus-one her college roommate, Issy Bisset. A perfect blend of French and Nigerian, Issy was a cool party girl at heart, and always down for whatever. Some of Jonathan's frat brothers came solo and there were a few other single ladies in attendance, but none of them could match the allure of Issy.

Riley had been hoping for a love match among their single guests during the weekend wedding celebration. But with Issy in play, it might be more like a quick hook-up.

When Issy appeared in the doorway with Sierra, Riley watched as heads turned and all eyes focused on her. Riley felt Jonathan's hand slip just slightly, but he recovered and she appeared unbothered. There had been rumors back in college that he and Issy had messed around, but he swore it was nothing and she chose to believe him. Mostly.

Sierra was always the wild card. She had your back in a bind, but she also had a talent for stirring up trouble. With so much history and more than a few rumors between their guests tonight, Sierra's simmering stew might prove toxic tonight.

Riley surveyed Issy in her fullness—a full and untamed jet-black thicket of soft, tight coils framing her perfectly dimpled face. She had the lashes, the perfectly arched eyebrows, flawless ginger skin, and shocking red lips. Riley willed herself to plaster on a smile before she leaned in and accepted Issy's embrace, welcoming her to the dinner.

"Everything looks perfect, Riley," she said. Riley thought there was just a little too much emphasis on the word *looks*, but she let it slide and graciously accepted the compliment.

Sierra was right behind Issy. She and Riley had known each other since they were freshmen. They had pledged their sorority together, and had made their share of mistakes together. Sierra had never been a fan of Riley's relationship with Jonathan, and Riley couldn't help wonder if her choice of a plus-one was an unsubtle warning.

Now standing face to face, Sierra knew Riley wasn't happy by her raised eyebrows and pinched smile. But it was too late for Sierra to do or say anything, so she opted instead to throw her arms around Riley and lavish her with compliments.

Freeing herself from Sierra's guilty grip, Riley watched from the corner of her eye as Issy embraced Jonathan, and he gave her the polite church hug.

Smart man.

As she walked away, Issy effortlessly slid her jacket off her shoulders, revealing a dramatic backless black sequined dress that hit her just below the knees and fit like a second layer of skin over wide-hips and an ample ass. Her strappy sparkling Louboutin sandals were at least five inches tall—five inches that transformed her 5'7 lean body into a weapon of mass destruction for any man in her path. Cardi B had called Louboutins "bloody shoes" — lyrics to a song that Riley would now always refer to as Issy's anthem.

Over the years, Issy's star had risen as a print model, and later as she began acting with a few minor roles on sitcoms, lots of commercials, and was now an influencer—whatever the hell that meant. If it paid the bills, Riley was happy for her. Any woman, but especially a black woman, calling her own shots and defining her own success got nothing but respect from Riley. Issy was no different.

Watching Issy own the red carpet, Riley was conflicted. Simultaneously she admired and was suspicious of the woman. Her instincts had kicked in and she had an uneasy feeling that Issy's presence meant trouble for some unsuspecting sucker tonight.

CHAPTER TWO

Gabriel

G abriel Laurent slowed his pace, wiping perspiration from his brow with the edge of his shirt.

Breathing heavy and his heart rate elevated, he had hoped he could outrun the difficult decision he would have to make tonight. Stretching his legs and arms, Gabriel faced the River Seine and watched its current—slow and deliberate, coming and going, connecting and dividing.

Everything in life was about choices. His was simple—well, not really. Should he return to his family business and take his place next to his father? Or should he accept the opportunity his company has groomed him for, proving they value his input and expertise?

Slowing his pace, he was happy to be home during his favorite time of year in Paris. The foliage alone was worth the price of the airfare. A splattering of white and Sakura cherry blossom trees blended with magnolias and plum blossoms at the river's edge and stretching along the length of the street. Each fragrance was distinct, but not overwhelming—each blossom unique and fleeting.

Wanting to lower his heart rate before walking back to his flat, he took a seat on the grass beneath a white cherry blossom tree not fully bloomed. But it provided just enough cover to meet his needs, and it was his favorite. Most people lingered near the trees with the most vibrant pinks or the fullest blossoms. But he preferred the soft white petals of the cherry blossom trees and their distinct branches cascading and nearly skimming the earth. It was a beauty that didn't scream out for attention in its perfection.

Settling in to think through his options, his solitude was interrupted when his sister called.

"Are you busy?" Juliette asked.

Swatting away a swarm of miniature insects, his quiet time was proving anything but.

"I'm never too busy for you, ma chère soeur," he said. "I just finished up an early evening run. How are you? Everything alright?"

"I just wanted to make sure you were still coming for dinner tonight," she said. "I know Papa has been pressuring you, but I really want to see you before you go back to New York."

Always a very clever girl, she was now an even more astute young woman, and despite his best efforts, he could never hide the tension with their father from her. He just hoped she didn't feel too affected by it.

"I'll be there," he chuckled. "And don't you worry about Papa. I can handle him."

"Oui. I know you can," she said, and then paused.

The pause worried him. The tension was spilling over and he hated it.

"It's just…" Juliette's voice softened and trailed off.

"Just what?"

"I don't know," she continued, her voice laced with concern. "He's been in a bad mood and I know it's because he wants you to come back to the family business. But you know his bad moods lead to bad decisions."

"You shouldn't worry, Juliette." He wanted to console her, but knew there was conflict and a reason to worry. He just didn't want her to do the worrying.

"Papa and I want the same things. We just disagree on the details. I want to make changes and he wants to keep everything just as it is.

Maybe we can come to a compromise tonight. At least I hope we can."

"Really, Gabriel? You want to come back to the company?"

He heard the anticipation rise in her voice and felt guilty. Wanting the same thing wasn't enough. There was a gulf of distance between them as wide as the river in front of him about how the company should be managed. His father wouldn't let go of the reins and Gabriel wouldn't settle for being a figure head just because it was his birthright.

"Yes, Juliette. I do. But on my own terms."

She sighed heavily into the phone.

"It's going to be a long night," she said.

Gabriel knew she was being serious, but he wanted to lighten the mood.

"You're right! Because after dessert, you and I are going to escape into your living quarters and you get to pick the movie. But I'm choosing the snacks."

"I'm going to hold you to it." He sensed her smiling through her quick agreement.

"I have no doubt that you will."

When they ended the call, Gabriel stood, his moment broken by Juliette's call and more people flooding the walk ways taking in the cool temperatures and the fleeting floral scenery.

Just as he started walking, his phone vibrated again. He didn't recognize the number, but answered anyway.

"Bonjour!" The voice on the other end was a little too eager, yet very familiar.

"Cecily?"

"Oui, Monsieur! How are you?"

"I'm fine. But how'd you get my number? And why are you calling out of the blue?"

Cecily Leroux was beautiful, a trendsetter, an heiress to her family's fortune, and his college ex-girlfriend. She was a lot of things, subtle was not one of them.

The wind picked up and clouds had started to move in. Rain wasn't in the forecast when last he checked, but the threat was obvious. So, Gabriel picked up his pace.

"Aren't you happy to hear from me? Your parents certainly thought you might welcome a call from your first love," she said, playing coy.

Gabriel hadn't spoken to Cecily in years. He was mostly based in the U.S. and Cecily was running the world of Paris high society. The last he heard she was playing a major role in le Bal des Débutantes. She had participated as a high school senior and always described it as the time of her life.

It was also how Gabriel met her.

He had been tapped to be a cavalier—the young men who escorted the debutantes—thanks to his mother. He was paired with Cecily because of their mutual family connections. Young, immature and boyish Gabriel liked her instantly. She was funny, smart, personable and without doubt, the most beautiful girl at le Bal. Everything in her life came easy, and he never saw her behave as anything other than a girl who knew the world would rise up to meet her and he was just along for the ride.

It was never lost on Gabriel that his mother tried to steer him away from Cecily, while his father approved of her in every way. But most assuredly, her greatest asset to his father was her family's business. For his mother, that was her greatest disqualifier.

Among her family's holdings was an outrageously profitable and upscale hotel enterprise. His father admired and coveted their properties—mostly because they weren't really in direct competition to our family's own significant portfolio. In all things, the business was first with his father.

When Gabriel and Cecily landed at the same college, they became an instant "it-couple" on campus. Their relationship had been completely orchestrated by Cecily—something he realized in hindsight. After college, he eventually found a permanent out—accepting a job with an American company. He knew Cecily would never leave Paris and she moved on quickly with a parade of celebrity suitors at her disposal.

He'd seen her in magazines and tabloids over the years, as beautiful and unburdened by real life as ever.

Her appearance now was definitely suspicious, but more inconvenient. He had a lot to sort through and didn't have the time or space to indulge whatever this was.

Gabriel changed his approach to speed this along.

"It's always nice to hear from an old friend, Cecily. What do I owe for this spontaneous call?"

She giggled. But her tone was uneven. Almost forced.

"Can't a girl reconnect with her old flame? I heard you were in town and wanted to catch up. Maybe grab a cocktail or a coffee. Maybe dinner and be each other's desserts."

Gabriel shook his head and smiled despite his irritation.

"Same old Cecily, I see. Why are you really calling?"

The sounds of the city had picked up as restaurants were opening for dinner and sidewalk cafe tables were emptying of their couples and groups of friends taking refuge indoors from the unpredictable weather. And Cecily was stalling.

"Hello," he said. "Are you still there."

"Why must you always question my motives? I called simply because I want to see you. I hear through the family grapevines that you may soon return to Paris to work with your father. If that's true, maybe there's a chance for us to reconnect."

Gabriel couldn't tell if she was being serious, or if she wanted something else. But what? She had everything she could ever want—including her pick of men. Why him? And why now?

"Ah, I see. You've spoken to my father." Gabriel navigated throngs of people on the slim sidewalks, stomach growling as he inhaled the sweet scent wafting from the small crepes cart that was always a block from his flat. He wanted this call over before he made it home.

"Talk of my return is premature, so sorry to disappoint. And if I do return, I'll be too busy to connect or reconnect with anyone."

Cecily interrupted him. "Don't be so quick to dismiss me. It's just a drink between old friends. How about tomorrow?"

Small droplets of rain now dotted the concrete and Gabriel picked up his pace. He wasn't against having a drink with Cecily, but he didn't know if he'd still be in Paris tomorrow.

"Maybe," he said, not wanting to seem too harsh. "My travel plans aren't finalized yet. But if I'm still here, we'll have a cocktail."

"Magnifique! I'll call you tomorrow! Enjoy dinner with your family."

The line disconnected.

He slipped the phone in his pocket and opened the door to his building. Sliding the key in his flat's door, Cecily's last words lingered.

How did she know he was having dinner with his family?

CHAPTER THREE

Riley

R iley couldn't wait to slide her exhausted body into a hot lavender bubble bath. Months of planning and she was less than 24 hours away from becoming Mrs. Jonathan J. Jasper, III, Esq. Yes, it was a mouthful. And no, Riley S. Jasper didn't have quite the same appeal as Riley St. James, but she was in love and that conquered all.

It had taken Riley months of debating with Jonathan about taking his last name. He took it personally that there even had to be a discussion, but she had spent years establishing her name in her field—a career she had worked damn hard to secure—as Riley St. James, Emmy award-winning broadcast journalist. So, they agreed that on paper she would become Riley S. Jasper, but in her professional life, she would remain Riley St. James.

This decision had made Riley's derelict mother ecstatic, who in turn offered just one piece of marital advice: *"A successful marriage is built on compromise. Learn to compromise, and your marriage can weather any storm."*

Now this was ironic coming from the woman who had abandoned Riley when she was still a child, and her marriage, to pursue a career as a European parfumeur. Early in her life, Roselyn Au Clair St. James had dreamed of reclaiming her family's legacy, a dream that had been deferred by pregnancy and then marriage. But dreams die hard, and claiming that motherhood and wifely chores were suffocating her, she packed her bags and set off for distant shores. She had opted out of the compromise solution when it came to her own marriage—even when her earnest and faithful husband offered to follow her. And like the fragrances she created, she was also beautiful, intoxicating, and fleeting. She could still enchant Riley, but she also eventually faded until you barely recalled her presence.

Yet, despite Roselyn's shortcomings, Riley agreed that compromise in a relationship was good advice and she swallowed it like the heavy thickness of castor oil her mother forced on her at the first sign of a sniffle or sneeze. The fact that her mom had been making an effort when it mattered most had softened Riley towards her, but not enough to vanquish the wish of her inner child that would forever wonder why her mother hadn't found a way to compromise with her father.

Which leads to another piece of sage advice from her mother: *Be willing to sacrifice for the desires of your heart.*

So, somewhere between her mother's wanderlust and wisdom, Riley found a man and a career she loved—both with heavy doses of compromise and sacrifice.

Before her leisurely soak in the tub, Riley went through her to-do list for the wedding day. She had tried to keep it short, but as the day wore on, she kept adding items. She had promised Jonathan no to-do lists on their honeymoon and to just go with the flow.

That was the plan, but rarely did anything really go as planned.

Piling her hair into a high bun, she surveyed her skin and her body. She wasn't perfect—because who is? But she looked damn good. She was born with some of it, and the rest of it she fought for every day. From workouts with a personal trainer, to following a strict Mediterranean diet, monthly facials and a twice daily skin regimen that rivaled whipping up a soufflé—she had fully committed to self-care and self-preservation. She was approaching her mid-thirties, but found small pleasure in those moments when she still got carded at the bar on her best nights.

She took a few seconds more to brush her skin all over, while the scent of lavender oil in the warm water relaxed her. She sang along softly to Sade's sultry voice filling the room from her mini-Bluetooth speaker and lit a cluster of candles on the counter for maxed out relaxation.

When she left the rehearsal dinner less than an hour ago, Jonathan and his frat brothers were drinking from the most expensive bottle of whiskey she had ever seen, Macallan Imperiale "M"—a bachelor's gift from his father. Some of the single ladies also remained, taking advantage of the view of the city for their selfies and IG posts. Saying her good nights to Jonathan, Riley noticed across the room that Issy was still there, but she had been on her best behavior all night so Riley gave her a pass. She had even eased into a comfortable conversation with her at one point after the dessert course was served.

Issy's family was also from New Orleans, and they commiserated over which was the better dessert of the night—the beignets or the bananas foster. While both were exquisitely delicious, they had agreed that you needed to be in New Orleans to experience the best of both. The desserts were as much about the place as they were the ingredients. Riley was a firm believer in food and music being the great equalizers.

She slid a little further into the warm water and let it envelop her body up to her chin. Mother Nature had been kind and paid her a visit a week before, so there was nothing preventing around-the-clock sex on their honeymoon. She relished the thoughts of what was to come, massaging her shoulders and arms and letting her hands slide gently over her body. Closing her eyes, she replayed Jonathan's pre-dinner kiss and tried not to get worked up.

But it was too late.

Tonight, her heart and her body had felt all the feels, and now she wanted and needed more.

Hopping out the tub, she quickly toweled off, lathered her body in honey cream and added a translucent layer of honey dust on her breast and neck. She quickly slid into a red lace bra and thong set, wrapped herself in her Burberry overcoat, stepped into the silver stilettos she'd worn at the dinner, and headed out the door.

On the elevator ride down, Riley's heart raced and she forced her hands inside her jacket pockets as her mind cycled through a host of excuses for where she was going dressed in Louboutins and an overcoat if she had a chance encounter with any of her wedding guests. Or God forbid, her parents. Her mother would instantly know and her father would pretend not to know what she was up to. It was the night before their wedding and Riley had demanded they obey tradition and not see each other. Now, the good Catholic girl would renegotiate her demands.

Her emotions were on one hundred, her body was on fire and she wanted him. She couldn't wait.

She wouldn't wait.

As the elevator doors opened, she heard the faint sound of a woman's laughter. Stepping out of the elevator, she turned her head towards the laughter and froze. Her breath was strangled with confusion as the voices registered.

She'd recognize the dress anywhere.

Issy.

And she was with Jonathan.

Her body was gripped with paralysis and her words caught in her throat. Before she could call out to him, Jonathan shhh'd Issy and laughed as they practically fell into his room.

The next sound she heard was an echo of the door snapping shut.

CHAPTER FOUR

Gabriel

Gabriel's family home was equal parts new world comforts and old-world charm and elegance. The high ceilings and windows were standard, along with elaborately carved moldings in every room, marble fireplaces throughout, warm herringbone oak floors covered with some classic and some contemporary floor coverings. But his favorite feature were the rooms in the back of estate with their wrought iron balconies looking out over the property. Whenever he invited his American friends to visit, they always remarked that it was just like in the movies.

Gabriel knew that it was, but it also wasn't. And that was because of his mother—Lady Simone G. Laurent. She had married a Viscount and assumed the title of Viscountess, but she was titled—and wealthier—before marriage, and could trace her family's lineage back centuries before his father's family. From her example, Gabriel understood how to value a woman, and his sister understood how to navigate her world of privilege with grace and intellect. And their mother ensured they had paths that led from the family's legacy if they so chose. She wanted them to guide their lives, which was not the case for her.

He had arrived just in time to join his mother and sister in the sitting room near the fireplace.

Gabriel leaned in to greet his mother, pecking both cheeks, "Bonjour mère." He took a seat next to Juliette on the sofa and the three of them nibbled on a spread of exotic cheeses, dried fruits, thinly sliced meats and crackers. One bottle of white wine was open and still half full.

Gabriel relaxed as they eased into conversation. His sister's presence was a gift, since she would typically be at school. But she had an internship in the city for the semester. She had so many stories to tell about her colleagues and the other interns, and they listened intently until dinner.

Gabriel's father joined them just as dinner service began, having just finished a conference call. It was after 7:00 p.m. and Gabriel settled in for what was likely to be three hours or more. A five-course meal, conversation, and a selection of wines would keep them engaged for hours. But he knew it wouldn't be quite so casual. His father, despite his mother's objections, wanted to talk business and was expecting an answer from Gabriel.

The evening moved along without incident, until his father found his opening before dessert service.

"You've had days to consider my proposal, son," his father started after a long sip of his deep red wine. Lord John Louis Laurent commanded attention in every setting, but Gabriel had long been unaffected by his father's posturing.

"I have," Gabriel acknowledged.

"Well, before you continue, I would like to sweeten the deal."

Gabriel lowered his own glass and leaned in. But before he could speak, his mother stood.

"I'm not staying for this," Simone said, sliding her chair away from the table and turning to Juliette. "Come with me, Juliette. Leave your father and Gabriel to talk."

"But, why do I have to leave?" She turned to Gabriel.

"Gabriel, tell her I can stay. Please."

Gabriel was torn. He wanted his sister to stay. But he knew whatever his father was preparing to say next wasn't good based on his mother's behavior.

Heat rising from his neck to his face, he forced a tight smile.

"Aller avec maman," he said to Juliette. "I'll join you when I'm done here for our movie. And I'll bring your dessert with the snacks."

Her eyes pleaded with him, but he didn't budge.

Finally, she stood and joined their mother. Together they exited the room, Juliette glancing over her shoulder before disappearing around the corner.

Gabriel joined his father at the opposite in of the table, standing near and hovering over him. He knew it was a ridiculous show of power, but he was at a loss.

"What is this offer that would make my mother excuse herself early from our meal?"

His father never looked up. He sipped his wine, and then he heard three faint voices in the hall. All women.

He hurried towards the voices and before he could leave the room, Cecily appeared and nearly tumbled into him.

"Cecily?" Confusion strangled him.

"Bonjour!" She wrapped her arms around him and squeezed, her perfume drowning out all the savory scents of dinner. "Are you surprised to see me? I really wanted to surprise you!"

Gabriel stiffened and negotiated his body out of Cecily's grip as anger raised, hot and sour from his gut. His father's plan was crystal clear.

Cecily traipsed over to the dinner table and his father stood to accept her greeting. She kissed both his cheeks and took Juliette's seat. "Did I miss dessert? Oh, please tell me there's more dessert."

Gabriel's eyes darted from Cecily to his father, not sure where to direct his anger.

"One of you better tell me what the hell is going on or I'm out of here."

"Son, please come join us at the table and you'll see, it's quite genius." His father's arm was outstretched, but this was no olive branch.

Gabriel took a deep inhale and decided to play along, walking back to the table. Now seated across from Cecily, he noticed that her deep brown eyes showed pinker than her usual bright white, and her hand shook just slightly as she poured herself a glass of wine in Juliette's unused stemware.

She didn't want to be here.

Gabriel turned to his father. "You have five minutes. What's your pitch?"

A grin spread across his father's face and he spoke with an arrogant assurance that always irritated Gabriel. "We're merging with the Leroux family of hotels."

"Great. But why is Cecily here?"

This time Cecily spoke.

"You see, love, my father has given me an ultimatum. Marry or else I'm cut off. Banished from the family fortune. Erased from our legacy. Distraught and…"

Gabriel interrupted Cecily's overly dramatic explanation. "Just so that I'm sure that I'm hearing this correctly, we are to be married so that our families can merge their companies."

"Yes." Cecily's tone had dropped so low Gabriel could barely hear her. She took a gulp of her wine.

"So, what do you think, son? You and Cecily back together. We merge to form the most prestigious portfolio of European hotels with you at the helm. Nothing but winners from my vantage point. You can run the company your way. Cecily gets a husband and keeps her family's fortune. And I can retire."

His father triumphantly leaned back in his chair and signaled to the serving staff to bring in the champagne.

Minutes passed by like hours as the servers popped the cork and added glistening champagne flutes to the table.

Gabriel had made his decision.

With all the glasses filled, bubbles rising to the edge of the glass, his father began making a toast to the merger. Gabriel didn't sip from his glass and Cecily swallowed her champagne in one gulp.

"May I add to your toast, Papa?" Gabriel said to his grinning father.

"By all means." He raised his glass as Cecily rushed to pour more champagne.

Gabriel didn't wait for Cecily to join. "To my father's vision for his company. May it rest in peace."

His father's eyes furrowed and Cecily nearly dropped her champagne flute. But Gabriel didn't stop there.

"And to me, for my return to the states tomorrow morning to take my place as the Senior Vice President of Hotel Development at the Élite Hotel Group."

Gabriel gulped his champagne and walked away, leaving his father and Cecily to fight it out.

CHAPTER FIVE

Riley

Riley stood, frozen in place, letting the scene sink in.

Part of her thought it was her imagination. That feeling was fleeting.

Right now, on the other side of that door, her fiancé was with Issy. Laughing and intoxicated. The night before their wedding. With the knowledge that she was just one floor above him not enough for him to show a modicum of discretion.

Nothing was ever enough for Jonathan Jasper, III, Esq.

Her face flushed with anger and the tears welling in her eyes threatened to spill down her cheeks. But she willed them back, choosing calm and cool calculation.

She pressed rewind in her mind and replayed the moment.

Jonathan's left arm around Issy's waist and his hand splayed on her hip. The same hand that she would accept in holy matrimony tomorrow. The same hand that would hold the weight of her hand tomorrow, sliding a ridiculously extravagant wedding band on her finger—a symbol of unending love and devotion. The same hand with fingers that just hours before were weaved and interlocked with hers. The same hand that lay comfortably, effortlessly, on the small of her back teasing her as they said their good nights after their Rehearsal Dinner and Soiree.

With one deep breath, she closed her eyes and stepped backward in retreat, letting the wall catch her. As the reality of what was happening settled in, her heart beat erratic as panic rushed through her. It was like witnessing her own death and she was unable to save herself.

Gravity pulled her head down, eyes landing on the ridiculous sparkling silver shoes. After all this time, she was instantly pushed back into feeling like a foolish girl for trusting and believing that he would love her and only her.

That he would keep his promises to her.

That he would choose her. Only her.

For every moment that she fought her insecurities and questioned her worth in his life, she had lost little pieces of herself. Relinquishing her independence. Scripting her existence in his world, desperate to feel good enough in his family and life of privilege. Pieces that would magically be put back together after they were married. After she had the proof of his love and devotion.

At least that's what she told herself.

Now, all the anxiety she felt leading up to this wedding weekend—and even a couple hours ago before their rehearsal dinner—made perfect sense. It had been a living, breathing part of her that she stubbornly ignored and kept hidden from the world. But over the years, it had grown stronger, giving her all the power now she needed to throw in the towel. To stop surrendering her full life to his square peg world.

Riley let the tears cascade down her face and onto the front of her overcoat. Too weak to walk and too hurt to care, she slowly slid down the wall and rested her weary body on the carpeted floor.

A mix of muffled voices, music, and televisions passed through walls and doors, mingling up and down the hallway. The only other sounds were her strangled breaths and the ice maker dropping periodic batches of cubes.

It was all very mundane on a night that was intended to be anything but.

Eyes locked on Jonathan's suite door, she wondered what she had done wrong.

Or, maybe the question she should be asking herself was what had

Issy done right.

She cycled through her own credentials.

She was successful. And not just a little successful. But like calling the shots successful, all built on her own intellect and drive—no reliance on a family name or an endowment or some other deceptive advantage. In all the ways that counted, she was actually more successful than him.

Him.

Everything always was about him.

Him, who had never known a day of truly wanting and working for something beyond his reach.

Him, who always had more than enough of anything and everything.

Him, who when someone told him no, he pushed and demanded until he got to yes. Of course, being told no had only happened once. And it was with Riley. She had the audacity to tell him no in college and he became obsessed with getting her to finally say yes.

And afterwards, she became just another thing to him, another conquest. It hadn't taken much to convince her, showing her the possibility of a life she only ever imagined happened in movies. And once she said yes to him, she had spent the entirety of their relationship in a perpetual state of yes.

Marry me—*yes.*

Change your name—*yes.*

Sell your condo—*yes.*

Dress sexier—*yes.*

Promise me forever—*yes.*

Each *yes* was a slice through her heart. The *yes* list could go on and fill the length of the hotel hallway. With each *yes* she willingly gave Jonathan, a little piece of herself was ripped away. Now, the wounds of every *yes* were exposed—too many to halt the bleeding.

Riley looked around and remembered where she was and why she was there, on the floor in an overcoat, Louboutins and lingerie—really just a costumed version of the modest college girl who fell for a boy's charms and had finally hit the hard ground of reality. Knees scraped—a girl still groveling for acceptance. Bruised ego—a woman who thought if she honored his every wish and looked the part, he'd fulfill her. Broken hearted—giving it away before she even knew what it needed.

She swiped the back of her hand across her face, erasing the salty tears that only agitated her wounds, and wondered why any reasonable person would want to *fall* in love. In no other circumstance would anyone willingly just *fall*. But we parade around, write books and songs, compose poetry and even chase the experience of falling in love. Fools. Every one of us, she thought.

In a matter of seconds—a flash of forbidden flesh dangled in front of him—and she'd gone from sexy to stupid. From being the prize to being a casualty of infidelity.

Wallowing in the grief of being deceived and disrespected in one careless act, Then, her grandmother's words gut-punched her— *remember who you are and whose you are.* Riley pushed her fists into the floor and forced herself up. Still undecided on her next move, but she couldn't just sit sobbing on the floor feeling sorry for herself. St. James women fell down, but they always rise like Maya, dance like Josephine and like Rosa, they only sit when it suits them. More of her grandmother's wisdom.

So, she took Granny Mae's advice and applied it to her boss chick life when faced with a dilemma: she weighed her options.

Bang on the door and let him scramble to try and hide Issy. *Nah, requires my energy to prove she's there. Next.*

Or, bang on the door and risk him simply not answering. *Too much opportunity to add insult to injury. Next.*

Or, stay in the hall and confront them both when Issy leaves. *Too passive. Next.*

Or, just walk away, pack my bags and leave without an explanation. *Dramatic, but still passive.*

All were viable options, some with just enough drama for good measure.

But none felt quite right. Because she knew Jonathan.

He was an attorney and argued his way out of any and every thing for sport. He would find an excuse and she would want to believe him so that she could wear her custom Nneka C. Alexander wedding gown, show off her custom wedding band alongside her gorgeous manicure from the Nail Picasso, save face, avoid emotional confrontation, and pretend as if none of this happened.

Doubt quickly morphed into all out anger. Her pulse raced as she got busy pulling her hair up into a messy bun and tightening the jacket's belt around her waist. A reservoir of unexpressed anger shot up her spine with each intentional footstep towards Jonathan's suite door.

As each step brought her closer to confrontation, she passed an opening along the hallway and barely glanced at it. Then something bright red caught her eye. She paused and took a few steps backwards.

And there it was…

A fire alarm encased in glass. A gift, really. All that was missing was a satin bow.

Before her better angels kicked in, she slid off one shoe and smacked the glass with her red-bottomed heel. Shards of glass fell to the floor, leaving a large enough opening for her to stick two fingers inside.

She yanked the lever.

The bells screamed and overhead lights flashed a bright, pulsing light.

Within seconds, guests were opening doors and stumbling out into the hallway.

Riley hid, tucked away and patiently waiting.

Ten…twenty…thirty seconds of watching confused and weary strangers walk by until finally Jonathan's suite door opened.

Stealing a peep around the edge of the nook, fire rose in her veins at the sight of Issy's tousled hair, smudged makeup and her sloppily worn dress slipping off her shoulders. A dress she had begrudgingly admired when Issy arrived as the plus one of her sorority sister, Sierra the shit-starter. Issy's presence had felt like an omen, but Riley ignored it and choosing instead to welcome her.

Jonathan had on the same pants and shoes he wore at their rehearsal dinner and a long-sleeved Under Armor shirt—Riley's favorite.

Asshole!

She popped her head back and waited. Watching the floor, she saw Issy's feet first—in the monogrammed slippers that were part of the honeymoon travel gifts she'd given Jonathan. Riley had a matching pair.

This seemingly innocuous pair of slippers covering Issy's feet drove Riley over the cliff of reason, and she timed her confrontation perfectly.

She stepped out in front of Issy, blocking her path and triggering a human train wreck. Riley's sudden movement caused Jonathan to bump into Issy, who blew out an exasperated breath.

"Watch where you're going!" Issy yelped, without even really looking at Riley.

Taking advantage of her nasty attitude, Riley reached her hand back as far as the socket would allow to get the momentum she needed to slap Issy's slutty ass across her dimpled cheek.

Issy's hand flew up to cradle her face and in an instant, Riley's face registered. Her eyes widened in recognition and her shoulders slumped, a physical confession of her misdeeds.

Jonathan, oblivious and irritated at being blocked from exiting, stepped around Issy and finally realized what was happening.

The three of them stood in silence for a few seconds, a mixed bag of anger, guilt, and desperation. Riley's palm tingled with little needle pricks reminding her she was alive. Her cheeks flushed crimson while her eyes, glassy and pleading, searched Jonathan's faithless grey eyes hoping for a sign of remorse or shame. But all she found was a cold emptiness, and she was gutted. She swallowed back her pain and it caught in her throat, poisoning her. Leveling her. She watched in revulsion as his eyes darted around for an excuse, a lie, or an angle. In this moment, it registered for Riley. He wasn't a man in love; he was an attorney about to argue his case. A cocky attorney who had never lost in trial. But he had never been the defendant on trial. Not until this moment.

His fortunes were reversed. He was about to take the biggest "L" of his life.

A decade of uncried tears streamed down Riley's face. Her chest heaved in and out and her fists clinched so tightly that her nails dug into the flesh of her palms.

"Riley," he finally said, landing on his defense. "What are you doing down here?"

The excuses and scenarios were percolating, brewing an explanation for why he was leaving his hotel suite with Issy.

"Isn't the better question *what are you doing here with her?*"

Issy had slowly slid to the other side of the hall, too afraid to try to walk away, but also staying far enough away from Riley to avoid another slap. The runway model turned low-level actress turned influencer— whatever the hell that meant—cowered against the wall.

But Jonathan stood his ground. "I can explain…"

"Don't bother. I've seen all that I need to see. I watched the two of you fall into your room. And I can only imagine what you fell into once you were inside."

"It's not like that, Riley," Issy managed to whisper, still careful to keep her distance.

Riley snapped her head towards Issy. "I'm not talking to you. Tomorrow isn't your wedding day and he isn't your fiancé."

Issy shifted a shameful gaze towards the wall.

"And your wedding day hasn't just been ruined by a cheap hook-up."

Riley knew it was a low blow, but Issy had chosen to be cheapened by a man who had never shown her any serious interest. There had been rumors in college about them, but Jonathan denied them, Issy wouldn't acknowledge them, and Riley chose to ignore them. It was crudely predictable.

Turning back towards Jonathan, Riley saw something new in him. Something she'd never seen. Panic.

Small beads of sweat had formed across his upper lip. Through labored breaths, his brows furrowed in frustration and his chest stretched out and in, straining against his shirt. His hand trembled as he reached out to her.

"Let's just go upstairs and talk about this, Babe."

Riley smacked his outstretched arm away.

"You mean upstairs to the suite where we were supposed to spend our wedding night? I don't think so."

"Riley, you're over-reacting," he said, taking one step closer to her. "Please, let's just go talk about this."

Now a couple feet closer, she could see up close his red lipstick-stained lips, beads of perspiration forming at his hairline, and a thick vein pulsating in his neck. For the first time since she'd known him, he looked unattractive.

"How could you?" No longer able to stifle her disgust, her voice raised an octave. "You made me promises. It's the night before our wedding. Nothing is ever enough for you!"

The question was genuine, but she didn't really want to hear his answer.

Tears began to well in his eyes as the magnitude of the situation was settling in as he wiped the back of his hand across the sweat on his forehead. And as she watched him, the anguish in his misty grey eyes, she wondered if the tears were for her or for the embarrassment of losing her on the eve of their wedding...for an old college fling.

And then, an unexpected realization struck her. She forced her head up and shoulders back, smoothed her jacket and exhaled. She was free of him. It was a freedom she never even knew she wanted—a freedom that scared her a little. Like an animal born caged and suddenly released into the wild.

Riley looked over at Issy and smirked. Issy bowed her head.

"Don't you dare," Riley said to her. "Don't bow your head in shame. Own your part in this."

She rolled her eyes at Riley, but kept her head up.

"My grandmother always said, 'If you can't be decent, at least have some dignity.'"

She looked back at Jonathan. All her tears had dried up and she was testing the waters of freedom.

"Here's what's going to happen, Mr. Jonathan J. Jasper. I'm going to MY suite to email our guests and tell them the wedding's off, but they're welcome to come to the reception and enjoy dinner and dancing—my treat. I'll inform my family and you can do whatever you like with yours. Then, I'll be taking that private jet to NYC tomorrow morning and flying solo to Bora Bora tomorrow afternoon. You are not to call me, text me, email me, message me, FaceTime me, tweet at me or drop in my DMs."

She paused, wanting to make her final words to him memorable.

"Riley, please…" His voice cracked and his shoulders curved from the weight of his indiscretion.

"Stay. Away. From. Me."

Jonathan dropped to his knees, burying his face in his hands.

"Please, Riley. Don't do this." His begging was too little too late.

She looked at him, and then over at Issy again. She knew she was letting her off too easy, but Issy hadn't made Riley any promises. It was a shitty thing to do to someone on the eve of their wedding, but it wasn't her fault. If nothing else, Issy was always the same. And Riley wanted her anger and the consequences to be directed at the right party: Jonathan.

But, just to be petty, she walked over to Issy and the woman flinched. Riley laughed and said, "You're not worth it. But those custom slippers on your feet, they are. Give them to me now!"

Issy awkwardly slid her feet out of the slippers and handed them over.

Riley snatched the slippers and gripped them to her chest like a shield. They were the only thing protecting her heart—broken, battered, and humiliated. A single droplet of perspiration slid down her spine as anxiety began to replace pain. Her breaths came quicker and her heart beat pulsed at double the normal rate in her ears. She knew she needed to get away from them, refusing to give him or her the pleasure of witnessing her anguish.

She turned her back on them both and as she walked towards the elevator, she used her trembling hand to slip that four-carat diamond off her finger and flung it over her shoulder.

When she reached the elevator, she looked back and Jonathan was still cowering on the floor, while Issy stood silent and barefoot clasping her jacket like a baby's blanket.

They had both succumbed to their worse instincts. The price they would pay was steep.

When the elevator pinged and the doors opened, Riley couldn't resist one final insult.

She stepped inside and poked her head out.

"Hey, Issy. He gave you what I'm sure was great sex—he's good at that. But I bet he won't give you that ring."

Satisfied, she stepped back and watched as the doors closed on that chapter of her life.

"Nowhere to go but up," she muttered into the empty space.

Riley returned to her suite a mixed bag of emotions. She was two parts angry and one part embarrassed with a healthy dose of disappointment, disillusion, and confusion. There was a small sprinkling of hope, but not enough to overpower the despair.

Logically, she thought it was good that she found out now—before she took those vows promising to love and honor a cheater until death do us part.

But, fuck that! Fuck logic!

There was nothing logical about what Jonathan had done, what he had risked—for a piece of ass. On the night before their wedding.

She let that sink in and told logic to go to hell and ring the doorbell.

Emotionally, she was a wreck, but she was never one to wallow in pain nor was she self-defeatist. And she certainly never played victim to someone else's failings.

So, she threw logic out on its ass and let emotion stay for the night. But not the sad, sappy, wallowing in self-pity kind of emotion. No, she chose the flipside of that coin and welcomed in angry, get-back, revenge emotion.

She grabbed her phone, opened her music streaming app, popped in her Air Pods and went straight to Beyonce's *Lemonade* album. Queen Bey had survived Jay's bullshit and gifted the world with a musical cocktail of endurance, affection, and fury. It was the appropriate soundtrack as Riley squeezed the sour out of her lemons—the first and main ingredient if she was ever going to manifest the tall, ice-cold glass of lemonade.

With *Hold Up* pulsating through her ears, she dismantled all that she had built around Jonathan. She ripped the pages out of her beloved wedding planning bible. She looped the custom, over-priced wedding bands through the ribbon on her wedding gift to Jonathan—a Cartier time piece with a message etched on its back: *Timeless.* When she purchased it, timeless was how she imagined their love would be. But the sentiment was still appropriate on the opposite side of that feeling.

Betrayal was also timeless.

Exhausted and sprawled out on the sofa, she felt a wave of disgust mounting inside at the sheer price tag of the three items. Between the wedding bands and the watch, someone could purchase a single-family home in many states across the country. It was a flagrant use of their money and a sad commentary of their relationship's reliance on status built on a concept of acquiring things.

Jonathan grew up in privilege, so it was his natural existence. But she had learned this behavior and was disgusted at her choices.

She forced those thoughts back and took charge of cancelling the disgrace that redefined her relationship with Jonathan.

She emailed all of her guests telling them the wedding was cancelled and inviting them to still enjoy dinner and dancing—minus the guests of honor and any wedding rituals. She visited her parents, told them the whole sordid story and asked them to play hosts to any guests who actually showed up tomorrow. In her mother's room, her custom, one-of-a-kind wedding gown hung limp on the closet door, and tears pricked her eyes. She wanted to burn it but instead instructed her mother to return it to the bridal boutique to be gifted to a bride of their choosing.

Her father, Sterling P. St. James, wore his anger on his sleeve and she begged him not to inflict any physical harm on Jonathan, before turning to her mother and convincing her not to confront him with one of her infamous tongue lashings.

Having barely kept her parents calm and completely exhausted from their energy, she opted to text her maid of honor and bridesmaids, relieving them of their duties and also inviting them to join her parents and family for dinner and dancing—minus a bride and groom. She had to promise them she would explain it all later, but just couldn't bear to face them.

She had been the envy of her friends, and now they would pity her. She was angry and embarrassed, sure. But far worse than either of those two emotions she felt—for the first time in her life—like an aimless fraud. Staring up at the ceiling, she faced her truth. She didn't want to see her friends because the mask she had begun wearing the minute she tied her life to Jonathan was now shattered, exposing the woman she needed to get reacquainted with on her own. She couldn't risk absorbing other people's emotions while hers were so raw. She had to process and reflect—undiluted and unfiltered.

Beneath her thigh, her cell phone reminded her that she was in the eye of a storm. In quick succession, a flurry of questions flooded her text messages—each one vibrating her phone like mini earthquake aftershocks.

She ignored them.

What she didn't bother with was reaching out to anyone in Jonathan's family. She gave him the choice of weaving a tale that involved her leaving him at the altar or being honest about what he had done.

She saved the call to her coordinator for last. She spared her the details, but told her to continue on with the reception as planned and to connect with her parents for any final adjustments.

Once she had cancelled her wedding, she rearranged the honeymoon plans, washed her flat-ironed hair and left it wet with her natural curls, got dressed, packed and ordered a car to Reagan National Airport with a 5:00 a.m. pick up. She wanted to be out of the hotel before the news settled over their wedding guests and eventually the public. A photographer from Washingtonian Weddings Magazine was scheduled to arrive at 8:00 a.m. and Riley the journalist knew she would report the lack of a bride back to the editor. Speculation alone would fuel the social media engine for the day.

She knew this because it's exactly what she would do. She made her living chasing and telling stories.

This weekend—she would be the story.

She knew how this worked and by the time news started to spread, Riley would be on her way to NYC to catch a flight to Tahiti. She'll have more than twelve peaceful hours in the air, disconnected from reality, alone in their business class seats with all the champagne she can handle and enough time to start plotting her next move.

The wedding was a bust. But Bora Bora would be her chance to reset and start over.

The caged bird would be freed.

CHAPTER SIX

Gabriel

Gabriel Laurent sat alone stoic and fixated on his work in his preferred business class aisle seat. He could never sit still on these long flights and hated to bother other passengers awkwardly sliding by them to stretch his legs. Or even worse, waking them for a bathroom visit.

But this flight was different. Or rather this trip was different. Weighty. After a decade working his way through the ranks at one of the most recognizable global hospitality brands, he was just one crucial step away from joining the executive ranks at the company. He'd worked his ass off. Put in his time. Paid his dues. All the bullshit clichés they slap you with when you're at the bottom of the proverbial ladder—he'd mastered them all. But he had a grander plan that required finesse and endurance, and this was but a rung on said ladder. This wasn't exactly end game for him, but it was definitely the right trajectory.

Now that the aircraft had reached cruising altitude, Gabriel pulled his training plan from his messenger bag for a final review. Just as he opened the document, the aircraft hit a pocket of turbulence and droplets of his black coffee hit the pages.

"Damn," he said a little louder than he intended.

A flight attendant headed towards him, cloth towel in hand. When she reached him, she dabbed at the pages and he watched as the pristine white pages of his immaculate training plan grew warped and stained, silently praying that this little mishap wasn't some type of omen.

He was headed to Tahiti for what was hopefully his last management trainer assignment. If all went well, he would be his company's next Senior Vice President of Hotel Development. The person currently occupying the position was retiring in three months, and Gabriel had made it his personal mission to always add value to the company in as many departments as they would indulge. He not only had a stellar track record of developing talent for the company, but he also scoured the trades for opportunities to grow the company's portfolio, collaborated with the sustainability team on energy efficiencies and reduced environmental impacts, and even helped scout new chef talents across the globe. They hadn't taken all of his advice, but everything he pitched was well-received—and that's more than he ever got from working with father.

Publicly, he was proud of what he'd accomplished.

Privately, some mornings he woke up asking himself what the hell he was doing. Sometimes moving too far up can deprive you of oxygen. He hoped that he wasn't trading the part of his job he loved most for a title and the appearance of success. And, as much as he hated to admit it, he hoped his father would take note and abandon his archaic business sense, letting Gabriel take the reins of their family company and secure their legacy.

But these were thoughts he dared not share with anyone. Inconvenient truths about executive promotions and being a reluctant heir apparent to a family business.

More than slightly irritated with the stains on his hard copy of the training plan, he slid it back in his bag and pulled out his laptop to continue reviewing his management trainee strategy for their signature property in Bora Bora. Gabriel had worked along human resources to perfect this strategy, keeping it fluid in recognition of seizing any opportunities for improvement. His new trainee, Simon Baxter, would benefit from this latest version of the strategy. And Gabriel planned to drill him and challenge him, while guiding him with a firm hand and observing him with a keen eye.

Simon was a rising star and reminded Gabriel of himself in many ways. He'd heard from colleagues that Simon, while talented and resourceful, could be a bit inflexible. But Gabriel could work with that. He wanted to give Simon all the tools he needed to be successful, and the permission to bend and the confidence to flex.

With each trainee, Gabriel adjusted his plans to customize areas of focus based on strengths and areas for improvement. He had met Simon several times as he was growing in the company, but this would be their first time working together directly.

They both had a lot riding on this endeavor.

Gabriel's focus, along with the monotonous sound of the aircraft engine and cabin air being recycled, was briefly interrupted by the flight attendant in conversation with a female passenger in the middle aisle on the first row.

She was seated alone, having boarded the flight from NYC before him. So far, he had only seen the back of her hair piled on top of her head five rows ahead of him, and he caught a quick glance of her face when she departed the restroom early in-flight and felt a hint of familiarity. There was no make-up, just beautiful bright eyes, enticing full lips and smooth golden-brown skin. He had smiled in her direction, but her eyes averted contact and then she was back in her seat.

During the first meal service, he could hear clips of her conversation with the flight attendant and noted that she spoke French. And not the choppy French tourists learn just before a big trip—this was smooth, conversational French.

Gabriel was indeed intrigued. Then he reminded himself this was not a vacation and he had zero time for a fling and no interest in sliding off course. He had a one-track mind—*get shit done.*

But what happened next surprised the man who had mastered the art of living a life at odds—unpredictable personal life, conventional professional life.

He exited the plane before the mystery woman, taking measured steps, hoping she would catch up and maybe pass him so that he could steal just one more glance. The fumes from the aircraft were thick and, in the distance, he could see the baggage handlers rushing towards the aircraft in their bag carts. As he walked, other passengers passed quietly by him in their comfortable shoes and whispered conversations.

But then he heard the tap, tap of footsteps. He knew it had to be a woman and wondered if it could be her. He stopped, stood his carry-on luggage upright while pretending to adjust the strap on his messenger bag, and glanced backward.

She had claimed the tarmac as her runway, a vision in white with oversized dark shades, ripped skin-tight jeans, a tank top revealing a beautiful neck covered by a thin, long white jacket bellowing behind her. Gone was the messy bun, released from its restraint into a tangle of golden-brown hair well below her shoulders, loose curls bouncing and a few escaped strands dancing across her face.

Not wanting to be obvious, he bowed his head and saw her white lacquered toes peeping through the clear strappy sandals as she quickly approached him.

He finally stood upright and she whisked right by him as if he were invisible. In her wake, the scent of vanilla and coconut lingered. He watched her walk towards the entry into the airport and caught himself smiling. Even the view from behind was spectacular.

And then, to no one in particular he whispered, "Flawless."

CHAPTER SEVEN

Riley

Riley arrived in Tahiti, her first stop in French Polynesia. She would spend two nights in Papeete at the Élite Papeete Resort and Spa before her final flight to Bora Bora.

She spent the flight in relative comfort—it wasn't the most luxurious business class, but the cocktails were exotic, the food decent, and she got swallowed up in the language of love. One of the reasons she had chosen the French Polynesian Islands was for the French influence. When she stepped onto the aircraft, American Riley melted away and her French alter ego rose to the surface. All of her conversations in-flight were in French—which also deflected attention from Riley St. James the broadcast journalist.

The sun had set when their Air Tahiti flight landed, and the air was warm but not humid. Riley had freshened up before they landed, and switched out of her comfortable travel gear into the casual white outfit she'd pack when she was a bride. No sense in letting a good outfit go to waste was her philosophy.

As she descended the staircase, she took a deep inhale and let the air of another world fill her lungs and ease her battled spirit. She had escaped. For now, at least.

Following her fellow passengers off the aircraft, hair blowing in the gentle breeze she recited her mantra: *You got this.*

She took long, dramatic strides with her head held high in oversized dark sunglasses, and her chunky heeled clear sandals tapping against the tarmac, while the lyrics to Rihanna's *Phresh Out the Runway* played through her Air Pods from her Brown Girl Dreaming playlist. The long, white silk jacket was light and the air caught it, forcing the front open and exposing her embroidered white tank top. The look was simple but trendy—sophisticated and subtly sexy.

The heaviness of disappointment in her chest eased and her breathing was smooth. She tilted her head upward and welcomed the light gusts of air releasing her from her emotional prison. This was a freedom like never before.

Keeping a healthy distance from the mostly coupled up passengers, she made her way through customs and towards baggage claim—blocking out thoughts of Jonathan, suppressing her anger, and leaving the pieces of her pain in the wind.

Riley stood waiting for her luggage—another reminder of how superficial her life had become. The new LV logo luggage with red leather handles and corners was a wedding gift to herself. It was an extravagant gift in hindsight—but it was all she had at the hotel back home, so she had to use it. She focused on the positive and found gratitude in the bold red accents that would give her the ability to quickly identify her bags on the conveyor belt. It always annoyed her when someone else grabbed her bag because it looked like theirs.

She adjusted the new duffle bag with the strap across her chest to improve her range of motion as she found a spot closer to the belt. Her white silk jacket, while dramatic and tarmac-approved, did not rate as practical. When she'd packed, Jonathan was supposed to be at her side handling all things luggage related. She didn't need to be practical. She just needed to be a beautiful, blushing bride. Now, she was a resentful runaway bride.

Riley shook off the thoughts of what was supposed to be and focused on what is. Her emotions were like a rollercoaster—one minute up and the next minute falling dangerously fast—minus the adrenaline rush of an amusement park ride. She wasn't anticipating the free-fall. Her arms weren't raised dangerously in the air, refusing the safety of the lap bar. And she wasn't laughing out loud. She wanted to pump the breaks on this ride, cling to the restraints, and reclaim her happy.

Alone, she watched as couples—there were a lot of couples—snagged their bags and headed out the airport terminal until finally, she was the last woman standing. The conveyor belt came to an abrupt halt, and her bags had not made an appearance.

The universe was conspiring against her. Losing a fiancé and your luggage in a 24-hour span qualified as cruel and unusual punishment.

Looking around, she located a customer service sign and walked in that direction. There was one woman on duty and no other passengers waiting. The agent lifted her head up from her desk when Riley entered and smiled.

"May I help you?" She spoke with a distinctly French accent and it put Riley at ease.

"Yes. It seems my luggage hasn't arrived. Is there some way you can check to see if it's delayed?"

"I certainly can. I just need some basic information from you to track your luggage."

Riley handed over her passport and airline tickets and in a matter of minutes, the mystery had been solved.

"Mademoiselle St. James, it seems that your luggage never left New York. It must have been delayed in transferring from your domestic flight to New York to the Air Tahiti Nui flight."

"Delayed?"

"Yes. I fear the baggage handlers did not hand off your luggage to Air Tahiti before your flight departed," she said with more concern in her voice than pity. Riley never wanted to be pitied.

"Okay. What do you recommend I do?"

"Well, you'll need to contact your domestic airline to locate your luggage and then they'll have to transfer it to Air Tahiti for the next flight out."

"Great!" Her mood lifted. This was simple.

The attendant tapped on the keyboard and then printed a sheet of paper.

"The next flight arrives on Wednesday…"

Before she could finish her sentence, Riley snapped. "Wednesday! What do you mean, Wednesday? I can't be here for four days without my luggage!"

"Mademoiselle, I know it's inconvenient, but that's why I'm here. To help."

With warm brown eyes and a comforting smile, she handed Riley the sheet of paper with all of the contact information she needed to make arrangements to receive her luggage and walked over to a shelving unit.

Returning to Riley with a small red bag she said, "This is a toiletry kit with enough of the basics to get you through the next few days."

"Toiletries?" The irritation oozed out before she could catch herself. Her duffle bag was full of toiletries, a valuable lesson she learned when her luggage disappeared for days at LAX. Skin products and hair products in airport-security approved sizes were always packed in a carry on.

She took a breath.

"Pardon, Mademoiselle."

"Ah, you speak French? No?"

"Oui, oui."

Riley relaxed, returned the attendant's smile and they continued the conversation in French.

Her name was Claire and she was just a young woman doing her job. Riley knew it would be a disservice to them both if she was hostile. By the time they were done, Claire had recommended two local shops where she could buy clothes and promised that there was a very nice hotel shop with beautiful items perfect for the weather.

Riley exited the airport terminal to her driver waiting outside with a sign — Mr. And Mrs. Jonathan Jasper. Suddenly, a rush of reality gut-punched her. She was solo on her honeymoon. She'd made the changes to their reservations using technology but how somehow neglected to think through the human element.

Another breath. And then her mantra: *You got this. You got this. You got this.*

So, what if the message about her solo arrival hadn't made it down the line to the driver. It wasn't his fault. Just like her MIA luggage wasn't Claire's fault.

If there was any blame to be placed, it was flatly on Jonathan.

She strode towards the driver and felt a hand on her shoulder. When she turned, she was faced with a couple with grins stretched across their faces.

The man spoke first. "My wife and I were on the plane with you from New York and we thought we recognized you."

Riley had foolishly thought she was home free and had made this trip virtually undetected.

She had been wrong.

CHAPTER EIGHT

Gabriel

G abriel headed towards the exit, searching the drivers with plac-
ards for his ride to the hotel. He spotted his name and headed
in that direction. As he drew closer, he noticed a small crowd of
passengers gathering in a circle.

He slowed his pace and as he got closer, he recognized her hair first.
It was the woman from the plane.

He caught the tail end of a comment from one of the women.

"Your hair is different, but I knew it was you! And weren't you
supposed to be getting married this weekend? They were talking about
it on the news that maybe your wedding was postponed. Are you ok?"

The confident woman he saw on the tarmac had been reduced to
speechlessness. She forced a smile and tried to continue to her car.

Gabriel looked in the direction she was headed, where her driver
simply stood back watching, unsure of whether to help or just wait it
out. It left just enough time for another woman to walk over holding
her cell phone eye-level and pointed directly at the beautiful damsel
in distress.

He hadn't recognized her as a celebrity, but the growing group of
curious passengers obviously had.

She pulled her sunglasses over her eyes, turned her head from the
woman aiming her cell phone at her and took a few steps forward.

Another man spoke through a big, goofy grin. "I knew it was her."

Gabriel had seen enough. He stepped forward, slid his arm across shoulders and guided her towards the driver. She initially resisted, but eased forward when she realized his intentions were good.

"Please open the door for Mrs. Jasper," he said, repeating the name on the placard.

The driver rushed around and said through a tight-lipped smile, "Sure thing, Mr. Jasper."

When she reached the open door, she paused, looked over her sunglasses at the driver, and spoke sternly. "Mr. Jasper won't be joining us. Please discard that placard." Gabriel watched his eyes widen as he slowly shifted his head towards him, as if he were also searching for someone to blame. He stammered out an apology as he relieved her of the duffle bag and Gabriel watched as she ducked down to enter the vehicle.

When the driver slammed the door shut, the woman just stared forward. Thankfully the windows were tinted and she was in relative privacy. He hoped that wherever she was headed, she has a nice, stiff cocktail.

CHAPTER NINE

Riley

Check-in had been uneventful and she was finally alone with nothing but her thoughts for company. Now, amidst the thoughts of Jonathan was the man that had come to her rescue at the airport. She didn't know why he did it or how he knew she needed rescuing. She was just grateful he showed up when he did. She hated not being able to thank him, and now she never could. She never saw his face, but she knew what the solid muscles in his arms felt like—protection.

That kind of attention wasn't unusual for Riley, but these circumstances were. She'd been disconnected from the world's 24-hour news cycle and hadn't bothered to try to rejoin the digital discourse. She thought she had time. She'd been wrong.

Rattled but not deterred and with very little to unpack, Riley arranged her toiletries and hair products on the bathroom counter. She pulled her cell phone from her bag and contemplated switching off airplane mode, but decided to wait. She was in no hurry for the bad news about her screwed up life. By the time she headed out to the hotel boutique, it was late, but the front desk clerk assured her she had about a half-hour to get in and grab a couple items.

Her suite was on the ground floor with a view and access to the beach and the pool. It was also a short distance to the boutique.

Once inside, she was pleasantly surprised at the quality of dresses, bathing suits and cover-ups. Claire had not steered her wrong.

While exploring a rack of dresses, a man approached.

"Mademoiselle, may I assist you?"

Riley rushed to turn in his direction and discourage any hovering when the accent registered. His voice sounded familiar but she couldn't be sure if it was the man that had helped her. She couldn't think every man on this island with a French accent had been her impromptu rescuer. Besides, she was a woman on a mission with a one-track mind, perfectly capable of choosing a dress without assistance.

But his accent hung heavy in the air. When their eyes finally met, she paused and let a slow inhale fill her lungs. Staring back at her were a pair of dreamy eyes the perfect replica of the South Pacific, as a tidal wave of longing coursed through her body.

Damn! He was fine! Like travel back to 2011, five o'clock shadow, Jason Momoa fine!

Her inclination to snap at him faded and was replaced by a girlish grin.

"No, thank you. I think I've got it handled." She practically giggled out the words, averting her eyes towards the rack and away from his gaze.

So, this is smoldering. Or maybe swoon-worthy. Or maybe a thirst trap.

He returned a dazzling white smile that reached his eyes on a canvas of sun kissed skin and a mess of raven black, thick, wavy hair. For the first time ever, she imagined pushing her fingers through someone else's hair and gripping it in a tight fist.

But she refused to let that particular stream of consciousness continue. Indeed, he was a thirst trap.

"I'm certain you do." He nodded his head forward and added, "Do let me know if you have any questions," before dropping his eyes in deference to her declaration.

Heat climbed her neck and reached her cheeks, while her eyes were forced upwards to meet his gaze. He was tall and lean, and she guessed her fluttering eyelashes were inappropriate at best, and desperate at worse. After a few awkward seconds of silence passed between them, he began backing away.

"I will," she said, redirecting her eyes and adding a smile for good measure, careful to balance between not too flirty nor too dismissive. "And, thank you."

Her internal temperature now matched her cheeks, a sensation that both surprised and intrigued her.

He turned and walked away and she couldn't help but watch his casual confidence. He lifted one hand, pulling his fingers through his thick, unruly hair and she thought he had read her mind.

Tall and clearly athletic, his baby blue linen shirt was untucked but fitted perfectly on muscular arms and across solid broad shoulders. She wondered again if that was the arm of her airport champion. A pair of beige linen pants hung loosely over brown slip-on leather designer shoes. She recognized his accent as French, but he didn't look Polynesian and he wasn't wearing an identifying staff badge, which she found a bit odd.

Any woman with eyes could appreciate this man—he had all the right attributes in all the right places.

And then she remembered Jonathan and his many fine attributes. She didn't need the French version of Jonathan. She needed an upgrade.

She physically shook off the reckless thoughts of this stranger and his unnatural good looks. *Everything that glitters isn't gold*, she reminded herself. She'd just run away from a glittering life; now was not the time to get distracted by the first shiny male object in her path.

Returning to her sensibilities, she continued sorting through the rack selecting two brightly colored and loose-fitting dresses, two tank tops, a golden bikini that matched her highlights perfectly and complimented her skin, a cover-up and matching straw hat, a pair of jewel-encrusted sandals and a multi-color straw beach bag.

Her hands full, she arrived at the counter and plopped it all down at once. She looked left and right, expecting her French mystery man to ring up her purchases, but instead a young woman approached the register. She charged her purchases to her room and left the store without another sighting of that handsome man.

Rushing back to her room, she cleansed her face and ran her fingers through her hair to loosen any tangles. She pulled her cell phone from her bag again, switched off airplane mode and saw 13 missed calls and more than fifty text messages—half of them from Jonathan. She ignored most of the messages but did text her parents to let them know she'd arrived safely and that she was going dark for the next few days. A woman of her word, she shut the phone off, threw it on the bed and headed to the bar.

She found a small table in a corner at the edge of the outdoor space and took a seat. It had a water view, but was tucked away and she hoped it gave her enough cover to avoid any unwanted attention and random cell phone camera photos. A waiter came by and took her order and as she waited for her cocktail to arrive, she took a few deep breaths and felt her muscles relax and the tension melt away. Her arrival hadn't been perfect, but this moment was. She acknowledged that she was hurting, but she wasn't going to let that ruin this beautiful trip.

When her cocktail arrived, she took a sip and let the cool liquid refresh and calm her. Faint island music played in the background and a group of women nearby periodically burst into fits of laughter. She turned towards them and smiled. They reminded her of her own group of friends and she felt a pang of loneliness.

She called over the waiter and sent them a bottle of champagne.

When it was delivered, the waiter pointed in her direction and she raised her glass. They each responded in kind and one of the women walked over to her table.

"Hi, I'm Charlotte!" Her deep southern accent and easy charm made Riley smile and think immediately of Reese Witherspoon.

"Hi, Charlotte. I'm Riley and you're from the south."

Charlotte laughed out loud. "I wonder what gave me away."

Riley chuckled.

"May I join you? I promise not to stay too long." Her voice was thick molasses sweet.

"Please do," Riley said, happy for the company and reminders of home.

"We just wanted to say thank you for the champagne and to invite you to join us…that is if you aren't expecting someone." She whispered the last part of her sentence.

Riley chuckled. "It's a long and sordid story, but no, I'm not expecting anyone. This is a solo trip for me."

Charlotte must have read something in Riley's eyes or picked up on her melancholy tone, because she didn't pry.

And then, as if a lightbulb went off over her head she said, "Did you say your name is Riley?"

Being inconspicuous was fun while it lasted, Riley thought.

"I did indeed."

Charlotte conspiratorially leaned in a little closer. "Are you Riley St. James?"

"I am. And if it's okay with you, I would love to be just Riley tonight."

"Oh, honey, that's fine by me. I've decided that I'm Charlie on this trip, so we can give you an alter ego, too, if you like."

They both laughed out loud.

"Well, *just* Riley, you must join us. This is our annual girls' trip, but this year we got really lucky. Our friend Savannah is a travel journalist and she's writing a series of articles on French Polynesia. Even she admits this was the trip of a lifetime and we all saved up our pennies and joined her. She upgraded her room to a suite so we could all stay together and we're having a blast."

She spoke so fast that Riley couldn't tell if she'd taken a breath between sentences and suspected it was the result of a few cocktails between friends.

"I love it!" Riley said, genuinely happy for the friendly foursome.

"I travel with my girlfriends sometimes. But it's never nearly enough."

"Amen to that, sister!"

Riley chuckled and for some reason felt a warmth and kinship towards her new southern acquaintance.

"If you're sure I'm not intruding, I'd love to join you and meet your friends. I mean, you all are the life of this party."

She looked around and there were only two other people in the bar, a couple obviously on their honeymoon because they couldn't keep their hands and lips off of each other. Riley definitely didn't want to sit and watch them for the rest of the night.

She pushed aside the thoughts of *what should have been* threatening to make an unwelcome appearance. Now was not the time. This was not a pity party; that would be the after-party when she would finally be alone in her suite with nothing but time and tissues.

Joining Charlotte and her friends, she'd hit it off immediately with Savannah, whom she suspected had also figured out who she was but didn't mention it. She also really liked Paige and Isabella, who didn't appear to notice, though Riley was sure Charlotte would fill them in later.

The four women were obviously close, but all couldn't be more different. Each was successful in different ways, and they looked like a mythical goddess delegation with a weekend pass from Mount Olympus. Riley lapped up their stories, a welcome distraction from her shitty situation.

Savannah Jordan, the travel journalist, was short and curvy with deep brown skin and long thin braids that constantly fell forward in her face. She was originally from California but now lived in New Orleans. She and Riley had lots to talk about.

Paige Maier was the seriously sexy one of the group—a literature professor with a Ph.D. at Stanford who could also double as a super model with her cute, blond pixie haircut and long lean legs poking through ripped denim shorts.

And Isabella Diaz was Puerto Rican and had recently returned home to help her family rebuild and to take a job as an executive chef at one of the top hotels on the island.

Between sips of champagne, she'd learned that Charlotte's family was in the sugar business, which was almost too spot on, and she spent her days working with nonprofits on a range of issues.

Riley had enjoyed laughing and talking to them, and having a glimpse into their easy comradery, born of their college days at Stanford. They were all whip-smart, but not the type to wear it like a badge of honor. It was just one of many things that made them who they were. Riley had chosen the HBCU route in undergrad, but did her journalism graduate studies at Columbia, wanting to prove that HBCU graduates could compete at all the levels. Looking back, it had been an unnecessary route to follow a bullshit prescriptive path to be considered a success in America. But she had learned a lot and made some friends for life. No regrets.

Riley sat with her new friends for about an hour before turning in and agreeing to meet up in the morning for brunch and a little island exploration. She was grateful to have met them. At least she wouldn't look lonely sitting poolside all day or wandering the island alone.

Back in her room as sleep gently claimed her—physically exhausted and emotionally compromised—she bargained with herself. Feel all the feels, but don't wallow. Invite hope and happiness into her situation, but don't be gullible. Put energy into healing, but don't define the parameters. And forgive, but never forget.

CHAPTER TEN

Gabriel

G abriel had a late morning flight to Bora Bora. He went through his usual morning routine of running on the beach and through the resort's tropical gardens, starting just before sunrise and finishing with the sun distant and high. Surrounded by hibiscus, palm trees, and a sprinkling of bamboo throughout the winding path made his morning run the best part of his day.

He took a cool shower and then ate a light breakfast of passion fruit and coffee at the lobby bar, to be followed up checking emails and a walk around the hotel property for an unofficial inspection.

Well, this was his usual routine whenever he was training managers at one of their island resorts.

This morning's routine was at the Élite Papeete Resort and Spa. He always felt like the many visitors to the French Polynesian islands were a captive audience as they began their trip with a night at this resort—really a best kept island secret. And for those who planned this as their final destination, often they'd be lured away to one of the other islands for day trips.

Traveling to the French Polynesian islands never grew old for him. He respected and admired the multi-island oasis as a woman who, above all else, understood her value—teasing her visitors with the promise of something spectacular, but making you work for it.

Many travelers ventured to French Polynesia for either the island of Moorea or its crown jewel, Bora Bora. But getting to either island was no cake walk.

The main island arrival was the Tahiti International Airport, just a few short miles from Papeete. Since most flights land at night, travelers at least get to spend a portion of their visit in the capital city of Tahiti. And this hotel property was the best on the island.

Gabriel knows his opinion was biased, but he also knew the lengths the company and the native staffers went into maintaining the cultural appeal of the island, not being a disrupter but rather serving as a connection between visitors and the local flavor. Not bending to travel norms, but rather opening up a world of possibilities for those willing to break through their comfort zones and experience a culture and lifestyle that defied stereotypes.

It began with the flights between the islands, where you could see the sky kiss the water and search, usually with little success, to find the delineation between the two. Or maybe it was the overwater bunga-lows, made famous in Tahiti, giving guests full access to crystal clear waters and exotic marine life. Or the simple luxury of Monoi oil, an infusion of Tahitian gardenias and coconut oil that could be used on every part of the body, including your hair.

And on the properties that Gabriel had in his portfolio, he insisted that the hotel blend into the island. And he checked them meticulously on every visit.

He had to admit, The Élite Bora Bora Resort and Spa was his personal favorite because it wasn't just pristine and otherworldly beautiful, but it was also wholly unpretentious. The vibe was warm and welcoming, the staff epitomized the island culture, and the food ranged from Tahitian traditional delicacies to French cuisine and classic American favorites.

And the over-water bungalows were unmatched.

But this morning his routine was different. He was distracted by the elusive Mrs. Jasper who must be some type of celebrity. He thought she looked familiar, but her name didn't match any celebrities he knew. Not that he really knew celebrities, but he didn't live under a rock.

When he saw her in the hotel boutique, it was clear she didn't remember him from the airport. But that was a bit of a blur and he never really looked her in the face. He just acted and whisked her away towards her car service.

It was muscle memory for him. It was true that he didn't really know any celebrities, but their hotels had certainly catered to them and had an entire protocol devoted to that specific clientele.

Gabriel had asked the hotel manager to meet him at the lobby bar to alert him to the mystery woman's presence at the hotel. He knew "Mrs. Jasper" could be a false name to hide her true identity, but she was definitely at the hotel and he didn't want the hotel manager blindsided by reactions to her presence.

What he wouldn't divulge to the manager was his hope for another close encounter with the mystery guest before he departed. He wasn't sure exactly what he'd say to her, but he felt like even another inconsequential conversation would appease his curiosity.

It was early yet, and most of the guests were still in their suites or bungalows. Only a few had risen to enjoy the sunrise, and a few more were getting in a run or walk on the beach and through the lush gardens.

His movements this morning were unsteady, maybe a result of his restlessness overnight. He had a lot riding on this assignment and he'd allowed himself one small distraction yesterday. That one tiny ripple in his plans had thrown him off balance and he had to get back on track.

Gabriel decided to start his inspection at the fitness centre. They had state-of-the-art equipment and the die-hards loved it. And this was the time of day it would be closest to capacity and therefore the best chance to see if guests were following the rules, if there were long waits, if towels were replenished and hand sanitizer was visible and being used.

He arrived at the fitness centre and just as he suspected, it was a full house. He pulled open the door and his gaze landed on a woman in the back, barefoot on a yoga mat stretching. He couldn't see her face, but somehow, he knew it was her. That unsteady feeling returned and despite his best intentions, he was like a moth to a flame.

Just him, though. No other moths drawn to this particular flame. It appeared that her identity hadn't registered with any of the other guests.

Gabriel had watched this woman walk away on the tarmac and had instantly memorized the curve of her hips, her thin waist and that beautiful, long thick hair. Even though she had it pulled up and off her face, the golden strands were untamed and unmistakable.

Then he had saved her from a growing crowd of unwanted attention. That same instinct propelled him now.

Literally, he had a few seconds to decide to continue his walk-through and possibly interrupt her, or worse, look like a stalker—or to simply take the cowards way out and retreat.

He chose the latter.

His desire to see her again was undeniable. But not like this. Not while she was working out, and not surrounded by a horde of hotel guests.

Not to draw unnecessary attention to himself, he glanced around the room and turned to depart. It wasn't a hasty exit, but he definitely didn't linger.

This is madness, Gabriel thought to himself. *I am a grown man and she is a grown woman. Why am I behaving like a lovesick teenager?*

He decided that he was going about this all wrong. Seriously. He was a hotel executive and had access to all sorts of guest information. Was he crossing a line? Maybe a little. But only to learn her name. Nothing more. Not her room number or how long she was staying or any really personal information. Just her name. Besides, the hotel manager would need to know. Only he knew it was really a pathetic excuse to unveil her true identity—a minor infraction, really.

Once he knew her name, he could satisfy one small curiosity, focus on his assignment and get his damn promotion.

But Gabriel also believed in listening to your intuition. There was something about her presence that stirred him, even on the plane. Sure, he was physically attracted to her. But there was something more. Like kinship. He couldn't explain it, so he embraced it.

He took a detour and went straight to the hotel boutique. The hotel staffer scheduled for the first morning shift was already inside neatly arranging and restocking clothes and accessories. He tapped on the door and she let him inside. They exchanged pleasantries and he went to the register.

"Just going to check the sales numbers for the week," he said out loud.

The staffer looked puzzled but smiled and nodded.

I'm an idiot! She doesn't care what I'm doing. Now I look suspicious. Am I trying to get caught?

Ending another pathetic conversation with himself, he entered his login credentials and pulled up the report from the previous night. And there, right at the top was her name.

Hello, Riley St. James.

CHAPTER ELEVEN

Riley's eyes fluttered open to strips of sunlight across her hotel room wall. Slowly she turned towards the window and smiled. The sun was warm across her face and shone so brightly that it lifted her mood just by its presence.

All things considered, she'd slept well. But she now wished she had reserved a spa appointment for a massage, or body wrap or even a facial. She was starting to relax but her muscles resisted, still tight and tense.

Absent a spa treatment, she decided a low-impact workout might help get the blood circulating, loosen her up a bit.

She checked the time on her watch and saw she had an hour before she would meet her new friends for brunch at one of the hotel restaurants. The waiter had convinced them last night that they must not miss it. He'd said the food alone was worth it, but there was also music and an authentic Polynesian dance performance, all while overlooking the infinity pool that appeared to spill right into the mouth of the lagoon.

She popped up, opened the blinds completely, allowing all the sunshine to filter in. Unable to resist the lush green plants and the sun slicing through, she stepped out on her balcony and took a deep breath in. Beyond her terrace she could see the lagoon with its vibrant shades of light turquoise and deep cobalt stretching as far as her eye could see. It was breathtaking.

Taking it all in, she allowed herself to imagine what it would have been like to experience this with Jonathan. She thought that they both had been looking forward to escaping their hectic lives for some downtime in an island paradise. She imagined his arms around her waist, light kisses on her neck and whispers of "I love you" sprinkled in between.

She did love him. Or some version of him.

There were the parts of Jonathan that she loved — the moments, however scarce, when he showed signs of vulnerability, like his fear of always living in the shadow of his grandfather and father. Or his devotion to building a life with her — however superficial it seemed in hindsight. His friendship with his fraternity brothers. She always suspected that some of them knew the real Jonathan, parts of the man that he never let her see. And she especially loved Jonathan the protector. He made sure she had the best legal representation money could buy so that she would never be beholden to any media conglomerate, unless it was a path she chose. If only he had worked as hard to protect her heart.

For these reasons, a part of her would always love a part of him. The other parts, the red flags in their relationship—the dark, secretive corners—that she blindly ignored, they were too big to dismiss. And it was that darkness in his personality that she could no longer ignore nor endure. His arrogance, though she suspected it's born of fear that he'd never measure up to the powerful men in his family. His selfishness that allowed him to think first of himself before their relationship. And his privilege that he wielded as a weapon.

These were the things that poisoned their relationship. Most people don't believe that light and dark can exist simultaneously. But Riley knew better. Jonathan was both, but one more than the other. She just chose to focus on the good in him and believed her love would smother the dark.

She gambled on him and lost. For all her trouble and trying to be the light, he had blown up their lives for a cheap one-night fling.

Her eyes welled with tears unspilled; emotions forced down.

She didn't feel strong, but she felt relieved. So, she let them fall and watched as each tear splattered on the ground.

Taking a step forward, she let her feet feel the cool and fertile earth, and chose to let her tears find a home in the rich soil. Tears didn't always have to be just a physical manifestation of pain, she thought. Tears can also open the door to progress. Tears can cleanse.

With her eyes closed, she did a quick breathing meditation and when she was done, wiped her face and stepped back inside.

There was no denying she hated that Jonathan left her feeling like she wasn't good enough. That no matter how hard she tried or how much she accomplished, he would still risk it all for a few minutes of stolen pleasure.

But there was a flip side. Without all of that negative energy, she wouldn't be here—in paradise with nothing but time on her side and the will to get her shit together.

She thoughtfully unpacked her duffle bag and had everything she needed. Luckily, she had packed one pair of yoga pants and a matching sports bra for the occasion. She'd learned some valuable travel lessons over the years, and having an outfit or two, along with facial and hair products, was essential in a lady's carry-on bag.

The quick five-minute cool shower was invigorating, and she pulled on her yoga gear and was out the door. She stopped by the concierge desk for directions and to confirm that her name had been added to the brunch reservation with her new friends.

Finding everything in order, she headed to the fitness center.

She entered, steps tentative and prepared to retreat if anyone recognized her and made this uncomfortable.

It was definitely the place to be in the morning. Every machine was in use and three people were using the free weights in different corners of the room. The back wall of the gym was mirrored and she located shelving with a collection of yoga mats and bricks, an assortment of balance balls, and a few weighted exercise balls. She chose a purple mat, found her spot facing the mirror, popped in her Air Pods and began a series of yoga poses she knew from memory. Completely unnoticed and unbothered.

She was interrupted once by text notifications, and paused to disable them but not before noticing that the text messages had doubled.

Notifications disabled.

As she transitioned from a plank pose to downward dog before going into warrior one pose, she caught a glimpse of a man through the mirror walking away. He wasn't moving fast, but intently with his head shifting left and right as if he were inspecting the space.

She couldn't take her eyes off of him and instinctively knew it was the man from the boutique. This time he wore loose-fitting athletic shorts, a short-sleeved shirt and athletic shoes. She wondered if he was there for a workout but couldn't get to the equipment he wanted because literally, everything was occupied.

Imagining him lifting weights, perspiration falling from his brow, his shirt clinging to what she was certain were washboard abs…

Stop it, Riley! She chastised herself for entertaining thoughts of another man less than 48-hours after calling off her wedding.

But it was a little odd, his appearance this morning. She'd met him working in the hotel shop and now he was in the fitness center. It didn't seem like common practice that hotel staff would workout with the guests. And, he looked rather official, looking around like he owned the place.

She became distracted and nearly lost her balance in starfish pose.

Damn it! This was not part of the plan. She was here to escape. To put her life back in order. Her perfect life had crumbled—or rather her illusion of a perfect life—and she needed to reset. And not with a man! No, she needed to reset alone.

She had never known what life was like alone. Jonathan had been a constant in her world since college. With him absent from the canvas of her life, she needed to know who she was without him. Not redefining herself, but re-evaluating her choices and her plans.

She knew that the perfect life she imagined was possible.

Last night before she drifted off to sleep, she sat in bed with her journal thinking about her role in what had transpired between her and Jonathan. What she found shocked and irritated her. It had all been about her choices.

She had *chosen* to allow Jonathan's obsessive pursuit of her in college. She had *chosen* to follow his lead in most things. She had *chosen* a career in DC to stay close to him, passing up other opportunities. She had *chosen* to accept his marriage proposal, sell her condo, and move in with him before she was really ready. And the list went on.

Being angry with Jonathan was easy and an obvious emotion. But checking herself—that's where the real work would happen. That's where the answers lived. Because her uncomfortable truth was Jonathan was exactly who she allowed him to be in her life.

She hadn't worked it all out yet in a night. But she had one big takeaway from that journal exercise: life is all about choices. Just as her choices had been the foundation of her failed relationship, so would they be for her healing. But this time, the result would be a contented Riley with the benefit of the lessons of this tortured failure, fully equipped to recognize the perfect man to complement her life—not control her life.

Defiantly, she skipped downward dog and went straight into full warrior pose with Alicia Keys serenading her and her choices with the black girl anthem, *A Woman's Worth*.

That's right, Alicia. Eventually, she thought to herself, she'd find a man who understood her value.

Just not today.

Not with a super sexy, French god in Tahiti. No matter how her body ached or her imagination ran wild, she would control those urges and focus on herself and her mission.

She stole one last glance through the mirror, just in case mystery man made another appearance. When he didn't, she took that as a sign that it wasn't meant to be.

Stretching her body out full on her back, she slipped into savasana and let a wave of relief slowly rise from the tips of her toes through her core and her heart, exiting with every measured breath. A sensation of peace covered her and she ignored that nagging voice inside counting her flaws and blaming her for her failed relationship.

She was enough.

CHAPTER TWELVE

Gabriel

Riley St. James.

He smiled, satisfied that he'd solved the mystery. He had no idea what came next, but at least he knew her name. That was something.

Then he paused. *Riley St. James? The* Riley St. James? He repeated her name a couple more times and then got slammed with a reality check.

Twitter trending hashtag *RileyOnTheRun* St. James?

Damn it! What were the chances that she'd be on his flight and staying at one of his hotels on the other side of the globe?

How had he not recognized her?

It was the hair. When she's on-air reporting the news, her hair is always straight, sleek and long. And her lips were always the perfect shade of red. The kissable shade of red.

This woman was the whole package. Smart. Successful. Beautiful. *Flawless.*

And now that he'd seen the contours of her body, he could add sexy to that list.

This explained the airport drama. Those people had recognized her. He had been singularly focused on removing her from that situation and hadn't heard anyone utter her name.

Gabriel did the math and realized this was probably her honeymoon. There had been social media speculation, but Tahiti was a trip too far for most media outlets to follow a hunch…in search of a woman determined to hide…with the resources to be anywhere in the world.

But she wasn't anywhere in the world.

She was here. In Tahiti. At one of his resorts.

He had to think. This was a tough call. Gabriel the executive knew the rules. Gabriel the man was intrigued by her presence.

Her presence. That will require special attention from the staff. *She hadn't requested any special treatment, but it was his job to ensure each guest is comfortable and safe on their properties.*

He'd seen her left hand in the hotel boutique. *She was not wearing an engagement ring.*

She had chosen to travel to Tahiti alone. *She was likely trying to escape the spectacle of whatever caused her to call off her wedding the night before.*

No, she didn't look miserable. *She's probably putting on a brave face.*

Suddenly, his curiosity about her identity was tempered, replaced with concern. He recalled her smile from the previous night, and wondered about the effort she made to be kind when she was obviously dealing with something ugly and painful.

He decided to stop there because this exercise was not getting him to the desired outcome—meeting and getting to know this woman who was no longer just a face he'd seen on television. And who definitely didn't deserve to be this week's social media drama du'jour…nor the object of his passing affection.

All signs pointed to him backing off and staying focused. She was intriguing, but her presence could be disruptive for other guests.

He checked his phone and it was nearly time for him to head to the airport for his flight to Bora Bora.

On his way back to his suite, he stopped by the restaurant to check on Sunday brunch. It was a traveler and local favorite. He was good friends with the hotel event manager and wanted to say good-bye.

The restaurant was already half full and guests were waiting to be seated. He found Victor standing near the bar.

"Hey, Vic," Gabriel said, extending his hand to his friend. "Looks like you're expecting a full house this morning."

"Indeed we are, my friend." Victor's English didn't have a distinguishing accent —unlike Gabriel—despite having been a child of the world. Not to mention, he spoke four different languages—fluently. His father had been in the military and they lived in countries all over the world. He said Europe always felt like home, London specifically, but you'd never know it when holding a conversation with him. That is, until he was having a few pints and his mostly British upbringing poured out.

"Are you here for a few days? If so, I have something big planned tonight…"

Gabriel stopped him.

"I'm actually on my way out, so don't try to tempt me," he said, casually leaning against the bar, his eyes scanning the restaurant guests. "I'm training the new manager at the Bora Bora resort for the next month or so."

"What a tough life you have," Victor joked.

Gabriel didn't respond, and conspicuously continued people watching.

"Why are you acting so strange? What's up?"

Without looking at Victor, Gabriel played coy. "Nothing's up. I'm just checking out the vibe. This brunch has become really popular."

"C'mon, man." His laugh was warm and easy. "I've known you what, ten years? And I know when you're off your game. So, I'll ask you again—what's up?"

This time Gabriel laughed.

"You got me. But it's a delicate matter." Gabriel lowered his voice as to not catch the attention of eager ears at the bar. "So, if I tell you, you have to swear to keep it to yourself."

"Is that even necessary? Seriously."

"Okay. I met someone last night in the hotel boutique, but I didn't get her name. She kind of brushed me off."

At this, Victor laughed out loud.

"Enough with the laughter double-o-seven."

Victor Toussaint was a man's man. Athletic, clean-cut, and tall with effortless charm and good looks. The first time Gabriel met him, James Bond popped in his head and now he was forever double-o-seven.

"I mean, a woman that can resist the charms of THE Gabriel Laurent. I like her already."

Gabriel turned and ordered a bottle of water, just to keep Victor in suspense.

"This is exactly why I didn't want to tell you."

"I'm just joshing. So, who is the mystery woman?"

Just as Gabriel raised the water bottle to take a sip, Riley appeared in the entryway of the restaurant. He swallowed and the water went down the wrong way and he started coughing uncontrollably.

To not draw Riley's attention, he turned to face the bar and Victor tapped him on his back.

"Damn, man. You got it bad."

"That's her. In the entryway waiting to be seated."

Victor turned in that direction and saw four of five women and thought it could be any one of them. They were all quite attractive.

But one did stand out. Her hair was full, almost wild but super sexy.

The suspense was now killing him.

"Which one? It's like a parade of women over there," Victor said impatiently.

Gabriel tried to play it cool and glanced in their direction. She was wearing one of the dresses she bought in the boutique, but the hanger had done it no justice.

The yellow cotton, floor length dress with wide sleeves hung off her bare shoulder. The fabric was sheer and the short tight garment beneath the dress hid all of her secrets and made him want to uncover each of them, one by one, inch by glorious inch. Slits on both sides revealed her bare legs, and she wore a pair of flat sandals that gave her whole appearance a sensually casual vibe. Around her neck, thin gold chains swept softly against her exposed skin and the oversized shades added a movie star quality.

Gabriel's distracted mind returned to his list.

She's not hiding her identity in that outfit.

This was a point in his favor—and made him forget that moments ago he had decided to back off.

"The woman in the yellow dress," he whispered to Victor.

"I kind of guessed she was the one. Not your typical type, but definitely stunning. Too bad you saw her first."

Gabriel nudged Victor. "Don't stare at her. Remember, I haven't introduced myself properly yet. And, she is a hotel guest, so show a little discretion."

He checked his watch and was out of time.

"Damn. I have to go or I'll miss my flight."

Victor turned back towards Gabriel. "So, who is she?"

"That's Riley St. James."

"Should I know who that is?" Victor took another peek back in her direction but didn't see anything familiar about the woman. But he also couldn't look away.

"Television journalist, Riley St. James."

"No way! But she looks so...different."

"It's the hair," Gabriel said as he pulled a few dollars out of his wallet and laid them on the bar.

Then he paused and pulled out five one-hundred dollar bills, forcing them into the palm of Victor's hand.

"Send them your best bottle of champagne, on me."

"And who should I say this expensive bottle of champagne is from?"

"Make sure Riley knows it's for HER and her guests. That's it.

"But, don't you want her to know it's you? I mean, otherwise, what's the point?" Victor was confused.

"I don't know how long she's staying, but we know it's at least until Wednesday. I'll be back before then."

And with that, Gabriel rushed out of the restaurant to catch his flight, stealing one last glance at a woman he was sure was the most beautiful girl in the world.

CHAPTER THIRTEEN

It was him. Riley was sure of it.

He was coughing or choking or both when she spotted him wearing the shorts she'd seen him wearing at the fitness center. Same dark hair. Same dreamy eyes. Same hot body.

He was with another guy at the bar and she guessed that they both must work at the hotel. The other guy was also handsome, and he had a name tag on his shirt. She was too far away to make out the words, but she knew it was a name tag.

It was just her luck that the hottest guy at the hotel was a staffer. Making him one hundred percent off limits, certain that the hotel had to have rules discouraging hotel and guest fraternization or some such thing.

Unlike last night, this morning she could look at him with lustful eyes concealed by her over-sized sun shades. She didn't have to adjust her body or tilt her head in his direction. She just cut her eyes to the left and got an eyeful.

He had a deep tan, making him almost a shade darker than her.

She made a mental note to get lots of tanning on this trip. When she returned to the city, she wanted the world to know that she had been bathing in sunshine, even if she was crying herself to sleep at night.

If she had met him anywhere other than the hotel, she would have guessed he was an athlete. Possibly a soccer player or maybe a professional swimmer.

He was a gorgeous man. But not pretty boy handsome. Like ruggedly handsome. This morning he was fresh shaven, and she kind of missed the stubble she'd seen on his face last night. She imagined what it might feel like to feel that stubble on the inside of her…

"What are you smiling at?" Charlotte's voice interrupted that thought with an accusatory twang.

Riley recovered quickly.

"It's just nice to be away from the city. I mean, look at this place. God probably vacations here!"

Charlotte laughed, but wasn't convinced. "With that sly grin I just saw on your face, I know you are not trying to bring God into this."

Riley laughed, but refused to take the bait.

By now, she knew they had probably figured out why she was there. The last thing she needed was for them to think she was about to have a fling or some type of revenge sex with a complete stranger.

And if she did decide to do either of those things, it would be nobody's business but her own.

"Right this way, ladies."

They were seated at what must have been the best table on the resort. With a perfect view of the pool and the lagoon and a gentle breeze off the water, Riley knew she had made the right decision to come.

Who could be sad and depressed when all around you were vibrant colors, warm smiles, impeccable service, and perfect temperatures? Besides, reality would be exactly where she left it when she returned home.

She took a minute to just appreciate her surroundings. The servers dressed in matching floral-patterned shirts or dresses, the women with one lovely accessory—island flowers perfectly set in their hair, either tucked behind an ear or in a pony tail. The seating throughout the restaurant was an inviting blend of warm cognac-stained wood with cushions of muted earth tones, surrounded by smaller tables for two or four with wicker chairs and simple white table linens.

They were seated at an oval shaped table with room for five and right near water. There was a stage nearby and a three-piece ensemble played island music with authentic Tahitian drums and wind instruments.

However, it was the view that was most striking. Riley had been intrigued last night, only able to see the gentle ripples in the water by lights strategically placed across the property. Even that was magical.

But this. This was spectacular. And it had been worth the wait.

She had planned to walk out to the beach once they finished with brunch, the pristine sand and crystal blue waters calling to her. She just wanted to feel the sand between her toes and the water splash up her legs.

Once they were all seated and situated, and had ordered the signature brunch cocktail—the Tropical Maitai—they relaxed and fell into an easy conversation. The mixtures of aromatic cuisine wafted all around them as servers with plates of food piled high with exotic fruits and steaming hot breakfast entrees passed by.

Within minutes, they were interrupted by the same man that had been standing near Riley's mystery man at the bar. Mystery man had disappeared, but the friend was standing right next to Riley's chair holding an ice bucket with a bottle of champagne.

Riley pushed her shades up on her head, pushing her hair back completely away from her face. She wanted to get a good view of his name tag. *Victor.*

"Well, good morning, Victor. Are you lost?" Riley teased and her new friends played along, with a whole lot of giggling and a little bit of eye-ogling.

He smiled and assured them he was not lost.

"This is for you, Ms. St. James. A gift for you and your friends."

Their waiter came up behind him with five champagne flutes expertly clasped with one hand.

"A gift? For me?"

"For you *and* your lovely friends." His eyes had darted towards Isabella more than once and she blushed.

Riley was enjoying this playful banter, but for a brief few seconds, she worried that Jonathan may have sent it. But rather than invite a cloud to their sunshine party, she kept at it and hoped for the best.

"And are you at liberty to share the name of my champagne benefactor?"

"Ah. I am not at liberty. He wishes to remain anonymous." He paused to pop the cork. And also, for a little dramatic effect. "He is your secret admirer."

This time, Charlotte got in on the fun.

"Now wait just one minute. We've been here for days and not once did any secret admirers send us champagne, cocktails, juice, or even iced water!"

They all laughed out loud, as now Victor's face was a bright shade of red.

Savannah piled on with, "Well, I guess we can't all be Riley St. James. We'll let her do all the heavy lifting and we'll be her beneficiaries."

Victor had recovered and spoke up. "Every lady at this table deserves her own bottle of champagne, but I guess there just aren't enough secret admirers to go around."

He poured each of them a glass and made a polite exit.

"Enjoy."

When he was far enough away, Charlotte pounced.

"I knew you were smiling like a Cheshire cat. Spill!"

Riley took a sip of the champagne. It was the good stuff.

"Seriously. There's nothing to spill." She took another sip to cool down her insides. Of course she knew exactly who'd splurged on the champagne. And it wasn't Jonathan.

"Nothing?" Charlotte and Paige said in sync, both dripping with sarcasm.

"You said it yourself. I've been here one night. And look around." Riley waved her hand. "This isn't exactly a singles bar."

"Okay," Charlotte said. "I know you're hiding something…" She stopped mid-sentence.

The table fell silent while Savannah shook her head and the others diverted their eyes away from the table.

But Riley genuinely liked them and wanted to come clean. She didn't want them to have the wrong impression of her. She was not pretending to be anyone other than herself. And she wasn't running. She was decompressing, reassessing, and planning her next move.

But she also didn't want to spoil the mood.

"Well, this is awkward," Riley dead-panned.

Savannah laughed first and then Isabella started to giggle. Eventually, all five of them were laughing into their champagne glasses.

"Look. I knew that after last night you all would figure out why I was here alone. And I appreciate you not peppering me with questions about it."

She hated having to expose this wound with them so soon. She was still quite embarrassed and hurt and confused and mad as hell. If she was measuring her mood by the five stages of the grief, she'd skipped the first one—denial—and went straight to anger. But she was smart enough to stifle her anger for her alone time.

"I just didn't want what happened to me to give you any reason to pity me. I wanted one night of relative obscurity, having a few cocktails with a cool group of women, laughing out loud and not dwelling on my tragedy of a relationship."

Riley pulled her glasses back down, just in case a tear tried to escape.

Savannah touched her shoulder and Charlotte touched her free hand. Her left hand with the bare ring finger that still had a thin stripe two shades lighter than the rest of her finger.

That small stripe of discolored skin was where the story began and ended. She'd worn his ring for nearly two years, covering the small space on her ring finger with the symbol of an empty promise. Now, in its absence, what remained was pale in comparison with her other fingers, having been denied sunlight for so long. That ended now.

Savannah spoke first, interrupting Riley's fixation on her now bare finger.

"Yes, we knew who you were last night. But it didn't matter. We liked you, too, and genuinely wanted you to hang out with us. We've known each other for so long, we needed to add a little fresh blood to the mix."

Paige, who seemed to always be measuring her words before speaking chimed in.

"Riley, we've known you less than a day and already know that whatever happened, you didn't deserve it and he's obviously..." She paused.

Riley was waiting for Professor Paige to whip out some multi-syllabic word that she'd have to google later when she was alone. But nope.

"...a stupid asshole."

They all laughed out loud.

The waiter came and took their orders, and when he left, Riley spoke up again.

"Let me just say this, and let's agree not to mention it again."

Every one of them nodded in agreement with curious and sympathetic eyes.

"He cheated on me the night before we were to be married. I caught him and confronted him and the object of his desire—who, by the way, is in our circle of college friends. And then I left him. I do love him. But I love me more."

Riley paused, clearing her throat to prepare the way for another of her tragic truths. This confession was the true origin of her anger.

"He was my first and my only. There's a crack in my heart—but it's not shattered. It's still beating and I'm still here. So, can we please just put this behind us? Let's drink all this alcohol and eat all of these carbs and do whatever the hell we want for the rest of the day. Cool?"

It was Isabella's turn. "Oh, mami. That's cool. But just one thing."

"What?" Riley was curious. Isabella's tone had turned serious.

"We must find this secret admirer of yours and fix that *first and only* problem!"

They laughed and ate and sipped cocktails and talked and laughed some more.

Riley was happy she'd met them. Like genuinely happy. Figured it was meant to be. These women didn't pity her. Didn't have complicated history with her. The Riley they were getting to know was version 2.0 They had front row seats to the start of her second act.

When they were preparing to leave the restaurant, Savannah pulled Riley to the side where she couldn't be overheard.

"What's up, Savannah?"

Savannah slipped her arm through Riley's arm and whispered. "I know we agreed to not talk about this again, and I don't want you to flip out. But I just think you should know that you're trending on Twitter."

"You can't be serious." Riley didn't know whether to be irritated or flattered. She'd had some trending news stories on Twitter—but that was a story, this was her life. It was personal.

Savannah tilted her head and shrugged.

"Like hashtag trending?"

"Hashtag *RileyOnTheRun* trending," Savannah whispered.

Riley threw her head back in laughter, surprising Savannah.

"I like that! Life dealt me lemons, but trust and believe, I'm serving lemonade!"

Arm in arm, Riley and Savannah joined Charlotte, Isabella, and Paige…Riley's lemon-yellow dress blowing in the wind.

CHAPTER FOURTEEN

Gabriel

G abriel had barely made his flight, and between reviewing his notes for his introductory meeting with Simon, he wondered if Riley had guessed who sent the champagne.

They had only a brief connection really. Nothing really. But none-theless, he felt drawn to her.

What he knew of her was basically public information. She was a high-profile journalist, well-respected and accomplished. He'd admired her and her obvious passion for her work. It was professional admiration.

But seeing her out of her element—without a microphone and cameras rolling, or sitting behind an anchor desk or across from polit-ical or entertainment celebrities coercing them to reveal their deep, dark secrets—he felt compelled to know more.

Riley St. James in-person was far more intriguing than the journalist the world knew from television. On her honeymoon alone was a bold move. Bolting from her wedding was a maneuver snatched right from the screen, like Julia Roberts in that movie where she kept getting engaged and then running away on the day of the wedding.

The fact that he even knew any Julia Roberts movie references made him smile—a testament to his relationship with his sister, Juliette, who devoured any and all romantic movies. She also had a big brother that would walk across hot coals for her—and binge watch romantic movies with her—therefore making him an expert on the likes of Julia Roberts, Reese Witherspoon, Kat Graham, Anne Hathaway, Zendaya, Amandla Stenberg, and a host of other American actresses he would likely never forget.

The small commuter jet was at full capacity today, mostly with travelers island hopping for the day. The couple on the opposite side of the aisle spent most of the flight with their heads aimed at the window, snapping photos of the spectacular view.

Gabriel was seated in the row of single seats—his preferred way to travel between the islands. With no danger of a stranger glancing at his phone, he logged into the Wi-Fi and opened Twitter. He had accounts on all the main platforms, but only sporadically posted. He preferred to be on the sidelines, checking out his friends and family, leaving messages on their posts, quietly envying their full lives.

He opted to check his sister's Twitter feed first. She had thousands of followers as a young European socialite with an opinion and far more purpose than he'd ever had. She supported all manner of causes from the environment to climate change, to clean water and health care, and social justice and cruelty free cosmetics. It was dizzying to Gabriel, but he loved her energy and her drive.

His father had groomed them both to join the family business, never missing a chance to give his *legacy and loyalty* speech. Gabriel had earned the ire of his father, refusing to play by his rules and escaping to a life in America. Now, it seemed his American life was becoming more permanent. His father had once told him he was his greatest disappointment. But he knew it was a manipulation from a desperate man. And, as for his sister, if his father thought she would be any easier to mold and manage, he was in for a rude awakening.

Juliette Laurent didn't play by anyone's rules—she wrote the rules, smashed them to dust and then threw caution to the wind. Gabriel couldn't wait to watch the fireworks between daddy and daughter. His money was on Juliette.

He opened the Twitter app and went to Juliette's profile. She hadn't posted since yesterday, and it was mostly shares of some philanthropic news and a new clothing designer repurposing recycled materials for accessories. He was happy she didn't let the fireworks from a few nights ago disrupt her life. They hadn't spoken since that night and he owed her a phone call.

He jumped over to search for sports updates and decided to check what was trending.

His eyes scanned the list and was about to move on when he saw her name. Well, not just her name, but her name blended into a hashtag.

#RileyOnTheRun was trending.

A rush of heat covered his face as the internal debate began. To look or not to look?

The pilot's voice interrupted the little angel and devil arguing in his head, both with rationales for taking a peek and avoiding it all together.

"The current temperature in Bora Bora is a warm and welcoming 85 degrees as we prepare for our descent."

Gabriel glanced out the window and knew the flight attendant would soon be announcing prep for landing. He had a rapidly closing window before he would have to shut down any activity on his phone.

The little devil won out and he tapped the trending hashtag.

A pang of guilt kicked at his gut, but his curiosity had already won the battle. He hadn't given much thought to why she was alone on this trip, but he guessed the likely cause was a betrayal too big to forgive. So big that a woman like Riley St. James would flee her own wedding.

Surprisingly, the social media snark wasn't too obnoxious. Riley was actually coming across rather favorably, he thought. The vast majority of women seemed sympathetic—many hilariously so. Which confirmed what he suspected. The fiancé had done something to blow up their wedding.

What an idiot!

He scrolled through the *RileyOnTheRun* hashtag feed, searching for a clue as to who the fiancé was and possibly what he'd done to drive away a woman as stunning as Riley. He knew he was biased against the man, but really…did he not realize what a catch that woman was?

He kept scrolling, knowing that there was really only one logical explanation.

He had cheated on her.

Then he saw it: a tweet from @JayJasper that tagged @RileySJofficial. But it wasn't an apology. It was a plea to their followers to give them some space to reflect and heal, and promising an official statement later.

Gabriel clicked on @JayJasper and scrolled. Pretty benign stuff. Nothing controversial. A few pics of him with Riley and his friends, along with some retweets. He was an attorney so Gabriel figured he knew not to use social media to spout any real opinions and risk tainting his professional profile.

Surmising that this guy was smart, and a little cocky, Gabriel had seen enough.

He shut down his phone and resolved to return to Papeete in two days. There were only two flights in and out of Tahiti per week on Air Tahiti Nui. If this were really her honeymoon, he couldn't imagine that she would have booked it for just four days. It took more than a half day just to fly to the island from New York. He didn't have a game plan yet, but he had a few days to figure it out.

Gabriel put his meeting notes away and spent the remaining few minutes in the sky wrestling with his thoughts about a woman who was basically a stranger. He was undeniably attracted to her, but he couldn't risk any distractions on this assignment and lose sight of his goal and his promotion—all because of a boyish lapse in judgment.

And yet, despite the logic lacing his thoughts, he couldn't shake her. If she wasn't Riley St. James, he might consider pursuing a harmless, off the books, on vacation only fling. But she wasn't just a beautiful woman. She was a high-profile journalist who just had a nasty break up that was quickly devolving into a public spectacle. This trip was probably her temporary escape to get her shit together.

She was the last thing he needed, and he was the last thing she needed. Without even knowing very much about her or what had just happened to her, he knew the stakes were high—for them both. Her relationship and his career were both on the line.

It was a line he wouldn't cross.

His flight landed and he took the boat over to the hotel. He never grew tired of this view.

This month he was training a new hotel manager who had transferred from one of their resorts in Honolulu. There were definitely some similarities between the cultures and the expectations for service, but some equally unique differences that might require the new manager to dig deep.

For one, Bora Bora was more secluded. There wasn't much of a nightlife scene, or casinos and high-end shopping. This resort catered to a different type of clientele. It wasn't elitist, more escapist.

Guests who traveled to Bora Bora wanted some solitude in peaceful and exotic surroundings. Couples on honeymoons, young families with small children, scuba enthusiasts, spa afficionados—that was the Bora Bora traveler profile.

Honolulu, Hawaii, catered to a broader range of travelers.

Neither was better than the other. Just different.

Gabriel was looking forward to working with Simon Baxter. He was building a reputation for himself in the company and if he kept on this trajectory, he may someday become the next Gabriel Laurent. Somebody would have to take over for him eventually.

The company was grooming Gabriel for a higher-level position in the C-Suite. For the past nine years, he had worked his way up from concierge, into mid-level hotel management, to land as one of the youngest regional directors with a portfolio of hotel properties that kept the back pages of his passport filled with international stamps.

This position was his last stop on his way to the top. He had worked hard, made the tough decisions and personal sacrifices.

Sacrifices his father didn't understand. Or chose not to understand. Hotel hospitality was in his DNA.

His family owned several boutique hotels in Europe, and his father had expected him to one day take the lead.

But the older Gabriel got and the more he experienced through his travels around the world, it became clear that his father's limited vision was smothering him. He was a citizen of the world with an MBA from an American Ivy League college. His vision for hotel management was expansive and knew no bounds. But, whenever he made recommendations to his father, they were met with skepticism and doubt, until finally he stopped trying and took a job with one of the most well-respected and successful global hotel and hospitality brands.

That was nearly ten years ago and his father still had not fully forgiven him. Whenever he visited his family for the holidays, his father had a new proposal to convince him to return to the fold.

But his father, the one and only Viscount Jean Louis Laurent, was old school. Like a relic almost. An affluent, sophisticated descendant of French nobility relic.

The senior Laurent's roots were in nobility, but his work was his own. He was a successful business man and Gabriel's work ethic and passion for his own career was a direct result of his father's business acumen and accomplishments. But he lacked a growth strategy. His father played it safe, clinging to old traditions and outdated standards. Gabriel played hard and lived for risks. They were polar opposites.

His last visit had not ended on good terms. That was typical, but this time was far worse. He'd since spoken to his mother, but he and his father remained at odds and disconnected. Gabriel's mother said they were mutually stubborn. Two sides of the same coin.

As Gabriel descended the aircraft stairs, thoughts of his father soured his mood. Their last encounter still affected him. His father had crossed a line and it would take some real work to recover. He had dangled Gabriel's dream of returning to the family business on his own terms, but anything that dangles always has strings attached.

It was the actual string attached to the dream that he couldn't abide. String can also be used to bind.

CHAPTER FIFTEEN

Riley

After her good-byes to her new friends and they confirmed their plans to join her in Bora Bora for an overnight visit, it was a quick flight on a tiny plane—the kind of plane you saw in bad movies that always crashed in a storm. Riley hated small planes, but the view more than made up for the inconvenience.

She watched in awe the crystal-clear waters and bright blue skies melting into each other. Small uninhabitable islands jutted up from out of the water, green and lush, while mountain peaks parted clouds against a clear blue sky, surrounded by an opulent turquoise ocean.

When they landed, she went straight outside to the pier where she was directed to the boat that would transport her and a few other guests to their hotel. She got the best seat on the boat while her travel companions negotiated all of their luggage. She only had a purse and a duffle bag. She had finally stopped fretting over the missing luggage the first night in Papeete and felt strangely unencumbered without the hassle of dragging the bags around from one place to the next.

Three planes and one boat later, she was finally in Bora Bora.

When the boat pulled into the pier, there were two Tahitian women in bright red grass skirts and matching head pieces, and a Tahitian god in a black linen cloth and an intricate tattoo the length of his right arm and shoulder greeting them. Behind them a team of hotel staffers stood waiting to greet and assist them. Riley needed the least amount of assistance since she had no luggage. So, she hopped off first and headed straight to check-in.

She was first to arrive in the lobby and was greeted at the counter by the hotel manager. She had changed the name on the reservation, but kept the large over-water villa because it promised a spectacular view of the Otemanu mountain and lagoon. She had contemplated moving to a smaller villa, but was glad she kept this one because she'd need all of that space to host her new friends.

"Welcome to Bora Bora. May I have your name?"

"Riley St. James."

The hotel manager, Simon, according to his name tag, tapped away on his keyboard. The expression on his face didn't change, but his cheeks began to flush just a little.

When he finally spoke, he said, "That's odd. I don't have a reservation for a Riley St. James. Could it be under another name?"

She couldn't believe this was happening. She had painstakingly made changes for every leg of the trip. How did they get it right in Papeete but not in Bora Bora?

"Maybe Riley Jasper." Her tone was clipped, but she maintained her tight but polite smile. A light breeze flowed through the open-air lobby carrying with it the faint scent of the exotic floral arrangements adorning table tops throughout the space—a reminder that she was in paradise and this was but a small misunderstanding.

His fingers tapped and tapped, heavier on some keys then others. After several seconds, he looked up.

"My apologies, Miss St. James. I don't have a Riley Jasper either. Could there be another name? Perhaps your husband?"

Her tight and polite smile fell and she rested one bent arm on the counter. Leaning in a little closer, a heat rising within that couldn't be tamed—not even by a floral scented Tahitian breeze—she spoke in a measured tone.

"I don't have another name and I don't have a husband."

The pink in his cheeks raised two shades brighter, clearly at a loss for what to do next.

When he didn't speak, Riley offered a suggestion, refusing to say the name of he who shall not be mentioned. "I just traveled here from your property in Papeete. Maybe you should contact your counterpart there to clear this up."

His demeanor was still pleasant, but he was now slightly anxious. Pulling his collar away from his neck with his index finger and tilting his head slightly right and then left, he exhaled a low sigh.

"Let me consult with my colleague who was just at the Papeete property yesterday. He'll be able to assist. Please excuse me one moment."

Other guests began to arrive and the lobby had come to life in under ten minutes.

Riley was getting impatient and started drafting a letter to hotel headquarters in her head to complain about this embarrassing mix up. Honestly, did Manager Simon really think someone would fly all the way to Bora Bora without a reservation?

Between guest chatter and background island music, two voices broke through and when she looked up, Simon was now walking towards her...with her French mystery man following dressed in a light grey linen suit and a white V-neck t-shirt that made his blue eyes even more distinctive.

Today, in this outfit, he looked more like the hotel manager than his counterpart, Simon.

Uncontrollably, she smiled. It never occurred to her that he might have transferred to another of their properties on the island. And while the clothes had changed, the butterflies fluttering around her stomach remained the same. She had found her mystery man.

But unlike their first encounter when he was flirtatious and his gaze melted her insides, today he was all business.

"Miss St. James, I apologize for the inconvenience. Someone neglected to change the name on your reservation in our system. It was our fault. So, to apologize for the inconvenience, we're extending to you a spa treatment of your choice and an additional full-day pass to enjoy the spa amenities, compliments of the Élite. Your villa is ready and if you require assistance with your luggage, one of our associates can bring your bags while you get settled."

He plastered on a passport photo smile and she stood in silence.

Here he was. Talking to her. Smiling at her. But it wasn't the same smile. She wondered what had changed. Where was that spark?

Now she felt a little foolish. Had she misinterpreted the connection? Was he attracted to her, or had he simply been doing his job? And why did she even care? She wasn't here for a fling. She had only just ditched the ring a few days ago. This trip was for a reset, not a rebound.

Her shoulders relaxed and her posture curved just slightly at the disappointment. But she managed to fake a smile. Tight but polite.

Finally, Simon came around the counter with a lei of bright pink passion flowers, his energy dialed up.

"Welcome to Bora Bora. As a guest of the Villa Laniakea, this special lei was created just for you." He placed it around her neck, while Gabriel stood back and watched.

"Here's the key to your villa and you'll find everything you'll need to know about the property in your room," Simon continued. He proceeded to give an overview of the amenities, a perfect presentation despite the rocky start. She accepted the key and told him she could manage on her own. She mentioned the issue with her luggage and he nodded while her mystery man remained in the background, hands clasped in front of himself, observing their interaction but not joining the conversation.

Riley heard every word of Simon's explanation, but she couldn't focus on him. She was distracted. Yesterday she was sure he had been the anonymous gifter responsible for the champagne. But now she questioned her assumptions, the butterflies, the temptation. She let her eyes shift briefly towards his direction and she read nothing in his expression.

When she turned to depart, the disappointment palpable, the mysterious Frenchman said, "Welcome to Bora Bora, and enjoy your stay, Ms. St. James."

CHAPTER SIXTEEN

Gabriel

Gabriel couldn't believe his luck!

No risky plan to return to Papeete necessary. Riley St. James was here. Alone. In Bora Bora.

And because of the mix up with her reservation, he legitimately knew that she would be on the property for ten days.

Ten. Whole. Days.

His confidence was elevated to an altitude requiring oxygen at the memory of her surprised smile when their eyes met at the check-in desk. A smile that eventually morphed into bewilderment, but he'd fix that.

He had the gift of time on his side.

Watching her eyes shift from bright and animated to bewildered and puzzled, he was forced to push down any indication of interest and stick to the formalities. He didn't know Simon well enough to be anything other than the consummate professional. And, he was expected to set the example and couldn't risk the appearance of impropriety with a hotel guest.

For the next hour, he mostly observed Simon and his interactions with guests and hotel staff. He seemed at ease, confident, and well-pre-pared. The confusion with Riley's reservation had been the only anomaly in an otherwise smooth check-in process.

When they were done, he walked through the remaining activities for the day with Simon and then excused himself.

He had a private tour to give of the property.

CHAPTER SEVENTEEN

Riley

Riley took her time walking to her villa, letting the peace of her surroundings cover her. Her senses were on overload.

Absorbing nature's decadence, she welcomed the breeze off the lagoon carrying the faint scent of salt blending with exotic floral fragrances, while small ripples in the water soothed her troubled spirit.

She paused and lifted her duffle bag off her shoulder, resting it on the wooden pier. Pulling out her phone, she switched it on, raised it above her head and snapped her first selfie. Over-water villas sat atop the lagoon and the water stretched as far as she could see. With each swoosh of air, curly strands of her hair whipped across her face, also happy to be free—from hair ties and flatiron heat.

When she reached her villa, she was at the tip of the pier.

This villa at this hotel is where she imagined Jonathan lifting her up and over the threshold.

As she approached the doorway, a sadness washed over her and her attempts to swallow back the pain and regret that bought her to this moment—alone and betrayed by the man she loved—were futile. Head bowed and her posture slightly curved, she stopped fighting and let the tears fall, giving her anguish the space to breathe, refusing to be suffocated by Jonathan's misdeeds. She instinctively knew that suppressing her pain and disappointment and confusion would delay her healing. And she was determined to be whole again.

After a couple minutes in therapeutic silence, the well of tears was again empty and she gently wiped away the damp trails from her face, regaining her composure. She crossed the threshold as a whispered gasp escaped her mouth.

It was breathtaking.

The view of the mountain could have easily been a landscape painting.

She didn't even bother walking through the villa. From her vantage point, the space was perfect. But there was something missing.

A certain someone was missing.

She allowed herself that moment of recognition and then stepped right out onto her private deck. Peering down into the crystal-clear waters was like standing in meditation. Small schools of exotic fish hurried by as tiny waves lapped against the deck's railings.

It was just her. Secluded in luxury. Surrounded by her new, temporary perfect world.

Always prepared, Riley slipped out of her jeans, pulled off her shirt and dived into the tranquil lagoon. She had the presence of mind to wear her bikini beneath her travel gear—the brand new, golden bikini that made her feel like a goddess in training.

The water enveloped her and she let the stress and strain of the last few days wash away.

She made her way back up to the surface, flipped onto her back and floated beneath the warmth of this new sun.

The thoughts of Jonathan slowly faded, replaced by a new smile and mystic blue eyes.

Maybe it really was time to get past the "first and only" and move on to the "next and new."

CHAPTER EIGHTEEN

Walking up the pier, Gabriel instinctively inspected each entry-way of every villa and found nothing out of order.

As he glanced to his right, something caught his attention in the distance.

He stepped closer to the railing and saw a woman floating in the lagoon.

Narrowing his eyes, he knew exactly who she was. He adjusted the collar of his shirt, failing miserably at trying not to stare. Her choice of a golden bathing suit was perfect—it nearly melted into her caramel skin while a soft brown halo of hair floating around her face. Riley St. James was a modern-day goddess.

He quickly turned away, remembering who he was and where he was. He needed to at least appear to be handling the business of the hotel property.

Continuing his walk towards her villa, he measured his steps to give her chance to make it back to her deck and inside, inspecting doorways and railings with surgical precision. He felt foolish, but decided even if she didn't make it back before he knocked on the door, he'd just wait. Maybe he would just check railings on both sides of the pier.

Riley St. James was worth the wait and pretense.

Several minutes later after a few distinct splashes in the water, he suspected that she was indeed headed back into her villa.

Standing in her entryway, he ran both hands through his hair and made sure there were no obvious signs of perspiration.

Gabriel was captivated by the golden bikini against her beautiful, supple breasts and the exposed curve of her hips and smooth, flat torso that dipped slightly at her belly button. The combined visual of her in the water and what he imagined he couldn't yet see went straight to his manhood.

If this were a game, she'd be winning.

He waited about a minute, maybe less, and firmly tapped on her door.

When she opened a few seconds later, she was wearing a multi-colored sheer kimono over her swimsuit, hair wet and pulled back from her face. He noticed a small dark mole beneath her left eye, a beauty mark that he'd never noticed watching her on television. Without meaning to, he dropped his gaze ever so slightly towards a sparkling navel ring, but then quickly recovered, not wanting to be offensive or too forward.

"Miss St. James. I wanted to extend an offer of a private tour of the property as a personal apology for your inconvenience today. I don't want your first impression at check-in to be a lasting impression of our beautiful resort."

He flashed her another smile. Not his hotel staffer smile, but the same smile from their first encounter in Papeete.

She returned a half-hearted, sly smile but opened the door wider. "Well, please come inside while I consider your invitation."

Just as he began to cross the threshold, she held out her hand against his chest.

Heat rushed up his neck and spread across his face.

"You have me at a disadvantage," she teased. "You know my name, my villa number, my exercise regimen…you even know where and with whom I brunch. But I don't even know your name."

As she spoke, her hand never left his chest.

"My apologies, Mademoiselle. My manners have escaped me. I'm

Gabriel. Gabriel Laurent. I am a regional manager for the hotel and it is my pleasure to serve you."

"Ah, Monsieur Laurent. C'est un plaisir de vous rencontrer."

When she spoke to him, fluently in French, he knew his heart was in trouble.

He smiled his appreciation. "Tu parles français?"

While he knew the answer to this question having overheard her conversation with the pilot on the airplane, he didn't want her to think he had been eavesdropping.

"Oui, Monsieur."

"Mademoiselle, I assure you, the pleasure is all mine."

She stepped back and allowed him inside.

He stood uncomfortably in the middle of the open living space, waiting for an invitation to sit and willing himself not to blow it.

"Please, Gabriel. Have a seat."

Intent on taking a seat in a chair to keep a safe distance between them, he walked to the living room area, careful to not overplay his hand. He focused on her delicate footsteps behind him and aimed his attention at the chair.

When he sat at the single seat across from sofa, his posture was precise to avoid appearing too comfortable.

She noticed.

She sat casually on the sofa and leaned back, tucking one leg beneath her body and pulling her kimono until it was closed tightly around her torso.

"Please make yourself comfortable, Gabriel. We're like old friends now," she said with a hint of humor and knowing.

He nodded and eased back into the seat, his legs parting with the movement. He noticed it was now her turn to drop her gaze, but she quickly recovered, pretending to adjust her kimono at her chest.

Gabriel rescued them both from awkwardness and broke the silence. "May I call you Riley? Or is that too informal?"

"Please, do call me Riley," she quickly replied through a warm smile.

"And tell me more about this invitation."

Gabriel sat upright and eased forward to the edge of his chair, his posture purposeful and his gaze intent. Like the delicate wings of a hummingbird consuming an enchanted nectar, Riley's eyelashes fluttered—her only reaction to his forward movement. But it was all the encouragement he needed.

"I propose beginning your tour at our world-renowned spa—the first of its kind in the world." He let his words flow soft and relaxed, giving him ample opportunity to focus on the contours of her face and neck, the curve and dip of her lips, the warm golden hues of her eyes, the light and dark brown tones of her hair, and most importantly, her smile.

"And, what makes it so unique?" She inquired, raising her dark eyebrows to match a smirk that was a cross between naivete and cunning.

"Slow down, Ms. St. James. I'm getting there," he countered with a smile to match her smirk. Studying the shades of amber and hazel in her inquisitive eyes, he imagined her strolling on sandy beaches beneath the sway of palm trees. Careful not to break their connection, he noticed in his peripheral her one exposed leg dangling from the sofa as she lightly tapped the tips of her toes on the rich wooden floor, impatient but obviously intrigued.

He remembered where he was—his purpose for this little visit—and continued with his pitch.

"The exquisite luxury, the attentive service, and options for pampering are unmatched. It was designed for a woman with high standards and exquisite style."

Riley shifted, lifting her exposed leg onto the sofa and letting her kimono fall open slightly, exposing a small section of her golden bikini top. Reflexively, she lifted her hand to adjust it, but paused and placed it back in her lap.

Gabriel sensed she was improvising and that he was being baited, maybe even tested. He wouldn't bite.

Through a smile she interrupted again, "Are there any services you recommend?" He sensed she was enjoying their tête-à-tête, even if a little nervous.

"There are a few I trust you'd enjoy," he continued, careful to not appear anxious by her movements. "The overwater bungalow massage over a glass bottom floor with a view of the lagoon is the most popular treatment at the spa, and it's very nice. But I think you might require something a little more…" He paused for effect, tilted his head slightly right and continued, "…discerning."

Riley leaned forward, marginally at first, and then with an uncontrolled flicker of her eyelashes asked, "What has given you that impression of me? Why, we've only just met, Monsieur."

The rapid flutter of eyelashes betrayed her otherwise sensual confidence—she was nervous. Sliding her legs off the sofa, she eased forward before crossing her right leg over her left, leaving them both completely exposed. The adjustment freed her right shoulder from the kimono and it fell midway down her arm. It was more skin than he was prepared to navigate so quickly. Her slender neck and barely there collar bone completely exposed. The whisps of curly hair tickling her shoulders and dimples that deepened with each movement of her lips.

She was exquisite—and now in complete control of this conversation.

Gabriel cleared his throat, adjusted his posture and made a snap decision to regain his footing.

"From the first moment I met you in the boutique in Papeete, I sensed your style by your choices in the attire you purchased."

Riley didn't respond. She just tilted her head towards her bare shoulder and crossed her manicured hands over the legs. Her breaths were heavier and her cheeks flushed.

"I felt your independence in your refusal of my assistance." His voice dropped an octave, and she smiled in confirmation.

"I witnessed your quiet—and likely hard-earned—strength and modesty in the fitness center." He didn't blink, wanting her to absorb his words and their meaning.

"And I saw it when you entered the restaurant for brunch in Papeete. Glowing, confident and yes…" He let his voice trail off to reveal a slight smile and then whispered, "…even a little vulnerable."

She didn't fight back the smile that enveloped that small dark mole beneath her eye, nor did she hide the flush in her cheeks. The seconds that passed between them felt like an eternity, filled with his hope that she felt just an ounce of his growing intrigue and might return his interest.

Because the truth was, without a signal from her of interest, he'd have to back off. He, after all, was an employee of the hotel and there were lines he couldn't cross.

Finally, she leaned back into the sofa, a physical invitation to continue, but not before adding, "So, you were the mystery champagne benefactor."

Gabriel parted his lips to speak and she interrupted him. "No need to deny or affirm. It's just nice to be able to say thank you."

He relaxed back into his seat and continued with his spa treatment descriptions of the rainforest showers with aroma therapy fragrances, the body scrub that included a full-body massage under a warm seawater shower, and the tranquil oceanside tea lounge.

Next to him, the sheer curtains at her balcony doors bellowed in bringing with them a warm breeze and the scent of island bliss. Their banter eased into a friendly conversation before they were interrupted by her phone vibrating. At first, she ignored it, but after multiple calls, the phone had inched its way to the corner of the table and fell off.

"Excuse me. I forgot to turn that thing off."

He watched her every movement, and then her body language changed, tensed, as she looked at the bright screen. She used her finger to scroll through and then held the side button to switch the device to the silent position.

"Let's make a deal," Still holding the phone, she turned to him and smiled.

"Okay," he quickly agreed. He didn't really care what she suggested. He was all in. His instincts about her had proven reliable. At first glance, he knew he wanted to know this woman. Now, in less than hour, he was more captivated and determined to get to the steamy hot core of Riley St. James.

"Today you'll give me a tour of the spa so that I can select my complimentary treatment. Then later this evening, maybe you can show me around the hotel restaurants and lounges and bars, and whatever other entertainment options are available on the property."

"I can accommodate your request," he quickly and decisively replied—possibly a little too quick.

She smiled bigger this time. "I'm not done with my deal yet."

"Oh, there's more?" This time he leaned back and nervously ran his hand through his hair.

"There's always room for more," she quipped, signaling a growing level of comfort with him.

"By all means, please continue, Mademoiselle."

This time, she stood—a move that commanded his attention and his eyes followed. She walked over the sliding glass door just as a breeze flowed into the space, catching her kimono and lifting it away from her body as she leaned against the door frame. He gazed in admiration while the soft scent of a floral bouquet wafted towards him, both seizing his senses. Her profile...the dramatic bellowing kimono against her illuminous skin...the intoxicating fragrance...distracted and vexed him.

She kept her body aimed out towards the lagoon, but when she spoke again, she tilted her head just slightly over her shoulder.

"Tomorrow, I'd like you to join me for breakfast and tell me all the best places to visit while I'm on the island." She paused and folded her arms, as if reconsidering, and added, "And not just the tourist traps. I'm talking real, authentic Tahitian experiences."

She angled her body so that her back was now against the door frame and tightened her kimono.

Gabriel rubbed his chin, truly perplexed. How could he explain eating breakfast with a female guest traveling alone? And not just any guest—Riley St. James—a famous guest that was sure to draw attention. If any of the hotel guests had seen social media in the last 48 hours, chances are they knew who she was also. His professional brain kicked in and he made a mental note to have a discussion with Simon about their special guest so that he could relay very specific instructions to the staff.

As if she read his mind, she embraced her modesty that he assumed was her true nature and added in a syrupy sweet tone, "I'll order room service and we'll have a private breakfast on my patio."

He welcomed the opportunity for some alone time with Riley, but his confidence was a little rattled, suspicious of her motives. Was he just a distraction from her very public personal problems? With so much at stake for him professionally with this last assignment, was he being foolish to take the risk?

But then he looked at her with her raised, eyebrows and a slight, but genuine smile, and he knew the answer.

Gabriel's apprehension faded and decided she indeed might be worth it. He wanted to get to know her and if she wanted to use him to pass the time and distract her from her real life, he was hers for the taking.

"You've got yourself a deal, Mademoiselle," he said, standing to walk over to her.

She stood upright from the door frame and accepted his extended hand. "Let's shake on it?"

She looked down at their gripped hands and then back up into his eyes.

A brief but fleeting moment of knowing passed between them.

Their brief encounter in the hotel boutique. The anonymous champagne delivery. Their eyes meeting in the fitness centre. She was a woman worthy of the desire he already had pulsing through his veins.

He started to release his grip, but then she sandwiched his hand between both of hers. Her palms were warm, and the gesture one more of gratitude than infatuation.

He added his free hand to their clasped hands, peered down and knew she had taken up residence in his thoughts—possibly permanently. He had wanted to wrap his arms around her waist since the moment she whisked past him on the tarmac. But those were the desires of a man looking with his eyes and not his heart. This moment was so much better.

When he looked up again, she was smiling. He allowed her to pull away first and then stepped back. He returned both hands to his pant pockets and returned her smile.

"Shall we begin, Mademoiselle?"

She cinched the string on the waist of her kimono, slid on her sandals and instructed, "Lead the way, Monsieur."

CHAPTER NINETEEN

Riley was having some sort of outer body experience.

She had always been a very confident woman as a professional. But she was still a work in progress personally. But today, in the presence of a strange man whom she'd barely just met, she flirted—just a little—finally understanding the allure that some women had and others could only admire.

Today, she felt like the object of someone's desire. Not an object to be possessed.

Gabriel was so damn sexy, but it was his subtlety that she found most attractive. It occupied his cool blue eyes. She sensed it in his restraint and his discernment—she might not have her luggage, but she still carried a lot of baggage. She felt it in the heat of his hands and heard it in the weight of his words. It wholly inhabited his demeanor, his mannerisms—his manhood. Any physical attraction he felt towards her, he suppressed in favor of getting to know her.

His regard for her was the permission she needed to release her inhibitions for once in her life and take a chance on something—and someone—that strictly made her feel good for the sake of feeling good.

Once they left the privacy of her villa, hotel staffer Gabriel switched on. He was all business, giving her the history of the hotel and the island and sharing the details about the range of guest amenities.

His English was really good, but she loved that his French accent was always present. And he didn't try to hide it.

As they reached the end of the walkway, a couple was heading in their direction. Gabriel reached out his arm to move her slightly to the left. The female smiled and nodded approvingly. Riley guessed she wasn't the only woman on this island that found her mystery Frenchman a delectable treat.

"The Deep Ocean Spa is ranked one of the top ten spas in the world," he recited. She smiled, realizing he was giving her the full pitch.

She was enjoying him turn on his work charm. It was a quality she recognized. She listened intently and stole a few sideways glances as they walked.

"It's the first thalasso therapy center ever built in the South Pacific, using the benefits of water drawn from the Pacific Ocean depths to deliver treatments unrivaled and unmatched."

"Sounds amazing," she said. "But, I'm curious. What exactly is your position at the hotel?"

Gabriel laughed before he answered.

"I'm a regional director for the company. I oversee a portfolio of our properties, including this one and all our other properties in the South Pacific, Australia and the Indian Ocean. I'm here for the next month to oversee Simon's training. He's the new hotel manager, recently transferred from one of our properties in Honolulu, Hawaii."

She nodded as he talked. He exuded the kind of masculine confidence she appreciated in a man. But on him, she sensed something different. There was a warmth to his presence. A warmth that put her at ease. A warmth that invited her into his space.

As they got closer to the spa, they stopped on small bridge expanse over a portion of the lagoon. On one end of the bridge post hung a fabric bag. When they reached the end, he stopped.

"Time to feed the fish," he joked.

"What do you mean by feed the fish?"

He leaned over the side of the bridge and her eyes followed. Below them were swarms of exotic fish, swimming in all directions.

"Reach into that bag and grab a piece of bread."

"Bread? We're feeding exotic salt water fish…bread?"

He laughed.

"Just trust me. They love it. You'll see."

She did as he asked and pulled a chunk of French baguette from the bag.

"First break it up into smaller pieces and just drop it in."

She was skeptical, but just as he said, the fish clamored for the bread pieces, devouring it as soon as it hit the water.

"I can't believe it! We share identical appetites," she joked.

"What do you mean, 'identical appetites?"

She chuckled. "I also like to devour bread," she said, avoiding eye contact. This all felt too natural. Too easy. Too comfortable.

It made her nervous.

They both leaned over the bridge, watching the fish jostle and dive for pieces of bread. It reminded her of her early days in the local broadcast newsroom. Editorial meetings could be brutal. If you weren't pitching a story idea, you were fighting for crumbs.

The cutest family of four wandered towards them, when the little boy broke away from his dad, eager to feed the fish. Gabriel handed him a chunk of bread and greeted the boy's parents. Riley stood to the side, pretending to watch the force of the oceanside waves, but really listening to Gabriel make kid-friendly excursion recommendations for the family. The mom eased over towards Riley, a curious smile on her face.

"I don't mean to be rude, but are you Riley St. James?"

Riley returned her smile and said, "Yes. And you are?" She held out her hand in greeting.

She quickly took Riley's hand and began shaking it a little too quickly. "I'm Justine, and that's my husband Paul and our boys Thomas and Nicholas. I told my husband it was you!"

Riley managed to free her hand from Justine's and asked questions to steer her away from any questions about her broken engagement. And Justine seemed perfectly content to talk about her boys and why she needed this vacation. When her family and Gabriel joined them, she teased her husband that she was right and Gabriel made a point of mentioning the tour of the property he was giving Riley to quell any suspicions of their rapport with hotel guests.

When Justine turned to leave with her family, she whispered to Riley, "Ignore the noise and enjoy paradise."

Riley smiled at her and turned to Gabriel, who had been watching the entire exchange. He didn't step in, but he appeared ready to leap if necessary.

As they walked towards the spa, he asked, "Is it always like that? People recognizing you and just starting conversations? And does it bother you?"

She dropped her head slightly, because it still embarrassed her. "People assume that because I'm a television personality of sorts, that I'm an extrovert. That I like the attention. It's really the opposite. I tolerate it and most of the time it's harmless. But sometimes…"

She paused, remembering the incident at the airport just a few days ago. "Sometimes people go too far and it can be draining. I don't know that I'll ever get used to it, but I manage."

"I hope you know that you're safe here. Our guests aren't typically starstruck. But if someone makes you uncomfortable, you just let us know," Gabriel said, obviously in his professional capacity.

She appreciated him asking and thanked him for his consideration.

He guided her to the spa's open-air entry where they were greeted by two women at the welcome counter. Of course, they all knew each other and Riley was sure one of the young women blushed when Gabriel addressed her.

"This is a special hotel guest, Riley St. James from the U.S. She'll be with us the next ten days and enjoying treatments at the spa. I'm giving her a tour of the property and wanted her to see the spa amenities before scheduling her appointments," Gabriel added. For the second time in a matter of minutes, he shrewdly averted any suspicion of impropriety.

And Riley understood the stakes were as high for him as they were for her.

The non-blushing staffer spoke up first. "Welcome to Bora Bora, Mademoiselle St. James. Please accept this welcome gift from us to you."

She handed Riley a small glass bottle of oil. Without looking at the name on the bottle, Riley untwisted the cap and inhaled.

"Wow! What is this? It smells amazing."

"It's Monoi oil, authentic to Tahiti. It's a combination of coconut oil and Tahitian gardenias and can be used on your skin, in your bath, or on your hair."

There was a mirror nearby, and Riley knew her damp hair was quickly drying in the heat. In all the excitement of her private tour, she walked out of her villa without adding any product to her hair. So, it was just wet with salty sea water.

"Mademoiselle, did you just come from a swim?"

Riley chuckled. "I did. I'm sure my hair was the biggest clue." Not to mention she was still dressed in her bathing suit and kimono, though she'd cinched it at the waist so that it doubled as a cute maxi dress.

"Why don't you go rinse your skin and your hair in one of our rainforest showers? There are only a few guests in the spa today and I'm sure you'll find one free."

She looked towards Gabriel.

"You go and I'll return for you in a half hour. These ladies will take great care of you, I'm certain. Then, we'll continue our tour."

"If it's not too much of an inconvenience." She hoped he would return, but didn't want to show it.

"Not at all, Mademoiselle." There was that familiar spark in his eyes as he smiled and she thought she might never tire of hearing him call her Mademoiselle.

"Merci," she said.

This time the blushing hostess came from behind the counter.

"Follow me, Mademoiselle."

She introduced herself as Clara and explained the various treatment rooms and lounges as they passed them by.

"These are the massage villas, and some have glass bottom floors to watch the fish swimming during your treatment. It's very relaxing."

"That sounds lovely," Riley said, slowing her pace to peek inside.

"So, you are friendly with Monsieur Gabriel?"

And there it was, Riley thought. She knew she had seen Clara blushing when Gabriel greeted them. But she was really young and likely had a very innocent crush on him. Riley understood. She was also nursing a crush, though it was far from innocent.

"Oh, no. He is just being nice to me. There was a problem with my reservation this morning and my luggage still hasn't arrived. So, he's taking pity on me."

She hoped she sounded convincing.

"He is a very nice man. And very handsome."

She was blushing again through a nervous giggle.

"Yes, he is very nice. And I guess he's also handsome."

The winding path they had taken was surrounded by a flowing water feature on the left. Clara explained that the water was extremely cold, meant to help detoxify the skin.

As she guided Riley through the tropical space pointing out the various rooms, she took the time to describe the exclusive treatments of a thalassotherapy spa including signature massages, body scrubs and wraps, bubbles for oxygenation, and seawater therapies and shower mists. Riley typically tried to limit her indulgent urges to designer bags and shoes, but that was all about to change.

Enveloped in a gentle warmth and surrounded by palm trees, exotic flowers, and a comforting blend of floral fragrances, she realized those were just things she was expected to have—this was therapeutic and something she needed to have. With each step on the tiled floor, she inched closer to reassurance—about her choice to flee and free the real Riley. This could very well be the inoculation she needed to prepare her for the real life waiting for her back at home.

Finally, they ended their tour at two shower stalls whose mosaic walls resembled the deep blue of the sea. After Clara explained the multiple features, she left and returned with a couple towels and a glass of water with starfruit slices floating inside.

"When you are done, just leave the towels in the basket and enjoy any one of the lounge areas. The Tea Lounge is nicest at this time of day. The glass doors are open to the beach and the breeze off of the ocean is very refreshing right now."

"Merci, Clara. And please let Monsieur Laurent know where I am when he returns." Riley was careful to keep her references to Gabriel professional.

"Oui, oui."

Clara disappeared and Riley slipped off her cover up. She kept on the bathing suit and stepped inside the shower. She chose the Brazilian rainforest treatment, a combination of air infused with passion flower and citrus fragrances, bursts of water from multiple shower heads caressing her skin, and a larger water feature sprinkled a light flow of water above her. She let her head fall back, reinvigorated by the water massaging her face and running through her hair. Her scalp tingled and she ran her fingers through her tangled mass of curls. Most days, she had a love-hate relationship with her hair. But since arriving in Tahiti, it was all love. She sometimes took for granted the versality that came natural with her hair texture because it was always so much work. But not today. Not this trip. There were no cameras and no lights. Just time in the sun, good food, good drinks, good company and a good time.

When she was done, she turned off the shower and squeezed the access water from her hair. Grabbing the bottle of Monoi oil, she poured half in the palm of her hand and massaged it through her hair and scalp. She poured a little more oil from the bottle, warmed it between the palms of her hands and applied it to her arms and legs.

Feeling refreshed, she headed to the Tea Lounge with her water, sipping the cool beverage along the way. When she entered the room, she thought that Clara had undersold the space.

A haunting sway of white sheer curtains around the open glass doors lured her in. The waves were a little stronger on this side of the property, aggressively splashing against the rocks and spraying water at least ten feet into the air.

She stepped outside into the cool sand and stared forward, half not believing she was here and half wishing she never had to leave.

With each crash of water against the stones, she wondered how their shapes had changed over time from the sheer force of the sea. Today, she felt more commonality with the rocks than the sea—repeatedly being battered until the shape of who she thought she was morphed into something new. She just hoped that the something new was recognizable.

She made her way back to one of the full-length lounge chairs and took a couple huge gulps of the water. She stretched her body out, closed her eyes to be fully present in the moment and gave thanks for her life—a life that wasn't always easy but one she worked hard at making meaningful. The sounds and the scent of the sea were all the therapy she needed.

But in true Riley fashion, her mind took over and was flooded with questions of what's next. Small droplets of water eased down her neck and dampened her kimono, pasting it to her body. With each burst of air off the ocean, the coolness kept her alert and oddly comforted.

The last few days had given her some distance from Jonathan, but the repercussions reverberated across oceans and countries. She didn't want the dread of the inevitable confrontation awaiting her back home to interfere with her chance to just be Riley. Not successful journalist, Riley. Not Jonathan's fiancé, Riley. Not never misbehaving Catholic girl, Riley. Not reliable to a fault, Riley. Not trusting Riley. Just Riley. It had been so long since she had the space to just be. This was her time.

But the planner in her wouldn't rest, so Riley indulged her impulses and cycled through all she had to do when she returned to the real world—mainly move out of Jonathan's and find a new home for herself. A sense of contentment returned as she sat up on the lounge chair and pulled her hair to one side, twisting the remaining water out, relishing the feel of the droplets trailing down against her skin. All around her, the combined scent of Monoi oil, lavender and orange permeated from her skin and her hair and she made a note to frequent the aroma therapy showers, daily if possible.

She let her shoulders drop and tilted her head left and right to release any remnants of tension. She was so far removed from her real life and didn't realize how much she would enjoy not being immediately recognized or bombarded with questions about some of the people she interviewed or the stories she covered or the state of journalism in America. Those things had taken a toll on her she hadn't considered until she was here, on the other side of the world.

Watching the waves wash in, she noted the sun sat lower in the sky. She didn't have a watch and had left her cell phone in the villa. This made her smile as she leaned back on the lounge chair. She had no place to be and no one waiting for her. She thought she could get used to this life.

A few minutes later, Gabriel appeared, casting his shadow across the length of her exposed legs.

"Mademoiselle St. James, are you ready to continue your tour?" he asked with his thick French accent—an enticement cautious Riley implored her to avoid. But new Riley was leaning into her curiosity about her mysterious Frenchman. As he stood a healthy distance away, she admired his professionalism and appreciated his regard for her personal space.

She was definitely feeling more curious than cautious. Practically daring herself to surrender to her desires.

Riley turned to face him and smiled as their eyes met. She let him catch her gaze as the silence suggestively grew heavy between them. When she finally looked away, it wasn't to break the connection, but to show some discretion.

"After that rainforest shower, the gentle breeze, some moments of contemplation, and this amazing view, I do believe I am ready for whatever is next," she elusively responded. She stood, slipped on her sandals and walked over to him. "Take the lead, Monsieur."

He turned and her steps matched his. He gently placed his hand on the small of her back, guiding her towards the exit. She slowed her pace to allow a little more pressure, to feel a little more heat from the palm of his hand. And giving him permission to keep his hand exactly where it was. At least until he couldn't anymore.

Neither of them spoke in quiet recognition of the moment they were sharing. They just continued that way until they approached the public space and he finally dropped his hand.

Without looking at him, she said, "I miss that already."

CHAPTER TWENTY

Gabriel

W hen they had completed their tour, they went their separate ways. Riley headed back to her villa and Gabriel still had work to do with Simon.

Problem was, he didn't know how he was expected to concentrate with thoughts of Riley's honey-coated thighs dancing in his head, and her sweet smile owning his thoughts. His attention was completely divided, and he had the added challenge of her being a high-profile guest. People—hotel guests and staffers—would be watching her every move.

When they ended their tour at the pool area, she invited him to join her for a glass of champagne later that night back at her villa. He promised to call her to discuss timing, which to be safe would have to be late so as not to risk being caught going into her villa while guests were still dining or mingling at the bars.

Riley had graciously agreed. After all, there was risk for them both.

He didn't know exactly what he wanted from her. He was conflicted. When he met her that first evening in Papeete, she was just a beautiful woman that caught his eye. But now that he knows who she is and what she's dealing with, he didn't want her to think he was a crude and insensitive opportunist, taking advantage of her heartbreaking situation. It was complicated and for now, he would settle for getting to know her.

When he made it back to the office, Simon was waiting.

"How was the tour with Ms. St. James?" he inquired.

"I believe it went well. She even spent some time at the spa. I'm grateful she agreed. I didn't want the mix-up with her reservation to leave the wrong lasting impression."

He hoped he didn't sound guilty or suspicious.

"It was definitely the right call," Simon said.

Gabriel was reaching for the property management manual when Simon spoke again.

"You do know who she is, right?"

He knew he had to play it cool.

"Yes. She's a television journalist. Which is one of the reasons why we must ensure she has a pleasant visit, free of unnecessary drama."

"True. But do you know this was supposed to her honeymoon? It's all over social media."

This time Gabriel turned to face Simon.

"Yes. I know that as well. And we should assume that other guests will also know and so we must remain diligent. We can't protect her, but we can make her stay as comfortable as possible. And we must discourage staff from engaging in idle gossip. She's our guest and whatever is happening in her personal life is exactly that—personal."

Simon agreed and they sat together for the next hour discussing evening activities and troubleshooting routine hotel matters.

He was distracted, but knew he had to get through the business of the day to enjoy the pleasures of evening.

Later that night at dinner service, Gabriel overheard two couples dining together casually chatting about Riley's situation. He positioned himself near their table to capture what details he could. He had opted to not ask Riley about what happened, truly believing it was a private matter and giving her the space to process and share when she was comfortable.

He still didn't know very much about her, but he knew she was in a vulnerable position—even if she tried to hide it. He sensed that the confidence she exuded as a professional woman in the spotlight, was now a shield in this personal scenario. She needed her confidence armor to cope, and hearing her name associated with gossip spread by people who didn't know her, wouldn't bother to know her, and simply only wanted to be entertained by the social media drama of the day, irritated him.

These strangers knew about as much as he did, but still managed to keep the conversation going by speculating. The two women were sympathetic to Riley, while the men insisted there were two sides to every story.

Gabriel recognized one of the women as part of the couple he and Riley passed on their way to the spa. She had smiled approvingly at Riley, and he wondered what it had meant. Was it encouragement? Approval? Solidarity?

Whatever it was, he felt a sudden rush of affinity with the woman and decided to send the table complimentary glasses of champagne.

But he also made a mental note to instruct the front desk staff to remind guests when they check-in to be respectful of all hotel guests' privacy.

The attention to privacy is not uncommon, and this hotel had gone to great lengths to build in privacy measures, including the strategic placement of its over-water villas. Each villa was angled outward and away from their surrounding neighbors. Meaning, you could walk out onto your deck without fear of your neighbor's prying eyes. You could certainly see other villas, but you could not see inside their space nor could you see what they were doing in the privacy of their outdoor areas.

And Riley's villa, the Villa Laniakea, sat at the tip of the pier, granting the most privacy of all the villas. It was also the largest. He made a note to ask her later why she kept so a large suite once she decided to travel solo.

All of the villas were nice, but that one had the best decor, flexibility, amenities and privacy. It was the privacy aspect that most attracted him at the moment. Riley probably thought so, too.

When he had called her an hour ago, she had told him she was taking dinner alone in her villa, not wanting to sit alone in the restaurant and be subject to whispers and questions. She had suspected that more of the guests would recognize her and she just didn't want the scrutiny.

He understood and gave her recommendations on the menu. They agreed that he would join her for a night cap at eleven that night.

Later that night, he changed into dark jeans, a black V-neck shirt and casual black leather loafers. All was quiet from Riley's neighboring villas, and he tapped on her door, unnoticed.

When she opened the door, his eyes and his heart dropped and she gave him a shy smile.

A hint of Monoi oil drifted from her hair, loosely knotted on top of her head and exposing her soft brown skin glowing against her dark strapless dress. His eyes shifted slightly down, admiring how the dress clung softly to her curves yet left a little something to the imagination. He didn't know what to expect from her tonight and had managed his expectations. Her brightly manicured toes peeped out beneath the soft fabric, and he wondered if she was the ticklish type—a thought that would keep him on a narrow path of good behavior.

"Bonsoir," was all she said, stepping back to allow him to enter.

He was a goner.

CHAPTER TWENTY-ONE

Riley

When Gabriel crossed the threshold this time entering her villa, Riley knew she was past the point of no return. She was throwing caution to the wind. She'd spent part of her day planning how to exit the life she'd carefully curated. Now, she wanted to experience life without a plan. It was, after all, a promise she made to herself about this trip. She wanted to feel all the feels—pleasure just for the sake of feeling good, minus any hidden or expressed motives.

The moment Gabriel appeared in her doorway, camouflaged in dark clothing to protect their secret rendezvous, she knew she was closing a door on a chapter of her life. But this was no re-write of her love life. This was all new material. Her sexuality had been trapped in third person.

That was then. This is now, and something had been stirred and awakened inside of her, something she liked. Something she was embracing. Something she wanted and needed.

As Gabriel breezed by her, she inhaled scents of coconut and shaving cream. She followed him towards the bar, struck by his form and his easy confidence, tempted to run just one finger down his chest.

In those first few moments, she knew where they were headed. She had granted herself adequate time to debate the pros and cons of sleeping with a man she barely knew. The pros won.

For years, she'd been following her man's lead. Responding but never initiating. Receiving but careful about how she was judged in her giving. Never too aggressive, but open just enough to ensure that he knew she desired him and only him.

And what had that gotten her? She had played it safe and it still wasn't enough. Playing it safe was no guarantee of life-long happiness.

She was over letting someone else narrate her life—living in third person.

Tonight's exploration would be in first person. For her pleasure—and his.

A bottle of champagne chilled in an ice bucket on the bar, with two empty champagne flutes waiting to be filled. The only lights on in the villa were over the bar and on her terrace. Her Bluetooth speaker was set to low and her Grown Ass Jazz playlist set the mood.

Tonight, she wore a simple, strapless black maxi dress that hugged her body in all the right places, imagining how it would feel to him when he eventually touched her.

If he touched her.

Up until now, she wasn't sure if her mostly subtle hints had served their purpose. She suspected that his presence in her villa coupled with his appraising eyes in the doorway was proof that maybe they had.

Gabriel broke the silence.

"Shall I pour the champagne?"

"S'il vous plaît, Monsieur."

When both glasses were filled, she suggested they retire to her terrace, where the evening breeze created quiet ripples in the lagoon and relaxed her.

He followed her to two lounge chairs at the edge of her private pool. She laid back, lifting the edge of her dress to expose her calves and propped one leg up.

Gabriel sat on the lounge chair next to hers, but chose to sit up—an attentive posture.

Heat rose as her confidence began to fade as she sat squarely in the middle of a scenario she orchestrated. It wasn't regret she was feeling, more like awkwardness.

His first question broke the ice and she recovered.

"So, you knew I sent the champagne in Papeete?"

She chuckled, taking a sip of her champagne before answering.

"I suspected it was you. I thought I saw you at the bar when we arrived, but then you disappeared and, in your place, appeared a bottle of champagne. When I didn't see you again, I guessed it was a parting gift."

She took another sip, giving him time to respond.

"Yes. I guess it was a parting gift. But it was also a clue."

"A clue? Please elaborate."

"I wanted you to know that I was interested in getting to know you, but I was out of time. I had a flight that morning and didn't want to embarrass you or myself in front of your friends."

Now he sipped his champagne, and she watched his throat as he swallowed a deep gulp.

He was also nervous.

Now, she was emboldened.

"I appreciate your discretion." She paused and sipped again. "And your interest."

He raised an eyebrow.

"Very good," he said. "And if you'll allow, I'd like to tell you specifically how interested in you I am."

He took another gulp of champagne, this time emptying the glass of his liquid courage and setting it aside.

She weighed her options. She was afraid and knew her next move would change her. But it might also reveal her.

"I have a better idea." She sat up, cautiously confident, and leaned in to kiss him.

Nothing too aggressive. Just a soft, sweet kiss on his lips and an invitation of her own.

"*Show me* how interested you are in getting to know me."

Her words trailed off and he pressed forward. When he opened his mouth to deepen their kiss, her moan encouraged him. Their tongues massaging and exploring, he cupped her face between his hands and her doubts fell away.

His hands trailed down her neck and across her bare shoulders. Her back arched, forcing her body forward and inviting him to move in closer. The sensations invading her body were intoxicating. A deep yearning rose from her core as she inhaled him, allowing her deepening desire to be freed.

Gabriel pulled back slightly and teased her lower lip before trailing kisses down her jaw and into the curve of her neck. She tilted her head, giving him full access while grasping a fistful of his hair and guiding the pressure of his kisses. He held her shoulders, the weight of his hands tightening as kissed and sucked at her neck.

The electricity between them emboldened her. She placed her free hand on his thigh, feeling his muscles tense beneath her touch as she slid her fingertips higher to feel him growing, throbbing and her body temperature elevating with each movement. The fire between them had started as kindling, slow and tentative. Now, the the flames danced and licked at them, torching any pretense of resistance.

Releasing her shoulders, he slowly traced his index finger across her skin and dipped it beneath the elastic holding her dress up. With a gentle tug, it fell away, exposing her breasts and taut nipples. He briefly pulled away to watch his now free hands cupping both her breasts. He softly squeezed and lifted them up towards his eager mouth and slid his tongue between them. Her breath caught as she pressed his head closer and he sucked and teased one nipple with his tongue and traced circles with his fingertip on the other.

Lightning rods of desire struck every part of her body beneath his touch, releasing a sense of absolute craving.

Her face tilted up to the dark, starlit sky, exposing her body and her desire to the night and this man that suddenly landed in her life, a channel to liberate her inhibitions.

As his kissing and sucking became more ravenous, she knew he was tasting the sweet honey dust she'd brushed across her skin—and he liked it.

He pulled back, pausing to catch his breath as his eyes drank in her body.

She was breathless and wanted more.

"You are so beautiful," he whispered. "And you taste so sweet. May I see all of you?"

At his gentle request, she stood and slowly slid the dress past her waist and let it fall into a pool of fabric at her feet. Like shedding a layer of skin, she was completely exposed and liberated.

He looked up into her eyes and she smiled in approval. She literally stopped breathing and the world paused with her. Her eyes soaked up the perfect tranquility, mentally recording this moment—her first—of emotional and physical honesty.

She finally exhaled beneath his gaze and felt her insecurity creeping in. Her hands moved on impulse to cover her most private place. No other man had ever seen her in the nude. But she sensed this man was different. His eyes never left hers, as if waiting for her permission to devour her or a cue to slow down.

The intensity in his blue eyes didn't plead, but were patient and shone affectionately in the cover of night. Beneath his gaze, Riley felt like the most beautiful and the most desired woman in the world.

Riley reached out and ran her fingers through his hair, and this time a guttural moan escaped from deep inside his chest and she knew he wanted her as much as she needed him. Her touch was the only permission he needed.

He turned his head into her outstretched arm and lightly kissed the delicate skin down to the inside of her wrist. She sighed and he pulled her forward. The warmth of his mouth found the heat between her legs and her fingers slid through his hair, grasping handfuls and directing his movements. He teased her with light, wet kisses until his tongue slipped out and began doing things to her that weakened her legs and made her whimper his name. Every cell in her body was awake, and she was delirious from excessive pleasure.

She moved her pelvis in motion with his mouth and his tongue, getting pressure in the right places and at just the right moment, until her body screamed out, begged and pleaded for more.

The background music changed, and Roberta Flack's sultry voice filled the cool air with *The First Time Ever I Saw Your Face*.

Riley's body softened as the lyrics permeated her senses and she pulled back from him. Lifting his face to look into his eyes, she murmured, "I need more of you."

At her desperate command, he released her. She stepped back, giving him space to stand. In one quick motion, he pulled off his shirt while she began unzipping his pants, finding a surprise inside.

Licking her lips as the head of his stiff cock immediately appeared, she teased, "No undergarments? Presumptuous much?"

He managed to pant out a reply, "I never wear undergarments."

"Wait," she paused for dramatic effect and looked directly into his eyes. "So, all day today while we were touring the property, you didn't have on underwear?"

He smirked. "That is correct, Mademoiselle," he said through a crooked smile. "Does that change anything? Shall we slow down?"

This time she stood on the tips of her toes, kissed him deeply and then whispered, "It changes everything," as she wrapped her hand around the length of him and felt him pulsate in her grip.

The warm night air and haunting melody inspired her. Now, with them both fully nude, she slid away and laced her fingers between his, leading him to the private pool at the edge of her deck.

She climbed in first, the cool water reinvigorating her as she dipped her head under. When she popped up, she pulled her hair free as Gabriel joined her from beneath the water. She leaned her body against the edge of the pool closest to the lagoon and pulled him in for a kiss as she admired the distinctive angles of his face, his thick black hair, now wet and wavy, and the perfect contours of his chest. She couldn't wait to feel the thick patch of dark chest hair pressed softly against her breast.

As he drew closer, she reached out her free hand and slid her palm down his chest and over his ripple of solid abs. A desperation and longing seeped from his skin and she finally let their lips reconnect. She felt him swell against her as his kisses deepened like this might be his only night with her and he didn't want to waste it. His eagerness was endearing, and a gift she never expected. The way he looked at her, spoke to her, cherished this time with her, attended to her body—it was everything she'd ever wanted and realized it was something she never had. Until tonight.

With the scent of coconut on his skin and the lingering taste of her wetness on his mouth, she took everything he was willing to give and returned it in kind, coaxed along by the incomparable Roberta serenading them.

Riley spread her arms across the edge of the pool, fully opening her body up to him. His hands caressed her breasts, her stomach and hips, and with the tips of his fingers, he teased and tempted the slit of heat between her legs. While he took his time enticing her, she let her hands feel every inch of smooth skin on his back, as his muscles flexed and tensed at her touch and she kissed and licked and nibbled on his neck. When she reached his waist, she let her hand find and grip his cock. She bit her lip and rubbed her thumb over the wet tip, and in seconds he grew and thickened as she stroked him until he couldn't help but grind against her in response.

His touch was synchronized to hers and exact, keeping the tip of his thumb on her clit while sliding his middle finger gently into the slippery wetness between her thighs. Instinctively, she pushed her hips forward to meet his touch.

Now moving in unison, their breathing heavy and erratic, and water splashing on the deck and over the side of the pool, she opened her eyes, wanting to feel and see their shared ecstasy. His eyes were closed and she watched as they twitched and his lip curled with each stroke of her hand on his cock. Satisfied that he was joining her right at the edge of explosion, she wrapped one buoyant leg around his waist and whispered in his ear.

"Did you bring protection?"

"As luck would have it, I did."

"Presumptuous?" she said teasingly.

"No. Just prepared," he said.

They paused while he reached over to pull a condom from his pants pocket. He ripped it open with his teeth and slid it on with one hand.

Riley raised both legs and wrapped them around his waist, giving him full access to enter her.

As he slid inside of her, he used a free hand to wrap a handful of her hair around his hand and gently pulled her head backwards, giving him full view of her neck. Every nerve in her body tingled as she licked her lips in admiration of the lean muscles in his arm tightening to hold her with every plunge deeper inside her.

"Oh, Gabriel. Give me more," she demanded through whispered pleas. He filled her, stretching her warm, wet tightness until she surrendered to her most primal urges. Riley swayed her hips and gripped him between her thighs, wild and dizzy with desire.

"Tell me how you want it," he whispered heat passing from his mouth into her ear. "Let me please you. Show you how much I want you."

She moaned. "Slow. Go slow, so that I can feel every inch of you."

He obeyed. He pulled back and watched as she let her head fall back, arms stretched wide to receive all of him. "You like this?"

"Yes. More just like that." She closed her eyes and soft gasps of air escaped her mouth with each stroke as he went deeper, slowly pushing her to her peak.

Their bodies met in a rhythm, her hips grinding against him while the water lapped against and over the side of the pool.

"Kiss me," she pleaded with him, raising her head to meet his gaze.

His eyes began to close as he reached in to kiss her.

"No," she demanded. "Keep your eyes open and kiss me. I want you to see me give my body to you."

He saw unfiltered desire in her eyes, and did as she commanded.

Eyes wide open, he began to slowly and softly kiss her, desperate to reach that place in her that's never been touched before. He gripped both hands on her ass and plunged deeper as their eyes locked, pushing their bodies beyond any physical limits and transcending into pure, unadulterated pleasure.

"I've wanted you to touch me like this all day," she whispered. "To feel what I'm feeling."

His gaze now piercing and gone far beyond a simple act of erotic love making, she felt them connecting. And it scared her. Physical connection was one thing, but emotional connection? She wasn't ready for anything more than this moment of selfish indulgence.

"I've wanted to touch and know you from the first moment I laid eyes on you," he confessed as he trailed kisses down her neck and across her bare shoulder.

She blocked those thoughts, refusing to be denied. Her moans grew quicker and louder, and she surrendered.

"More," she demanded, her breathing and movements firing at a rapid pace.

He was more than willing to oblige. He met her every movement and she could feel him pulsating and nearing release. Pulling out fully and plunging deeper inside her, he sped up each motion as she pressed against him. Unable to keep his eyes open, his breaths became groans and his back curved with each thrust. His grip on her ass tightened and he spread her legs wide until her back arched and her head heavy on the deck. Pounding deeper, she opened wider and made room for him. She felt the tiny nerves swelling on her clit and forced herself up. Wrapping her arms around his neck, she sucked on his earlobe, panting, gasping and trembling as she reached her climax.

When she screamed out in pleasure, he let himself go and held her as her body shuddered against his.

Slowly, she slid her legs down his and rested her face between his neck and shoulder, steadying herself with one arm over his opposite shoulder. She could feel his heart racing as fast as hers against her breast, and his breathing was heavy.

Perspiration dotted his forehead as he buried his face in her hair, gripping the back of her head.

She took a deep breath in, inhaling their bodies now drenched in chlorine.

When he pulled back, he looked into her eyes, smiled and said, "You are a goddess."

She smiled back at him.

"Yeah, I'm trying something new," she joked.

"This is something new?"

"It's all new," she said

"Tell me more."

She didn't want to get too heavy with him, at least not right after. So, she played coy and set the stage for more.

"Not here. Let's get cleaned up and if you're nice to me, I'll tell you more…after round two."

He returned her smile and followed her out of the pool.

"Oh, I'll be nice," he promised.

CHAPTER TWENTY-TWO

Gabriel

B ack inside the villa, Gabriel poured them both more champagne while Riley left him alone to fill the tub for a hot bath. He only had a couple minutes to regain his composure. The fire flickered on a small vanilla-scented travel candle atop the bar, and he inhaled to let it calm him.

They'd left the sliding glass door partially open and the air had grown thick and humid and the soft white curtains swayed and rippled. Gabriel wiped his brow and slowly ran his hands through his wet hair, forcing his heart rate to slow and wiping away any evidence of his nervousness.

He walked over to the sofa with the two full champagne flutes and sat, debating between leaning back comfortably, or sitting closer to the edge of sofa, eager. Then he remembered, it was too late to appear eager—he'd removed all doubt of his intentions out on her deck. So, he shook it off and slid back halfway—a compromise—replaying in his mind what had just happened just as the track on her playlist shifted to an unfamiliar song blending Caribbean rhythms with jazz. He smiled at the pleasure of this unexpected moment.

Shifting his body, Gabriel peered out the glass doors, eyes trained on the bright moon perched high above the island. Beautiful and completely out of his reach. But he still admired its wonder.

He heard Riley's light footsteps as she returned, wrapped in the plush complimentary robe. She joined him on the sofa and they sipped their second glasses of champagne.

Gabriel had so many questions for her, but he didn't want to over-whelm her. But he also didn't want to sit in silence and appear to only have sex on his mind. Sex was definitely on his mind, but it was because she intrigued him and he wanted to feel every inch of her body, know the crevices of her mind, feel the depths of her heart, and be the keeper of her secrets.

Watching her get comfortable on the sofa, face flushed and move-ments unsure, she was a walking contradiction—and it captivated and worried him in equal measure. When she thought no one was watching she was modest. But when they were alone, sensuality seeped from her pores. She was confident and bold, but her eyes held curiosity and uncertainty. She was overtly beautiful on camera, and naturally beautiful away from the camera. And, she was self-contained, private and undeniably alluring.

But before he could break the silence, she turned to face him and slid her legs beneath herself on the sofa and said, "Shall we address the elephant in the room?"

Meeting her gaze, he wasn't sure what, or which, elephant she was referring to, but he was fine with letting her guide the conversation.

"Sure," he hesitated. "But I'm not sure what you mean by elephant."

"Let's see. Number one: You knew my name before I knew yours. Number two: You've seen my reservation in your system, so you know it was changed. And number three: You introduced me at the spa as a special guest of the hotel."

She paused. "Have I missed anything?"

He thought for a second, wondering if this was a trap and conflicted by the sudden change in her demeanor.

"You're correct on all three counts, but I still don't see the elephant."

This wasn't exactly true, but he didn't want to identify the wrong elephant, so he dodged.

She didn't respond and stood up. "Excuse me while I shut off the bath water."

When she left the room, he sat upright and debated what he should say next. She seemed irritated and he needed to think quick and recover the mood.

As she walked back towards him, she wasn't smiling. He needed to bring her smile back.

She sat back on the sofa, but this time she didn't face him. She leaned back with her arms folded in her lap.

"Riley," he said. "Look at me."

When she didn't respond, he reached for one of her hands and squeezed it tight. She still stared forward.

"I know who you are and I know that you were supposed to get married last weekend. I didn't know any of that when I came to your aid at the airport—that was instinct and common decency. I also know that you canceled your wedding the night before and that this was supposed to be your honeymoon."

He paused, wondering how far he should go. When she dropped her other arm, he knew he was making progress.

"I also know that you're trending on social media, but that you haven't made any kind of a statement about your situation. That's what I know. And I'm sorry if I made it difficult for you to say whatever you were trying to say. I just didn't want you to think you had to say anything until you were ready."

Still looking forward, she said, "Are you done?"

He nodded.

"Thanks for being honest," she said, turning to face him. "And yes, that was the elephant in the room I was referring to. And I only wanted to clear the air because eventually I'm going to leave this villa and walk amongst the living, and someone might say something stupid, or insensitive, or supportive. Or, they just might want to take photos or just stare until I'm uncomfortable. Mainly because of social media."

He didn't say anything—not wanting to interrupt her and signaling that he was there to listen.

"My fiancé cheated on me, so I called it off and left. Risky, I know.

But most of life is risk, so my chances of my walking away from my relationship working out in my favor are fifty-fifty."

She traced tiny circles on her thigh and gazed out the sliding glass door in crushing silence. When she finally spoke again, her voice was low and laced with trepidation.

"I don't know what this is between us, if it's anything at all. But I feel comfortable with you and I like you. You made me smile when I thought I would drown in the pain. And, you protected me when you didn't even know me."

She paused again and he didn't take his eyes off her. Her head dropped slightly and she continued the slow and repetitive circle motions with her finger. "What happened between us tonight is a first for me, but I don't want that to scare you off. I enjoyed you and I hope you enjoyed me. And right now, that's enough."

Her eyes remained downcast, like the answers were in her lap. Then, she looked up at him, eyes piercing his and said, "It has to be enough."

Gabriel smiled tentatively, and though the ambiguity made him want to bolt, he didn't want to lose the connection. Her response was laced with one part regret, one part fear, and two parts definitive. She hadn't planned this and neither had he. All he could do now was give her some assurance. She had confided in him, shared her body and now her story with him. But what had he given her in return? She was vulnerable, but so was he. She had also been honest about their encounter and put his expectations on notice. He respected and feared that kind of strength and self-awareness.

For him, time stood still as recognition set in. This was a defining moment. Did he leave her swimming in uncharted waters exposed and alone, or did he dare peel back his own layers and dive in with her?

She broke their gaze first, looking away from him, from this. His eyes searched her face in profile—her cheeks flushed and her once confident posture curved into uncertainty. She had drifted into the deep end, but she didn't need rescuing this time. She needed a companion.

"I first saw you on the flight from New York to Papeete, but you didn't see me. I slowed down on the tarmac to catch a glimpse of the beautiful woman who conversed with our pilot in French with a tangle of hair piled high above the seat."

When she didn't look at him, he continued, slow and steady.

"I never expected to see you again, but I was drawn to you. Certainly, you being beautiful is an obvious attraction," Gabriel added, his tone lighter. "But there was something else willing me closer to you. When you exited the plane draped in all white, windswept hair and resolve in your footsteps, it was like watching a tidal wave—dangerous but awe-inspiring. One half of me wanted to run and the other half wanted to ride the wave."

Her finger paused its motions on her thigh, and she tilted her gaze towards him, the beginnings of a smile taking shape.

"No pun intended," he said through a crooked smile.

She smiled back at him and sat up, attentive and inviting Gabriel to continue.

"Why did you want to run?" Her curiosity was piqued, an indication he had met the moment.

"I didn't know at the time who you were," his voice trailed off, careful to not be offensive. "You were a gorgeous woman who caught my eye, which would have been fine any other time and any other place."

She raised an eyebrow, teasing him. "Don't stop now. This is getting good."

Her teasing made him more comfortable, less guarded.

"I have a lot riding on this assignment this month. I'm in line for a corporate-level promotion, and I really can't afford any distractions."

Riley interrupted, "Is that what I am? A distraction?"

Her tone was neutral and he didn't know her well enough to read her. So, he chose transparency.

"In all honesty, hell yes! You have taken up residence in my mind rent-free since I laid eyes on you on the tarmac."

This time she chuckled.

"But seriously," Gabriel continued, wanting to share as much with her about his situation as he knew about hers. "I've been with the company for a decade now, having walked away from my family's hotel business—and my overbearing father, Viscount Jean Louis Laurent—to prove myself. That wasn't easy and I had to pay my dues. It's my time for something bigger, and this is the last stop before I arrive. It's also my chance to prove to my father that I'm an asset and not a puppet. That I'm not just a younger version of him. That my ideas have merit. That he can't control my decisions or my life."

Riley's eyes softened with understanding. Up until this very moment, these were his private thoughts, words that never crossed his lips but kept his mind racing at night. The discord with his father wasn't by choice—his father was stubborn and a creature of habit and archaic traditions. As much as Gabriel wanted to honor his family's legacy, he wouldn't compromise himself. Not for his father, not for an inheritance, not for anything.

The song changed again, and Dinah Washington's distinctive, high-pitched voice took control of their story with "What a Diff'rence A Day Makes."

"Then, you appear. My mind screams run, but everything else in me says take your shot." Pulling closer to her, he reached for both her hands and held her gaze. "And here we are. My emotions have officially overtaken my mind. I don't have a reasonable explanation. But I also don't have any regrets. Under any other circumstances, I wouldn't be conflicted. I would pursue you and see where it leads. But neither of us is in a position to flip a switch that might illuminate our interest."

A heaviness floated all around them, matching the humid air seeping in from outside—an acknowledgement that they both were headed towards the deep end of the ocean. Either by choice or sheer force of nature.

Riley broke the silence. "Well, Monsieur Laurent. Seems we might have a few things in common. Except for your father's royal title," she teased. "I'm definitely curious about that legacy, but another time."

Gabriel nodded his consent.

"And, I think we can both agree that what we did tonight was risky and neither of us can afford a scandal," Riley continued. "I've only been de-coupled for a few days and you have a career to protect. I hope we can continue to get to know each other without paying too high of a price."

Gabriel wasn't expecting her to be so matter-of-fact, but he appreciated her candidness.

"Before you continue, can I say something?" he asked, wanting to offer some reassurance and salvage their night.

"Sure. But make it quick. Bath water's getting cold."

"You're not playing fair. How am I supposed to be thoughtful and poetic if you're going to place images in my head of your body in a tub of warm water?"

She shrugged. "I never said that I played fair."

"Well, I'll keep it quick. I agree with you—I want us to get to know each other, but discreetly. What's between us is between us and doesn't need to be defined. And this being a first for you doesn't scare me—it just makes me like you more. Whatever you want this to be is enough for me."

He let his last words linger, giving her some time to digest it. When she didn't speak, he lightened the mood.

"So, can we go enjoy each other in that tub of likely lukewarm water now?"

She reached over and brushed light kisses on his lips and chin, drifting slowly down his neck. He used his free hands to untie her robe and caressed her, sliding the robe off her shoulders. When she moaned into his mouth, he pulled her closer to him, wanting to feel the warmth of her skin against his own. He was sure she had no idea just how beautiful she was, or what her touch did to him.

"Take me to bed," she demanded.

"Your wish is my command."

He stood first and helped her off of the sofa. When she was in a standing position, he lifted her up and tossed her across his shoulder.

"This is more Neanderthal than French," she joked.

"Wait until I get you to bed," he said, carrying her down the hall into her suite.

CHAPTER TWENTY-THREE

Riley

They never made it to the bath tub.

Gabriel quietly crept out of her villa at 3:30 a.m. and she slept until eight.

Standing in her shower, the warm water soothed and relaxed her as she replayed her night with Gabriel.

She had never had a one-night stand, so she had nothing to compare it to.

But lacking a comparison didn't prevent her from remembering every muscle, every scar, the feel of his skin against hers, the first traces of stubble on his chin pressed against her cheek. She knew him physically, and knew she had only skimmed the surface on the rest of his life—his real life. In many ways, he was still a mystery to her. A mystery she wasn't sure she had the energy to solve. She had opened up to him a little last night, and he had shared his very valid apprehensions about pursuing her.

Walking into this, her eyes were wide open. She knew this was a vacation fantasy come true and nothing more. She knew she needed a no-strings-attached release of her sexual frustrations. And she knew there was no real danger of it developing into something she wasn't ready for because there was literally a world of distance between them.

She was playing it safe and living on the edge all at the same time.

Besides, it was just one night. Now she was relaxed and she could maybe flirt with him a little, but she thought once was enough. Well, technically twice, but who's counting.

But would one night be enough? She couldn't deny their physical attraction, but there was something else about him that she hadn't quite figured out. Her journalist senses piqued as she listened to the short and sweet version of an undoubtedly more complicated story with his father—something she could relate to with a mother who was opinionated yet largely absent. And paying your dues was her career trajectory on repeat.

But she picked up on something else in his voice when he mentioned his family's hotel business. A melancholy mix of disappointment and pride hinted at things unresolved.

He was a protector. He was protective of his future and their reputations. He had wanted to protect his family's legacy, but on his own terms. He was protecting his career and his commitment that he made to himself and the company. He was protecting his time and her space. He had protected her even when he had no clue who she was or why she needed protecting.

It was an admirable trait. But she wasn't looking for a protector.

She hadn't been *looking* for anything. But yet, here he was.

Mentally, she prepared a to-do list for the day. She was trying to keep the promise she had made to herself—and her cheating fiancé—about living in the moment. And for the most part, she had.

But old habits die hard. Besides, a mental to-do list is an improvement over a daily, handwritten list that required early morning planning and day-long tracking.

While she shampooed and conditioned her hair, she considered the day ahead of her. It was time for her to come out of her protective shell. This had been an easier task in Papeete thanks to her new flosse posse—the solo honeymoon edition. But here in Bora Bora, she was primarily alone.

Her only acquaintance on the island was Gabriel, and they could only exchange pleasantries while out in public. She began counting the days until her new friends arrived for a proper girl's trip.

As for today, there was only one item on her to-do list. Spa treatments!

She stepped out of the shower and toweled off. She was famished after that marathon night, and decided to head to one of the hotel restaurants for breakfast.

As she dressed, she noticed her cell phone on the night stand charging. All notifications were shut off and she had adjusted it back to airplane mode, not wanting any disruptions. She was a news junkie at heart, but the last year in the field had been physically and emotionally draining. The silver linings had been few and the cultural tensions had been high. She had planned this honeymoon in part to disconnect from the cacophony associated with a reality laced with distress, disharmony, and disinformation. When she chose a career in journalism, it had been fueled by idealism. Now, a decade later, her hands were filthy from digging through the mud to find the bright stories to share with the world.

Now, a story was probably being told about her, and not a bright one.

Gabriel's admission last night danced across her psyche. A creature of habit, she was tempted to check her social media accounts, but something buried deep inside screamed out in warning. Not knowing went against the grain. But knowing—that had the power to unravel what little progress she had made.

Gabriel had seen posts about her on social media, but he didn't elaborate. She didn't know if that meant he was being polite and didn't want to share bad news. Or, because she didn't ask so he didn't tell.

Gabriel the protector.

As she massaged Monoi oil onto her bare legs, she decided that there was no better time than the present to face the social media music.

She pulled up her Black Girl Magic playlist, connected it to her Bluetooth speaker with the volume on high and Nicki Minaj's *Your Love* streaming through the room. She sat down on the edge of bed, bracing herself for the worse, and unlocked her phone.

As soon as she disengaged airplane mode, a wave of text messages poured in.

Her parents, Jonathan, Sierra, her sorority sisters and cousins. But one name stood out.

Her producer had sent only one message in the tidal wave of texts. Six words in all caps.

JEREMY: CALL ME. THE EXECS ARE CONCERNED.

That was curious. Riley couldn't fathom what they had to be concerned about. She was on leave for the next month—leave she had earned and had every right to use, even if she didn't get married. So why would they be concerned?

Riley debated whether to ignore the message or respond.

Jeremy Wilson was not prone to the dramatic. He was always direct, brutally honest, politically savvy, and unquestionably her biggest champion.

No, Jeremy would not text her unless there was really a problem. She decided to respond. The other messages could wait.

RILEY: What's up, Jeremy?

She stared at the phone, impatient and willing a response from Jeremy.

Less than a minute later, he replied.

JEREMY: YOU'RE TRENDING ON SM AND THE EXECS WANT YOU TO RESPOND.

Her fingertips snapped across the phone screen, matching her mood.

RILEY: Why?!?! It's my personal biz.

A few seconds went by and Jeremy continued.

JEREMY: NOT ALL OF IT IS FLATTERING IN THE DEMOGRAPHICS THAT WE'RE ALREADY LOSING.

RILEY: And they think that's my fault?

JEREMY: NOT YOUR FAULT. BUT YOU'RE A
CONTRIBUTOR.

RILEY: Again—why? And can you please lose the all-caps.
It feels like you're yelling at me and I'm not in the mood.

JEREMY: You're trending and it's not favorable for the
network.

RILEY: They do know that I didn't get married, right?

JEREMY: They know.

RILEY: Well, I can't control people on social media.

JEREMY: You can issue a statement. Like Jonathan did.

Was Jeremy trying to piss her off? She stood and paced around the
room, gripping her phone instead of screaming out loud, thumbs
aggressively pressing into the mobile screen. All the men in her orbit
seemed to want something from her to benefit themselves—their
reputations, their careers, their bottom line. Well, maybe not *all* the
men. Gabriel was an exception, but he didn't really count. He had
proven to be the temporary soft landing she needed.

RILEY: Pardon my French, but f*ck Jonathan.
He's a cheater trying to save face.

JEREMY: Doesn't matter why he did it.
You need to say something. Anything.

RILEY: WTH do they want me to say? I know they've told
you something. So quit stalling and give it to me straight.

JEREMY: They just want you to say you would like some privacy and time to heal. Maybe that you're heartbroken.

RILEY: Really? Play the victim? That's what they want?

JEREMY: They want audience sympathy on your side.

RILEY: The TRUTH is on my side.

JEREMY: Well, are you willing to risk putting the real truth out there and spark an entirely new trending hashtag?

RILEY: Would serve Jonathan right. The only reason I'm #RileyOnTheRun is because he is #cheaterinchief.

Jeremy didn't respond with an LOL or an emoji. He kept it straight, no chaser.

JEREMY: I know it's not fair, but it has to be done. It's your job—our jobs—on the line.

RILEY: Wait. What? Our jobs on the line? WTH?

JEREMY: News is no longer just news and you know this. News is interchangeable with entertainment and journalists are the new celebrities. A scar for you is a scar for the network.

RILEY: I get it. But seriously…it's only been a few days.

JEREMY: So, you'll do it?

RILEY: I'll do it, but I don't have to like it.

JEREMY: When?

Riley swallowed back the frustration and anger mounting in her chest. If women aren't carrying the weight of the world, it's the fate of the future or the pressure to perform—always at death-defying speed.

RILEY: Damn, J! I just agreed. Now you need a timeline?

JEREMY: Yes. I need to report back with status.

Status? Report back? She couldn't believe the audacity of any of them. She's cheated on and humiliated the night before her wedding and she has to play defense. Her career and reputation in jeopardy, all at the hands of men. An ex-fiancé who wanted to control her, and now a group of network executives who want to control her narrative. It was all such bullshit.

But she wasn't going to take her frustrations out on Jeremy. None of this was his fault. He was just the intermediary. And, he wasn't just her producer. He had been a good friend over the years.

RILEY: I'll do it today, J. But for the record, I'm doing this for us...for now. When I'm back in the real world, we need to talk exit strategy and new moves. This might be the end of the rope at this network.

JEREMY: You're the boss, RSJ. Where you go, I go. Thanks for doing this. I didn't want to bother you, but the block is hot.

RILEY: LOL! Have you been watching old BET movies? The block is hot?!?! You crack me up! I'm glad you're there to have my back. I'll let you know when I post.

JEREMY: Cool. And for the record, I haven't been watching old movies. I've been on a Lil' Wayne throwback tour.

She giggled, imagining Jeremy sitting in the studio offices with his headphones on blasting Lil' Wayne. All the anger she was feeling minutes ago slid off her like water on her coconut oiled skin. She stepped out onto the deck and let the view remind her of where she was—despite the reasons why.

RILEY: Gotta go, J. Paradise is calling!

JEREMY: So now we're rubbing salt in wounds.

RILEY: You started it with this statement mess!

She watched the screen as the little typing bubble floated, waiting for Jeremy's response.

JEREMY: ENJOY!

Riley clutched her mobile phone and walked to the edge of the deck, grateful to have an ally back at work, but still disheartened that she had to make a statement about something so painful in her personal life. A statement that basically would provide cover for the misdeeds inflicted on her. A statement that would be more fodder and less resolution.

Breakfast would have to wait.

The sun sat bright and high in the sky, and the temperature was rising. She slipped out of her cover up to soak up some sun while she contemplated her social media post.

On the bright side, at least it wasn't an official statement to the press. It was just social media and she could post, turn her phone off, and remain secluded—mostly—in paradise.

She decided to check some of the other text messages, just in case there was another fire that needed her attention.

There were multiple texts from Sierra, and her feelings were mixed. She knew Sierra would never intentionally cause her harm, but she had never been Jonathan's biggest fan and Riley wondered if she also had suspected him of messing around with Issy.

Well, today would not be the day that she'd get answers from Sierra. Not a priority.

There were multiple messages from her parents and she texted them back on their group text. Her mom responded first and broke the news that she was still in D.C. with Riley's father—her ex-husband. This both shocked and amused Riley. Their shared concern for her probably allowed them to put their differences aside and stand in solidarity with Riley.

She assured them both that she was fine, thanked them for always putting her first, and promised to call them in a few days. She snapped a couple pics with her phone of the mountain in the distance and her feet in the crystal-clear waters as proof that she really was in the best possible place to heal and plan her next move.

While snapping pics, her phone rang. It was an unknown number and she considered not answering. But she remembered that there was still the issue with her luggage and the airline had promised an update. Reluctantly, she answered.

She was grateful she didn't duck that call. Air Tahiti Nui had located her luggage and it would be delivered Thursday morning.

That was good news, even though Riley had practically forgotten she didn't have her luggage. She'd found some cute bathing suits and cover-ups in the hotel boutique, and she'd picked up a few silk sarongs at the market in Papeete that when tied creatively, doubled as dresses.

There was little need for lots of clothing. Her life of excess was slowly but surely being replaced by a new minimalist mindset. A mindset that she would work to fold into her regular life. She would always love nice things, but too much of anything can be more harm than good. She now had first-hand experience.

The news about her luggage was a welcome distraction from what she knew she had to do—had promised Jeremy she would do right away.

Sitting on the edge of her pool, she let her legs rest in the water while she opened up her Twitter app. She went straight to her very own trending hashtag and couldn't believe the number of posts. People clearly had too much time on their hands.

She scrolled through, skimming several of the posts and she saw what her network execs saw. Of course, it was the men questioning her motives, accusing her of being another black woman who didn't know what she wanted, berating her for disappearing and leaving Jonathan to clean up the mess.

Disgusted, she opened her notes on her phone and began crafting her post. She didn't dare type directly in the app for fear of posting before it was finished or she was ready.

After 15 minutes of drafting and revising, she was finally satisfied with her post. And, to keep from having to post on Facebook and IG, she set her account to post the message automatically to those accounts and she would be done.

As she copied and pasted the message into Twitter, a wave of sadness suddenly rushed over her. She couldn't believe that in a matter of moments her whole life had been ripped apart by someone who claimed to love her. And that she had to share that wound with the world, and plead for privacy while she worked out her feelings.

For the first time in her entire career, this felt like a price too steep for a job she loved.

When the tears began to well in her eyes, she didn't fight them. She let them fall freely, not bothering to wipe them away. She was allowed to feel the sting of a betrayal so deep, to cleanse her soul of it so that she could begin to heal.

Jonathan had been the love of her life. Her first and only love. She had given him all that she knew how to give and accepted him just as he was. She had tried desperately to live up to his expectations, even when those expectations threatened her own sense of self-worth and value. So desperate to be loved, to be enough, that she fiercely gripped at that love until it was deprived of oxygen—that's what she had done. Willingly.

Through bleary eyes, she looked at the words on her phone screen.

Thanks for your support during this challenging time & for

giving me the privacy to heal. There is nothing quite so
raw as the first days of love lost. But life is made of equal
parts rain & sunshine. As I learn to dance in both, send
good vibes my way.
Not #RileyOnTheRun.

All she could hope for now is that the sentiment wasn't met with cynicism. She toyed with the idea of leaving the hashtag off the message, but if she wanted the masses to see her statement, it needed to be in the feed.

She had purposefully left Jonathan's name out of the message. She wanted him to know he was no longer a consideration nor a priority in her life. She really did him a favor because she could have put his cheating ass on blast. But Riley was classy. She wasn't going to feed the beast by airing their dirty laundry.

But she was also no shrinking violet. She wasn't running from her problems. She was reflective and giving herself the space to begin to heal. On their honeymoon in Tahiti.

But was she healing or avoiding? When her thoughts slipped towards Gabriel, she considered the new x-factor in this scenario. Distraction or well-deserved indulgence? She wasn't sure. But in her otherwise heavily planned existence, meeting him and being so attracted to him was unexpected. And sleeping with him—well, unexpected was an understatement.

No one would ever describe her as a prude, but she was definitely cautious. Men were always attentive, and she had considered a fling once or twice. But she was faithful to Jonathan and always realized that in the end, good sex with someone she couldn't see in her future wasn't worth losing her man or the life they were building together.

And Jonathan for his part had certainly kept their sex life spicy. But he controlled it and she allowed it. Rarely did she initiate sex. And the few times she had, he was distant and it left her feeling cheap. Which is why his cheating on her the night before their wedding was especially painful.

She was one hundred percent out of her comfort zone the night she pranced down to his hotel suite in her blood red bra and panties, shielded only by an overcoat, prepared to take the lead. Now, in a span of days, she felt that same desire again with Gabriel and had nearly pulled back. It was risky, and he had lots of legitimate reasons to reject her. But she abandoned her cautious default and led with her longing. Thankfully, Gabriel more than met her halfway.

But with Jonathan, she had been too late. He had made the blatantly obvious choice of sex with a woman who was somewhat of sexual legend. Issy had always been sexually free and took no prisoners. She wasn't looking for love—strictly pleasure. She didn't need a man, but she wanted what they had to offer in the bedroom. Riley once heard her joke that she never took a male plus-one to any event because she didn't want to miss out on a new encounter.

Most men liked the idea of women like Issy. With them they could be raw and unfiltered. There was no emotion in the way.

And women like Issy found their own freedom in deciding who and when and for how long. A small piece of Riley envied her for walking boldly in her truth. But Riley also knew that one day Issy would wake up and want more. Or she would meet her match and her perspective would shift.

But the thing that Riley didn't want to face yet was Jonathan's *why*. Why had he done it? Why did he risk it all?

But worse than the question was the possible answer.

Was it because she was an inexperienced aggressor in bed? Had he been secretly longing for her to take what she wanted from him? Had she waited too long to reveal that unfiltered side of herself?

And if the answer was yes to any of these questions, did that make this outcome inevitable? And was it to some degree her fault? Had she failed him and their relationship?

With these questions swirling around in her head, she looked back at her phone and with the flick of her finger, hit send on the official end of her and Jonathan.

CHAPTER TWENTY-FOUR

Gabriel

G abriel had practically passed out when his head hit the pillow back in his suite. Two hours later when his phone alarm buzzed him awake, he was surprisingly energized, though also sleep-deprived.

At a half-hour before sunrise, it was already a balmy 80 degrees and his morning run around the hotel property provided fresh air to fill his lungs and images of Riley to divide his attention.

They had only spent a few hours together, and somehow, she was consuming his thoughts. Her very presence intrigued him and had unleashed a desperate curiosity in him to know more. She was sexy, but with an alluring innocence—like she didn't fully grasp her power over men. She was observant and funny. She appreciated luxury but was equally comfortable improvising. She had good taste, but not in an obnoxious and arrogant kind of way. Her smile was warm, her kisses sweet, her body a weapon, and her surrender to their lovemaking was pure pleasure.

Every one of his senses was on overdrive from the sound of her voice, the touch of her hand, the scent of her hair, the look in her eyes while he entered her, the sweet taste of her skin—he had to remember to ask her about that.

But would he have another chance to ask her? They had spent one night together, but hadn't made any definitive plans beyond that. She expressed wanting to see him again—discreetly. But something bothered him. Or maybe it was just his ego, but he couldn't help question her motives. Maybe she had just needed to blow off some steam last night. Or maybe she wanted to have revenge sex to hurt her ex-fiancé. Maybe she was planning to go back to him, but wanted a secret of her own.

Damn!

His pace quickened as he wondered if he was being presumptuous to think that he'd get another opportunity to ask her such an intimate question?

He had missed his chance to confirm another date.

Again, too presumptuous. And could they even consider last night a date?

How could he have been so stupid? One night with her may have to be enough.

Breathing heavy with sweat dripping in his eyes, he took a break to wipe his face and let his heart rate slow down. He bent over slightly, hands on his knees and just listened as waves softly lapped against the sand, breathing in the scent of hibiscus and Tahitian gardenias from the nearby garden.

This was by far his favorite time of day. Quiet enough to hear birds chirping and the wind whistling through the trees. The island was beginning to wake up and he had the best vantage point.

Soon, cutlery would be scraping against plates, glasses would be filled with ice cubes and fresh juice, servers would be taking orders and pouring coffee, and the die-hard sunbathers would be claiming their lounge chairs around the hotel's popular infinity pool.

There was always a sprinkling of early risers, headed out for water sport excursions or fishing on the other side of the island.

As a small crowd of people with scuba gear began boarding the boat transport, he got an idea.

He had to work with Simon this morning until about noon and then he was free.

It was true that he and Riley could not be seen being too familiar around the hotel—but they could leave the property and venture out to the other side of the island. And he knew just the place.

Back in his suite, he showered, dressed, and plotted how he would invite Riley to lunch. He decided on the simplest method—a phone call.

Just as he went to dial her villa, his cell phone rang. He checked the caller ID and saw it was his sister. So, he answered.

"Bonjour, ma belle!"

It was Juliette.

"How are you? Is everything alright at home?" It was an unusual time for her to call, so he suspected she was calling to report drama on the home front.

"I am fine, mon frere."

"Mama and Papa, they are well?"

"Mama is well. It is Papa that concerns me."

"Is he ill?" Gabriel was angry with his father, but he certainly didn't want to think he was ill and hadn't bothered to contact him.

"No. He's just stubborn," Juliette added.

"Well, then everything is the same. He's always stubborn."

Juliette hesitated before she spoke again. "I'm worried that he's planning something that spells trouble, Gabriel."

"Something like what? And trouble for who?"

"It's definitely something with the business and I think the trouble involves you."

"Me? How could he cause trouble for me?"

Gabriel was trying to remain calm, but he knew his sister's call meant that whatever was happening, she was worried. And her instincts were usually spot on.

"He's been talking to Cecily's father a lot more lately."

"Is that all?" Gabriel was relieved. His sister wasn't yet a part of the business, but she would take on a greater role once she graduated college. She didn't fully understand all of the innerworkings of the company, and definitely not all that would be involved with a merger.

"Well, they are considering a merger, so that involves lots of meetings."

"Yes," she said with a hint of exasperation in her tone. "I realize that. But these calls are happening in the evenings and on the weekends. And whenever Mama or I enter the room, he gets nervous, raises his voice and changes the subject. I think he's up to something and I think you should find out what."

Gabriel didn't want to belittle her concern, so he asked her to tell him specifically why she thought it involved him.

Her voice took on a more concerned tone, and he didn't like it. Whatever was happening at home really had upset her. Turned out, she was worried because of the ambush her father led him into with Cecily on his last visit.

"I didn't want to admit this, so you have to promise that if you speak to him or Mama, you won't divulge my secret."

Gabriel agreed and she continued.

"I overheard one of his calls with Cecily's father. He promised him the merger would happen and that you would marry Cecily. He said he had a plan but it would take a few weeks to finalize."

She paused and Gabriel asked, "Is there more?"

"Unfortunately, yes." Her voice lowered, edged with concern as if she were disgraced by what she was about to say. "I heard him say that Cecily should schedule time with our jeweler to have great-grand-mother Antoinette's heirloom ring sized and that the attorneys should begin drafting the merger agreement."

Seemed Juliette's concern was valid and that their father hadn't played his last hand yet. Gabriel knew how much his father wanted him to return to the business, but he couldn't imagine what plan he could have conceived that would cause Gabriel to switch course.

He listened intently as she voiced her concerns, and promised he would call their father to reinforce his position. A lot of good it would do with a man as stubborn as their father, but he promised her he would try.

Once the drama du'jour was over, they talked a few minutes about her internship, and he told her about his recent visit to New York, wanting to keep their conversation routine and alleviate her concerns. As usual, she asked about his love life. She was desperate for a sister, and realized that the only way that would ever happen is if Gabriel got married. He knew this was the one area that he was a disappointment to his sister. Sure, she'd been able to travel to some of the most luxurious hotels in the world because of his position in the company, but that was the only personal benefit of his work. He had sacrificed his time, relationships, friendships — most things personal — for his job. The jury was still out on whether those sacrifices were worth it. And if the promise of a promotion really meant as much to him now as it once did.

He decided to give her a little something to nibble on, and confessed he was thinking about getting back out into the dating scene. He didn't dare give her any real details because one, she undoubtedly knew exactly who Riley St. James was, and two, there was nothing to tell absent his rescuing Riley from some obnoxious admirers and a long night of extraordinary sex—which wasn't the sort of story he'd share with his little sister.

When they hung up, Juliette was satisfied and he was somewhat concerned. His father had been trying to convince him to come back to the company practically since he walked away. He had grown accustomed to his schemes.

But something about this had Juliette spooked. So, he was going to call his father and get some answers.

Later.

Right now, he had another far more important call to make—inviting a beautiful woman out on a lunch date.

CHAPTER TWENTY-FIVE

It only took Riley a few minutes to finish dressing, drop a few items in her bag in preparation for some much-needed poolside sunbathing and cocktail sipping after breakfast.

She made it all the way to the door and realized she should take her straw hat, and turned around to grab it from her bedroom.

She stepped one foot out the closet and her phone rang, startling her.

Who would be calling on the villa phone line, she wondered? Then she remembered that the hotel staff was coordinating with the airline regarding her luggage, so she thought the call might be related.

"Bonjour! Riley St. James speaking."

"Bonjour, Mademoiselle St. James."

It was Gabriel. Once again, he had managed to surprise her. But more surprising than his call was the heat rising up her neck and causing her face to flush.

"Monsieur Gabriel. What a surprise." Her voice was steady, but she was not.

She needed a new mantra, she thought. *Pull yourself together, Riley.*

"Well, I hope it's a pleasant surprise."

He paused, waiting for positive affirmation.

She let him sweat a few seconds and then said, "A pleasant surprise indeed. How can I help you this morning?"

She didn't mean to make it sound like a business call, but she didn't have a lot of experience with the morning after a booty call. She was navigating unchartered waters. She fidgeted with her cover-up and her bag slid off her shoulder, pulling the garment with it and tilting her slightly off-balance.

"It's more like, how may I help you."

"I'm listening," she said through a growing smile as she rearranged herself. She was happy he'd called. Their night together was beyond memorable but she had no expectations beyond those few hours. But his call made her feel like more than a one-night stand.

"If you'd allow me, I would love to take you to lunch this afternoon. There's a place on the other side of the island that I think you'd like. It's casual, fun, a little tourist-y, but worth it for the best damn Bloody Mary you'll ever drink."

Her smile had grown into a gaping grin.

"I'd love that. But do you think it's a good idea? What if hotel guests see us?"

"Just dress casual and I'll do the same. Hopefully we won't be recognized. Besides, the rush doesn't usually start until late afternoon after the scuba excursions."

She thought about it for a few seconds, debating whether she should go for it or play it safe. It was definitely risky. But she did want to see some of the island beyond the hotel. And she was willing to bet he knew the island as well as the locals.

"I'm in," she said before she could overthink it. "But what time and how will we get there?"

"We'll meet there at noon. You'll take the shuttle service and I'll drive one of the hotel's cars. Then, we'll ride back together."

"I can do that. If you're sure it's not too big of a risk." She knew that there was so much that could go wrong. But it felt worth it in the moment. She welcomed the chance to sit and have a meal with a handsome man with no pretense and no strings attached.

"Mademoiselle, anything worth having in life involves a risk. And trust me, you're worth the risk."

"You're good," she said through a laugh. "Pouring it on pretty thick, but I'm in the mood so I won't tease you. At least not too much."

Gabriel laughed. "It is the truth. And you may tease me as much and as often as you like."

So last night wasn't an anomaly. He was still flirting with her. A rush of relief passed over her.

"I'll be sure to remind you of that when the teasing commences."

He laughed again. "I look forward to it. See you at noon."

"See you then."

She hung up the phone and let her body fall across the bed, arms stretched wide and open to this new world of possibilities. She turned her head left and stared out the bedroom window, drinking in the blue waters and matching sky.

The morning had started out rough, but she was recovering—in small part due to some welcome attention from Gabriel.

Now that she had a lunch date with the dreamiest man on the island, she could push down thoughts of Jonathan's betrayal, rethink her wardrobe choices and catalog all the questions she had about Gabriel Laurent—his life, his family, his dreams, his secrets. Last night, she had gotten to know Gabriel on a very physical level—a level she wouldn't mind repeating. But she was still a creature of habit and her life revolved around asking the right questions. So, if he wanted to continue to get to know her, he would get the full Riley St. James treatment.

She ordered room service, turned on her playlist and began styling her incognito lunch outfit dancing around the room to Prince crooning *U Got The Look.*

CHAPTER TWENTY-SIX

Gabriel

She was seated at a high-top table for two in the back of the restaurant near a window. Just as he suspected, Bloody Mary's had only a handful of people, and no one he recognized from the hotel. At least for now, they were safe.

He casually glanced around the restaurant as he headed towards her. She hadn't seen him come in, staring out the window, lost in her thoughts.

When he suggested she dress casually, he should have suspected that on a woman as beautiful as her, nothing really looked casual. But he knew she had tried. Her caramel legs were crossed and bare up to the top of her thigh where her grey shorts were matched with a basic white cotton shirt that hung off one shoulder. He immediately wanted to greet her with a soft kiss on her exposed shoulder but knew it was too soon, not to mention too risky.

Her hair was up in the same style she wore on the plane with her sunglasses balancing on top. The simple gold and diamond hoop earrings complimented the gold strands of hair that never seemed to all make it inside the bun and a thin gold chain with small diamonds hung low from her neck.

This woman was like this island personified—every time he saw her, she was more beautiful, and every time he left, he couldn't wait to get back to her. He was mesmerized or smitten or infatuated or intoxicated or all of the above with her. Last night all he could think about was touching and kissing and feeling her. Today, he just wanted to look at her and listen to her talk.

She turned her head towards him just as he approached the table and smiled.

At this angle, in that light, she was radiant. She looked relaxed, and somehow still very sexy in shorts and t-shirt.

"Bonjour. Even dressed casually, you are stunning." Gabriel fought the urge to kiss her, not wanting to cross a line or be too presumptuous.

Riley blushed. "Well, I like you in your casual gear. And the baseball cap was a nice touch. Very incognito."

He slipped the hat off and hung it on the back of the chair. "That is high praise from a woman as beautiful as you."

"Still pouring it on thick I see."

They both laughed and eased into their conversation about the menu and the history of the restaurant. Once they had ordered, and before Gabriel could get his questions out, Riley jumped in.

"So, tell me about Gabriel Laurent. Do you live in Tahiti? And what exactly is your job? Where's your family?"

Her questions rushed out in rapid fire, like she was playing catch up or they might run out of time. Her interest in him caught him by surprise—but it was a happy surprise.

"I see you have lots of questions. And so do I. So, I propose we make a deal."

"I'm listening," she said, taking a sip of her Bloody Mary that was just delivered to the table. She closed her eyes as she took a long sip through the straw and moaned as she swallowed.

Gabriel had a flashback and had to adjust himself beneath the table.

Regaining his composure, he said, "For every question I answer, you have to also answer one of my questions."

She swirled her tongue around the straw and looked up at him. She was teasing him.

"It's a deal," she said. "You first. Do you live in Tahiti?"

He was now drinking from his glass, skipping the straw and tilting the glass to take a few gulps.

"No. I split my time between New York City and Paris. I have an apartment in Manhattan and a flat in Paris. I travel a lot and most of the hotel properties I manage are in this part of the world."

"Wow. New York and Paris. So, you travel a lot?"

She was already trying to wiggle out of the deal, but he wasn't letting her off the hook. He respected that she was a journalist and asking questions was like second nature to her. But there was so much he wanted to know about her—questions he couldn't ask when she was in the nude, making his mind pure mush.

"It's my turn. Where did you learn to speak French?"

"Growing up. I've spoken French since I can remember. My mother is French Creole and French was her native language. She grew up in the countryside of France and moved to America when she was a teenager. She met my father fresh out of college, got pregnant, so they got married. She spoke French a lot around the house and I picked it up. I guess technically I'm bilingual, though I don't get to use my French as much as I would like."

She paused and sipped her drink again.

"Until now. Until you appeared at my side in a hotel boutique."

"It's funny you should mention that," he said. "That was *your* first encounter with me. It wasn't my first with you, so I needed to give you a chance to catch up."

"Very funny," she deadpanned.

"Don't worry. You were more beautiful each time."

She smiled. "So, you were stalking me?"

This time he laughed.

"I was not stalking you. But you kept appearing—teasing me. First on the airplane. Then I waited to see you on the tarmac before rescuing you from that small mob of fans—which was pure instinct."

Stringing all those moments together made him feel like a creep, and he hoped she didn't share the sentiment.

But in Riley fashion, she made him sweat. Only a few seconds passed, but it felt like an eternity.

"So, you were my stalker and my knight in shining armor?" A wicked smile spread across her face and reached her eyes, and her laughter reached her shoulders and chest.

She was making fun of him. That was a good sign.

"I don't know if I'd go that far, but you were hard to ignore and the situation with those peopled seemed uncomfortable for you, so I stepped in. It was just the decent thing to do."

She hadn't looked away from him, now with a slight grin and her hand idly tapping her straw against the bottom of the glass as the silence stretched between them.

Gabriel held her gaze and wished he could know what she was thinking. And then she finally spoke.

"First, let me say thank you. I should have thanked you last night. You probably don't think what you did was a big deal, but it was for me. I was unprepared and had no idea what was happening on social media."

She dropped her eyes and her shoulders tensed. He knew he had to say something. To save her from going to a place she was probably trying to avoid.

"Hey," he said, reaching his hand across the table to hold her hand. "You just needed some space, and I got that for you. As for the idiots surrounding you, well you know they don't matter and social media matters even less."

She looked up and he made his next move. "Besides, what man wouldn't want to whisk you away from the roar of the world? I did the moment I saw you own the tarmac."

Through a growing smile, she fell right back into their rhythm. "So, you weren't saving me, you were pursuing me?"

"Not intentionally. At least, not at first." That was a piece of brutal honesty he hadn't planned to share with her.

"And, now?"

"Now, I will only pursue you if I have your permission. And, you've asked too many questions of me and I've only gotten one response from you."

"Since you're keeping score, you may continue," she teased.

The waiter arrived and delivered their meals. They took a few minutes to get situated and continued their conversation over poisson cru, a Tahitian dish similar to ceviche but with raw tuna marinated in lime juice and coconut milk, followed by breaded fish wraps and deep-fried shrimp.

"What would you be if you weren't a broadcast journalist?"

She didn't look up from her plate. She cut into her fish and said, "I don't know if I've ever thought about it. As a girl, I thought I wanted to be a singer. But I fell in love with journalism in college when I joined the school newspaper. Didn't take me long to realize that the news was another way to tell stories. I love the pace, the nuance, the thrill of shaping the world narrative, the secret sources, the camaraderie with other female journalists—it's an adrenaline rush. And I've done it all. I've been a newspaper reporter, a digital news reporter until finally I dabbled in broadcast. Some doors were opened for me, and some others I had to kick down. Sometimes I wonder 'what if?' But not often. What's the point, right?"

Riley paused and he didn't push. She seemed reluctant to say more. He imagined the road hadn't been easy. Her tone lowered just a little at the end of her answer, and he wondered if she really loved the news business or the storytelling. If the news was like a necessary evil for the gift of telling the stories.

Gabriel broke the silence. "So, you can sing?"

"Nope. It's your turn to answer a question," she reminded him.

"Now who's keeping score?" he quipped.

"What would you be doing if you didn't work for this hotel company?"

"That's easy. I'd be working for my family's hotel company." He took another gulp of his Bloody Mary, which was almost gone now.

"Wait," she said. "Your family owns hotels? And you work for this company? Why?"

He was used to being questioned about his decision to abandon his family company, and usually he had a stock answer—more opportunity to grow and learn. But he didn't want to give her the fake answer. He wanted her to know the truth. He wanted one someone in the world to know his whole truth and she was the safest choice.

"I left my family's company because my father, Lord Laurent, wouldn't let me make any changes. He prefers tradition over trends, so I left and joined this company and am on my way to becoming an executive in the corporate office. They've given me opportunities and trusted me to make changes that enhanced our hospitality service and our properties. My father just hasn't been willing to do that. Until now."

She stopped short of taking a forkful of vegetables.

"Until now? What does that mean?"

"He's planning to merge with another high-profile hotel chain in Europe with a more diverse portfolio, and he wants me to take over. Says I can manage it my way without his interference."

"So, what am I missing?" She had sat back in her chair and was sipping from her drink.

"There's a catch. With my father, it's never black and white. There's always an angle."

"What's his angle? And before you answer, can we order dessert?"

He laughed, grateful for the moment of levity.

"Order whatever you like."

"Great. So, back to your father's angle."

"He's offering to give me what I want, but in exchange, the patriarch of the other company wants something in exchange that I just can't give him."

Riley raised an eyebrow, waiting for him to continue.

When he didn't continue, she asked, "Well, what does he want? Your first born?"

Gabriel laughed.

"It's too absurd to even mention. Just know that I told my father I wouldn't concede to his demands and that he needed to find another way to orchestrate the merger."

"So, you're really not going to tell me what the grumpy, rich relic wants from you?"

"Trust me. It's too foolish and unreasonable to even entertain."

Riley leaned in, her curiosity piqued. She was a journalist he reminded himself and probably could sniff out a story in any situation.

"By the way, Riley," he added, "this is all off the record."

She flashed him her dazzling smile and eased the tension that was building.

"With all that's happening with my own personal life, do you think for one minute I'd turn your little story of hotel intrigue and family drama into a news story? It could be very intriguing, but not really newsworthy when you leave out vital information. Just more First World problems of the rich and privileged."

"Wait, that's not fair!"

"It's a joke. Chill out." She laughed and tried to change the subject. But he wondered if that's how she really saw him. But worse, was it true?

"How long have they been friends—your father and this other man?"

"I'll answer, but for the record, you haven't answered a question since your journalism origin story."

"So that's on the record?" she joked.

He grinned and said, "I'm clearly out of my depth up against an award-winning journalist. So, I'll keep going."

"Handsome and smart. I like it."

Gabriel continued. "They've been friends since I can remember. I went to college with his daughter. We dated for a while, but it fizzled out fast once we graduated and both happily went our separate ways. She's a socialite, hotel heiress. And I'm a hotel executive. But she's a party girl and according to my sister, her father is threatening to take it all away if she doesn't settle down."

Worried that he'd said too much, he paused. When the waiter

appeared, Gabriel had to force down a sigh of relief.

Wiping his mouth with his napkin, he laid it across his plate while the waiter took her dessert order.

"Seems like there's a gaping hole in your story, but I won't push. It's your business. But, you know, it would make a great reality show. I'd watch it."

He almost choked on that sigh of relief he forced down. She was suspicious, but she didn't seem angry. More like cautiously curious. Was it because she didn't really care because, well, this is just a vacation fling? He knew that's what this thing was, but still…a part of him wanted her to care enough to push. But he knew not to poke a bear, so he took the get out of jail free card and let the moment pass.

"I'm glad my father's antics are entertaining for you. But he's a pain in the ass. And now my little sister is worried that he's still planning something that involves me."

"You have a sister? Is she your only sibling?"

"Yes, and yes. And I am one hundred percent wrapped around her pinky finger."

"That's sweet," she said. "So, what are you going to do now?"

"Nothing. What is there to do? I'm going to call my father and reiterate that if he wants me to come back to the family business, it has to be on my terms. I know he won't change, so I'm just focused on my work here until I am promoted."

Gabriel looked across the table at her, and she looked contented. Her lipstick had faded during the meal, more strands of hair had escaped, and she slurped the last bit of her Bloody Mary.

"Now that was delicious," she said.

He laughed and asked, "Do you want another?"

"No. I'll have my dessert and drink some water. I have to save room for champagne later."

"You're having champagne again tonight?" He was fishing for an invitation, but didn't want to come across as too forward.

"No. *We're* having champagne again tonight."

Now he could really relax. She had just committed to seeing him again tonight, and he would use that time to convince her to see him again and again until she left the island.

Playing it cool but keeping his attention on her, he switched subjects.

"So, what's on your playlist?"

"Which playlist?" She raised one eyebrow and smirked.

"How many playlists do you have?"

"One for every mood."

"Whoa. I have one playlist that I just keep adding to whenever I hear a song or artist I like. It has hundreds of songs but no real focus beyond music I like."

"See," she said. "I'd call that My Favorite Things playlist."

"Okay. I get it." He was intrigued by how she organized her music, kind of like how she organized her life it seemed. "So, do you have a playlist that's like your go-to? One that gets the most air time?"

"As a matter of fact, I do. It's really two playlists for my most dominant moods."

She paused.

"Are you sharing, or is it a secret?"

She laughed. "I didn't know you wanted details."

"I want all the details," he added.

"Be careful what you ask for. I can talk for hours about the music on my playlists."

He leaned in with his elbows on the table and pushed his ears forward. "I'm all ears."

"Sexy and goofy? I like you even more now."

"So, you think I'm sexy?"

Her face flushed and then she leaned in. "I thought we were talking about my playlists."

"You have the floor, Mademoiselle."

"I have a Brown Girl Dreaming playlist for when I need some motivation. And when I'm in the zone, I listen to my Girl on Fire playlist."

"No romantic playlists—you know, to get you in the mood?"

She didn't respond immediately and he wanted to kick himself. Romance was probably the last thing she wanted to think about. He needed to slow down and remember that she's only been single a couple days—and it wasn't exactly by choice.

But she surprised him. Or she was just being polite when she responded.

"Not what people would typically consider 'in the mood' music. I have a Sentimental Mood playlist, but it's all jazz. And not that fake smooth jazz, radio music. It's Miles and Coltrane and Ella and Monk."

"So, basically the legends," he added.

"You know jazz?" She was pleasantly surprised.

"The Paris jazz scene on some nights can rival New York and New Orleans. I'm into the straight-ahead jazz, not that—what did you call it?"

"Smooth jazz?"

"Oui, oui. Where they take pop tunes, turn them into instrumentals and call it jazz. It's a hard pass for me."

"Well, Monsieur Laurent. I'm impressed. We do have something in common."

"We have a few things in common, Mademoiselle."

Looking at her across the table, he saw a woman comfortable in her own skin yet still unsure. She was sweet and sexy, smart and accomplished, gorgeous and generous. She was opening up to him today despite all she was dealing with in her personal life. She had taken a chance to share a meal with him—and peppered him with questions. Last night, she had enticed him. Today, she had captivated him with her easy manner, curiosity and a smile he suspected was reserved for only those she trusted. He started this just wanting to get to know her—now he wanted to be her safe place. If this were another time, and they were in another place, he would have his seat right next to hers so that he could drop his arm behind and down her back, resting it right at the curve of her spine as he leaned in for a long, lingering kiss. Just a kiss.

"What are you thinking?"

She had caught him. "Umm…"

"Ever heard Prince's *Dirty Mind* album?"

"I can't say that I have. Why? Should I add it to My Favorite Things playlist?"

She chuckled.

"Maybe. But whatever you were just thinking, I know it was dirty."

He picked up his empty Bloody Mary and licked the Old Bay spices from part of the rim. Now, when his face flushed, it was the spice—and not her—that caused it.

"Lucky glass," she teased.

"If you let me, I'll make you a lucky girl later."

"You have my permission, Monsieur."

He sat the glass down and smiled at her. She smiled back, twisted her body in her chair so that her legs were freed from under the table.

Her skin was smooth and slightly browner since her arrival. She'd gotten some sun since landing in Tahiti and it looked good on her.

"So, do you have a favorite artist?"

He turned his attention away from her legs and said, "Yes. Sade."

"That was fast."

"I don't need to think about it. She's the whole package. Her voice, her music, her band. She doesn't try to be anything other than who she is. She is reserved, but not in an uptight way. In a more mysterious way. She leaves you wanting more, and yet, she waits years and years before she releases new music. She's a class act."

"I can agree with all of that," Riley said. "Have you heard her collaboration with Jay-Z for *Moon and the Sky*?"

"I have not." The girl in her that thought she wanted to be a singer was sitting across from him right now. Eyes sparkling, voice raised an octave higher, and a childlike enthusiasm reaching into her bag for her phone and Air Pods. In a few seconds, she'd opened up an app, scrolled through and gave him one of the Air Pods. She kept the other one.

They sat across the table listening and he watched as she closed her eyes. He wished he could melt his thoughts into hers, know her mind and her heart, fix what was aching, be the salve for her wounds.

When the song ended, he handed her the Air Pod back and she put everything away.

"It's beautiful and sad," he said.

"That's true. But it's also hopeful."

"Hopeful? In what way?"

"It's obviously the story of two people who couldn't make it work, but they still ended up with something beautiful and lasting in the end. Every hurt, every heartache doesn't have to leave a scar. Sometimes it leaves a gift in its place. A lesson."

He sat quietly, contemplative, giving her the space to process. Because that's what she was doing. She was making sense of her life in this moment and was sharing that precious space with him.

CHAPTER TWENTY-SEVEN

Riley

On the drive back, they continued their conversation, sharing their favorite things — music, movies, food, drinks, activities, family memories and books. Not only was he a Sade and jazz fan, but he was also into musicals, Maroon 5, Drake, nineties hip-hop, Rihanna, Corinne Bailey Rae, H.E.R. and even turned Riley on to Romy Rose and Dorely, two French artists giving Caribbean and hip-hop vibes. He was mostly into non-fiction books, while she was a fiction girl to the core. They got into a debate about book publishing, specifically publishers trying to balance their political titles and whether that was the right choice. We agreed that the theory was admirable, but disagreed on how it should look in practice. His movie tastes were all over the place, but so were Riley's depending on her mood and he was surprised that she considered herself a self-taught mixologist that could mix a cocktail to match a personality. Of course, he challenged her to create a cocktail that captured him, and she had accepted.

Gabriel connected Riley's playlist to the car's sound system, but kept the volume on low. As he talked, she watched him as he nervously pulled his free hand through his hair whenever she challenged him with a question. His eyebrows were thick and she envied their perfect arches, but not the break in the hair, a cut he got skateboarding as a teen, and the hair never grew back she'd learned. His eyelashes curled and his dark brown hair had natural cinnamon-colored strands peeking through. His facial structure had perfect symmetry with smooth skin, full lips a shade darker than his skin, a straight nose, and perfect white teeth. Riley had seen his five o'clock shadow and wondered how he would look if he just let it go. When he turned in her direction, a sly smile crossed her face and she looked away.

"What?" he asked.

"Nothing," Riley said. "Just admiring the view."

He kept his eyes on the road, but his cheeks lifted when he smiled and shook his head.

"Are you flirting with me, Riley St. James?"

"What if I am?"

"If you are, you have my permission to proceed."

She wanted to scoot in closer to him. Feel his arm around her shoulder and nuzzle into his broad chest with her legs curled beneath her in the seat. But it felt too intimate. Too presumptuous. Too much. So, she settled for a safe distance, the scent of his cologne, a nice breeze, and a little innocent flirting.

The lunch away from the hotel and from the curious eyes of guests, plus the ride back, was just what Riley needed. Gabriel was the perfect distraction and she was happy to keep their secret. Getting to know him like this, with no friends and family influencing, interrupting, interjecting, or interfering should be a prerequisite at the start of every relationship.

Relationship?

How had that slipped into her consciousness? This was definitely not a relationship. Just two people getting to know each other in a confined space with a finite amount of time, she reminded herself.

Part of the ride, she just sat quietly, taking in parts of the island not overrun with tourists. It wasn't an awkward silence, more like two people comfortable with having some space and not feeling the need to fill every minute with words.

When they arrived back at the hotel, Gabriel parked the car in what she guessed was an employee lot. As they're exiting car, Riley noticed

Simon talking to a guest in the lobby area. Little beads of perspiration gathered on her back and her face flushed.

"Gabriel," she said. "Don't look now, but Simon is in the lobby with a guest. I don't know if he sees us, but he might."

"Don't concern yourself with Simon," he said. "There's no reason for Simon to be suspicious. And if he asks me, I'll tell him that I saw you eating alone at Bloody Mary's and offered you a ride back to the hotel."

Maybe he wasn't concerned. But up until now, as far as she could tell, she was the only person of color at this resort. Now there's at least one more and she didn't want to be connected to anyone just by proximity. But Gabriel would be completely oblivious to this—those in the majority usually were.

"You seem to be good at evasion," she said, projecting her angst and agitation on him. She adjusted her tone because what was the point.

"Do you make it a habit of pursuing hotel guests?"

She was only half joking. It was uncomfortable to imagine herself as just another woman in a long list of women he seduced at one of his hotels. Plus, he was cagey about the ex-hotel heiress.

None of it really mattered, she told herself. Their game of seduction was equally shared between them.

"I can assure you, Mademoiselle. You are the only woman I have ever pursued while working in my official capacity. You are indeed special."

She raised both eyebrows suspiciously, but added, "Thank you for saying that."

"You don't have to thank me for telling you the truth."

Truth. Now there's a concept.

But, had he told her the truth about the deal with his father? Or just a half-truth? Men pretend that they don't think they're lying when they leave big chunks of the story out—waiting to be asked a very specific question before telling a truth that might be damaging. That's what she thought Gabriel was doing with his ex-girlfriend.

Riley didn't push it. She had her own secrets about what happened between her and Jonathan hiding out in the recesses of her mind.

Not being one hundred percent sure that she wanted to get married. Not giving herself to him completely. Being suspicious of him and Issy—since college. Never feeling like she was enough and wondering if that, in the end, had been their demise. No. She kept those secrets in a place where she could control them and how she reacted to them.

But that control didn't erase the sting of betrayal.

She'd always trusted that Jonathan was telling her the truth. Now, she didn't know with any certainty which parts of their relationship were real, and which parts he was faking. Ever since she'd rushed away from Washington, D.C., the questions around his betrayal nagged her.

And the questions always circled back to whether it was the first time.

Then there was the imagery—Jonathan's hand splayed across Issy's hip and his sloppy handling of their secret rendezvous—that played on a continuous loop as she drifted off to sleep every night since it happened.

Could she ever again trust that she was being given the whole truth? Or would she be better off keeping a healthy dose of skepticism in her back pocket at all times?

She looked across at Gabriel as he locked the car and adjusted his baseball cap. She desperately wanted to believe that he was telling her the truth. And that desperation made her want to reach out and hug him, feel his arms around her waist and his lips and breath on her neck.

A part of her knew it was the alcohol contributing to this mood—along with the raw wound of Jonathan's betrayal that left her feeling insecure.

As they walked away from the car and towards the lobby, she was hesitant. Her pace slowed and Gabriel noticed.

"There's nothing to worry about. Simon will only be suspicious if we look guilty. And we've done nothing wrong. We had lunch together and I gave you a ride back."

She knew he was mostly right. But maybe she was feeling guilty because this felt like more than just lunch and a ride back. And maybe it was too soon. Or maybe it was exactly what she needed.

"You're right," she said, and resumed her pace.

As they got closer to Simon, he turned towards them.

"Perfect timing," Simon said, looking at Gabriel.

Gabriel smiled and focused his attention on Simon.

While Riley focused her attention on the man he was talking to — her former classmate. And boy, had he matured. Tall and dark with smoldering obsidian eyes, Donovan Alexander had shed his awkward, boyish looks and lanky body and morphed into some serious eye-candy. She had seen photos of him over the years as he was building his hotel empire, but they had not crossed paths and those photos had not done him justice. Or maybe she just wasn't paying attention.

He had her attention now. *How was he here?*

"Gabriel, meet Donovan Alexander. Donovan owns…"

"Monsieur Alexander needs no introduction," Gabriel said, stopping Simon mid-sentence. "He's owner, founder and CEO of the Alexander Group. It's nice to make your acquaintance."

Donovan extended his hand to Gabriel and they shook.

He then turned his attention to Riley.

"And hello, Riley. What a happy coincidence running into you on the other side of the world."

Riley—award-winning broadcast journalist, weaver of stories, talking head and one of the most in-demand speakers on the circuit—was speechless.

How was it possible that of all the hotels in the whole wide world, that Donovan would land at the exact same location at the exact same time as her?

This couldn't be a coincidence.

"Donovan!" She walked closer and reached in to hug him. "It's really good to see you. What are you doing here?"

"It's really good to see you, too," he said flashing that warm smile that took her right back to their college campus and all the long nights they spent in the library—her researching and him helping her with math. Back then, his smile was a work in progress, covered in a grill of braces.

Gabriel jumped in, eyes darting between them both. "You two know each other?"

Riley could see the blend of confusion and panic on his face.

"We sure do," she said. "We're old college classmates."

"Speak for yourself," Donovan quipped. "I'm not old. I'm just getting started."

They both laughed, and Gabriel offered a curious smile.

"So, what are you doing here? Seriously! In Bora Bora!"

This time, Donovan turned toward Gabriel.

"I'm here chasing down this gentleman."

"You're here to see me?" Gabriel shifted his weight and slid both hands in his pocket.

Riley was still getting to know Gabriel, but she knew enough to see that he was genuinely confused.

"Yes. About a business collaboration. I was in Australia for two weeks, and the flight here was only a few hours away. My contacts in Australia told me you were here for at least the next month, so I thought I'd take a chance on you sparing some time for a discussion."

Riley looked at Simon, who tried to remain neutral, but his slightly raised eyebrows betrayed him. She didn't know exactly what was happening right now, but she knew she needed to regroup. Her entire flow had been disrupted by a blast from the past standing in close proximity to the man in her immediate present, leaving her in quite the predicament.

Simon excused himself first as Riley nervously sought her exit. "Well, I won't let your business interfere with my fun. So, if you'll excuse me, I'll retreat to my villa."

Gabriel was silent, probably torn between the revelation of Donovan having a business proposition for him and Riley being friendly with the very same Donovan.

"How about we have dinner this evening," Donovan said to Riley. "We should really catch up. And if not tonight, then maybe tomorrow. I plan to stay for a few days." He turned and looked towards Gabriel and added, "Or at least until I can convince this hospitality phenom to come work with me."

Gabriel laughed and Riley thought she saw his cheeks redden just a touch through his sun-tanned skin.

"Dinner tonight sounds good. Just give me a call in my villa and we'll confirm a time," Riley said.

Now Gabriel was looking between Riley and Donovan, a new reality setting in. He no longer had Riley all to himself.

"I'll call when I'm done here. It really is so good to see you." He flashed her a smile that gave her warm fuzzies.

Riley had missed Donovan's smile and his friendship. She wasn't surprised that he was so successful. He was super smart and focused. And he believed in dreaming big. He came from humble beginnings—they had that in common—so that made his success that much sweeter. She was proud to know him.

"You, too."

She turned to Gabriel, wanting to reassure him without being too obvious.

"Monsieur Laurent, merci pour le retour. The car was definitely far more comfortable than the shuttle bus."

He smiled, and she knew he took the hint.

"C'est mon plaisir, Mademoiselle St. James. Enjoy the rest of your day."

This time Donovan laughed. "You've finally found someone to talk to you in French. Watch out, Gabriel. She'll talk your head off!"

She laughed with him. "Well, we are in the French Polynesian islands. So, what do you expect?"

"Ah, now I get it! You're here for the French!"

They both laughed and hugged again before Riley walked away.

She started walking towards her villa to change into her bathing suit. When she was a few feet away, she turned back in their direction. Both men were watching her exit.

She smirked and used her free hand to loosen her hair and let it fall around her shoulders. She reached in her bag, pulled out her Air Pods and opened her playlist to Lizzo's *Good As Hell*.

Riley St. James was back.

CHAPTER TWENTY-EIGHT

Gabriel

G abriel and Donovan agreed to meet at one of the hotel lounges
in an hour, giving Gabriel time to shower and change.

And some space to figure out if he should be worried about Riley's
connection to Donovan.

Just when he thought they were moving closer to…something. He
didn't know exactly what to call a connection with a complete stranger
on an island while he was on official hotel business and while said
stranger was a famous hotel guest.

There was so much wrong with what they were doing.

But it also felt right.

They had ended their lunch date with loose plans to connect again
tonight. But with the sudden appearance of her college friend on the
island, at the same hotel and with a proposition for him, there was a
new and unpredictable obstacle.

He had watched the way Donovan looked at Riley with instant
recognition. Donovan's eyes looked at her the same way he had looked
at her.

She said they had been college friends. But had Donovan been
pining away for Riley over the years?

And then it occurred to him that Donovan might know about her
break up with her fiancé and wanted to help her pick up the pieces. He
had been in Australia—not under a rock.

Gabriel ripped a shirt off a hanger in his closet and slammed the drawer after he took out a pair of pants for his meeting with Donovan.

How was he expected to focus on business when he couldn't stop thinking about Riley and what Donovan's true motives were in showing up in Bora Bora now?

Gabriel showered, shaved, and hastily dressed for his impromptu meeting with Donovan. He was curious. Even though he wasn't looking to leave his company, it couldn't hurt to entertain discussions with hotel executives with their fingers on the pulse of industry trends.

Over the years, Gabriel had followed Donovan's career. Donovan had bought his first hotel in South Beach. It had been abandoned and was considered a distressed property. It wasn't on the most popular street in South Beach, but it was just a block over and a mere few minutes' walk to the iconic beach.

He made headlines because he had struggled to get the financing he needed to make a go of it. Until a professional athlete stepped in, loaned him the balance of the start-up capital he needed and the rest is history. The athlete remains a silent partner in the enterprise and Donovan now has 17 boutique hotels in his group.

Gabriel read an interview with Donovan discussing his next phase—ventures that would move him beyond the U.S. territory. Gabriel wondered if Donovan—who was connected and savvy—had heard about his father's attempts at a merger.

Dressed and ready to leave his suite, Gabriel decided to call Riley. He wanted to lock in the loose plans to meet later. And, he was man enough to admit that he wanted to do a temperature check, see if she had cooled down since Donovan was now on the scene.

Her suite phone rang three times before she answered, out of breath.

"This is Riley St. James."

"Bonjour, Riley. Did I catch you at a bad time?"

"Is there ever really a bad time in Bora Bora?" she joked.

He breathed a sigh of relief.

"I'm on my way to meet your friend, Donovan."

"Okay. Hope it goes well."

She wasn't going to make this easy for him. She had given him zero openings.

He squeezed his eyes shut and dived in. "So, at lunch you mentioned us having champagne later. Same time as last night?"

"So, you did remember." Her tone was playful, sweet.

Another sigh of relief.

"Of course I remembered. Who could forget anything coming out of the mouth of the most unforgettable woman on the island?"

"Just on the island?"

Now she was teasing him.

"Pardon, Mademoiselle. On any island in any part of the world ever."

"I can live with that. I'll expect you at eleven tonight."

"It's a date."

"Is it?"

She was teasing him again.

"How about this. It's a promise."

"I hope you aren't making promises you can't keep," she added, her voice tender and low. He was instantly reminded of all that she'd been through over the past several days and he just wanted to keep giving her reasons to smile.

"Never. I'll always keep my promises."

"You know. I think I believe you."

He was so grateful she couldn't see the big stupid grin on his face. He broke the awkward silence and added, "Can't wait to see you later."

It was nearing 4:00 p.m. and guests were beginning to congregate in the lounges for pre-dinner cocktails. A live Tahitian quartet added to festive mood, while some families still lingered poolside, the laughter of kids chasing each other, diving in the pool and splashing water everywhere. The adults kept a watchful eye between sips of cocktails and sodas. The infinity pool gave the illusion of pouring into the mouth of the lagoon. The gradient shades of blue began as turquoise at the edge and ended in deep azure with frothy white tips as far as the eye could see. There were very few places on earth to experience this kind of natural beauty.

Gabriel searched the lounge area and found Donovan at a table for two furthest from the music. He had also changed his clothes, and Gabriel felt a hint of jealousy rising inside. Donovan hadn't changed for their meeting; he changed for dinner with Riley later.

Walking towards him, perfumes and colognes blended with the floral arrangements, and it was almost sickly sweet. He swallowed back whatever was churning inside, and pushed down thoughts of Donovan and Riley. He was not in competition with this man, because Riley wasn't a trophy. She was a woman whose heart had been broken just a few short days ago. She didn't deserve to be objectified and if Donovan showed her some attention, gave her more reasons to smile, then Gabriel was happy.

At least that's what he was telling himself.

"Monsieur Alexander. Sorry to keep you waiting."

Donovan stood and met Gabriel's eyes. They were the same height, and when he reached out his hand, they exchanged firm handshakes.

"Please, call me Donovan."

Gabriel couldn't help but to take measure of this man. He wasn't sure if it was because of Riley, or if it was because of all that Donovan had accomplished, on his own, with no family legacy or money behind him. He had a lot of respect for a man that blazed his own path and pushed his way through doors that had been locked or blocked for many.

They sat and Donovan asked what he was drinking. They both decided on bourbon and Gabriel added an order of goat cheese stuffed dates wrapped in prosciutto.

"Nice pairing," Donovan said.

Just one more thing they have in common, Gabriel lamented.

"It's my favorite appetizer when I dine here." Gabriel leaned back slightly in his chair and crossed his legs. "So, let's cut to the chase. Tell me why you're here."

Donovan smiled. "I like your style. We would make great partners."

"Partners? You're a self-made man. Why would you take on a partner now? And why me?"

"So, you've done your homework. Another favorable asset."

The waiter arrived with their drinks and appetizer, and Gabriel took advantage of the distraction to survey the room. Their guests were smiling and laughing, and the restaurant staff was polite, professional and punctual. Simon was behind the bar overseeing every aspect of the space, and Gabriel felt a sense of pride.

Out of habit, Gabriel examined the appetizer plating and inhaled the scent rising from the dish, mostly an earthy fragrance from the goat cheese. It was, as expected, impeccable.

When the waiter was gone, Donovan continued.

"I've heard through the grapevine that your father is looking to merge his company with another brand to diversify. I know he wants to move into some new markets, and so do I. We have a common goal. But I think your father's goal lacks vision based on who he's pursuing as merger material."

Gabriel was intrigued. His thoughts were similar, except that he did think his father's target had some merit if he was at the helm.

"How so?" Gabriel wanted Donovan to be specific. Wanted to follow his train of thought.

"The two companies are practically the same. Sure, the other company has a few properties outside of Europe, but I've seen their numbers and they are barely in the black. It's like churn. Everything they're making, they are putting it back in to stay afloat. Just one dip in the market and in two fiscal quarters, they're in the red. You know this business. It's feast or famine."

"And how did you come about this information?" Gabriel leaned in and crossed his arms on the table's edge, suspicious of Donovan and how he acquired intimate details of Cecily's family's business.

"My silent partner and I are also silent partners in that company.

Mostly for my expertise, which they haven't leveraged. The family patriarch is a bit of a relic and is slow to change."

Gabriel laughed. That was all the proof he needed to confirm that Donovan was legitimately connected to Cecily's family.

"Everything you say makes sense, and you're absolutely right about the family patriarch. It's one of the reasons he and my father are considering a merger. They are cut from the same cloth."

Donovan sat his glass of bourbon on the table and also leaned in, almost conspiratorially. "That's what I suspected. But I can't get close to your father to get him to consider my offer because he's convinced that he has a deal and that you're going to return to your family's company to lead the new merged brand."

Gabriel laughed and this time took a gulp of his bourbon, loosening his posture.

"Yes. My father is delusional. I have no plans to return to the family business because he added a stipulation that I just can't abide."

"A stipulation?"

Gabriel emptied his glass and held it up for a refill.

"Yes. See the two relics have conspired to not only have me return and run the merged company, but to also marry the daughter of the patriarch as part of the deal."

Donovan was silent.

Gabriel raised his eyebrows.

"You aren't kidding, are you?" Donovan finally said.

"Do you think I would conjure such nonsense?"

"They do know this is the 21ˢᵗ century, right?"

Gabriel smirked. "You and Riley really are friends."

Damn! He might have gone a step too far.

"You told Riley about it?"

He had to think quick. He hadn't intended to expose their connection. It was her business to tell.

"I saw her eating alone at a restaurant on the other side of the island today and I joined her. We traded sob stories and she also was shocked that families would still try to arrange marriages."

Donovan's eyes narrowed with suspicion. A momentary lapse in an otherwise consistent demeanor.

"I'm glad you were there to keep her company. She's going through a hard time."

"So, you know about her non-wedding?"

"Is there anyone who doesn't know? Truth is, I never liked Jonathan for her. I always suspected that he was cheating on her, but I didn't think he was stupid—or arrogant—enough to try something the night before their wedding. And with the most obvious girl in the room. He couldn't even be bothered to be creative. He just went with the easy target—a girl he had toyed with in college."

Gabriel took a gulp of his bourbon and leaned back in his seat, shifting his weight. He was uncomfortable, but Donovan's tone was covered in irritation, possibly even some frustration.

Donovan averted his eyes and Gabriel broke the silence. "And Riley caught him with this woman?"

"Red-handed." Donovan turned back towards Gabriel, his tone nostalgic. "I always knew she was too good for him. But she had this idea of a perfect man and a perfect career and a perfect life. She was obsessed with her image and he fit her ideal."

"That's too bad. She seems like a lovely woman." That's all Gabriel managed to say. He was afraid to say anything more for fear of Donovan reading too much into it.

"She's better than just a lovely woman." Donovan sipped his drink and Gabriel thought he saw something in his eyes—possibly a little more than friendship.

Gabriel watched Donovan as he turned his head towards the lagoon and gazed forward. He was contemplative and Gabriel didn't want to interrupt him. But it made him uncomfortable.

Finally, Donovan turned his attention back to their conversation.

"So, back to my proposition."

"Yes. What are you proposing? And how does it involve me?"

"I'm proposing that your father merge his company with mine and that I remain CEO of the American Division, you become CEO of the new International Division, and your father remain on as Chairman of the Board of Directors. You've done your homework, but so have I and I know talent when I see it. I am well aware of the improvements you've made to this company, and I also know that you're ready—or dare I say—hungry for more."

Donovan definitely had Gabriel's attention. It almost sounded too good to be true.

"I'm intrigued by your proposal. It doesn't just make good business sense, but it also would satisfy my father's desire to have me return to the company and would get him to let go of the foolish idea that I marry a woman for business."

"Exactly." Donovan reached down and opened a leather satchel. He pulled out an envelope and placed it on the table.

"I know that I'm poaching and it doesn't show respect for your company. So, we're going to end this conversation with a copy of what I propose in writing, as well as a thumb drive containing a digital copy so that you can have it reviewed by anyone of your choosing. I just wanted to meet you face-to-face and make my pitch. Now that I've done that, I hope you'll give it some consideration. I'll be here for the next few days and if you want to reconnect, we can. And if you'd prefer to wait until you're back state side, I respect that and am in no hurry."

Gabriel accepted the envelope. Just touching it made him feel dishonest. As much as he'd like to deny and suppress his traitorous deliberations, he couldn't. Because he was literally considering another offer on the property of his current employer, and without his father's consent. Yet despite his trepidation, something about Donovan's offer felt liberating.

His thoughts, tangled with *what if* and *why not* scenarios, were slammed back into the reality of the moment when he saw Simon, his expression stoic and his posture formal, with a gaze like a video recorder. Gabriel didn't know how long he had been watching them, but he knew that whatever he'd witnessed, he had committed it to memory.

Nervously, Gabriel returned his attention to Donovan and tried to remain indifferent.

"Thank you for coming all this way and for your interest in not just my family's company, but in my expertise. I have a hell of a lot of respect for you and what you've accomplished. And I agree, we would work well together. But I do need to think about this. It's a lot to consider."

Donovan nodded. "I wouldn't expect anything less."

Gabriel laid his palm flat on the envelope and looked back at Donovan, whose eyes were now diverted towards the pier. Like a scoop of ice cream melting and pooling in a bowl, a smile began to spread across his face and Gabriel turned to see what he was looking at...or rather, *who* he was looking at.

CHAPTER TWENTY-NINE

Riley

This was the entrance of every girl's dreams. And yet, it had come together effortlessly.

After a long, leisurely swim in the lagoon, Riley had soaked in the tub and selected one of the silk scarves she'd bought at the market in Papeete. Following the instructions from the young Tahitian woman at the stand, she knotted two corners of the scarf across her chest, which gathered most of the material in front of her, but left an opening that only became visible when she walked.

The distance from her villa to the restaurant was like a long fashion runway. With the sun beginning to fade behind Mount Otemanu, she glided in confidence knowing that the deep tangerine silk hugged her curves in all the right places—luxuriously soft and somehow comfortable all at the same time.

With each step, she felt the soft material caress her skin, revealing the full length of her smooth legs, accented in her tall, clear acrylic heels. Although it was nearing sundown, the temperature was still warm and she kept her pace slow to prevent any unnecessary perspiration from forming in problematic places.

The drama of the leisurely pace was an added benefit. A light breeze wafted and caught her messy up-do, casting whisps of hair strands across her face. Several thin gold chains hung at multiple lengths from as far as her belly button and up close to her collar bone. She had chosen a pair of dark amber, dangling earrings that skimmed her shoulders, glowing with sparkling gold body butter. The finishing touch was a light coating of nude lip gloss on her lips and a hint of dark brown mascara to make her lashes pop.

Riley was regaining her stride, and she felt absolutely radiant.

Once she got closer to the restaurant and lounge area, she saw Donovan seated at a table with Gabriel, both men looking in her direction. It made her think of Jonathan, who always made her feel desired, but she couldn't remember the last time he looked at her the way Gabriel and Donovan were watching her now. She had imagined Gabriel's gaze, but was a bit surprised at Donovan's intensity. But they had been friends disconnected for so long, she assumed he was just as happy to see her as she was to see him.

She hoped it was just that.

Donovan stood first and hurried to her side, while Gabriel hung back, collecting an envelope and talking to a server.

Her heart sank just a little when Gabriel didn't rush over to greet her, but remembered they had to play it safe.

"Riley," Donovan took her hand between his. "You look absolutely stunning. You are literally glowing."

His smile was so big and genuine, and she was instantly taken back to their college days. This was a man that she trusted implicitly. He had always been a real friend and never tried to cross a line with her. He had respected her and her choices in college, and probably put her up a little too high on a pedestal.

Now here he was, a decade later all smooth bronze skin, Colgate smile, broad shoulders, a successful company, and giving Morris Chestnut vibes. And not *Boys in the Hood* Morris—*Best Man* Morris effing Chestnut. The brother was undeniably fine in every way that mattered.

"Thank you, Donovan. You don't look so bad yourself."

He guided her towards the bar and pulled out a bar stool for her, before taking his seat. The bartender took their orders—chardonnay for her and another glass of bourbon for him.

He spoke first. "So, how are you? And not just broadly. But really. I know what happened and I'd be lying if I said I wasn't a little concerned for you, hashtag *RileyOnTheRun*."

"You were always a straight shooter," she said, grateful that her wine had arrived. She had wanted champagne, but decided to wait and share that later with Gabriel.

"There's something to be said for consistency. So, stop dodging."

She chuckled. "I'm not dodging, and I'm about as good as to be expected. I needed this down time to reflect and figure out my next move."

"And begin healing, I hope," he added.

"Definitely. I'm hurting, but I'll survive. I'm disappointed, but am looking forward. I'm angry, but I'm not letting it consume me. I'm also confused, but I've accepted that I may never have the answers to why this happened to me." She slid back in her seat and let her gaze fall downward as she swirled the wine around in her glass. Feeling like a victim was an uncommon emotion for her, and the blend of her emotions was just as intoxicating as the wine she was about to gulp down.

"Feeling like a victim makes me uncomfortable, but not much I can do about it."

Donovan nodded as she spoke. She could tell he wanted to say something, but was holding back.

"Well, I guess some things do change. Donovan Alexander at a loss for words?" she teased.

"Not at all. I just want to choose my words carefully."

"Thanks. Wish I had chosen my life partner more carefully." This time she sipped her wine, rolling her eyes up and shaking her head.

"That's just it, Riley. I tried to warn you away from Jonathan years ago. I knew he wasn't right for you. And all these years, I was hoping that I had been wrong back then. Turns out, I wasn't. And now one of my dearest friends is paying a price too steep for anybody's love."

Riley let his words sink in. He was right, of course. But it wasn't exactly what she wanted to hear right now. She knew Donovan meant well, but where the hell has he been all these years? Damn sure not being her friend...not a real friend, anyway.

Riley huffed, a smirk of annoyance spoiling her mood. "That's interesting you should refer to me as one of your 'dearest friends,' because I haven't heard from you in years. Now, you come along and tell me 'I told you so.' That's so not cool."

Now Donovan was quiet. The waiter came over and told them their table was ready and escorted them to the restaurant in silence.

When they sat down, he spoke up.

"You're right, Riley. I did kind of ghost you the last few years. But you had to know that it was hard for me to sit on the sidelines as a spectator in the Riley/Jonathan show. I cared about you and I never trusted him. I didn't want that distrust to ruin our friendship, so I backed off."

"You could have told me that," she said.

"No. I couldn't. You would have accused me of being jealous or over-protective or overly critical of Jonathan—none of which is true. Well, maybe I'm a little over-protective. But I knew you and I knew him. And when I heard about what he did with Issy..."

"What do you mean, you heard?" Riley cut him off. How could he possibly know about Issy?

"Come on, Riley. You're not that naive. People talk. *Issy* talks."

"This is such bullshit." The happiness she had felt at their chance encounter was quickly evaporating.

"Since when did you start listening to gossip, Donovan? That's not your style." Her anger was bubbling up to the surface. And not just a little anger, but the anger of the last five days was threatening to explode all over Donovan.

"I don't typically listen to gossip. But Jonathan and I are frat and everybody that was there that night saw him leave with Issy. And everybody knows their history. How this is breaking news for you is distressing. It doesn't take a rocket scientist to put the pieces together,

Riley. Or maybe you never wanted to piece it together."

She didn't say anything. She looked out at the ocean, wishing she could just dive in and swim until her arms gave out and she could float away into oblivion.

"Riley, this isn't your fault." Donovan's tone was softer. Honest. "This is all on Jonathan. And people aren't really gossiping. They're confronting Jonathan and Issy on your behalf. Even I confronted Jonathan."

Riley exhaled, furious, as she turned towards Donovan. She leaned in, hands firmly on her hips and eyes laser-focused on him. "You did what?"

"I confronted him. Called him out on his shit and told him what an asshole he was for hurting you and that he deserved whatever punishment you dished out."

"And what did he say?"

"Doesn't matter."

He was being cagey.

"It matters to me. What did he say?"

"He accused me of harboring feelings for you and hung up on me."

This time he looked away and the silence between them was palpable.

She sipped and sulked. And then pressed rewind on their friendship. His presence brought flashbacks of memories she had stored away for safe keeping. Her and Donovan making macaroni and cheese in the communal microwave of his co-ed dorm. Their sophomore year as mentors when they introduced the inaugural freshman orientation scavenger hunt. Jogs at dusk around campus, racing against a setting sun. Up all night drinking Pepsi and eating cold pizza with pepperoni and pineapple, just for the alliteration. Singing karaoke at the local sports bar on Wednesday nights. Him a focused business major and Riley a hard-core journalism major and editor-in-chief of the school newspaper, but secretly taking creative writing courses. Donovan was there as she grew from a girl to a woman, holding her hand, keeping a watchful eye, redirecting unwanted advances.

"Donovan." When she said his name, he redirected his attention to her. She searched the contours of his face looking for the youthful boy beneath the masculine transformation. "We're friends, right?"

"Of course," was all he said.

"And you know that Jonathan was just deflecting when he accused you of having feelings for me, right?"

This time he smiled. "Riley, what he said was partially true. There was a time when we were young and racing around campus together that I had feelings for you. I didn't know what I was really feeling and I never wanted to risk our friendship by tainting our connection with adolescent angst."

He paused and emptied his glass. She didn't speak because she could tell he wasn't done yet.

"It was part of the reason why I backed off and let you go figure out your life with Jonathan. I knew he didn't want me hanging around. I mean, he's mostly the reason I waited to pledge our fraternity in a graduate chapter. I knew he would block me in college. So, I faded into the background of your life. But I'm here now. And I know you must be hurting. And this isn't about 'I told you so.' This is about a long, lost friend who saw you barreling towards a painful reckoning in pursuit of perfection a long time ago, here now—by pure coincidence—to help you pick up the pieces. That's it. That's all."

He looked away again, holding in a sigh of relief against the heat rising at the back of his neck—and in desperate need of another bourbon.

"Thank you for being honest with me," Riley said. "If I'm being honest, I think I loved you back then and just loved the idea of Jonathan. You were right. Jonathan checked all the boxes. But you were the genuine article. And you know I've never been very patient and am an admitted perfectionist."

He laughed. "I'm glad you can finally own up to being a perfectionist. It's past due."

She shook her head and smirked, a mixed bag of emotions. She noticed that he didn't acknowledge the 'loving him' part of her admission. But that was cool. She didn't say it so that they would spend hours talking about what ifs. She just wanted to be equally honest with him.

"True that." This time she gulped her wine, and he laughed out loud.

"Now that we've cleared the air and are both in need of another round, how was your meeting with Gabriel?"

"Oh, so you're on a first name basis with the dashing, French hotel executive? The plot thickens."

Riley had to think fast. She had just unintentionally revealed a familiarity with Gabriel and she needed to twist and bend her way out of it.

"He's been looking out for me. There may have been an incident at the airport with some unwanted attention that he rescued me from and some harmless banter over lunch today, but that's it."

She could feel the heat rushing up into her cheeks and hoped Donovan didn't notice.

"So, if it was just 'some harmless banter' over an innocent lunch, why are you blushing?"

Damn it!

"Seriously, Donovan. I'm not blushing. It's just a little warm out this evening." She turned to get the attention of the server to buy some time.

"One—you are blushing. Two—you deserve some fun, and maybe even some revenge sex. And three—he's a good dude. I am familiar with his family and have followed his career. He's legit smart, driven—and his French is better than yours."

At this, she laughed. They were falling back into their old familiar rhythms. So, she decided she could trust him with her secret.

"A decade may have passed between us, but you my friend, can still read me like a book."

He ordered them another round.

"Spill," was all he said.

"It's true, Gabriel and I did have lunch today and we did share some

enthusiastic banter. But lunch wasn't a coincidence. We planned it."
She paused and took a deep breath, building up the strength to get to
the juicy part. "After spending the night together last night."

Donovan's expression didn't change. He sat completely still, staring
at her through squinted eyes.

She adjusted herself nervously in her chair.

"So, let me get this straight. You spent the night with Gabriel? And
then went on a lunch date? And now, you want to know about my
conversation with him?"

A trickle of perspiration eased down the hollow of her back. She was
literally in the hot seat and went on the defensive.

"I should have never told you."

"Damn! This is a new record. I made Riley St. James sweat in under
thirty minutes." He burst out laughing—a deep, velvety laugh that was
the opposite of his voice when he was growing into manhood.

But that didn't make her not want to toss her glass of wine at him,
just to shut him up.

"You're an a-hole!"

"Riley, I'm happy for you. You deserve some no-strings-attached
sex and whatever else he's serving on the side. Everybody doesn't know
you like I do. And I know that once you went there with Jonathan, you
were one hundred percent his. And I'm pretty sure that Mr. Gabriel is
one of just two men to know you intimately."

She eased back in her seat, relieved to have shared her secret with
someone who really knows and gets her.

"You might know me best of all Sir Donovan. This thing with
Gabriel is temporary. Let's just call it an entanglement. But I like him.
I'm having fun and he's making me laugh and doing things to my body
not appropriate for public discourse. So, this experience is my new
definition of perfect. Perfect for right now."

"I'm happy for you."

She looked into his eyes, searching for any sign of unrequited love or dodging of the truth. There was nothing there but genuine concern and happiness.

"Thanks, Donovan. And what about you? Are you going to be an eternal bachelor? Are you too busy building your empire to find love?"

"I'm glad you asked, Ms. St. James. As a matter of fact, there is someone special. And when I get back to Los Angeles, I plan to propose. Also, I'm so damn happy I don't have to call you Mrs. Jasper. So bland and pedestrian."

She chuckled then bolted upright in her chair, his last sentence registering on delay.

"What! Way to bury the lead! Who is she? Tell me everything!"

And just like that, they slid right back into their groove. They laughed and talked until the dinner service was over and half the guests had retired either to their villas or the lounge. They decided to keep their reunion party going and headed to the lounge area.

Gabriel was there, behind the bar with Simon flipping through a large binder. He didn't notice them come in, and so she stole a few glances of him in his natural habitat. He did own whatever space he was occupying. His presence wasn't obtrusive, but it was discernible.

"Should we hit the bar?"

She thought better of it. She'd had a few glasses of wine and she didn't want to get too comfortable with Gabriel while Simon was so close by.

"No. Let's grab a table."

They found a table for four, but sat side by side on the leather bench.

Donovan was scanning the room, and then suddenly stood up.

"Where are you going?"

"There's a piano!"

"Oh, no! We're not doing that tonight!"

"Just one song, Riley. Come on! Can you really say no to your long, lost friend who just swooped in to save the day?"

She laughed. "That's a bit of an exaggeration. But okay. I'll play along. Just. One. Song."

Donovan sat on the piano bench and began tapping away on the keys. All eyes turned in his direction, including Gabriel's. Then his eyes began scanning the crowd, and she smiled.

He was looking for her.

This time she stood, made brief eye contact with Gabriel, and then walked over to the piano. She slid in beside Donovan and nudged him with her body.

He still had it. His fingertips danced across the keys and her body matched the rhythms filling the air.

Somehow, he still remembered that her favorite songs with piano accompaniment were Alicia Keys. So much of her music could be recreated just with piano, and it was really the only way Riley would sing outside of the privacy of her home.

When he tickled out *If I Ain't Got You*, she felt the music rising inside. Through the melodies and notes, she felt them being transported right back to college, the dynamic duo in the music room before rehearsals for whichever musical they were performing in that semester. They always had a warm-up song before rehearsals—and it was usually Alicia Keys, Prince, or John Legend.

She closed her eyes and let the music envelope her. Swaying left and right, she started out with a hum, rising in pitch as Donovan played on. They were always perfectly synced.

At the perfect moment, she opened her mouth and let the words pour out. Soulful lyrics about fortune and fame, the trappings of love, and the idea of having it all. It was perfect for this moment, for this space where she was releasing her ideals and embracing what it means to really connect to a person. Not just a romantic connection, but genuine, authentic human connection.

Despite the years between them, her connection to Donovan had remained intact, even without nurturing it. And over a few days on the opposite side of the world, she had connected with a man she barely knew.

She allowed herself one glance in Gabriel's direction as she belted out the chorus. She smiled through lyrics, seeing a look of appreciation in his eyes that she'd never seen before from a man. Not even Jonathan.

Gabriel was equal parts soulful and sexy. He respected her and didn't crowd her. He could read her mood, be vulnerable and mysterious. He accepted her terms for their island fling, but still made her feel like she was the most important person in the room. He confounded and charmed her all at once. He was on a mission, but still made time for her and let her in. She was more than a bit damaged, and he seemed content to help her lick her wounds—minus any strings. He was exactly what she needed through this pregnant pause on her life.

Breaking the stolen moment with Gabriel, she turned back towards Donovan, who had the biggest, dumbest grin on his face. But he didn't stop playing.

She continued to sing through her smiles, and finally turned her gaze towards the other guests in the lounge. People were standing around, watching and listening. Some got closer while others never left their seats, but swayed and sang along to the song. She noticed a table nearby of two couples. One couple was grinning, holding hands and fake serenading each other. But the other woman held her mobile phone up and pointed in their direction. She wore a big smile, and Riley realized what was happening.

She had let her guard down and gotten too comfortable. Now, she and Donovan were being recorded, and there was nothing she could do about it.

CHAPTER THIRTY

Gabriel

Gabriel helped Simon and the lounge manager on duty close out the night and rushed to his suite to shower and change before seeing Riley.

He had watched her that night at the lounge, mesmerized by her voice and completely smitten with everything about her. His jealous streak was pulsating right at the surface, but he forced it down—at least until he could talk to Riley about her relationship with Donovan. He didn't want to jump to any conclusions, but the two of them looked very cozy. He kept telling himself they were only friends whenever he looked in their direction. But then, they sang that song together and he thought he was dead in the water. He could never compete with that kind of bond. That history.

By the end of the night, he was convinced that she had changed her mind about seeing him later. He was steeling himself for the bad news when her and Donovan walked over to say good night. But instead, she gave him a hug and whispered in his ear, "See you at eleven."

He cleared his throat and nodded nervously, straining to maintain his composure.

Donovan reached out to shake his hand and then leaned in to add, "Be good to her."

The handshake grounded him, even though he was surprised that Riley had shared their secret with Donovan. But he considered it a good sign and said, "Count on it."

He knew all that he needed to know.

Confident of his standing in her life, however temporary, he rushed to get to her villa. But he wasn't as careful as the night before. He missed the soft billow of cigarette smoke at the edge of the lagoon and Simon's curious eyes.

This time when Gabriel knocked, Riley yelled for him to come in. The door was slightly propped open with the latch.

He stepped inside, shut the door behind him, but didn't see her.

Looking around the room, he noticed chilled champagne in an ice bucket, a bottle of Chambord, a small bowl of raspberries, sliced kiwi and pineapple chunks, a bowl of deep red sorbet, and two champagne flutes with rims coated in what he guessed was sugar.

He walked over to the bar to inspect the set-up and wondered how she had pulled it off.

He was careful not to touch anything because she obviously had something planned and he didn't want to ruin the surprise.

He heard Sade's voice pour out from the bedroom and he dipped his head and smiled. She had been paying attention when he told her Sade was his favorite singer.

When he looked up again, Riley was leaning one shoulder against the doorway between the living space and bedroom, draped in an emerald green oversized scarf that she had tied around her neck and was wide open in the front. A small triangle of black fabric sat between her thighs and his breath caught.

"Bonsoir, Monsieur Laurent."

He was speechless. He took a few steps forward until he was standing directly in front of her. But she didn't move. He cupped her cheeks in his hands and began placing kisses all over her face—grateful that she thought enough of him to plan something nice and relieved that she still wanted whatever this was to continue. When she moaned into his mouth, he was sure they wouldn't get to have whatever decadent cocktail she was planning to make for them.

"I guess you're happy to see me," she said between his kisses and her smile.

"What gave it away?"

She reached her hand down the front of his body, past his waist band and paused. No words were necessary.

He laughed and pulled back, but never taking his eyes off of her.

"May I have this dance, Mademoiselle?"

"You may, Monsieur."

She gently laid her arms around his neck, and he placed his hands around her waist, palms resting on the curve of her hips. She began kissing him slowly on his neck as they rocked to Sade's *Sweetest Taboo*. When the song hit the chorus, she sang the lyrics and he pulled back to look at her.

"I want you to sing to me all night."

"Still so presumptuous," she joked.

"Not presumptuous. Cautiously hopeful."

She rested her head on his chest and they stayed that way until the song ended. When the next song began, she took him by the hand and led him over to the bar.

"I want to make you a drink, before the sorbet melts."

"How did you get all these ingredients?

"Room service, of course."

He sat on one of the stools and watched as she dropped a spoonful of sorbet in each flute and began her presentation.

"The sorbet is really just the French translation of the English word for sherbet. It represents our connection."

Using a shot glass she obviously bought from the hotel's boutique, she began adding the Chambord.

"This ingredient celebrates your history and regal ancestry—a raspberry liqueur that originated in France and was made popular by King Louis XIV."

He was in awe and completely entertained by her knowledge, her thoughtfulness, and the details.

Next, she grabbed a handful of bright red raspberries.

"The fresh raspberries are symbolic. They are a symbol of kindness—which is what you've been to me. Even before you knew me. That's a quality that can't be faked."

Finally, she gripped the bottle of champagne and poured, the effervescent bubbles pushing the raspberries to the rim of the glass.

"This is where I come in," she said through a warm smile. "I'm the ingredient that spices up the recipe—makes it sparkle."

She handed him his first, and then she held up her glass for a toast.

"To new friends and new adventures. And may all our glasses be rimmed in sugar as a reminder that life is sweet."

They touched glasses and sipped.

And then he raised his glass again.

"My turn."

She lifted her glass and looked into his eyes. He almost forgot what he wanted to say.

"To risks and rewards. And the moon and the sky."

"I can definitely drink to that." She took a sip and added, "I see my playlist is already pulling you in," acknowledging his reference to the Sade and Jay-Z song they shared over lunch.

They finished their first round and she poured them another. Tonight, they weren't in a hurry. They had lingered on the sofa and then took their second round out onto her patio and sat on the edge, their legs swishing through the water.

He told her about his talk with Donovan, and she told him what Donovan was like in college. He talked about his younger sister, and she told him about her new friends in Papeete that were coming to visit in a few days.

As she spoke, he remained solely focused on her. She was like two sides of the same coin. The public persona that had come to define her was still there, but on the backburner. A more relaxed, less intense Riley sat beside him now, legs dangling and sharing small pieces of her life like she was telling a bedtime story. He was sorry he'd spent any time wondering about her and Donovan. He was just happy that she had someone from her past that knew her history with her ex-fiancé and could provide another kind of comfort for her. And he loved how she listened as well as she spoke. He knew that was the journalist in her—asking all the right questions.

The more she shared, the more he wondered how a man could need or want anything more in or from a woman. When he first saw her, the physical attraction was natural. As he observed her, he wanted to know more. When he touched and kissed her, he never wanted it to end. But talking to her and getting to know her mind and her heart, that was the real magic. He knew this would be the part of her that he would remember most. And that he would miss the most.

Taking a chance, he asked her how she was holding up otherwise, and she showed him her social media post. Together, they looked at some of the comments, waffling between laughter and shrieking and cringing.

When they were done with round two of their champagne cocktail, she escorted him into her bedroom, lit only by a small candle on the night stand and the moon's imprint against the lagoon. Gabriel's sensibilities screamed this was a bad idea, to keep falling in deeper with her. But those thoughts were quickly banished when she untied her scarf and it floated to the floor. He took a step closer and kissed her, his hands slowly caressing every inch of her, committing each curve to his memory.

He finally lifted her up and gently laid her on the bed. He pulled a row of condoms out of his pocket, slowly pulled off his shirt and slid out of his pants, giving her ample time to see all of him. In this moment, all of him belonged to all of her.

She watched, breathless and biting the corner of her bottom lip, as he ripped open a condom with his teeth and took his time sliding it on. A soft moan escaped from her and he kneeled on the bed, slowly lowering his body onto hers. Heat rose from her skin, drawing him in closer as he kissed and licked and sucked her taut nipples, drowning in pleasure at each gasp and moan she made. Her reactions to his touch were genuine and unfiltered, filling a gap he never knew existed.

She wrapped her arms around his neck and her fingers gripped and tangled in his hair, urging him forward, faster. She lifted her legs around his waist in one swift movement, making room for him and inviting him inside.

He was already on the edge of ecstasy when he slid up her body and pressed his mouth to hers, swallowing her passionate whimpers. He desperately wanted their emotional connection to mirror this undeniable physical connection. He felt her response as her nails dug into his back, pressing him closer and arching her back until he had no choice but to slide inside the warmth between her thighs. He lost himself to her gentle movements, and inhaled each breath that she released, hoping to capture droplets of her essence to keep for himself.

Slowly, they found each other's rhythms while their hands explored their bodies. Their kisses were deep and lingering, as the surface of their bodies became slick with moisture from their thrusts and retreats.

When her body began to arch, he knew she was nearing release. She called out his name over and over again, digging her hands into his hair, gripping and pulling until she couldn't hold back any longer. With each motion forward, he plunged deeper and she moaned louder. And as her body began to quiver, he felt his release rising to the surface and pulled back and then slid his full length inside her. With a handful of her hair gripped tightly, he pulled her head back, sucking and licking her neck as she scraped her nails down the length of his back.

Exhausted and satisfied, he pulled out and turned over on his back, his breaths heavy and labored. She turned over on her side and laid her head across his chest. With his right hand, he massaged her scalp until he heard her breathing slow and he knew she had drifted off to sleep. He lay staring up at her ceiling, wondering what he had done to deserve these stolen moments with this amazing woman. He had no way of knowing how long this would last, but he didn't want to waste time dwelling on the unknown.

Instead, he focused on the here and now. She was here with him and she wanted him now. That was all that mattered.

But was this *all that mattered*, he wondered? Or could there be more? He had dated a lot of women and knew if they were really into him. But Riley was different. He didn't know if he was just a convenient distraction. Or, if he had been so enamored with famous Riley that he was taking uncalculated risks.

He buried his face in her hair and she stirred, stretching her leg across his.

He pulled her closer, knowing that she could be wallowing in self-pity, but instead she was shaping a new happy for herself. And she chose to let him be part of that new happy. He was all in.

An hour later, he felt her slide out of bed. She blew out the candle and he thought she was headed into the bathroom. Moments later, he heard a faint splash into the water. He sat up and peered through the wide-open window and there she was. In all her naked glory, swimming and then pausing, and then diving underwater again.

There was a faint glow in the water from the lights beneath her villa, and when she swam close to it, he could see the curves of her body ripple just below the surface.

She dipped back under and swam away from the villa, where the water was darker and deeper. He sat up fully and slid to the edge of the bed, just to keep an eye on her. The water wasn't just deeper that far out, it was also cooler and she might not be expecting that.

Seconds passed by like hours while she was beneath the surface, and he stood, prepared to dive in if she didn't come up for air soon. He pressed his face against the glass and saw her arm pop up in the air and wave at him.

An invitation?

He didn't stop to consider the risk…or to put on a robe. He stepped out onto her patio and dived in. When he came up for air, he didn't see her. He dipped back under and swam further forward. This time when he came up for air, she was nearby floating on her back and completely still, her breasts perky and hair drifting around her. He swam closer, loosened his muscles and joined her floating on his back.

Above them, a sprinkle of stars lit up the night sky and they were adrift in a state of suspended animation. Seconds became minutes, and he drank in this moment, unsure of how he got here and certain that in a few days, she would disappear from his life as quickly as she had appeared. The fact that he was choosing this uncertainty for himself made him uncomfortable.

"What are you thinking?" She broke their silence, her voice as wistful as his thoughts.

"I'm going to take a chance here and be honest."

"I could use some honesty in my life."

"Just thinking about what happens when your trip ends."

"What would you like to happen?" Her tone didn't change, but he thought he heard her voice catch just a little.

He didn't have an answer. At least not one he was willing to say out loud.

"Honestly, I don't know. Your life is a world away from mine. We have careers, family and friends, plans—all waiting for us when you leave this island."

"Don't forget the eventual reckoning with my ex-fiancé. I have a big mess waiting for me when I return to Washington, D.C."

Gabriel didn't say anything to that. He knew in some ways she was running from her problems. But she had run right into his arms. What was he supposed to do now? Let her slip free or hold on tighter? And more importantly, what did she want?

She took advantage of the quiet space between them, and let her body descend into the water. He decided to join her and let his full weight drag him under. With a couple feet of water above them, he could barely make out her silhouette in the water. He reached forward and they found each other. Kicking their feet, they pushed themselves up to the surface and let their bodies float closer until there was no space between them.

Riley put her arms around his neck and kissed him. He held onto her waist, gently nudging her forward to feel his excitement growing.

Her kisses grew firmer, her tongue probed deeper as she wrapped her legs around his waist and he pulsated against her. The water glided between them and rippled around them. Her breathing intensified, and her soft sighs enticed and begged him for more. But he knew if they continued, his desire would swell and that was too big of a risk. They were completely unprotected and he had to find some will power to withhold.

As if she had read his mind, she lifted her lips from his and drew her torso back, stretching her body out in the water. Her legs clinched tighter around his waist and the motion of her body matched the waves. Droplets of water trickled off her breast and she stretched her arms out and behind her, vulnerable and exposed before him.

There was a shift in the universe, and their connection intensified.

He held her back with one hand and used his free hand to massage the smooth skin on her stomach and breasts, memorizing every inch of her body, the rise and fall of her chest, the euphoria captured in the slit of her eyes. But he was one hundred percent present, and knew that they both needed a healthy dose of reality. He didn't want to disturb the tranquility, but he also didn't want them to wake up tomorrow with regrets.

Their physical connection morphed into something spiritual, their bodies enveloped in the warm, opulent Polynesian cove, just the two of them in the solitude of night.

He imagined what being inside her—raw and unprotected—would feel like and if she had touched him, his orgasm would have shaken the ocean floor. But those were dangerous thoughts, and before his will power faded, he released her. His head fell back and the stars winked at him.

At first, she didn't move. He was worried she might be upset with him because he had broken their connection. He let his body join hers, floating slowly beside her as her eyes fluttered open.

Sheepishly, he said, "I'm so sorry. I really want to…"

She dipped her body underwater and popped back up wearing a smile so wide it met her eyes.

"Don't apologize."

"But I want you to know that I would love to be with you fully—no barriers between us. But we can't afford the risk."

She paddled closer to him again, and planted a sweet kiss on his cheek.

"I know," she whispered. "You saved us from what could have been a huge mistake with far-reaching consequences. I don't have a lot of experience expressing restraint, so please don't apologize. I have no regrets."

She smiled at him, and he didn't read any disappointment in her eyes. Then she added, "Besides, I had a back-up plan."

He smiled back at her and tried to let it go. He was still angry with himself, but he had acted on behalf of them both.

Together, they swam back to her patio and pulled their bodies up on the ledge. She stayed seated while he went in to get them towels and robes.

Once they dried off and wrapped themselves in the robes, they cuddled up on the sofa outside with just their breathing and heart beats between them.

Gabriel finally spoke.

"So, you remembered that I like Sade."

He could feel her smiling against his chest before she responded, "I added her to my playlist."

CHAPTER THIRTY-ONE

Riley

When she opened her eyes, she was in bed, her nude body half covered by the crisp white sheet. She stretched and turned over, half expecting to see Gabriel beside her. But she was alone.

She knew he had to leave before sunrise, but she wished that he had kissed her good-bye before he snuck off into the early morning. This was a new feeling for her. She knew they had to be careful, but giving herself to a man that wasn't still beside her the next morning felt cheap.

Curling up, she pulled the sheet up to her neck, and let that negative thought train run off the track, and instead smiled and then giggled just a little. She replayed their last waking moments together from last night and was struck by how comfortable she was drifting off to sleep in his arms.

It was the first time since she'd left D.C. that Jonathan and Issy weren't tormenting her on a continuous loop as she drifted off to sleep.

Remembering Gabriel's arms around her, his gentle kisses and the way he worshipped her body during sex, a small but very present glimmer of hope rose in her. Just enough to remind her that she would one day love again.

Having a sexy stranger pursuing her when she was feeling the least desirable wasn't just good for her confidence, it was good for her recovery.

Gabriel was a distraction. But he was also a balm for her wounded ego.

What she wasn't ready to tackle was the question of what happens next. It was too big of a question with too many implications that she just wasn't equipped to deal with in her current state of mind. She knew he was thinking about a what's next. But she couldn't. Not until she knew what she really wanted out of life for herself.

And Gabriel's life wasn't exactly an open book either. There was definitely something he was hiding about the ex-girlfriend. And maybe it's as simple as a wounded heart or a bad break up.

A wound inflicted by your first love—now that was something she could relate to thanks to Jonathan.

She and Gabriel were quite the pair. Two wounded souls that find each other on an exotic island and connect in the quick exchange of a glance in a boutique.

Sure, she knew that what they were doing was risky because of his position at the hotel—and her job and reputation, too. But they were being careful and it really wasn't anybody's business as long as it didn't interfere with how he did his job. And she would never do that to him or anyone else.

She turned over towards her night stand to check the time on her phone and saw a handwritten note on the hotel stationary.

Bonjour, ma belle. Here's my number. 210-555-4342. Text me "our" playlist. Gabriel

He hadn't kissed her good-bye this morning. This was better.

She propped herself up in bed, dialed room service to order breakfast, and then turned off airplane mode on her cell phone to text Gabriel.

As soon as her phone came to life, a flurry of text messages popped up on her screen and her mood instantly went grey. She didn't want to deal with her real life. She just wanted to be here, on this beautiful island basking in its splendor, peace, and quiet.

A text from her mother in all caps made her pause. All caps were not her mother's style. Actually, texting wasn't her mother's style. So, she opened her message app to read her mother's note.

Just as she started reading—CALL ME AS SOON AS YOU GET

THIS!—there was a loud knock on her villa door. Startled by the force of the knocking, she sat upright and looked around for her robe. She found it at the foot of the bed and headed towards the door.

The knocking didn't grow louder, but it was definitely quicker.

"I'm coming, I'm coming." She knew it was no way this was her room service order. And if it were, she'd take her complaint straight to the top.

She opened the door and found a disheveled Donovan on the other side.

"Donovan? What the hell! Why are you knocking on my door like you're the cops and I'm America's Most Wanted?"

He didn't answer and just pushed past her and entered her villa.

"Sure, come on in."

She shut the door and turned to face him. He was pacing and rubbing his head, his shirt partially tucked into khaki shorts and his sneakers were untied.

"Donovan, what's going on? Why are you acting so strange?"

He stopped pacing and pressed his hands on the back of her sofa. Dropping his head like he was in prayer, his back curved and tense. When he finally spoke, the words slid out heavy and thick like glue.

"Somebody took a video of us last night."

"Who is *us*?"

"You and I. You singing, me playing piano."

His head was still bowed and Riley was starting to get nervous, his angst starting to stick to her.

"Okay. And how do you know about this video? And why is it freaking you out? We were just singing." She walked closer to him and placed a hand on his back. His breathing was heavy and slow like a wrecking ball swinging until it would finally hit its target. Keeping him calm was her strategy to remain calm. She thought back to the woman pointing her cell phone at their performance, and her stomach turned.

"One of these fucking busy body guests posted it on IG. Now it's everywhere."

She stopped rubbing his back, but didn't lift her hand. She was stuck to him, his words, and this moment. Last night had been laugh-out-loud fun with a long-lost friend—singing their way down memory lane back to a time when life was easier, less complicated, and the world was waiting for them with open arms.

The reality of the imagery struck her like a lightning bolt. She knew the power of an image. It was a power she yielded over audiences every time she stood in front of a camera reporting on the world's latest disaster or the moments that define history.

In her mind, she was writing the script of that moment as an image absent of any context. Without having seen the video, she knew what the world would see, would assume, would accuse her of—without any context.

The world didn't know where she was. She was #RileyOnTheRun.

Now, they know.

The world knew that she called off her wedding, but they didn't know why.

Now, it looks like an affair with another man is the reason why.

Yesterday she asked for privacy and the space to heal.

Now, she looks like the villain and Jonathan the victim of her betrayal.

She removed her hand from Donovan's back and stepped away from him to get her phone, tightening the belt on her robe, her steps heavy and quick. For days, she had been playing hide and seek with her life, her family, her friends, her career. Existing in secret on this island. Letting Jonathan's betrayal play the leading role in her otherwise carefully crafted life. Ignoring what and who was important. Having sex with a practical stranger. All while pretending to be getting her shit together.

Now, her friend had innocently been dragged into her mess of a life and it has him distraught.

Scrolling through the avalanche of text messages, she realized that the common theme was danger ahead. Most of the texts from her family and friends had been warnings—mostly. Some of them—many of the most recent messages—accused her, but some were congratulatory.

Her anger was too raw to even begin to formulate a cohesive response.

"This is bad," Riley said out loud, eyes darting across her screen, fingers feverishly scrolling to read threads of messages before moving on to the next. "This. Is. Really. Bad."

Oddly enough, there were no messages from her father. But he had predicted that her life with Jonathan would be short lived. What had he called it? *A catch and release scenario.* Why had she not realized that anytime she and her mother agreed always spelled disaster. Sometimes you want something so bad you overlook all the red flags of warning. Agreeing with her mother was definitely a red flag she foolishly ignored.

And yet, despite their differences, disagreements, and the gulf of distrust she had allowed to grow between them, her mother's voice was the only one she wanted to hear right now.

But there was Donovan to deal with—an innocent by-stander in her drive-by life.

She looked at him, still hunched over her sofa. His breathing had slowed and the curve of his spine had straightened and he stood slowly, metal rod straight. He wasn't a man that easily bent to the will of circumstance. He just needed a few minutes to remember who he was.

"Yes," he finally said. "It's not just really bad. It's the fucking worst."

He walked over to her bar where the remnants of last night's champagne cocktails were scattered and half used. The champagne bottle now floated in an ice bucket of chilled water and the glasses were smudged with sorbet residue and wilted raspberries.

Donovan pulled the bottle from the ice bucket, droplets of water landing on the hard wood floors, and lifted it to his mouth.

She watched his throat as he gulped the flat champagne until the bottle was empty. When he was done, he dropped it back in the ice bucket and water sloshed over the side.

"I never made you for a sloppy drinker," she said in a half-assed attempt to lighten the mood.

"Well, I never made you for a woman who would finally see through Jonathan's bullshit and drown your sorrows with the first French dude to land on your doorstep."

Riley stopped smiling.

"That's fucked up, Donovan. Seriously."

He pulled out a bar stool and slid back onto the seat. He leaned back on the bar and his head fell back, like it was too heavy for his shoulders to hold up any longer.

"Sorry, Riley," he whispered. "You know I didn't mean it—well not really, but a little bit."

"What the hell, Donovan! Last night you encouraged me to spend time with Gabriel. Now you're acting like I'm disinvited from the cookout."

He leaned forward and laughed.

"Nah," he said. "You're still invited. But Gabriel's going to have to earn his invite."

Now they both laughed and she walked over to the sofa, taking a seat and angling her body towards him.

The silence that stretched between them was thick like the last piece of bubble gum being split between friends.

"My girl saw the video." His voice was almost a whisper—low, thick and heavy with the debt of remorse he didn't owe.

Riley let the weight of his words sink in. Last night he had just told her that he was planning to propose to the woman he was dating. The golden flecks lit up in his hazel eyes when he talked about her, and Riley had known he had at long last found the real thing. Through the years when she thought about Donovan, she thought that his work had consumed him and that it would be his only real love. He had proven her wrong and found his soulmate. And instead of making plans with Donovan to meet the love of his life, Riley was now the object of her hurt and embarrassment.

It was a feeling she knew all too well. It was the exact feeling she had run away from six days ago.

Her guilt formed in her throat like a tangle of weeds pushing up and strangling her words. She didn't know what to say.

She started slowly. "Just start with the truth."

It had been Jonathan's insistence that she shouldn't believe what she saw with her own eyes that had only added salt into the wound. *It's not what you think, Riley.* When really, it wasn't about her thoughts in that moment. It was about what she could see, what was tangible and as plain as the nose on her face.

Adding insult to injury never ends well.

"I did. And I think she believes me. But she's embarrassed. Her family has seen the video and, in her words,—*My family saw what I saw. Devotion in your eyes when you looked at Riley. If she's only your friend, you might want to remind yourself.*"

His words oozed out like venom, the bags beneath his eyes weighted in anguish. The stubble on his chin and cheeks, along with the pink in his eyes told a story as old as time. He hadn't slept all night and it was because of a relationship.

Riley thought about this for a minute and chose her next words as carefully as she had chosen all the important things in her life.

"Give her time, Donovan. She just needs some space to process. Once the shock of it has worn off, she'll be ready to talk. And when she's ready, I'll be there with you to reassure her that we're just friends and that you only have eyes for her. That what she saw in your eyes when you looked at me was a friend relieved that his best friend from college was finally ridding herself of a man that was never good enough for her."

He tilted his head up and looked at her, wearing the grin of the less confident Donovan she remembered from college. That she remembered even from last night.

"If I didn't know your true age, I'd call you a wise old woman, Riley St. James."

"Thank you, I think."

She stood and walked over to him, taking both his hands in hers.

"I'm going to have to cut this trip short," pulling his hands back from her.

"You absolutely should. Let her know that you are there for her whenever she's ready. Don't let her drown in a sea of doubt because you're on this island with me. Go. Home."

Donovan shook his head in acknowledgement.

"I'll call the airline and see if there's a flight out today and get packed. I hate to leave when we were just getting reacquainted. I feel like I'm just getting my friend back and now we're being torn apart again by circumstance."

"You never lost me, Donovan. If anything, I lost myself. But that's too much of a philosophical debate to have under duress. We're always going to be friends. But now, we're going to be present as friends in each other's lives, no matter what."

Before he could respond, there was a tap at the door. "Room service."

"I forgot that I ordered breakfast."

Riley opened the door and instructed the servers to arrange breakfast at the table on her patio. Donovan watched from his bar stool, still very much in a daze.

When they were done, she stepped back inside.

"Join an old friend for breakfast?"

"I could use some food and some coffee."

She waffled between guilt and pity, as she watched her friend move in slow motion, a man on the cusp of losing the most important thing in his life. It was a feeling she understood. Her wound was still wide open, the pain oozing out after losing what I thought was the most important thing in my life. It made her wonder if Jonathan wore this look on the Sunday after their abandoned nuptials. Or, if he stayed true to form, and stepped out in his bronze perfection, undeterred and pretending to be perfect.

Riley decided that she wouldn't let Donovan lose the woman he loved, and she'd do whatever was necessary to keep them together.

As they sat down to eat, she sat her phone on the table next to her water glass.

"Shouldn't you respond to some of those text messages," he said as he poured them both coffees.

Without responding, she flipped the phone over and began scrolling through the messages. Not to respond, but hoping that one name in particular wasn't there. Deep down, she knew it would be. Jeremy.

CALL ME. THEY'VE CALLED AN EMERGENCY MEETING WITH CORPORATE AND EDITORIAL. I'M NOT INVITED BUT HAVE BEEN TOLD TO BE ON STANDBY. CALL ME!

It was her producer—shouting at her—and she knew that a statement on social media wouldn't be enough to wipe this away.

She flipped the phone over. He had texted her nearly two hours ago and she knew that by now, her fate may have already been sealed.

Dread pooled in her stomach, but she took several sips of coffee, hoping the warmth and the acid of the caffeine would melt away her anxiety.

Not wanting to worry Donovan any further, she smiled across the table at him and said, "It can wait."

As soon as Donovan left, she hopped in the shower, changed into a bathing suit and cover-up and headed out to the patio to take in some sun—all delay tactics. She had to call Jeremy back.

The shower calmed her—a little. But sunshine was the ultimate therapy and right now, the temperature was just right and with just a small adjustment to one of the lounge chairs, she positioned herself to soak it all in.

Today, she would fuel her body with all the Vitamin D the sun had to offer.

She opened her phone to another influx of text messages, and bypassed them all and went straight to her phone app.

She tilted her head up just as a cluster of clouds began forming around the sun and pulled up her recent calls. She selected Jeremy's name and mobile and he picked up on the first ring.

"It's about time!" he shouted. "I texted you hours ago! Damn it, Riley! This is serious!"

"Well, hello to you, too, Jeremy."

"Riley. There is no time for pleasantries. While you're down there playing sun goddess, the good 'ole boy network up here is meeting in the morning to vote on whether to release you from your contract. Our contract!"

"You can't be serious. They can't be serious. Over a stupid video of me singing with a college friend?"

"That's not how it looks from this angle, Riley. You look guilty AF."

"Guilty of what? Singing a song?"

She could hear the exasperation in his voice as he rushed through every word. His sentences running together with no pauses for punctuation.

"You know what it looks like, so don't feign innocence. It's an insult to my intelligence and is beneath you. Plus, Jonathan isn't helping."

"What does Jonathan have to do with it?"

She eased up in her lounge chair, cloud cover now completely blocking the sun. She could smell the moisture in the air.

Jeremy heaved a heavy sigh and Riley said, "Spill. Just tell me what Jonathan's done now."

"He commented on the video and pretended to be torn up by what he was seeing. Then followed up with a dramatic announcement that he was taking a hiatus from social media. Asshole."

Riley felt a drop of rain land on her cheek, and another on her thigh. Turning towards the sky, the pale blue cover had morphed into an ominous grey. The clouds cloistered, moving fast and chasing the sun away.

She stood to take cover inside, taking the pot of coffee with her.

"I'll deal with Jonathan. I need you to get an update on what's happening in the meeting. I'll reach out to my lawyer to discuss options."

"I just wish you were not half a world away. Not now. I know you needed to put some distance between you and Jonathan, but that distance has caused a chasm in your professional life and resolving it from a secluded island won't be easy."

Standing at her bar, she poured herself another cup of coffee, her mind racing and her adrenaline on overdrive.

"I know." She looked at the time on her phone. With a six-hour time difference, it was after 2:00 a.m. in Washington, D.C. "But we have a few hours before their meeting. Let's talk strategy. They may think they're in control, but nobody but Riley St. James controls my career."

A crackle of thunder and a bolt of lightning cut through the darkened sky. Just minutes ago she had been bathing in the warmth of the sun, and now, hovering storm clouds had erased her perfect morning.

Watching rain droplets bouncing off the deck planks and rippling in the lagoon, she was reminded of that old saying when life took a turn for the worst.

It's always darkest before dawn.

When Riley finished her conversation with Jeremy, she called her attorney with an update. They agreed that her attorney would join—uninvited—the executive meeting, as was Riley's right to have legal representation present when her contract was on the agenda.

Her attorney, the brilliant Stanford law alum Octavia Gray by way of Detroit, commanded attention in board rooms and court rooms. Tall and curvy, packaged in tailored suits and monogrammed white shirts that popped against smooth skin like midnight, eyes like golden orbs, a cold, calculating smile and a tight 'fro that let any and all coming for her clients know that she was the first line of defense and would be the last woman standing.

Riley and Octavia talked through their strategy for an hour, and she was satisfied with the direction they would propose to the boys in suits. But she kept hidden from Octavia her fear and focused on the red-hot anger and outrage.

Anger and outrage were tangible; fear was vague and showed weakness. This was not a time for weakness. She reserved those feelings for the moments late at night when she shed the remnants of the day and lie still in bed with only her emotions for company. That's when she invited in fear, in the solitude of darkness where it could be released in a controlled environment. Where she could take the bandages off the wounds and let them bleed. Where tears flowed freely and doubt danced around the crevices of her mind. Fear was her secret. It always was. And this storm wouldn't change that.

Riley had opted not to give Jeremy all the details of the plan with Octavia because she didn't want him to panic. She was panicked enough for them both.

As a woman of color in broadcast journalism, every time she stepped in a newsroom, it was a balancing act. She had to play by a set of rules designed for a standard that didn't always value diversity—of appearance, thought, opinion, education, or background.

Riley had learned to compartmentalize every slight, microaggression, or flagrant -ism of the day. It was the "Three 'F' Rule." *Face it, fight it, or flip it.* Not in any particular order and they could be mixed and matched as needed. All battles weren't worth the energy to fight. And winning could be a double-edged sword.

She had faced and fought against bias her entire career. She had to fight with her colleagues about how they covered marginalized communities while balancing not being marginalized herself in the newsroom. She had to fight with producers about the angle of stories that led with assumptions about marginalized communities and not facts. She had to fight with editors about language. She had to fight with sales executives about advertisers unaligned with diversity and equity standards. She had to fight with the marketing team about how they positioned her and other women and people of color as assets to ensure fair and balanced news coverage. She had to fight in editorial meetings for the right to report on stories that were deemed controversial because they didn't fit a mainstream narrative and against stories that advanced stereotypes. She had to fight with hair stylists and make-up artists about her hair and her skin. And she had to fight, every day, to apply her authentic voice and her authentic lived experiences to a national news lens or risk losing herself to an industry still trying to live up to a standard not yet met.

But the difference between how she fought and how the decision-makers in the industry fought was fairness. Riley fought fair and within the confines of their rules. She had to or else lose the opportunity to be a journalist of color swimming in a sea of white. They didn't have to fight fair because they made the rules, and could change them on a whim.

What Riley was now facing was a choice. Not a choice between whether to fight or give up. No, giving up was never an option. Her choice was about what she was willing to fight for—and against. And whether she was willing to buck the rules in favor of her conscious.

She found herself fearful for the first time in her career. There was so much at stake. So much she could lose. But she had to consider what might be gained. Forever a balancing act. She might need to apply the full "Three 'F' Rule."

She sat at her dining table with her laptop open and drinking ice water while she re-entered the real world—as defined by social media. Posts about her and Jonathan, and now Donovan, were a combination of entertaining, laughable, insufferable, and bizarre. The video that had been posted to IG looked incriminating, but she watched it with a fondness shared between friends despite the controversy it was causing. Through all of the posts and the comments, she controlled the urge to respond—mostly on the advice of her attorney. Octavia had explicitly forbidden her from engaging, and she was pissed about it. Riley was a fighter, and if she couldn't fight for herself when necessary, what was the point of even being in the ring? But she knew, logically, that Octavia was right. But emotionally, she was feeling more ratchet than responsible. The rules keep changing and the bias against women, and particularly against women of color, remained the same.

Riley was no shrinking rose. She was a journalist always looking for the angles, seeking out both sides of a story. Now she had to apply those same skills to her life. Absorbing the good and the bad, the sweet and ugly. The storm had picked up and the symphony of raindrops swelled across her deck and rooftop, its steady rhythms soothing the weariness of the moment. She slid open the patio door to amplify the splattering sounds and to let in the cool breeze carrying stray raindrops that would soon evaporate leaving behind small stains as the only proof of their existence. She breathed in the scent of fallen rain and felt oddly refreshed.

An hour later she'd seen enough and there would be no more social media until she was back home. She had thought about cutting her trip short and going home to deal with the fallout, but she decided to stay put. She would not allow Jonathan's false narrative to dictate her behavior. She needed this time. Hell, she deserved it. He had already taken so much from her. This was where that ended.

The rain was easing, the droplets smaller and their force softer as they fell and blended with the lagoon. She watched as the clouds slowly began to creep away from the sun and what was grey was pale blue again.

Some storms are temporary and some leave lasting damage. Riley knew that she was living through a severe storm with a mix of hovering clouds, torrential down-pours, the threat of lightning strikes, and ominous skies. And if she weathered this storm, the sun was waiting on the other side—exactly where she'd left it. The terrain would be different in its wake, but the storm would pass.

She shut her laptop and then texted her parents. She wanted to talk to them later that night to share her plans and ease their worry for her. She had been dodging them, too. She knew they had so many questions, but she didn't have many answers. Answers were elusive, still only trickling in. But a trickle was better than living with no direction—even on her high-jacked honeymoon.

There were a ton of text messages remaining to answer, but she wasn't ready. One thing at a time. Slow and steady.

Plus, she still had to deal with Jonathan. She knew she should call him, but her attorney had also advised against that, citing his social media influence and the impact his narrative was having on her company's executives and their decision-making.

Deep down she always knew that Jonathan was self-serving. She'd seen it in how he navigated most of the relationships in his life. But he'd never used it as a weapon against her. Until now.

In time, once she was back at home, she'd deal with him.

But for now, she had to send Gabriel "their" playlist. Through all this madness, she was grateful for how his presence gave her reasons to smile. How he was willing to take risks, put it all on the line for the things he wanted for himself, for his life. It was refreshing.

But it also reminded her of how easy men had it. He could take risks because there was a built-in safety net for him. He had a family business he could fall back on. He had Donovan trying to poach him. And, he was being groomed for a promotion. Three very solid options…all with safe landings.

No such safety net existed for her as a woman of color in an industry still heavily dominated by men at the top. Those men were making decisions that could upend her life and her options for how she chose to make a living. All because of optics and the choices she made after another powerful man had wronged her. She was now the villain in this story. But given the choice between villain or victim, she'd play the villain every time.

Having done all she could to head off complete disaster, she planned to keep her date at the spa for a facial and hydrotherapy treatment, to be followed up by finalizing the plans for the arrival of her new friends Thursday afternoon.

She tried not to think about it, but she knew she was almost half-way through this trip. Soon she'd be back to her grind. She stood and walked out onto her patio to let the gentle breeze off the lagoon wrap around her body. The water below was calm and crystal clear. If only her next steps were as clear, she thought.

CHAPTER THIRTY-TWO

Gabriel

Morning breakfast service was in full swing when Gabriel arrived. His morning run, coupled with his night with Riley, had his energy dialed up and he was looking forward to a productive day. There was still a nagging worry about their encounter last night in the lagoon, but Riley said it was all good.

She had already gifted him two nights of her life, and each time sent him spiraling down a rabbit hole in search of a new excuse, a new way to tempt her into spending more time with him. His craving for her touch, her nearness, made him raw with emotion and unsettled. With each passing hour, his desire to be in her space grew. Even more than the physical intimacy, he just wanted to talk and laugh with her, to learn more about the woman she was when she wasn't breaking down barriers and calling out bullshit for the masses, and how that woman came to exist. He wanted to hear about her dreams and her fears, her life as a child, her friendships and her enemies, the people she's loved and all that she's lost. He wanted to pull back every delicate layer and take his sweet time memorizing the contours of her life.

But she'd have to want that, too. Want him. Her body's response to him showed evidence of possibility. But in 48 hours, trying to read what's in a woman's heart—that's something entirely different.

The challenges for them were as plain as the rising sun—obvious, yet hopeful.

With a smile plastered on his face and euphoria floating through his veins, he alternated between the indoor restaurant and the outdoor seating, greeting guests, refilling coffee and juice, and chatting with the staff. Simon was busy managing the restaurants and the lobby, demonstrating the demeanor, hospitality, and attention to detail that had fueled his steady climb in the company.

Gabriel nodded in his direction, a signal that the service was going well. But Simon's response appeared tight and restrained, if not a bit distant. He chose not to focus on it, assuming Simon was distracted with learning the rhythms of the hotel.

Walking over to the bar to place a mimosa order for a guest, Gabriel overheard two of the servers whispering about a video. When he turned in their direction, they went quiet and dropped their heads. They were breaking rule number one about hotel guests—keep your personal opinions and observations to yourself. Unspoken rule—especially in front of the boss.

But Gabriel wasn't a fool. He knew that anytime you combine videos and whispers, disaster usually followed.

In the distance, he noticed a cluster of dark clouds drifting in their direction. As a precaution, he would instruct the staff to begin relocating diners on the patio into the covered restaurant.

He delivered the mimosa and found one of the servers he caught whispering to remind her of the standards they were expected to meet, and to find out exactly what the whispering was about.

"There's a video, Monsieur Laurent. Of Mademoiselle St. James and her friend singing at the lounge last night. Someone at the hotel posted it on social media and everybody is talking about it."

A wave of panic rushed through Gabriel, but he couldn't let the server see any change in his demeanor. But he was worried about Riley—she had enough social media drama with her break-up. This was like pouring gas on a fire.

And then there was Donovan, an innocent bystander who was only there to meet Gabriel. A literal victim of circumstance.

Gabriel had expected to see them both for breakfast this morning and now wondered if this video surfacing is what kept them away.

"I don't know anything about a video. And I suggest you behave as if you don't know either. Understood?"

"Oui, Oui."

"And tell everyone else to ignore whatever they hear or see. I'll handle this with Simon. In the meantime, begin relocating the guests from the patio inside. Looks like rain is coming."

Gabriel sent the server back to work and couldn't decide whether to speak to Simon first, or to slip off and call Riley in her villa. Just as he decided that he should check in with Riley first and headed towards the office, Simon appeared in front of him.

"May I have a word, Gabriel?"

"Simon. Of course. I was going to find you to warn you about a situation with one of our guests," Gabriel said, even though Simon was second on his list of people to talk to this morning.

"Would this warning concern Mademoiselle St. James?"

"Oh. So, you're aware of the social media video circulating amongst guests and staff?"

Simon chuckled, and Gabriel noted a hint of sarcasm in his tone.

"I have not heard anything concerning Mademoiselle St. James. But I have seen something that I suspect may involve her."

Unsure where Simon was headed, Gabriel didn't want to risk anyone overhearing a conversation that might prove delicate concerning another guest. He kept smiling as his eyes scanned the room. No one was looking in their direction, but speaking out in the open about private matters made him uncomfortable.

Gabriel slid both hands in his pockets, transferring the perspiration forming to the fabric lining. His eyes darted left and right as he lowered his voice. "Let's discuss this in the office."

The two men crossed through the lobby and entered the office. Gabriel sat behind one of the four desks shared between the hotel's managers, each with an extra chair next to the desk for impromptu meetings. He invited Simon to sit.

Simon declined.

"I'll stand, if you don't mind, Monsieur."

"If that's your preference, of course."

There was an awkward silence as Gabriel took a pen and pad from the desk drawer to take notes. Whatever Simon had to say, he wanted to be sure to have a record of it. And he wanted Simon to know that his observations were important by modeling behavior he'd expect of Simon once his training was over.

"So, tell me about what you've seen that may involve Mademoiselle St. James."

Having a few minutes to think about what Simon had witnessed, he wondered if it involved Donovan. If there was a video making waves on social media, Simon may have seen something that might reflect negatively on the hotel.

"I did not see Mademoiselle St. James," Simon said.

Gabriel's left eyebrow raised in confusion. "But you said you saw something involving Mademoiselle St. James."

"That's correct. It involves Mademoiselle St. James, but I saw you."

Gabriel paused, his breath caught in his chest. Panic pressed down on him and heat rose from his neck and splashed across his face. His confident, unflappable demeanor had been reduced to massive uncertainty. Small beads of perspiration began dotting his hairline and he sat back in his seat, resting the pen down on the pad. Rarely is he surprised by much. But this—this was serious with severe consequences. The many ways it could go wrong and hurt him and Riley started running through his head all at once like a movie on fast-forward.

Folding his arms across his chest, he asked, "What exactly do you think you saw?"

He didn't want to appear angry, but he was definitely on the defensive and out of his depth. Had Simon been spying on him? Or had he gotten too comfortable in Simon's presence while Riley was nearby? Maybe Simon read the expression on his face? Maybe he was just making an assumption? Or maybe, Simon had saw something—which was the worst-case scenario.

"Not think. *Saw*. I saw you leaving your suite late last night. I was out on the beach having a smoke after the lounges were cleared and all the guests were back in their villas. Dressed in dark clothing, you walked down the pier and turned in the direction of Mademoiselle's villa. And you didn't return."

Gabriel had to think fast. He had two choices. Come clean or make up an excuse for visiting a guest at that hour. Both options were dire.

Fuck!

Training Simon this month was meant to be the final step in the process towards him joining the c-suite. He had allowed a distraction to challenge his focus when he was so close to everything he wanted.

For fuck's sake!

He knew seeing Riley on hotel property was a risk. But he thought they had been careful. Then that movie started playing in his head again, but this time on rewind. In a flash he knew, they weren't kidding anyone. They had been anything but careful. And each time, they had been less careful.

Gabriel decided to follow his conscious.

"I won't deny it."

This time it was Simon who raised an eyebrow. After a few seconds of a silence so heavy Gabriel thought he would suffocate from the weight of it, Simon pulled the chair next to the desk away and placed it in front of the desk where Gabriel sat. His body must have also felt the weight of the awkward silence, because his body slammed into the seat.

"You don't deny it, Monsieur? Are you sure? Because you know what this means, correct?"

"I don't deny it and yes, I know what this means. You have to report it to headquarters and I won't try to stop you. My only request is that you give me a day to warn and prepare Mademoiselle St. James."

When Simon didn't speak, Gabriel continued, trying to offer an explanation.

"When we first met, neither of us knew who the other was and it escalated quickly. It's no one's fault, really. Well, I guess it's my fault somewhat, because I know the rules. But I don't want her to suffer another ordeal on top of everything else she's already dealing with on this trip."

Simon dug his elbows into his knees and clutched his head between the palms of his hands.

"I'll give you a day," he said when he looked up, shaking his head.

"I apologize for putting you in this position," Gabriel added.

"I really hate to have to report this," Simon continued. "I really like you and was thrilled when they told me you'd be training me. You're a legend with the management training cohorts. And I know this sounds weird, but I think Mademoiselle St. James is a nice woman and doesn't deserve what's happened to her. No one does."

"Thanks, Simon." It was all Gabriel could say. His emotions had started roiling in his stomach and had made their way up and threatened to spill out if he tried to choke out anything more.

"And for the record—I think you two would make a handsome couple."

Somehow, Simon had added a moment of brevity to the situation, and Gabriel chuckled.

"You think so?"

"I do, Monsieur. Under better circumstances."

Gabriel let Simon's words sink in. *Under better circumstances.* What better circumstance could begin to match the stolen moments he'd had with this enchanting woman in what is arguably the most beautiful tropical paradise in the world? When would he have ever had the undivided attention of a woman like Riley? In what world would their paths have ever crossed and allowed them the space to get to know each other's minds, bodies, and spirits?

"Perhaps you are correct, Simon. Thank you for understanding. I'll speak to Mademoiselle St. James and you can make the call tomorrow."

Gabriel leaned back in the chair and let his shoulders drop. He had been carrying the tension of the moment and now, he felt a much-needed release.

Simon stood and said, "I'll give you some time alone. I really am sorry about all of this, but I have to do what's right."

"You don't owe me an apology. I took the risk and dare I say, I believe she's worth it."

Simon's eyes softened and he bowed his head as he made his exit.

For the next half-hour, Gabriel sat in quiet contemplation weighing his options.

He knew that he might lose his job over this indiscretion—or at the very least, his promotion—and he had mixed feelings about that reality. He had worked hard for the company, put in a lot of time and energy to take what was good to great. He had been singularly focused on his advancement to the corporate rankings the last few years, to the detriment of all else in his life.

There had not been a woman in his life in the past five years—at least not any that lasted beyond six weeks or so. He had a posh flat in Paris, but was rarely there more than a few weeks every year. He only saw his family occasionally and he sometimes made time for his friends when he traveled on business.

The decision to leave his father's company had started an avalanche of risk in his professional and personal life. That one choice fueled all other choices, and in a matter of days, just when he was on the brink of reaching the pinnacle of his success, he risked it all. For a woman he barely knew.

When he told Simon Riley was worth it, he meant it. But he didn't know if he was worth the risk to her. And yet, he would do it all over again if given the chance.

He needed a back-up plan.

He had an offer on the table—a damn good offer from Donovan. But it was dependent on his father, who still wanted him to marry his ex-girlfriend and merge with her father's company. If that didn't work out, he could ask Donovan for a job to focus on business development and help him find another company to merge with that met his standards and business goals.

There were also other hotel companies that he could consider. He had a stellar reputation among his peers. But this indiscretion with Riley might have added a layer of tarnish that wouldn't soon fade.

He could also make a deal with his father to rejoin the company without the merger and keep his head down until the time came when his father stepped away from the company and he would have free reign.

As he continued weighing his options, the phone on his desk rang. He watched as it rang, the green light urgently flashing. But he didn't answer it. He let it go to his voicemail, not in any mood to talk to anyone.

He shifted from his professional worries to the more personal issue of telling Riley about this new development. Thinking through what he might say, he noticed that the voicemail notification was now lit on his phone. Whoever had been calling left a message.

Grabbing the pen and pad, he dialed into the voicemail and let the message play.

Hi. This message is for Gabriel Laurent. My name is Carmen Berger and I'm a reporter with...

Gabriel disconnected the call once he heard it was a reporter. He didn't know what she might be searching for, but he was in no mood for talking to the press about anything. And he knew if it was related to the hotel, their public relations team would reach out to him with instructions and talking points.

When he stood to leave, he noticed that the voicemail notification light on his phone was still lit, even though he had technically listened to the message. Assuming a glitch, he ignored it and headed out to the lobby area.

There were two staffers behind the check-in counter and one person at the concierge desk. He stopped to make small talk and was interrupted by his mobile phone vibrating.

Stepping away, he pulled the phone from his jacket pocket half prepared to see an unknown number. *Jefferson Saxton.*

He answered right away.

"Jefferson, old friend! What a surprise to hear from you!"

Gabriel and Jefferson were college mates and had competed as teammates on both the rugby and the rowing teams. The last time he had seen Jefferson had been in London nearly a year ago, so his call was unexpected.

"Good to hear your voice, mate!" Jefferson replied. "I hope you're well."

That was a loaded statement, but Gabriel wasn't about to dump his drama on his old friend.

"I'm good and can't complain."

"That's good to hear. Look, I only have a few minutes but I need to ask you a favor. It's a really big favor and if I'm out of bounds, please just let me know."

Now Gabriel was really curious. He hadn't heard from Jefferson since London, which wasn't unusual. He was a busy man, executive producing some of the highest profile, award-winning news and entertainment programming in Europe.

"Ask away." Gabriel would be happy to help his friend in any way he could.

"I just learned that there's a guest staying at one of your hotels. Riley St. James. We're trying to reach out to her but just keep hitting brick walls. I'm not asking you to do anything unethical, but if you could confirm she's guest, we can take it from there."

Gabriel was quiet. He hoped his friend wasn't planning to send a news crew to ambush Riley. But he wanted to give Jefferson the benefit of the doubt.

"What's this about?" Gabriel could feel anger simmering just below the surface. The urge to protect Riley was strong. She'd been through enough. "It must be serious if you're asking me to share personal information about a guest."

"It is rather serious. We've been following the fallout from her break-up..."

"Let me stop you right there," Gabriel said. "I can't let you ambush a guest. And I can't believe you'd even ask me to be party to something like this."

"You didn't let me finish, Gabriel. We've been following the fallout and want to talk to her about a job."

"A job? She has a job." Now Gabriel was really confused.

"Look, my friend. News travels fast in our industry, and we're hearing that her network wants to release her from her contract. If that's true, we want to make our pitch before all the other blood hounds start sniffing around."

"So, let me get this straight. You want me to confirm if Riley St. James is at one of our hotels so that you can offer her job. In Europe?"

"Yes, and yes. Can you help me out, mate?"

Gabriel paused before answering to consider the facts. He'd just learned about this video of Riley and Donovan on social media, which meant more bad news for her if her career was now in jeopardy. And if that's true, she might want to know about this offer. He made a snap decision.

"I can confirm that she's at one of our resorts. But I won't reveal which one. Give me the official contact information and I'll see that she receives it. Let her come to you if she's interested."

"You sound like you know her. Have you met her on this trip?"

"I have. And she's a lovely woman and doesn't deserve the cards she's been dealt. You'd be lucky to get her."

"Hey, I don't need you to tell me. We want to build a show and a brand around her. This is a legitimate offer I can assure you."

"Sounds great. But whomever does the pitch, make sure it's the best you have to offer. She's a woman who knows her worth."

"Thanks, Gabriel. I owe you. Big!"

"I'll be ready to collect the next time we're in Paris."

"I look forward to it. I'll email you the information in the next few minutes. Talk soon."

When the call disconnected, a smile crept across Gabriel's face. His day had started bright as the early morning sun, and just as quickly descended into darkness. This call from Jefferson had added some calm to the brewing storm. He still had a lot to deal with, but knowing that a silver lining was on the horizon for Riley was good enough. It might take some time, but he'd find his silver lining.

Thoughts of Riley and their night together filtered through and his emotions were mixed. Their souls had connected beneath the stars—of this, he was sure. Now, he'd have to go to her and share the bad news about Simon and tempt fate. They had only known each other a few days and she could very easily decide he wasn't worth all that she was risking. He trusted Simon to keep quiet and follow the appropriate protocols. But he didn't have any idea what might happen once it left Simon or how many people would get involved.

He hated the idea of becoming another problem for Riley. If she decided this was too much, he'd understand and step back.

Hoping he was wrong, he mustered up a smile and headed back into the restaurant. The sun was shining at full strength, and the familiar smell of roasted coffee and sweet pastries welcomed him back into his routine while he considered how to approach her about the video and Simon's revelation.

Walking towards the bar, he felt his phone vibrate in his pocket. He weighed not checking it, fearful that it might be more bad news and his hands were already full of crap. But hiding wasn't his style, so he pulled out the phone to find a notification from Riley. When he unlocked the phone, it was a text message and link to her playlist with a note—**I added a little bit of you to MY playlist. You've still got some proving to do for this list to become OUR playlist. Show me what you got!**

That was really all he needed to confirm their connection. Despite what he had just endured with Simon and the revelation that tomorrow, everything might change for him, a three-sentence text from Riley eased his anxiety. He still needed to check-in with her about this video and Simon, but now he was a little less nervous—but definitely still worried. This thing between them was one big risk and he still thought she was worth it. And based on her text message, some part of her—however small—thought so, too.

CHAPTER THIRTY-THREE

Riley

Riley had spoken to Gabriel only once after she texted him. He called to check on her after he heard about the video—the next chapter in her epic social media saga. She assured him she had it under control. It was a strangled truth—covering her uneasy sense of pending doom. While it slithered up and around her consciousness like a poisonous vine, she grasped and pulled at it, refusing to let it win.

But Gabriel had buried the lead.

Learning that Simon had seen Gabriel headed in the direction of her bungalow was a setback—and while suspicious, it wasn't a provable offense without her corroboration. But Gabriel had owned up to it without bothering to check in with her first. Now, on top of being a runaway-bride-gone-viral-on-video and a soon to be unemployed journalist, she might be the cause of someone else losing their livelihood and even worse, add more speculation about another man in her life and cause further damage.

Her escape to paradise had officially failed.

When she hung up with Gabriel, she was a tangled mix of emotions. She was angry at his thoughtlessness. Did he not consider what his admission of guilt meant for her? This felt uncomfortably familiar— another man making decisions for her. But she was also pleasantly surprised that he owned up to spending time with her, after only a few days that were mostly nights. And then there was that pinch of guilt she felt knowing that he had consciously jeopardized so much for her. He wasn't ashamed of their relationship—if that's what this was—and was even willing to risk his job and his reputation to protect her—even if a touch misguided. She didn't need rescuing and it was more than she could expect from a man she'd only just met mere days ago.

But the elephant in the room was the stark contrast between Gabriel and Jonathan. When faced with choosing to protect his reputation or hers, Gabriel chose her—which was more than what Jonathan was willing to do for her. She sat with that revelation for a few minutes. The man who professed to love her had chosen to go all in on his scoundrel persona and instead of owning his part in the demise of their relationship, had latched on to a false narrative to cover his own misdeeds and put her reputation at risk.

These were two very different men.

And in a few days away from her real life, she was becoming a different woman.

She had done all that she could to tame the beast of public opinion that was threatening her perfectly constructed world. She had to release her fear and apprehension and press on. She had an appointment at the spa—that she needed now more than ever. She had preparations to finalize before her vacation posse arrived tomorrow. And, she needed to check in with her parents.

Yes, it was sort of a to-do list. But not really because she didn't write it in her journal. So technically, she was keeping the promise she'd made—initially to Jonathan, but now to herself. It was an uncomfortable shift, leaving her feeling in limbo at times. But it also opened her up to spontaneity.

She got out of her head and went to change into something more spa-appropriate. As she picked through the few items she had, she silently celebrated that her luggage would arrive tomorrow.

She changed and headed to the spa. For the next three hours, she would tune out the noise and soak in all the luxuries of paradise.

She'd spent the better part of the afternoon at the spa. As the masseuse kneaded the mass of knots in her upper back, she watched as schools of fish swam by beneath the glass-floored overwater bungalow and let the heavy scent of lavender soothe her. She was willing herself to relax, but she couldn't shake the feeling that everything had changed. And she wasn't sure if that was exciting or terrifying.

While soft island tunes streamed throughout the room, she made a quasi-attempt at considering her options by cycling through the scenarios waiting for her back home.

Home. Her home had been with Jonathan. She had given up the first place she owned—a condo in Center City D.C. —to make a life with him. Now, she would have to find a new place to call home, which would have to wait until she knew if she had a job or not. As much as she wanted to hit rewind and go back to undo all the mistakes she had made—especially giving up that luxurious condo—she needed to keep facing forward. Now was not the time, not yet anyway, for looking back.

Her job. The one constant in her life. The one place where she knew what to expect—the good, bad, and indifferent—was also at risk, like sand slipping through her fingers. The years of sacrifice. The indignities suffered while fighting for stories that meant something. Triumphing over newsroom politics and refusing to meet the inequitable demands that she do more with less and for less. How she defined triumphant varied, and some days it wasn't even possible. She paid her dues with soft news and local controversies from school board meetings and puppy adoption events, to festivals, concerts, and groundbreakings. She aggressively fought for the bigger stories, and when her time finally came, she shined and never looked back. When the network finally took notice, it was her work ethic, her creativity, and her skill at uncovering the truth no matter how heavy the rocks she had to turnover that got her foot in the door—and contributed to the network's bottom line. Her ratings were always in the top tier—but one personal issue and she was on the chopping block.

The last few years of #MeToo had bought some heavy-weight industry men to their knees. There were investigations and public scrutiny, and it had taken time for them to be pushed from their pedestals. But inequity persists, and in under a week and absent any form of investigation, she was being cut from the story.

She knew she should be angrier, but maybe she had been fully seduced by this island—and Gabriel. She was relaxed and comforted knowing that she had made all the right decisions before accepting that assignment with the network. She had the best legal counsel, her contract was airtight and if they wanted her gone, they had to pay.

But what would be the ultimate price she would pay for loving and trusting Jonathan? For running away from their wedding? For hiding out in paradise?

Riley St. James, award-winning journalist, was on the verge of losing it all—for a love that wasn't true.

There had never been this much unrest in her life, and she wasn't sure if she was sinking or swimming. But right now, she could feel the tension being released through her pores thanks to some very fragrant almond oil. Closing her eyes, she drifted off into a meditative state, pushing away the negative noise and welcoming in the good vibes.

Riley left the spa and was hit with a light breeze off the lagoon and a gorgeous bright sun on the horizon. She heard kids splashing in the pool in the distance saw couples returning on jet skis from one of the many island excursions. The smell of what she was sure was barbeque wafted through the air, and it made her hungry for a hearty meal. Wanting to enjoy more of the same, she decided she'd have dinner at one of the restaurants—alone—at a table closest to the beach. It would be the perfect way to end an otherwise turbulent day.

She ended her musings and headed directly to the concierge desk to finalize plans for her guests arriving the next day, and to check the status of her luggage. She had gotten comfortable with the few items she had bought on the island and didn't really miss all the outfits she'd packed. But now, the need for the luggage was urgent. She needed the comfort of the familiar.

Seated at the concierge desk, she saw Gabriel and Simon walk by. She nodded in their direction, forcing a strained smile. They both greeted her in unison but didn't pause for small talk.

It was for the best, but it made her feel like the elephant in the room. And no woman anywhere ever wants to be the elephant.

The lobby and outdoor areas were buzzing with activity, and guests walking by looked in her direction a little too long. Maybe she was being paranoid, but she was sure some of the women even whispered as they sauntered past her. What began as her sanctuary now felt like a fish bowl. Guests kept their physical distance, but there was no escaping prying eyes or unfair judgments. For a few seconds, she played out a scenario where she would just pack up and leave on the first flight out. But then she'd miss out on more time with her new friends. And, she decided to stay. The vultures might be circling, but she wasn't dead yet.

She changed her dinner plans and decided she would order room service and dine on her deck. That was the practical choice. She still needed to call her parents, check-in with Savannah about their arrival the next day, and possibly respond to emails from her attorney. Because no one left Octavia Gray waiting. Ever.

Riley showered and changed into lounge wear. She carried the room service menu and cell phone out to her deck to enjoy the gentle wind and sun drifting towards the horizon. She was in the mood for something filling, a decadent dessert, and a full bottle of wine. Scanning the menu, she dialed her father first and smiled when he answered. His deep baritone voice immediately put her at ease and she hoped just seeing her phone number had done the same for him. She was a woman in her thirties, but to him, she was still his little girl. Still her protector, her biggest fan, her champion, and her confidante. His presence both soothed her and made her nervous. She still sought his approval and the idea that he might be disappointed in her made her heart ache.

He spoke, and she could feel the words pouring through his smile. "Hey, baby girl. I'm glad you called. We were worried about you."

Before she fully absorbed his words, she responded, "Hi, Daddy."

"You doin' okay? We saw something on one of those entertainment shows about you, but I told your mom we couldn't believe that stuff."

"You spoke to mom?" In the span of thirty seconds, he had used *we* twice.

"She's here with me now."

He said it so plainly, like it was the most natural thing in the world. When the reality was, Roselyn Au Clair St. James was rarely present, and definitely not alongside her dad.

"Mom? She's with you now? Where?" She felt panicked and protective. Her mother was unreliable at best and obnoxiously beautiful with a compromised attention span at worse. While her father's mild-mannered demeanor and track record for forgiving too easily made him easy prey.

"We're at my place. She decided to stay just in case you needed her. With so much going on, baby girl, she wanted to be close by."

Riley was silent. Suddenly, all of the men in her life were behaving like lovestruck teens. Jonathan was lashing out. Gabriel was playing the hero. Donovan was sulking. And now her dad, the solid and congenial Sterling Paul St. James, was hosting the wife that had abandoned him and their only child to embrace more creative pursuits—because where's the creativity in raising a child and being a good partner to your husband. It was a bit much to digest on a day when she had to launch a defense to protect her career.

She had planned to check in with her mom after she spoke to her dad, expecting her to be back in Europe by now. Far, far away from her father, and mostly unavailable to Riley—back to their decades long reality.

"You still there, baby girl?"

"I'm here. But I can't believe that mom's still there. Is everything okay with you two? And where is she staying?" The questions spilled out, the words a desperate tumble of confusion.

"We're fine, and she's staying in my guest room. You have enough on your plate. Don't spend a minute worried about us."

Now they're an *us. What in the hell is happening?* They usually tolerated each other for Riley's sake, but Riley wasn't around. What were they doing?

But those were questions she didn't really want the answers to, so she stuck to the basics.

"Daddy, I'll be home in a few days. There's a lot happening and I don't know if I'll have a job or where I'll be living. But I promise you I'm fine. And don't believe anything you hear on television. I'll tell you everything you need to know. Okay."

"Sure. We'll just wait to hear from you." He paused and then finally said, "You want to speak to your mom. She's worried sick about you."

This was all too much for Riley. Too many *we's* in sentences where they didn't belong. Her absentee mother sticking around and her doting father in the mood to forgive two decades of that absence.

More upheaval. Riley couldn't stand another part of her life in disarray. She depended on her parents as they were—divorced, on different paths, loving her the best way they knew how—separately. Now, they were together and getting along. She needed time to process this new development.

But not today.

"Just tell mom I'm fine and I'll call you all in a couple days."

"Okay, baby girl." His voice dropped almost to a whisper, but he didn't push. "But she'll be disappointed."

"She'll be fine. And a little disappointment might be good for her.

Daddy, you just be careful."

"It'll take more than a week of your mother to knock me off my game. Don't you worry about me. You try to relax and then get home safely. Call us back any time. Promise me you will."

Riley let her head fall back onto the back of the lounge chair. Water lapped against the bungalow's stilts and she closed her eyes, imagining she was drifting away along with the waves.

"I promise, Daddy. Talk to you later. Love you."

"I love you, too, baby girl. All the time."

She disconnected the call, pulled up the playlist on her phone and went to her Brown Liquor playlist. The Isley Brothers' *Footsteps in the Dark* was first in the rotation, and she let Ron Isley's voice take her to a place where she could imagine her parents as they might have been, before her, before they fell apart. She barely remembered them as a couple, but she knew that her father still carried a torch for her mother. He had dated a few women through the years, but none of those women lasted more than six months. And deep down, Riley knew why.

Her thoughts were interrupted by her bungalow phone ringing. She stepped inside to answer it and Gabriel's voice on the other end made her smile.

"Good afternoon, lovely lady," his tone laced with happy and anticipation.

"Well, hello handsome."

"If you don't already have plans, I'd love to have dinner with you tonight."

He sounded genuinely interested in seeing her and not at all anxious about what tomorrow might hold for him.

"I'd love that. But please join me. I'm ordering room service to get a break from the unwelcome attention." She hoped he wouldn't pity her.

"I understand." There was no pity in his voice. "I'll join you for dinner."

She paused a few seconds and then asked, "Are you sure we aren't being reckless, given recent developments?"

He assured her they were not and that he felt a weight lifted now that Simon knew that he was seeing her. While she was flattered, she was also naturally a skeptic. This was all happening way too fast—like a speed boat jumping waves. Exhilarating, but also dangerous. But the adrenalin had kicked in and she decided to go with the flow.

"Okay. I'll see you at seven."

Refusing to overthink it, she dialed Savannah next to finalize their plans. Of course, Savannah had been following the news and Riley assured her she was fine and that she would fill them in once they were all together.

Next, she checked on Donovan. He was staying until Friday, still hoping to convince Gabriel to join his company. His girlfriend—soon to be fiancé, he hoped—was at least talking to him and had promised she wouldn't make any decisions about their future until he returned. She respected his work and didn't want him to abandon his mission. But he had to promise to not be caught in anymore compromising positions with Riley. That would be easy enough.

With her mental to-do list complete for the day, she placed the room service order and prepared for her dinner date with Gabriel.

Dinner date?

It was the first time she'd thought of spending time with him as something more than a convenient distraction. But she couldn't trust her feelings. Not now with so much falling apart around her. So, she pushed any thoughts of Gabriel's presence in her life into the deep, dark depths of her mind and chose to be in the moment.

She only had a few full days left on the island. She wanted to enjoy these last remaining days, and thinking about Gabriel as anything more than a fling was more than she could manage. No, she'd indulge in him just one last night, and then she'd close the door on this chapter of her life.

It was a good plan. But nothing had gone as planned since last Friday. Why was she expecting this to be different?

CHAPTER THIRTY-FOUR

Gabriel

Whh hen he entered Riley's bungalow, the sun was bidding the day farewell on the horizon while Marvin Gaye's hypnotic voice was urging *Sexual Healing* out on her deck. Seeing her in a thin, soft pink dress that brushed the floor just slightly, with tiny straps on her suntanned shoulders and her nipples pressing against the fabric, he wasn't sure if they'd make it through one glass of champagne, and certainly not an entire meal.

"You look delectable," he whispered.

"And you look famished. Shall we eat?" Her voice was silky soft as her eyes took his full measure. When she smirked, he knew she was equally famished and he was prepared to serve her all night.

Before they stepped out onto the deck, he told her about his call from his friend Jefferson, and gave her the contact information. He had printed the information out and promised her it was legit. She scanned the document and promised to hand it over to her attorney. He had expected her to be more excited, but she was already juggling a lot and she hadn't been released from her contract. At least not that she'd shared with him.

The deck was softly lit, and as she stood near the table pouring the first glass of sparkling Rosé, the silhouette of her fully nude body beneath her dress erased everything around her and caused his groin to pulse in his pants. He lowered his head to focus and fight back his growing desire—the night was young and he wanted to savor every moment with her.

He stood at the threshold of the deck's sliding glass door, drinking in the view of the most amazing woman he'd ever met and admiring her in all her fullness. He barely knew her, yet he felt as if she was meant to be part of his life. She had certainly taken him by surprise and thrown him off his game.

Everything felt disjointed and while it would be easy to place Riley at the center of that, he knew that wasn't really the truth. He was in control of his life, his decisions, but none of them were what he truly wanted. He hadn't *wanted* to leave his family business. And he hadn't *wanted* to sacrifice a personal life in favor of working around the clock.

But this trip was proving to be pivotal. Because he was finally exploring what he truly wanted—by circumstance and consequence. With Riley, he was opening up to wanting a real relationship. With Donovan's proposition, he could reclaim what he really wanted professionally—to make his family business more successful. And by being honest with Simon, he wanted to prove he was a good man—with some flaws—that accepted the consequences for his actions.

He watched the ease of Riley's movements this evening, so unexpected. He was expecting tension, at least some trepidation from her. But she seemed more relaxed tonight than any of the other nights they'd spent together. He knew she had spent time at the spa, and thought maybe that was the reason for this transformation. Or maybe he had just been projecting. He had a lot on his mind—the future of his job with this company, Donovan's offer, his father's reaction when he proposed the merger.

Both champagne flutes now full, she turned in his direction and smiled—a girlish grin on a grown ass woman. He melted.

She propped her hand on her hip, pulling the fabric tighter over her golden skin and he returned her smile with a sly smirk.

"Are you just going to stand there all night, Monsieur, or are you going to join me?"

She was tempting him. And he was in the mood for all the temptation she had to offer.

He walked over to her, took her free hand in his and squeezed. Their
fingers intertwined, she returned the pressure and leaned in a little
closer, her breasts barely grazing his chest. Whisps of her hair caught
in the wind and tickled the side of his face as he drew his face closer to
hers. She looked up at him through her long lashes, an invitation to
take more. But he wasn't ready to kiss her yet. He just wanted to share
a quiet moment with her and commit it to his memory.

He turned his head slightly and used his free hand to draw her closer
at the nape of her neck. He splayed his fingers and pushed his hand up
and deep into her tangle of hair, and she rested her face on his chest.
Now, there was no space between them and he felt her release a soft,
deep breath while sliding her hand from her hip and around his back.
Their bodies swayed slowly to the music and in unison with the waves,
while the breeze off the lagoon caressed their exposed skin.

Gently massaging her scalp, he inhaled the floral fragrance of her
hair and closed his eyes, grateful for this perfect moment. Their hands
still gripped, she held onto to him as tightly as he was holding onto her.

He felt something changing, growing between them. She had sauntered into his life, wounded but not irreparably. Hurt but not resentful.
Confused, but very much in search of clarity. And yet, somehow in spite
of all odds against it, they had made a connection—a connection that
he couldn't imagine ever being severed. At least not for him.

How she felt about him, he couldn't be sure of because of her situation. He didn't know if he was just a port in a storm, a transition man,
or just a vacation fling. And he was afraid to ask.

When she began to hum along with rhythms of the song, he smiled
and pulled back. She lifted her head off his chest, dreamy eyes meeting
his, yearning matching his. Now, he needed a kiss.

She wore a delicate, barely there smile that was sweet and seductive
at the same time. He smiled back and leaned in, gently touching his
lips to hers. She opened her mouth slightly and let her tongue trace the

curve of his lips. Every nerve in his body was on edge, but he didn't dare move. He let her explore until finally he pulled her closer and pressed their mouths together, sliding his tongue against hers slowly, tentatively, not wanting to seem too eager. But she was having none of it. She devoured him, squeezing her body into his, demanding his attention. Sparks of fire ignited just beneath his skin as she slid her hand up the back of his shirt, and massaged the palm of her hand across his back until she reached his shoulders and felt the contours of his muscles. She squeezed and his manhood rose against her body while she pushed up on her feet until he was perfectly positioned between her legs. The fabric between them stretched and pulled, and she moved her pelvis in slow motions, left and then right and back again.

Refusing to release her hand from his, he slid his free hand from her hair, down the curved spine of her back and gripped her ass in his left hand adding pressure to her movements. She released a soft moan in his mouth and he slid his hand between her bare cheeks and down to the heat between her legs. The skin on the inside of her thighs so soft, he was desperate to feel her skin. He yanked at her dress, gathering fistfuls of the fabric until the length of her was exposed. Sliding his hand between her legs, she was slick with desire. He slid the tip of his middle finger inside her and her breath caught. When she released it, she closed her lips around his tongue and sucked it in and out of her mouth, sighing in rhythm to his finger teasing her, entering her and retreating.

"I. Want. You," she pleaded between breaths.

"I just want to please you," he returned. "Will you let me take care of you?"

When she breathed out a moan in response, he pleaded with her. "Please, let me take care of you."

Her chest rising with each breath, she forced out a soft, guttural, "Yes."

Pulling back from her, but still not releasing their intertwined hands, he walked her over to one of the deck's walls, and sandwiched her body in. Their kisses grew aggressive, and his manhood pushed against her softness. As much as he wanted to be deep inside her, he wanted to see pleasure slide across her face.

He pulled his lips away from hers and began kissing her face—her cheeks, her forehead, her chin—and down to her neck. She smelled like sweet honey and vanilla, and he wanted to devour her. With his teeth, he pulled one thin strap from her shoulder and let it fall, exposing her hard nipple. He covered it fully with his mouth, sucking and licking, gripping the fullness of her breast with his hand while her head fell back and she lifted her hips further into his crotch. He pressed further into her, his heart throbbing to match his pulsating between her thighs.

He let his hand drop down to her waist and gathered the fabric of her dress up into his fist. With one leg now completely exposed, he kissed down her torso until he was firmly planted on his knees. She reached her free hand around and grabbed the fabric from his hand, giving him full view of the sweet, hot wetness between her legs.

Gabriel whispered, "You're so beautiful."

He slowly slid his middle finger down her slit, adding a little more pressure on her clit before dipping it slightly inside her.

"Mmm. You're so wet. May I taste you?"

She sighed and thrust her pelvis forward.

He slid his finger out and brushed it against her clit, at first slowly and then a little faster with more pressure until her back arched and a moan escaped between soft thrusts. She used her free hand and grabbed a handful of his hair, guiding his face between her legs.

"I need to feel your mouth on me. Please, baby."

Gabriel greedily obliged. He parted his lips and slid his tongue up and down her clit while sliding a finger deep inside her. Her hips rose and fell, and he grabbed her ass to take control of her movements and her pleasure. He alternated between nibbling and sucking her clit, adding another finger insider her, plunging deeper with every thrust forward. As her body began to stiffen at the edge of her explosion, she began grinding her hips into his mouth and he flattened his tongue, applying pressure to her clit as his fingers went deeper and faster inside her. Her body surrendered as her thighs tightened and she screamed out in ecstasy, leaving him breathless and oddly satisfied.

As her body went limp against the wall, he realized their hands never broke contact. She was still holding on to him, and he never wanted to let her go.

He slid his fingers out of her, pulled his head back and gazed up at her, watching her chest rise and fall. When she finally looked down at him, he slipped his two fingers in his mouth to taste her wetness.

She bit her bottom lip and watched him lick her off his fingers.

He smiled up at her and said, "I said you looked delectable."

She giggled and retorted, "And, I said you looked famished."

"Guess we were both right." He stood to his feet, still clutching her hand. She stared down at their fingers intertwined and squeezed.

He kissed her softly on the lips, and pulled her over to the table.

"Let's sit and enjoy this meal, and then we can enjoy each other for dessert."

She smiled and finally, their hands slipped apart. He pulled out a chair for her and she slid into the seat. He took the seat across from her and she reached across the table for his hand. He accepted her hand and she blessed the food. When he took his first forkful of flaky white fish, no longer even warm, she looked across the table and said, "You'll be my dessert."

"Whatever you desire, Mademoiselle."

When they finished dinner, they took what was left of their sparkling Rosé back into the bungalow and relaxed on the sofa. Riley had changed the playlist and Miles Davis' *In a Sentimental Mood* poured throughout the space as they got comfortable on the sofa. Both of them barefoot, he sat at the far end of the sofa and she laid out on her back, her head in his lap with her hair pouring over his lap and her eyes closed. The gourmet meal had more than satisfied them, and now it was nice to just be still in the quiet.

After a few minutes, her eyes fluttered open and she broke the silence.

"So, are you going to tell me what's up with Simon? Are you okay?"

He smoothed her hair with his hand, buying time before he spoke. He wanted to say the right thing. He didn't want her to worry and he didn't want to scare her. He was keenly aware of what she was navigating with her own job and didn't want to pile on.

"Yes, I'm okay. And as for Simon, he's a good man and a professional. He didn't earn this position by breaking the rules. I kind of feel bad for him."

She cut him off. "You feel bad for him? Why?"

"He's in a tough spot. It's not like he wants to report me. But in his position, it's exactly what he should do."

She was quiet and then asked, "What would you do? Would you report him if the roles were reversed?"

"Depends."

"On what?"

She really wasn't letting it go. "I'd give him a chance to end it. If he'd be willing to do that, I'd give him another chance and not report him."

"Did he give you that chance?"

"He didn't. But it wouldn't have mattered. I wouldn't have agreed to that."

This time she propped herself up on his knees and looked directly at him, confusion dancing across her eyes and her tone accusatory. "You wouldn't have agreed? Not to save your job?"

He didn't want to rush his answer, because something told him this might be a turning point. He couldn't appear too eager, but he also couldn't be too flippant.

"Some things are more important, Mademoiselle St. James." He hesitated, and reached in to kiss her. When he pulled back, he didn't take his eyes off her and added, "You're more important."

There it was. It was out there in the universe. He had owned his feelings and he was at her mercy.

She slid back down and closed her eyes. He studied her face, the shape of her lips and their two different shades of pink, her perfectly arched eyebrows, the small black mole beneath her eye, her distinctive nose and sharp chin. The pieces of her were as beautiful as the wholeness of her.

Her eyelashes fluttered and one single tear escaped down the side of her face. His chest tightened and a flash of anger rose inside him and ended across his face. That one tear carried with it the pain she brought with her to this island. He wished he could get inside her head and live in her heart, protecting her from anyone that would threaten her.

He wiped the one tear away, and hoped it wasn't a bad sign for them. And then she spoke.

"Gabriel, you'll never know what that means to me." Her voice cracked, and he knew she was choking back emotions. "But I can't let you jeopardize your career for me. I don't even know what I want. I would be lying if I didn't admit that I desire you and want to keep learning all the parts of you. But I can't commit to anyone or anything right now. Knowing you might lose your job over me is just one more trauma in my already chaotic existence. More proof that I've lost complete control over my life."

It wasn't what he wanted to hear, but he wasn't surprised. He knew he was passive-aggressively pursuing her. Making himself available. Relinquishing his control over their situation. He wanted to explore more, but he also wanted to explore more with a whole person. Riley wasn't whole right now. That both hurt and angered him.

He lightly touched her face, but she kept her eyes closed. The silence grew heavy between them, and he knew that something had shifted. Maybe it had become too real. Maybe his declaration had come too soon. He searched his soul and found no regrets.

"Riley, you aren't responsible for me or my choices. I'm not asking you to make any decisions about me or what this is or isn't. I just want to spend time with you and let it go wherever it's going to go. Please don't add me to your list of troubles. I want to be the opposite for you. I want to be your safe space. You just have to let me."

This time, tears fell from both eyes. He wiped them away and rubbed her face with the back of his hand. When the tears continued, he let them fall and played his part. When she was all cried out, he whispered, "Let's get you to bed."

She opened her eyes, and they were pink with raw emotion.

He smiled to reassure her, and she smiled back.

She sat up and he stood, taking her hand in his. He helped her stand and they walked hand in hand into her bedroom. She slid out of her dress and crawled beneath the sheets in a fetal position. He tucked the sheets around her and kissed her forehead.

"We'll talk more tomorrow, if you're in the mood."

She turned her head toward him. "Stay. I don't want to be alone." She paused, closed her eyes again. "Stay and just lay beside me."

Gabriel didn't utter a response. He just laid on top of the duvet and pressed his body into hers. He gently rested one arm across her and she slid her body back closer to his.

"Good night, Riley," he whispered,

"Good night, Monsieur. And, thank you."

He lay in the darkness beside her, physically close but feeling her emotionally slip away. He pressed his face closer to her, and she smelled like the island. She had been using the Monoi oil in her hair and on her body—becoming one with her home away from home. He hoped that it was as comforting to her as it was for him. When he finally drifted off to sleep, he was hopeful but not assured. Tomorrow was a new day that held new opportunities. She might not be ready right now, but he was willing to wait. She was worth it.

CHAPTER THIRTY-FIVE

Riley

Riley's eyes lazily fluttered open. The warmth of the sun rested on her face, and its brightness enveloped the room. She stretched long and deep, and threw the bedding off her body. With both arms now wide across the bed, she realized she was alone. She vaguely remembered asking Gabriel to stay last night, and him laying down beside her as she drifted off to sleep. But now she was alone. She hadn't heard or felt him leave in the dark of night or in the clarity of morning. Unlike the prior mornings, she didn't feel cheap at being left alone. Rather, as she gathered the sheet up to her neck, she felt respected, and considered, and safe.

She turned over on her side to check her night stand, and there was a note.

Mademoiselle Riley—

I hope you feel rested this morning, and that the arrival of your guests is smooth today. Thank you for another beautiful night, and if I can be of service to you and your friends, don't hesitate to ask.

Affectionately yours,

Gabriel

She smiled at the note and was comforted by its sentiment. She was also struck by his salutation. *Did he feel like he belonged to her? Was that even possible?* So little time had passed. She could as easily count the time that they've known each other by hours as by days.

But these thoughts reminded her that what she was really dodging was how she felt about him. She didn't want to feel anything. She was still numb and Gabriel had been an easy and conveniently available distraction. She wasn't ready to feel anything for anyone. Except for herself.

Pushing those thoughts away, she focused on her day ahead. It was still early and she had time to get in a swim and a decent breakfast at the hotel restaurant. She wanted to sit at a table in the sand right at the edge of the water—alone with her thoughts. Her friends—along with her luggage—would arrive around noon, and the real fun would begin.

As she changed into her swimsuit, a rush of excitement surged through her as she anticipated the antics that might ensue over the next couple of days. She tried to focus on the good, because she knew that a huge dose of reality would get mixed in. Her attorney had met with the network executives and nothing had been decided. To buy her out of her contract wouldn't come easy or cheap. But falling ratings shook them more than the dollar signs attached to her contract. Knowing Octavia was on it was her security blanket, and gave her some space to enjoy her last days on the island.

It was kismet meeting Savannah, Charlotte, Paige, and Isabella. Like the stars had aligned just right to meet a need she didn't even realize existed. She could really use some girl time and some advice. She couldn't risk confiding in her friends back home and having them get the wrong impression and add fuel to the speculation flames. But her new flosse posse knew the deal and had actually encouraged her to have a little extracurricular activity—not as revenge, but as a long overdue treat to her body and her shattered ego.

And Gabriel had been the perfect means to that end. It seemed so easy at first. But now it was complicated like the rest of her life. They both had successful careers that were now in jeopardy—his because of her presence in his life, and hers because she had a sorry ass fiancé that instead of coming to her defense, had chosen to play the victim.

But this morning wasn't the time for dwelling on the choices men around her were making.

Her thoughts were interrupted by her phone ringing. She answered, and Donovan was on the other end.

"Hey, Riley." She thought he sounded better, and was hopeful that meant that he'd worked it out with his girlfriend.

"Donovan! I'm so glad you called. How are you?"

"I'm good, thanks. I just wanted to let you know that I'll be leaving tomorrow afternoon. I'm still working on Gabriel, and Estelle is feeling better. So, we're good, but she's going to want to meet you SOON."

Riley laughed. "Cool. I'm down."

"So, how are you? Have you spoken to Jonathan's wimpy ass? I saw what he posted on social media. He's a real asshole, Riley. I know it might be too soon for this, but I'm glad you're done with him."

"You're right and it's not too soon. I haven't spoken to him and don't intend to. He'll be hearing from my attorney when I'm back home to arrange my move out of his house. And that will be it."

She was wearing her tough girl mask for Donovan, but deep down, the upheaval was scary. But she didn't want Donovan to worry any more than he already had on her behalf.

"Good, Riley. You deserve better."

"I know. And I'm working on that."

"What's up with you the Frenchman?"

"That's another story entirely that we don't have time for now. I'm about to get in a swim and go get some breakfast. I would invite you, but since we're an internet sensation, I don't want to add another chapter to our scandalous reunion."

Donavan laughed. "Yeah, probably not the best idea."

"But my new friends are coming today. You should join us tonight for cocktails in my villa. I'll text you the details."

"Cool. Leave it to Riley St. James to make not one, but multiple new friends on the other side of the world."

"What can I say?" Riley joked. "I'm a woman of many talents."

"That you are. Have fun today and I'll check in with you later."

"Thanks. And, good luck with Gabriel. He might be a little more open to your proposal today. You've got this." She didn't want to spill Gabriel's business. And she didn't really want Donovan to know that Gabriel might be a free agent because of his association with her.

"I'm not even going to ask what that means. But, thanks for the vote of confidence."

Riley had been seated at a table for two right at the edge of the hotel's private beach. The restaurant decor was simple yet casually sophisticated. With seating on a pristine beach, a stunning view of Mt. Otemanu, and hypnotic blue hues of the lagoon, any meal became a one-of-a kind experience.

And this morning, she was famished—starved for nutritional sustenance and natural splendor. She ordered coffee, yogurt, exotic fruit, eggs over easy, and croissant with butter and jam. She'd end her meal with a mimosa, take a barefoot walk along the water's edge, ensure everything is in order for her guests, and prepare for their arrival.

Looking out over the lagoon, trying not to worry about what was happening with her job and finding comfort in Octavia's superhuman legal skills, she sipped on her mimosa and mentally scrolled through her daily to-do list. Her quiet time was interrupted by Simon.

"Good morning, Mademoiselle St. James. I trust you found everything satisfactory with your meal this morning."

She hadn't heard him approaching, and was caught off guard by his sudden appearance. Standing on the opposite side of her table in a neatly pressed, light grey two-piece outfit and white boating shoes, he was immaculate and she was at a loss for words. She didn't know if he was judging her. If she should mention Gabriel. Or, just return his polite inquiry with pleasantries. She chose the latter.

"And good morning to you, Monsieur Simon. The meal and service were impeccable. Not to mention the weather and the view."

"Ah, yes. Morning is my favorite time on the island. Watching everything waking and coming to life is rejuvenating. A new day always brings with it new opportunities." He smiled at her through his words, but she saw a hint of regret in his eyes.

"I couldn't agree more."

He began pouring her more coffee from her carafe, and it seemed like a nervous gesture.

"Thank you." She raised her half-consumed glass of mimosa to toast him. "Cheers to a new day and new opportunities."

He smiled at her, his eyes pleading for understanding. And she did understand. He was an honest man trying to do the right thing. Trying to be good at his job. Half of her felt a pang of guilt, with the other half wished he would give Gabriel a little more time. Or another option.

He clasped his hands in front of him, and bowed slightly. "Cheers, Mademoiselle."

And then he was gone.

A couple hours later, she stood at the dock awaiting the arrival of her fancy new luggage and her new friends. She would be beyond thrilled to see both. She really needed some female energy in her space. Besides, she had grown bored with her limited wardrobe and was in desperate need of a fashion injection. She'd packed some nice pieces just for the trip, and she planned to not let those outfits go to waste.

As the boat drew closer, she recognized each woman—mostly by their hair. Charlotte's rich auburn hair blowing carefree in the wind; Savannah's braids piled high atop her head in bun; Isabella's dark, thick curls pulled up and back in ponytail; and Paige's platinum blond short pixie cut, now sleek and brushed back away from her face. Every woman Riley knew experimented with her hair—color, length, texture, styles—and no woman wanted to be caught dead without their products. Riley had improvised for the last few days, but couldn't wait to get her hands on her Tracy Ellis Ross products to redefine her mess of untamable curls.

She waved her arm high, and in unison, they all began waving back. She also noticed another vaguely familiar face on the boat. *Was that Victor?*

When the boat docked, they rushed off, one by one, each with just one bag that they carried themselves. As they hugged and laughed, the hotel staff removed Riley's two suitcases from the boat and told her they would deliver them to her within the hour. And then Victor paused to say hello.

"Greetings, ladies. It's nice to see you all back together again." He was addressing the group, but looking at Isabella.

Isabella blushed and Riley raised an eyebrow.

"Good morning, Victor. It's nice to see you again also," Riley said.

Eyes deadlocked with Isabella, Paige stepped in…literally.

"That's enough. Let's get going," she said, putting her arm through Isabella's and looking back at Victor. "Maybe we'll see you around the island."

"Nothing would please me more."

The women exchanged curious glances between themselves and gathered up their bags.

"Let's go!" Riley said.

When they hit the edge of the pier to turn and go in the direction of Riley's villa, Gabriel was walking towards them. She smiled politely, but felt her cheeks flush. Riley threw up her arm to wave at him, but didn't stop. Savannah caught up with her.

"What was that about?"

"What was what about?" Riley feigned ignorance.

Savannah kept her face forward and said, "Okay. Guess you're not ready to talk about the mysterious Frenchman who magically appeared in Bora Bora after sending you champagne in Papeete. But it's cool. I'm a patient woman. I can wait."

Riley chuckled and took the lead towards her villa to get the festivities started.

Waiting for them when they arrived, a young, handsome bartender had prepared five cocktails on the rocks with rum, amaretto, cranberry juice, sprite and more than a couple maraschino cherries. There was a spread of fruit, cheeses, nuts, and desserts on the table, and Megan Thee Stallion serenaded them through Riley's wireless speaker—a tribute to their mini-Hot Girl Summer. They might be older than Megan, but they had the spirit and bodies to be hot girls. At least that's what they told themselves.

They dropped their bags near the door and gasped.

"Well, damn, girl!" Charlotte's southern accent stretched the words out like taffy. "Now this is how you honeymoon!"

Paige nudged her in the shoulder as they both headed towards the spread on the dining room table, and Savannah just shook her head, walking out to the deck. Isabella had made her way over to the bar—either to get the first sip of the cocktails or to call dibs on the bartender. Or maybe both.

Riley was smiling so hard, her cheeks ached. This villa felt strangely alive with the arrival of her friends, and she knew that this was exactly the energy she—and this space—needed.

"Make yourselves comfortable. I'll show you our sleeping arrangements after we catch up, but thought we could have some cocktails, soak in some sun, take a tour of the resort, hang by the beach and get ready for dinner. I have a spectacular evening arranged for us, and tomorrow we're going on an afternoon excursion around the island before another fabulous dinner.

Savannah walked back in from the deck. "Riley, this is amazing! Do you mind if I take a dip in the pool to cool off?"

"Yeah," Charlotte chimed in, "this makes our water front hotel suite in Papeete look like a studio apartment."

"Riley, it really is beautiful," Paige added. "Thank you for having us."

Isabella was engrossed in whatever conversation she was having with their bartender, and hadn't said a word.

"I'm glad you all like it and of course you can take a dip in the pool, but you might want to try the lagoon first. You can get in a pool at home. Where else will you get crystal clear, calm, cool water like this back home?"

Savannah looked back over her shoulder and agreed. "You might be right," she chuckled.

"What a view," Paige whispered.

The sun was set high in the sky, and the water was almost completely still like a sheet of rippled glass. The soft blue of the lagoon blended into the sky with no obvious point of delineation between the two. Two vastly different elements existing in perfect harmony.

"But before you dive in, can we have a toast?"

They all joined Isabella at the bar, each took a cocktail and held their glasses up eye-level. Riley spoke first.

"To new friends and new adventures, mixed with good vibes and good times!"

They touched glasses and all said, "Cheers to that."

"Can we throw in a few good men to the good times," Isabella joked, and they all laughed.

"Sure, Isabella," Paige said. "To good men who only bring the good vibes. And to Isabella, who we hope will leave some for the rest of us."

They clinked glasses again to laughs and smiles, and eased into small talk.

Savannah escaped to the deck, pulled down her shorts, slid her sheer cover up off, loosened her braids, and dived into the lagoon. What Riley assumed was a vibrant orange tank top was really a gorgeous, high cut, one piece bathing suit with a dangerously low plunge in the back that accentuated her curves and smooth brown skin.

"Well alright, Savannah," Riley said as Savannah hit the water.

"Oh, she's been turning heads all week," added Paige. "Men *and* women."

"I can see why. She's a damn goddess," Riley added.

The four women had exited to the deck to sun bathe on the lounge chairs. The sun was out in full force, and soon they were all peeling off their clothes and taking the plunge.

Five grown women regressed to their girlish selves far out into the lagoon. They splashed, raced each other, disrupted whole schools of fish, and laughed until their bellies ached. All the anxiety of the last week fell away from Riley, and she felt a freedom and a calm like never before.

CHAPTER THIRTY-SIX

Gabriel

G abriel greeted Victor at the edge of the pier and they exchanged fist bumps. Like Savannah, Victor had noticed the swift wave from Riley towards Gabriel, and dived right in.

"So, what's up with you and *Riley On the Run*? I saw her wave at you, but she certainly didn't slow down to allow for small talk."

"You don't waste any time, do you?" Gabriel hadn't been prepared to discuss Riley so soon with Victor. He wanted to ease into a conversation, perhaps get a little advice. Maybe over cocktails.

"Time waits for no one. So, what's up?"

Gabriel could always count on Victor to be a straight shooter. He never minced words. You never had to guess what he was thinking. He was calm in the most challenging of circumstances, and damn near psychic when it came to relationships between men and women. But he was glad he came to hang out for the weekend. He needed some male energy that wasn't judging his every move.

"Well, it's complicated."

"Tell me something I don't already know. Guests are off limits, and that didn't stop you from chasing her down in Papeete. Now, you've been on this island with her for days and I know you haven't just been making sure housekeeping cleaned her villa extra special."

Gabriel laughed. Victor was right, but there was the whole business of being caught going to see Riley that he was reluctant to share. Not because Victor would judge him, but he didn't want him to be disappointed if their work relationship would be severed as a result.

"So, you're right. I have been secretly seeing Riley and it's been great. Actually, it's a lot more than just great, but that's not the most important part."

"Okay. Well, thanks for confirming. I wasn't sure because I saw that video of her with some other man and I wasn't sure what to think. People are saying she left her fiancé to be with the guy in the video. I guess that's not true if you've been seeing her. But I can see how that confusion might be useful to keep your thing a secret."

"Take a breath, man!" Gabriel said, patting Victor on the back and chuckling. "You just devised a whole scenario with no input from me. Slow down so I can give you the details and hopefully, you can help."

"Cool," Victor said. "I'll keep my mouth shut and listen. But don't try to take advantage of my silence and drag this story out. I have opinions, advice, and a big imagination. It's a burden that I have to release."

They both laughed, and Gabriel continued as they arrived at his villa door. Once inside, he grabbed two beers from his fridge and they went out to his deck.

As soon as they sat down, Victor continued his line of questioning. "Gabe, I appreciate the attention and you letting me stay a few days, but shouldn't you be working? I didn't expect you to take time off to entertain me."

"You don't miss a thing. That's what I was working up to."

"Okay. Well, get to it."

"Simon caught me going to visit Riley a couple nights ago and reported it to headquarters." He sipped his beer and looked towards the lagoon.

Victor nearly choked on his beer. "Wait. So, you've really been spending time with her? Like—intimate time?"

"I don't kiss and tell, but let's say we've grown close." Gabriel paused and added, "Sort of." He felt vulnerable, and weird, and a little foolish. This whole being honest about your feelings was like a burden.

He was trying to embrace it, but it wasn't easy.

"Just so that I understand what you're saying—you've been sneaking off at night to spend time with Riley on the Run, got caught by Simon and he reported you."

"That about sums it up."

"So, what happens next? And how do you feel about it? I mean, you've worked hard for this company. Is she worth throwing it all away?"

Gabriel didn't speak. It was an honest question that he thought he knew the answer to.

Victor wasn't deterred by Gabriel's silence, and dug in deeper. "I mean, she's a beautiful woman. Successful, and definitely wife material. But do you think she could even begin to see you as a life partner? She still hasn't settled things with the fiancé she ditched back in Washington, D.C. I just want you to be realistic about all of this."

Victor's tone took on a seriousness that gave Gabriel reason to pause and take stock of his decisions.

Gabriel turned the beer up and drank until the bottle was empty. When he asked himself if she was worth it, it was a resounding yes. But when he heard it from Victor, his firm *yes* felt more like definitely *maybe*.

Victor also knew how to read a room, and gave his friend some space to process. Gabriel stood and got another beer. Just as he closed the fridge door, his phone rang. It was the company's chief of staff and general counsel. Dread sank in and he felt like he was having an out-of-body experience. Like his soul was watching his physical body screw up their lives.

He sat at the small desk in his villa and listened intently as the man on the other end of the line outlined the consequences of his dalliance with a guest, disgust and anger rising to the surface.

His promotion was on-hold for at least another year and he'd have to attend training on workplace conduct, added to a quarterly check-in with the Chief of Staff. They were giving him 48 hours to respond by signing a performance improvement plan.

Gabriel slid one arm out of his linen blazer and let it hang off his opposite shoulder, suddenly too hot for an extra layer of clothing. He was incredulous. After ten years of immaculate service, they wanted to put him on a performance improvement plan. If he performed any better, he'd be the damn CEO.

But what pissed him off the most was they didn't even ask to hear his side of the story. They just took Simon at his word — the employee he was there training — and made a blanket decision. They couldn't even be bothered to investigate—question him or the guest in question. Just a blind assumption that Gabriel had acted in bad faith.

Gabriel took notes, pressing the pen deeper into the pad with each bullet point. He agreed to respond within the allotted timeframe and ended the call without saying good-bye. When he hung up the phone, he smacked the beer bottle off the desk and it crashed to the floor, a pool of liquid and foam spreading across the surface.

Victor rushed in and saw Gabriel with his head buried in his hands. "What happened?"

"I think I'm on an unofficial probation. And, there will be no promotion. At least not in the next year or so and pending the outcome of my one-year performance improvement plan."

Victor walked around the liquid mess on the floor and stood near Gabriel. Not sure what to do, he patted Gabriel's slumped back.

"That's not too bad. At least they didn't fire you."

"I guess." Gabriel lifted himself up and Victor's hand slipped away. "But there's still something I haven't told you."

"Damn, Gabe. This woman has your life twisted."

"This isn't her fault. I pursued her."

"I guess," Victor added, not really buying Gabriel's defense of Riley. "But she could have said no and none of this would be happening."

"That's true. But this might be the push I need to get out of my comfort zone."

Now Victor was confused.

"I thought the promotion was you getting out of your comfort zone."

"It was." Gabriel continued as he went to get a towel to clean up his mess.

"But the reality is the promotion is basically a desk job with the perks of traveling, but not nearly as much as I travel now. And that's what I love about this job. But who keeps doing the same thing year after year when there are other opportunities to grow?"

"So, what are you saying?" Victor sat on the couch and took another sip of his beer.

"There's a CEO from another boutique hotel company here—on the island—trying to recruit me away. The only problem is, the owner wants to merge with my family's company and move into the European market."

"Okay. I'm listening."

"It's an intriguing offer," Gabriel continued. "But I'd have to convince my father, who wants me to come back, but to merge with my ex-girlfriend's family business. He actually wants me to marry her. I've said no on many occasions, but he keeps pushing it and now, Cecily's on board because her father is threatening to cut her off financially if she doesn't marry soon. That hasn't helped matters, but I know I'm not marrying someone for business."

"Damn, Gabe. Your life is like a reality television show."

"Not helpful, Victor."

"Okay. Let me put on my advisor hat." Victor sat his now-empty beer bottle on the table and began to outline a dual track plan.

"First, you have to decide if you even want to keep working for the company. While you're considering that, you have to talk to your father about this possible merger. He might surprise you."

Gabriel considered Victor's advice, and found it sound.

"That sounds right," Gabriel said. "But what about Riley?"

Victor exhaled deep and long. "For now, she can't be a priority. Just think about it, you don't even know if she'll want to see you after this trip is over. Are you really going to make life-altering decisions for yourself based on a woman who might not really be available to you? You have to know that she could work things out with her fiancé."

Gabriel knew deep down that Victor was right. At least that's what his brain told him. But for the past several days, it's been his heart—and his cock—that had been in the driver's seat. And he didn't know if he could just turn those two things off and let his sensibilities take control.

Victor had changed out of his clothes and was now rotating between swimming and floating across the lagoon. Gabriel was happy to have a friend nearby. Even if they might not exactly agree.

Gabriel decided to take the few minutes of alone time to phone his father. Like ripping of a Band-Aid, you never know what's going to be waiting for you beneath, but there was always a little pain in the process of getting there.

His dad answered on the first ring and Gabriel swallowed hard. His father preferred his conversations in French, so Gabriel dived in with the offer. His father listened and was strangely quiet. Gabriel couldn't tell if that was a good sign, or if he was so angry that he was driven to speechlessness. When he did finally speak, he had lots of questions and Gabriel did his best to sale the idea as the best of both worlds. After all his questions were answered, he told Gabriel he'd think about it but reminded him that he was putting him in an awkward position since he was already in talks to merge with another company and there was the heart of a woman also waiting for an answer. When Gabriel pushed back on the marriage angle, his father snapped. All the anger that had been simmering beneath the surface bubbled to the top and was now boiling over.

Gabriel wasn't surprised by his anger, nor that his father mentioned Cecily. He wouldn't soon let that go. But he was surprised that it was the Cecily marriage issue that angered him the most. Gabriel was reminded of his conversation with his sister Juliette and wondered if there was more to the story than his father was sharing.

If he removed Cecily from the conversation, their talk hadn't gone as bad as he had expected. He still didn't have the answer he'd hoped for either, but knew his father was stubborn and fickle and he might go either way.

With that conversation marked off the list, Gabriel reached out to Donovan, who invited him and Victor to dinner at the hotel restaurant. He now had to have a plan to pitch Donovan on the idea of hiring him absent his family company if his father wasn't in agreement. That didn't make him as nervous as the fallout he could expect from his father if he walked away from the company again. Their relationship might be irreparably damaged.

When he hung up with Donovan, Gabriel realized that he wanted more. More than what he was getting from the company he had served well. The kind of more that Donovan was proposing. He had 48 hours to make a decision, but he had already made it.

Looking out the sliding glass doors at Victor on his back, the sun in his face and floating in place, Gabriel decided he needed a refresh. He dressed in his swim shorts and joined Victor. Once he was out in the water, he swam as far down as he could and let the force of the water be a refuge. Beneath the surface he welcomed impaired senses in a place where there was no sound, there was nothing to smell, his vision was blurred and he had no voice. Just his muscles pushing him down and then back up with his hair raising and floating with the current and his movements. He was but a small speck in this one giant organism. It humbled him. Gave him perspective.

When he bobbed above the surface, he wiped his drenched hair out of his eyes and back, and he looked across the lagoon towards the sound of voices. He could vaguely see Riley and her friends enjoying the water and the weather—also free of the world's distractions.

Victor caught him looking and must have been able to read his mind because swimming closer, the next words out of his mouth to Gabriel were, "It would be nice to join them."

Gabriel agreed but cautioned against it. "Last night she told me she didn't know what we were or what she wanted. That she couldn't make any more big decisions. I know you think I shouldn't be willing to risk too much for her, but she didn't just walk away from her wedding. Now her job is also on the line."

"Why?" Victor seemed seriously confused. "He cheated on her, right? And either way, it's not *your* fault. Your employment issue *is* her fault."

"Not exactly, but we'll agree to disagree. Once that video of her and Donovan hit the internet, the story shifted and now she looks like the cheater."

Victor dipped under water and when he popped back up again, Gabriel continued. "And by the way, Donovan invited us to dinner tonight. He's Riley's college classmate, but he's also the owner of the company trying to recruit me away."

"More intrigue," Victor responded. "Count me in."

And then, just like they had regressed to being boys without a care in the world, Victor challenged Gabriel to a race.

"Last one to the deck buys the first round tonight."

Before Gabriel could say, "I'll take the bet," Victor was already in full arm stroke towards the deck.

Once inside, Gabriel saw a missed call on his cell phone from an unfamiliar number. Whoever it was had left a voicemail. He was in no mood to entertain strangers about anything, so he just ignored the call.

CHAPTER THIRTY-SEVEN

Riley

While they dressed for dinner, Riley put on her Black Girl Magic playlist, filled with anthems, revenge lyrics, sexual empowerment, self-love and power moves. As they danced and sang along to the tops of their voices, Riley remembered her night beneath the stars with Gabriel and how he was so close to penetrating her— unprotected. With her luck, she'd have the first modern day immaculate conceptions just from being rubbed against. As a precaution, she opened the side zipper inside her largest suitcase and pulled out a bottle of morning after pills. She swallowed the pill and sipped from a glass of water when she thought Savannah wasn't watching.

She was mistaken.

"What was that?" Savannah asked, walking towards Riley standing near the night stand.

"What?"

"What did you just take? Are you not feeling well?"

"I feel fine," Riley responded. She decided be honest without giving too many details. "Just a little precaution."

"Precaution? For what?" Savannah slapped one hand on her curvy hip and was incredulous. "I know you haven't lost your entire mind with that Frenchman. Please tell me you aren't down here having unprotected sex."

"I am not! And please, lower your voice, Savannah."

But it was too late. Isabella was already dressed and had just been on the other side of the door making a cocktail.

She popped her head in. "Who's having unprotected sex?"

Riley plopped down on the bed.

"Damn," she said. "I couldn't wait for you all to get here and now, I'm reminded exactly how much we are all up in each other's business."

"That's a good thing," Savannah said. "Sometimes our friends are the voice of reason."

"And sometimes they're like me," Isabella added. "Unreasonable, unrestrained…"

Before she could finish, Savannah added, "…and unreliable!"

They all laughed, and Riley propped herself up against the head board. Savannah sat at the foot of the bed and Isabella laid on her stomach next to Riley, head propped up and looking Riley directly in her face. She didn't want to miss a word of this.

"We got carried away one night out in the lagoon, but stopped before it went too far. We hadn't planned it, but we got caught up beneath a starlit night, a soft breeze and gentle current swaying our bodies closer and closer together. It was reckless and actually, *he* stopped us. But it was fucking magical."

"Wow…" Even the quick-witted Isabella was reduced to a one syllable response.

"I guess I kind of understand," Savannah added. "He is fine as hell."

"What do you understand?" Charlotte walked in with Paige in tow.

"And why are you all crowded in on Riley's bed?" Paige wanted to know.

"We're talking about Gabriel," Riley offered.

"And their unprotected sex," Isabella threw in for good measure. As if the mention of sex hadn't sufficiently surprised them.

"Well, sit up Isabella and make room for us," Charlotte demanded. "That man's a tall glass of sweet goodness and I'm glad someone got to get a sip."

They all laughed and then Riley got serious.

"First, we almost had unprotected sex. But seriously, you all don't think I'm crazy for engaging in a little extracurricular activity with a man I barely know? I mean, I only just broke up with my fiancé last week."

"For the record," the reliable and matter-of-fact Paige jumped in. "You technically didn't break up with your fiancé. You ran away from your wedding. You haven't dealt with him at all. But you will."

Riley thought about that for a minute. Paige was right. She had told Jonathan there would be no wedding and that she was leaving. But had she explicitly said it was over between them? That night was now a blur and eventually, she would need closure. He would need closure, too.

Savannah piled on with her opinion. "I don't think you're crazy, but I do wish you had been more careful."

"Honey, you don't even know the half of it."

"Whatever do you mean?" Charlotte's sincerity wrapped around Riley like a warm blanket on a cold night. It was genuine concern from a woman she hadn't spent more than two days with.

"Well, Gabriel got caught coming to see me a few nights ago, and his colleague reported him. Apparently, there's a fairly strict no fraternization rule with guests, and now he's facing a reprimand." She paused, closed her eyes and dropped the real bomb, "He could lose his job."

"Oh, no, mami," Isabella said.

This time Paige stood and smoothed out her belted red jersey dress with a plunging neckline headed so far south it nearly reached her belly button. Her green eyes sparkled and her pixie cut had little spikes at the top that made her look like a dangerous seductress.

"Enough of this pity party. Trust me. A man like Gabriel will land on his feet. I'm more worried about Riley and her reputation. So much of our news now is more entertainment than journalism. I, for one, need more women like Riley covering national and world events. Journalists who still care about balance and fairness, and who operate with integrity. We lose a Riley St. James, the next one coming behind her has it tougher and that glass ceiling just keeps rising."

She said her peace and walked into the living area, her voice trailing,

"Let's go enjoy this extravagant evening Riley has planned for us."

Riley sat upright in the bed and fully absorbed Paige's declaration. It was true. Gabriel already had an opportunity just waiting for him to accept it in the form of Donovan—not to mention a family safety net. Meanwhile, Riley had to send in her attorney to negotiate on her behalf. She already suspected they wanted to release her from her contract, and at least she had a legal warrior fighting for her and with her. She had no reason to feel bad about Gabriel's prospects. He was a man and he would land on his feet.

"Paige is right. Let's get out of here and head to the restaurant. We've got a long night ahead of us."

They all stood and prepared to leave. Savannah hung back to have one final private word with Riley.

"Don't you dare feel guilty about indulging in a little sexual exploration with Gabriel. You deserved it. But don't let your judgement get too clouded either. You'll be back home in a few days, and if this thing with Gabriel is real, that distance will give your answer."

Surprising Savannah, Riley reached in and gave her a big bear hug. She'd been so disconnected from her real life, she had forgotten how important that girlfriend wisdom was when shit hit the fan. Her heart was filled with gratitude.

"Thanks, Savannah. That means a lot."

Savannah wiggled herself free from Riley's embrace and looked her in the eyes. "I know we don't know each other that well, but I've got your back." She tilted her head to the side of Riley and added, "They've got your back, too. And we decided before we even came here that a crew of five was better than four. Now somebody can break our ties when we're arguing."

They both laughed and headed out to join the others. They grabbed their evening bags and stepped out—beautiful and bold, fearless and fabulous. Riley's phone began to vibrate in her purse. When she removed it to see who was calling, it was an international number. Assuming it was a wrong number, or some overzealous European tabloid had tracked her down, she ignored the call and joined her friends outside.

When the five women stepped off the pier, it was an understatement to say they literally turned heads. Early evening diners watched as one by one, a parade of gorgeous, grown ass women in a kaleidoscope of dresses sauntered into view.

Donovan, Gabriel, and Victor had already arrived and were talking amongst themselves. It made Riley smile seeing Donovan and Gabriel together, secretly hoping that they could come to an agreement and work together. They had so much in common, and their personalities and drive would ensure their success. She decided she was staying out of it, but hoped they both got what they wanted.

Riley had taken the lead down the pier, in a sheer, textured chartreuse dress with braided spaghetti straps and a plunging neckline that stopped just above her navel. She opted to forego the bra, and let her perky breast take the lead. There was a braid across the bottom of the top where the fabric gathered, and beneath it, pieces of the bottom half of the dress attached to the braid, leaving sections of skin around her torso exposed. She wore black, low waist panties beneath the sheer dress that drew the eye to her most delicate places. Her skin glowed and sparkled, accented by her hair piled high with whisps of tendrils dangling just above her shoulders. With thin gold earrings grazing her shoulders, she felt like black girl magic personified.

Savannah had chosen a vibrant tangerine skirt with a matching, loose crop top that exposed just a hint of her toned midriff. Several strands of thin gold necklaces layered and looped just below her breast, and her braids were parted in the middle and held back with gold and silver barrettes.

Paige dazzled in her spicy red, and Charlotte's southern charm lit up the night in a strapless bright yellow baby doll dress that barely covered her cheeks, paired with what she called her silver "fuck me pumps."

And Isabella was walking fire. Her full-length, high-waist white skirt had a slit up to the very top of her right thigh, and her exposed leg was further elongated in clear platform heels. She paired the skirt with a regal purple, haltered bra top that left a sensuous, diamond shaped patch of midriff skin exposed. She had parted her midnight black hair down the middle and pulled it back, leaving her curls full and cascading down her bare back. Elegant and oozing sex appeal. When she stepped off the pier, Victor's mouth dropped open and he couldn't take his eyes off of her. Even Donovan seemed a little mesmerized by Miss Isabella.

But Gabriel only had eyes for Riley. The smile that spread across his face made her breath catch. It was the look from a man that she never knew she wanted—never knew she was missing. As she drew closer to him, she could see he was dressed in linen from head to toe. His crisp white long-sleeved shirt was unbuttoned midway to his chest exposing a tan that practically matched her own. The shirt hung loosely over dove grey pants, and was unbuttoned at the bottom. The bulge at the intersection of his thighs was visible, she hoped only to her. He hadn't bothered shaving, and his five o'clock shadow made her deliriously aroused. She instantly imagined the stubble against the inside of her thighs and moaned quietly to herself.

Or, so she thought.

"I heard that," Savannah mused.

The men rushed over as they each began to step from the pier to the walkway leading to the beach, lending a hand to smooth the transition.

Gabriel's hand was warm and he held onto hers a little longer than was necessary. She smiled at him and made a half-hearted attempt to make polite conversation.

"I see you received your invitation." She bent her head down slightly to navigate the walkway. "I'm so glad you could join us."

"Oh, you mean my invitation from Donovan? Yes, it was received and I'm thrilled to be joining the most beautiful woman on this island."

"Donovan may have asked you to join," she teased. "But rest assured, the invitation was from me. I am the hostess of this private soiree, and you are among my special guests."

They walked side-by-side until they turned a corner where their table awaited.

The long communal table was draped in a white table cloth, and wide wicker chairs for eight surrounded the table. Down the center of the table lay a runner of palm leaves with a mix of soft white candles in tall- to medium-height floating glass votive holders interspersed with fresh pineapples adding a natural pop of color. The dancing flickers of fire matched the waves of a light breeze off the lagoon carrying an intoxicating scent of salt, coconuts and a blend of floral fragrances.

A small round table was off to the side also covered in white with platforms draped in pink holding charcuterie platters of cheese, fresh fruit, nuts, dried fruit, and slices of salted meats. The centerpiece offered a vibrant mix of tall palm leaves, orchids, hibiscus, and birds of paradise flowers—a not so subtle reminder of their island oasis.

Dotting the edge of lagoon were multiple tiki torches, providing an additional touch of ambiance as the fire flickered with the crystalline water as a backdrop. As waves lightly lapped at the beach's edge, the motion was a soothing reminder to relax and enjoy paradise.

A small bar with two bartenders was set-up at the end of the walkway, and Riley invited everyone to head in that direction to start their evening with a carefully curated cocktail, compliments of the hostess. A dollop of pineapple puree was added to the bottom of the champagne flutes, rimmed with sugar and coconut flakes held in place with a mixture of honey and rum, topped off with sparkling prosecco.

Riley recognized one of the bartenders as the young man who had greeted them in her villa earlier in the afternoon. She wondered if he had volunteered for this assignment, because he was slightly distracted by the presence of Isabella, who was holding court with Donovan and Victor. Gabriel had walked over to introduce himself to Savannah, Paige, and Charlotte, and Riley giggled as Charlotte slid her arm between Gabriel's and gave him a nice squeeze. He smiled graciously as they eased into a light conversation. He seemed very comfortable and unburdened. Like his job wasn't in jeopardy.

Riley assumed by his presence he either made a decision about Donovan's offer, or the company had made a decision for him. When Donovan mentioned he was having dinner with Gabriel and Victor, Riley thought it made sense for them to join their table. Now, she questioned that choice. She didn't want to make matters worse for Gabriel.

She took a minute to scan her surroundings and noted Simon nearby orchestrating in the background. There had obviously been a development she wasn't privy to—but she'd also been out of touch today with the arrival of her friends. She was certain Gabriel would share any updates.

But maybe he wouldn't. She had pretty much put him on ice last night, admitting she was confused. It was a painful truth. But damn, she was into him. *Really* into him.

She looked over at him as he laughed and got to know her new friends. So confident, so charming. She knew they were lapping up that thick, smooth accent of his. For his part, he appeared to not have a worry in the world. And while she was pretending to be fine with whatever was unfolding for her career, she really wasn't. And, her relationship with Jonathan was garbage, but she still had to get closure. With these things coupled together, she knew that she was on the verge of losing it all and being forced to start again. It was unsettling, but she put on a brave face and her big-girl panties, and kept moving face forward.

And planning this little impromptu soiree had been a good and easy first step. She needed something to remind her of who she was and of the blessings that continued to pour upon her. She was on a beach in Bora Bora, hosting a gathering of friends, dressed like a goddess, and still smiling. She had stumbled, but she had not fallen.

Getting out of her head and back to her guests, she looked at both clusters of people and knew that Isabella the firestarter needed a wing woman. So, she chose to add a little more estrogen to their conversation, and simultaneously remind Donovan that he wasn't quite out of the doghouse yet with his girlfriend.

"Hey, guys!" Riley cheerfully interrupted. "Are you all keeping our fair Isabella entertained?"

"Of course," Victor added. "She's quite beguiling, your fair Isabella is." He looked towards Donovan and added, "Wouldn't you agree?"

A nervous Donovan chuckled. "Yes, beguiling. She's definitely that plus some."

Riley nudged him and they both laughed.

"Did Donovan tell you all that we're old college friends? That before this trip we hadn't seen each other in like ten years?"

"Funny," Isabella said, her eyes meeting Donovan's before taking in his full measure as she sipped from her glass. "He hadn't mentioned it."

Riley made a mental note of that move. Isabella was good. She should teach courses.

"Well, he might be a little shy about it since we became overnight internet sensations."

"Yeah, let's not talk about that," Donovan jumped in. "I'd rather hear more about Isabella's new restaurant."

"Beguiling and a good cook," Victor added, his eyes undressing Isabella right in front of us.

"Perdóneme, papi," Isabella corrected, her accent thickening as if on demand. "I'm a chef. A Michelin-starred chef I might add. I am not a *good cook.*"

"Apologies, Mademoiselle," Victor cowered just a bit. Not all men were built for women like Isabella. He best tread lightly.

Donovan shifted the conversation to Puerto Rico's recovery and the rest of the guests joined them. Everybody had lots of questions, and Isabella was happy to regale with tales of triumph over all that the island had endured, and her part in the return to not just normalcy, but vibrancy.

Riley excused herself to consult with the lead server, and returned to ask her guests to be seated.

She took her seat at the head of the table and guided Gabriel to the opposite end of the table. She asked Donovan to sit to her left and suggested Paige sit at her right. She hadn't spent enough time with Paige, and wanted them to have a chance to chat. And, she thought Donovan would enjoy getting to know her as well.

Over a five-course meal combined with local specialties and French cuisine, they talked, toasted, laughed and just enjoyed time together. It was an eclectic group, full of energy and zest for life. As she glanced at them all, she realized that Donovan was the only person at the table that really knew her. Sure, they knew her public persona—but that was about a job, not who she was as a woman. And even Donovan only knew the Riley barely out of her teens. With this group of people, she was like a blank canvas. That was an invigorating thought. A blank canvas has nothing but space for new and imaginative exploration.

Following dessert and coffee, Riley invited everyone to the champagne bar for an after-dinner aperitif and more cocktails for those with a strong enough tolerance. She also invited Simon to join them, assuring him that he was welcome. Thirty minutes in to what had become a revelry involving her guests and other hotel guests, Simon joined them, loosening his collar and throwing back a couple of beers.

Moments like these were pure perfection for Riley.

She headed over to the bar to order a glass of champagne, and was approached by a woman. She had seen her poolside at the hotel, and also at dinner the night she was with Donovan.

"Hi," the woman said. "I'm Rebecca, and that's my husband Rick throwing back shots with whoever that is."

They both laughed. "That's Victor. He works at the hotel in Papeete."

"Okay. Well, he should be harmless."

"Mostly," Riley joked, and they both chuckled.

"Well, I wanted to introduce myself and to apologize," Rebecca said, lowering her eyes.

"Apologize for what?" Riley now turned to face her.

"I posted the video to social media. Now I know I shouldn't have done that, and I'm sorry."

Riley was quiet for a few seconds, not wanting to respond out of the anger that instantly rose to the surface. She wanted to choose her next words wisely.

"Why did you post it?"

"I know this will sound crazy, but I wanted the world to see that you were not some wounded woman. That you were not hiding, but getting on with your life. More women need to see that side of a break up." She paused. "My intentions were good, I swear. But this is your private life, and that was an invasion. I hope you can accept my apology."

Riley turned away from Rebecca and got the bartender's attention. "Make that two glasses of champagne."

"Oh, no," Rebecca insisted. "Make mine sparkling water, maybe with a twist of lemon."

She turned back to Riley, "I'm pregnant."

"Really? But you've been rocking bikinis every time I've seen you. You definitely don't look pregnant."

"I know. We found out right before this trip—like two days before because I kept vomiting everywhere."

"Wow! Congratulations! You must be so happy."

"I am." She glanced over at her husband and giggled. "He's happy, too. And maybe just a little nervous."

When their drinks arrived, they both took a sip. Riley had just taken the morning after pill. The thought of what could have happened scared the hell out of her. Her life was a damn three ring circus. Broken engagement. Job jeopardized. Social media madness. There just wasn't space for anything else.

She chose not to dwell on it, but she knew she and Gabriel had run their course.

They had shut down the bar, and Riley was ready to kick back and relax back in her villa with her friends. As everyone began saying their good nights, they had all agreed to meet up in the morning for breakfast, barring any significant hangovers. Gabriel, Simon, Donovan, and Victor were saying good night to Isabella and Paige, while Savannah and Charlotte waited patiently on the walkway.

Riley walked over to speed up the good-nights, and Gabriel asked if they could take a walk. The silence that fell over the group hung heavy and she fidgeted with her purse, her palms damp. Her eyes darted around her new friends, and every pair of eyes was on her. She was never this nervous in front of camera—but in this moment, she wished she could just click her heals and disappear.

"Of course," she said, looking cautiously—or maybe it was pleadingly—at Simon, whose smile was warm, genuine, and signaled approval.

She handed her villa key to Paige and quipped, "It's time for all little mousies to go to their own little housies." They all laughed, while Gabriel took her by the hand and led her to the beach. She didn't dare look back because she was sure they looked like some romcom couple walking off into their happily ever after. If only it were that easy.

"Nice job tonight," Gabriel said, still holding her hand. He had slid his fingers between hers and her body immediately time traveled back to last night when he drove her to the edge of ecstasy and pushed her right over.

"Thank you," she said. "It was a lot of fun. Just what I needed."

"I think it was just what we all needed. Even Simon!"

They both laughed.

"Speaking of Simon, you seemed pretty at ease tonight. And he definitely loosened up after a couple beers. Did something happen I should know about?"

They had reached the edge of the water, and she so desperately wanted to dip her feet in. Reading her mind, he led her to a nearby lounge chair, guided her to sit, and proceeded to slip off her Louboutins. He slowly massaged both her feet, noticing for the first time a delicate flower bloom painted onto her toes.

"Are those flower petals?"

"Yep. Cherry blossoms to be exact," she smiled remembering the blooming trees back home.

"An interesting choice," he said.

"They are a big tourist attraction in D.C. But I've loved them since I was girl." Her happy thoughts were immediately replaced with the wedding and the life she left behind. She could see things clearer now and she knew that running in that moment of panic was a necessary choice to put some distance between herself and the situation, but that she still had to face Jonathan. And she had more grieving to do for that relationship. She didn't want him back. But she wanted that sense of security back.

"Let's dip our feet in the water?" Riley said, changing the subject.

"Your wish is my command, Mademoiselle."

Hand in hand, they walked to the water's edge and let the soft waves cover and then retreat a few times before she continued.

"So, tell me about you and Simon."

"Right. So, he followed the company's handbook and reported me to headquarters. They have outlined the consequences of my actions, and I have 48 hours to respond and sign a performance improvement plan." He used air quotes when he spoke about the plan, but beneath the sarcasm, she could tell he was disappointed.

"I'm so sorry, Gabriel. I didn't mean for any of this…"

He stopped her. "No apologies necessary from you. This is not your fault. Number one, it's an outdated mandate. Number two, I made a choice. I don't regret that choice. Now I have to decide if I can accept their punishment."

They were quiet again until she asked, "What do you think you'll do?"

He hesitated, splashing the water with his left foot, trying to keep his balance.

"Honestly, I don't think I can accept their terms. I have my reasons—and there are many—but I think I'm ready to turn the page. The promotion I've been angling for is not even something I really want to do. It's just something different."

Her happiness for him was mixed with just a hint of resentment. What must it feel like to just change lanes in your career, to just choose something different? What a luxury. A luxury reserved for men.

"Well, then I guess it's lucky that Donovan stuck around. Did you all talk tonight?"

"We did and I had an initial conversation with my father today. I don't know if the grumpy old man will lean in to this offer, but I have a back-up plan that I'm going to pitch to Donovan tomorrow after breakfast."

"Wow! It's all working out for you." That hint of resentment was rising and she let her hand slip away from his with the pretense of gathering her dress up and away from the water. In all that he just shared about his next move, there was no mention of her. She knew she wasn't being fair because she had started pushing him away last night. But she quietly hoped he might think her worthy to fight for.

Gabriel picked up on the change in her tone.

"I'm sorry. I didn't mean to dominate the conversation. What's happening with you and your situation?"

"It's not a situation. It's my livelihood," she said, swallowing back bitterness and softening her tone. None of this was his fault.

"My attorney is in play and she'll likely negotiate an exit strategy for me. Beyond that, I don't know. Unlike you, my options are limited. First, I'll have to deal with the fallout of my break-up, let an appropriate amount of time pass, then start working on my next move. And, I have to find somewhere to live."

He put his hands in his pockets, obviously speechless.

She turned to walk back towards the lounge chair, feeling disappointment but also some relief. She was ready to end this night—that was one thing she could control. With her back to him, he reached out and grabbed her hand, pulling her into him.

She didn't turn around to face him, her breathing labored, chest visibly rising and falling while an ocean full of tears welled in her eyes.

Gabriel wrapped both arms around her and squeezed. She let her body relax and leaned back into him. She felt like she was falling, and it felt like he was catching her.

"Riley, I'm trying to respect you, your feelings, your situation. But I want you so bad. I know you aren't sure right now, so I won't push. But please don't walk away from me tonight believing that I don't want you, because I do. More than anything I've ever wanted before."

One tear escape and she was sure it landed on his arm. But it was too late to take it back, to wipe it away.

Her breath caught and the more she fought against the tears, the more physical her emotions manifested themselves. She lifted her arms and held onto his, feeling completely safe for the very first time in the arms of a man.

"Just know that the only thing I want more than you, is for you to be happy," he continued, emotional but not desperate. "If that includes me, I'm yours for the taking. And if it doesn't, you still have a friend for life. You came crashing into my life and a life I never knew I wanted suddenly appeared. A life that includes you. But not half of you, Riley. All of you."

She could tell that he had said his peace. She took one last squeeze before swallowing back the urge to keep falling.

"I know you care about me, Gabriel. And I know this because you know that I'm not whole. I'm far from it. But I'll get there."

She didn't know why this was so hard. Earlier she was so sure she could let this go. Now, she was finding it more difficult to walk away from this man she had only known a few days than it had been to leave Jonathan. But neither of those women were whole. She needed to be whole again—without a man.

"You have shown me so much affection and attention. You have listened to me and sacrificed for me. It's more than I could have ever imagined, and definitely not what I expected. You made me feel again, and reminded me that I can and I will heal. But that's a journey for one. What's happening now is just too messy for me. I need to rid myself of some of this chaos so that I can see and choose with a clear mind."

She had gotten it out. Somehow, she held back the tears long enough to free him to move on, and to take the time she needed to process all that she's lost.

His arms loosened and slid away.

"Riley, life is sometimes messy," he said, still standing behind her. Still ready to catch her.

"It's not always perfect, but we can find perfect moments. If nothing else, I know we shared some perfect moments. And I guess that will have to be good enough."

His final words—*good enough*—lingered in the air as she stepped away from him, grabbed her shoes and her evening bag and ran towards her villa, leaving him with only his thoughts and the expanse of ocean and open air as consolation.

She had settled for good enough with Jonathan. She wanted and needed more.

CHAPTER THIRTY-EIGHT

Riley

Just as they planned, they all met up for breakfast. The restaurant had placed three tables together so the large group of seven—minus Gabriel—could be together and not spread out at different tables. They kept the same seating arrangements as the night before and the conversations picked up right where they left off.

Donovan spent quite a bit of time chatting with Savannah about her life as a travel journalist. He shared stories about the boutique hotels in his portfolio. Riley and Paige both were completely absorbed in the conversation when they were interrupted by a bit of a commotion.

Riley stretched her neck to see what was happening, and she caught a glimpse of Gabriel walking towards the disturbance. When she saw him again, a tall, dark and handsome man was right on his heels.

It was Jonathan.

Whether it was force of habit or if she just needed an anchor, she latched on to Donovan's hand and he whispered, "Just breathe."

"So, it is true!" Jonathan shouted loud enough for all of the dining guests to hear.

Frantically, Riley looked left and right, hoping and praying that no one was filming the latest episode of her reality television show life.

"You came on our honeymoon to be with fucking Donovan."

Donovan slid his hand away from Riley's and stood, chest out like full armor ready for battle.

"Watch your mouth, *Frat*."

Jonathan stepped closer. "Nah, don't bring the frat into this. This right here—her" he pointed towards Riley, "is between you and me."

In the blink of an eye, Gabriel slid his body between the two men.

"Let's everyone calm down and bring it down a notch. You're disturbing other guests, and we can take this somewhere more private."

This time Riley stood and walked around the table and planted herself right next to Jonathan. She glanced around the restaurant at the other guests, now their audience. There were no phone cameras in sight, but she knew it was only a matter of time.

"Thank you, Gabriel. I can take it from here," she said. Gabriel and Donovan slowly stepped back, but hovered nearby.

Riley turned to Jonathan. "First of all, you need to lower your voice. I don't need any more viral videos to explain away."

Jonathan's face softened and he measured his breaths. She took him by the hand and walked him away from the outdoor dining space. When she turned to address him, he smiled and squeezed her hand.

"Wipe that smile off your face." She yanked her hand from his grasp. "This is not a reunion, and no, Jonathan—my being here alone has nothing to do with Donovan, but everything to do with your cheating ass." She poked him in his chest, and his eyes softened. "I don't believe you have the audacity to show up here and accuse me of having an affair, with Donovan of all people. This is all you projecting your bullshit on me. But it's not going to work. Not this time."

Savannah stood first, followed by the other three women while Jonathan scanned the table.

"Who the hell are all of these people?"

"They're my friends and of no concern to you."

Savannah went and stood next to Riley, squeezing her hand. "You cool?"

"I'm good," Riley responded. She looked at Jonathan. "We can go somewhere private and talk, but you will not embarrass me any further. Does that work for you, Commander Jonathan, or would you prefer to continue ruining my life out in full public view? Answer wisely, because if I go down, we're both going down in flames. Comprende?"

Before he could answer, there was another set of raised voices coming from the direction of the hotel lobby.

"Are we on the set of the real housewives of Tahiti?" Isabella quipped.

Gabriel slipped on his executive manager hat and headed towards the newest disruption. But before he took the first step up the small set of stairs towards the lobby, he abruptly stopped in his tracks.

A beautiful young woman ran towards him and threw her arms around his neck. "Gabe!" she cried out.

"Juliette! What are you...."?

He didn't get to finish that sentence. Behind Juliette were a distinguished older man, a stunning young woman, and a tall, elegant woman with short grey hair wearing a wrinkle-free white linen dress. Immediately, Riley knew this was Gabriel's family. They were all present and accounted for...except for the young woman with platinum blond straight hair matching her rail thin body.

When Juliette released Gabriel's neck, the young woman stepped up, threw her arms around Gabriel and embraced him. When she released him, she simply said, "We need to talk."

CHAPTER THIRTY-NINE

Gabriel

Gabriel looked from Cecily to his mother and father, and back to Juliette.

"What are you doing here with my family, Cecily?" He didn't raise his voice, but his cheeks went from tanned to crimson, and he fidgeted with the buttons on his shirt.

"Your father invited me. The two old gents have reached a deal and we have to work out the details." Cecily spoke as if she truly believed what she was saying.

Gabriel looked around the restaurant, searching for Riley. When their eyes finally met, hers shot daggers at him.

He pleaded with her as best he could with his eyes and mouthed, "I'm sorry."

Riley was stiff, her eyebrows furrowed with one hand firmly planted on her hip. She shook her head and responded. "You lied." She turned back towards Jonathan—she had her own fire to put out.

He gripped Cecily's arm and pulled her towards his parents. Juliette clung to his free arm.

"Bonjour, mère et père." Gabriel greeted his parents through clinched teeth. He felt a vein pulsating in his neck and was sure it would burst. Which would be appropriate because this was an emotional massacre, minus the blood.

They returned his greeting, while Cecily tried to squirm out of his grip.

"May we please retreat to my office?"

"Oui, oui," his mother responded for all.

They followed Gabriel to the office and he locked the door behind them.

"What the hell is going on? Why are you all here?" Gabriel noticed Cecily's left hand for the first time and his eyes widened. "And why in the hell is Cecily here wearing the family jewels?"

His questions poured out fast, blanketed in anger and confusion.

"We are to marry, no?" Cecily chimed in first. "Our families agreed. Why are you so angry? I thought that you had agreed."

Now Cecily looked confused, her gaze shuffling between Gabriel's father and his mother.

"Will someone tell me what's happening?" Cecily demanded.

Gabriel took a deep breath and decided to focus on his parents.

"Mère, pourquoi êtes-vous tous ici?"

His mother didn't answer, but pointed to his father. She instead pulled out a chair, took a seat and began flipping through a fashion magazine she pulled from her bag. His mother had mastered tuning out her father, and Gabriel was usually amused by it. But not today. He needed her help.

"Papa, please tell me why you're here."

Juliette still had her arm through his, and her presence was the best part of this surprise visit. Arm in arm, they were on the defense. She whispered, "I told you he was planning something."

With as few words as possible, his father explained the agreement with Cecily's family for the merger, and marriage was a condition. He made it clear that all had been forgiven and that he expected Gabriel to consent and fly back home with them to begin preparations for the business and the wedding.

"Papa, I mean no disrespect, but I am not marrying Cecily and therefore, there will be no merger with her family. I've given you a perfectly generous alternate offer that you've refused to consider. I am your son and I want to take over the family business. I really do. But on my terms. And definitely not like this."

He waited for his father to speak, who had taken the executive chair behind the desk — always a man in charge.

"Where is this other offer?"

"It's in my villa. And the owner of the company is here and ready to open negotiations. Please just hear him out, Papa. Give him a chance. Give me a chance. Trust me just this once." Gabriel's pleas were genuine, and this time was different. He was fighting for his family's legacy. Not running from it.

"Wait a moment," Cecily chimed in, turning her attention back to Gabriel. "You aren't on board with this marriage? This merger?"

Gabriel realized that she was also a victim of his father's delusions, and he felt genuinely sorry that she'd been dragged into this mess.

"No, Cecily. I told you before and I keep telling my father, I will not be forced into marriage so that he can merge with your father's company."

"But he said you had a change of heart. That you apologized for the Paris fiasco." She looked at Gabriel's father, who just tapped his fingers on the desk. She walked to the edge of the desk and leaned in. "Do you hear me? Did you lie to me? To my father?"

Gabriel knew this would not end well if he didn't intervene. "Wait, Cecily. Before you accuse my father of anything, you could have called me anytime to confirm—to talk it out since we would be most affected by this decision. But you chose to follow his lead—even after I told you and him it would never happen."

Cecily looked pleadingly at Gabriel now. "I did call you. More than once. But you never answered."

He had been avoiding calls from unfamiliar numbers and he rarely checked his cell phone.

"Okay. That's my fault," he conceded.

She looked at him with pleading eyes. "If there is no merger, then there is no marriage. And if there's no marriage, I'm cut off. I thought maybe you had reconsidered—for me. We do have history, Gabriel.

You once cared deeply for me."

Gabriel approached her. "Cecily. You are a beautiful woman and men will form lines down blocks of streets just to have one date with you. You don't want to marry me. You want your father's money."

A heavy silence sat in the room while Cecily considered Gabriel's last words.

Tears had begun to well in her eyes, and when the first one fell, she laughed out loud.

They all just stared at her as she turned and sat on the edge of Gabriel's desk.

"That's a terrible thing to say, Gabriel." She paused and pulled a handkerchief from her purse. "It's also a terrible truth."

"Yes, on both accounts. So, you just need to find a man that wants you and your father's money."

She slid the engagement ring off her finger and sat it gently on the desk.

"Don't blame a girl for dreaming. And you know we could have been happy. Would've been the hottest couple in Paris, just like college. And our children would have been cover models by the time they were out of diapers. I guess it's your loss."

"Sure," Gabriel conceded. "It's my loss."

He hugged her and she pushed him away. "Don't. You'll wrinkle me."

Now that was the Cecily he knew.

A tap at the door startled them all, and Gabriel opened it to find Victor standing on the other side.

"Everything good in here, mate?" he asked.

Cecily stepped up and slid Gabriel to the side. "No, everything is not good. Please save me from this life of disappointment and point me to several glasses of mimosas."

She slipped her arm through Victor's, he shrugged and away they went.

Gabriel sighed in relief, just slightly concerned for Victor.

"Let's get you all checked in. You do have reservations, don't you?"

"Of course we don't have reservations. This is your hotel. You'll find space for us," his father demanded, behaving more like the Viscount than a parent.

Gabriel shook his head and guided them out to the front desk.

He tried to keep his attention focused on getting his family settled, but thoughts of Riley forced themselves forward. She was definitely angry, and a small part of him thought that might be a good sign. An angry woman is at least a woman with feelings towards him. Being angry is typically prefaced by a source of joy.

He thought maybe there was still a chance for them.

CHAPTER FORTY

Riley

Riley was a ball of confusion. The fiancé she ran away from was standing in front of her accusing her of having an affair with her college friend, while her secret lover was in the arms of another woman with a diamond engagement ring that rivaled the Crown Jewels.

Riley watched the beautiful woman smile at him while he squirmed out of her embrace, and she remembered the holes in his story about his ex-girlfriend. This had to be her. There was no other explanation. And if she was right and they were engaged, had she just switched places with Issy? And could he really have another woman in his life, waiting for his return, while he was declaring feelings for her? It didn't seem plausible. But she had to believe with her eyes, not her heart, on this one.

Shit just got real.

But there was no time to get swept up in Gabriel or Jonathan's drama. She had plans for the day with her girlfriends, and men were not on the menu.

She turned to Jonathan. "We'll talk later. Maybe even tomorrow. Right now, I have plans with my friends. I suggest you get some plans of your own that do not involve me."

"Wait, what? Where are you going, and where am I supposed to stay?"

She laughed. "I know you did not fly half way around the world with no hotel reservations. Well, now you have plans. Go book yourself a room somewhere, anywhere, away from my villa. I'll reach out to you later. Waaaaay later."

She gestured for her friends to walk with her and they started towards the pier.

"Riley, you can't just leave me…"

She paused and gave him her left hand. "See this left hand? It is ring-free. You no longer dictate what I can and cannot do. I'm not leaving you, Jonathan. That would just be repetitive. I left you back in D.C. Now, please do yourself a favor and locate some overnight accommodations."

This time when she turned away, she didn't look back.

The five of them rushed to the shuttle bus that was scheduled to take them to begin their afternoon excursion. Riley had reserved a half-day, open-air four-wheel drive tour of the island to see more of the island and capture some really good photographs. Her outfit now matched her mood—complete disarray. The nerve of Jonathan to show up and accuse her, deflect from his deceitfulness, make a scene, embarrass and humiliate her—again.

Every breath she exhaled was weighted, heavy with shame and anger. Her insides were aflame and her head ached from the strain of toxic male bullshit. But she pressed on, mostly in silence. Her new friends seemed to understand that she needed some time to process.

But once they arrived and were settled in to the vehicle, she had calmed down and the questions and commentary rolled in. Her answers were as bumpy and precarious as the roads they were traveling. And they tried to bring some levity to the situation—though at moments totally misguided.

"Jonathan is fine," Isabella said. "Must have been hard to walk away. And so direct and masculine and muscular."

"Shush, Isabelle," Charlotte added. "Everything that glitters isn't gold. Or some such thing."

"Forget Jonathan," Paige joined the conversation. "Who was the super model slobbering all over Gabriel?"

"Yeah, Riley." Savannah said, her question filled with more concern than curiosity. "Who was she? Has he mentioned a fiancé to you?"

Riley should have known they also saw the damn ring. You could see the diamond from the moon. She tilted her head back, closed her eyes, and let the warm air wash across her face. These were all good questions, none of which she had answers for, which just made her frustrations mount.

The fumes from the vehicle caused her to cough—a short reprieve from their questions.

"I know this is all exciting and dramatic, but please remember it's my life."

"Oh, honey. Of course." Charlotte's voice was like sweet molasses, and Riley wanted to drown in it. "We're here for you, Riley. Nothing else. And if you don't want to talk about it, we can just enjoy these views, get some beautiful selfies to make the people back home thoroughly jealous, and block all this mess out."

"Exactly," Savannah agreed.

"Besides, my hair has been on its best behavior since I started using that Monoi oil, and I need all the pics I can stand," Isabella said, always finding a way to lighten the mood. "I hope you don't mind that I borrowed some of yours…and we're almost out."

Riley forced a smile and felt a little better. There was no space for misery in Isabella's presence. And knowing that she could just push the events of the morning away—even if just for an afternoon—lightened her load.

The driver of the open-sided SUV pulled over at various stops where they gazed out and over the famous Bora Bora turquoise lagoon. From the different lookouts — East Matira, Faanui Canon, and Amanahune Bay — it was a completely different experience from all the angles.

Stunning views over lush foliage that surrounded the deep blue ocean was like an out of body experience. They stopped by an open-air market where local artists crafted jewelry, painted and weaved tapestries, tie-dyed sarongs and made coconut oil. They skipped the war memorials—they saw enough of that on the news—and instead opted to stop at a local plantation that offered a tasting menu of tropical fruits and dessert wines. All throughout, their tour guide shared stories of Polynesian traditions, and they embraced a respect for the island that was more than just an admiration of its beauty, but was now saturated with a profound regard for the island's history and culture.

That night, they ordered dinner on Riley's deck, drank prosecco, and sat up talking all night. She wasn't in the mood for rehashing the morning events earlier in the day—she had needed some time to process. Between the impromptu photo shoots on their afternoon excursion, the welcoming spirit of the communities they visited and the pure beauty of the island, Riley was able to count her blessings and find an assurance that she would be okay.

She knew she had to face Jonathan, and she would the next day. And she was still in limbo about her job, but suspected she'd know her fate within hours. Those were the things she could control.

Savannah caught her deep in thought and sat next to her. After a few minutes, Savannah gulped what was left of her prosecco and sighed.

"I had a bad breakup and a miscarriage two years ago. I was devastated. I tried to keep my shit together, but failed miserably."

"Oh, Savannah. I'm so sorry."

"Thanks for saying that. But let me finish."

Riley nodded and squeezed Savannah's hand.

"When I started avoiding my family and friends and stopped doing the things that I loved, someone spoke power into me. My baby sister said, 'You need to see a therapist.' She left a business card on my kitchen table and it sat there for weeks. One night, when the pain was too much to bare, I opened another bottle of wine in the kitchen and lost control of the opener. The red wine spilled and cover the business card.

I grabbed it and rushed over to the sink to rinse it off. I saved that card and the next day made an appointment to save myself. I don't still have the card, but I have the wisdom."

Savannah faced Riley, her own agony at the edge of release, and said, "You need to see a therapist."

They sat quietly, and Riley knew Savannah was right. But she wasn't ready.   And as far as Gabriel was concerned, seemed his family—specifically his father—had chosen a fiancé for him. Riley had gotten to know Gabriel over the last week, and she doubted he would fill her head with fantasies for sport. And, she knew from recent experience that everything you see isn't always what it seems. She was blinded by the diamond and caught up in her emotions over Jonathan's abrupt arrival. Gabriel was just an easy target. But with a few hours and some distance between them, she knew she was just projecting on him.

But even if that's all true, his life is equally as messy as hers. And, he probably has a new job that will demand most, if not all, of his attention. He said he wanted to be with her, but there was really no space in his life for her. And she still had to recreate a life for herself.

Maybe ending it now was all for the best, she thought.

CHAPTER FORTY-ONE

Gabriel

The boat to the airport was leaving at 9 a.m. Gabriel, his sister Juliette, and Cecily walked Victor to the pier to board. Cecily and Victor had spent the day together yesterday and had dinner last night. They appeared quite fond of each other, which was alright with Gabriel.

As they hugged good-bye, Riley and her friends approached. They were also saying their good-byes, and Gabriel watched the care and comradery between the women. He was happy Riley had them by her side this weekend. Her life just seemed to continue in a downward spiral, despite his best efforts to be her port in the storm. But he heard her loud and clear Thursday night. She needed time and space to process, and that didn't include him.

He respected her choice, but it cut deep. He had spent nearly every night with her since she'd been on this island, and he missed her. The warmth from her body pressed against his. Her hair splayed across the pillow, scented with island oils. Her soft breathing and the stillness of her slumber. Their long talks and her infinite playlists—one for any and every mood. Her creative cocktails, and the way she listened. He recalled their first night together. She had tossed and turned along with uneven breathing and pure restlessness. But each night after, she eased into her sleep and he hoped that his presence had been a comfort to her.

Last night, Gabriel's sister had kept him up half the night, peppering him with questions about Riley. Her eagle eye had caught their eye contact at the restaurant and she knew he was keeping secrets. He gave her just enough information about his time with Riley for her to be hopeful, and she gave him advice on how to win her back. She had fallen asleep propped up on sofa pillows, her last words slipping out as gibberish. He covered her with a blanket and watched her sleep. He loved his sister, and she loved him without any conditions or pretense or judgement. She'd been so giddy about Riley, and he had to promise to make an introduction. She was a true fan. And that was truly scary.

Gabriel joined Riley and her friends, and wished them well on their journeys back to Papeete and ultimately home. He'd given them each his personal business card and invited them to look him up when they were next in Paris. Charlotte was practically salivating.

When the boat departed, Riley was left alone with Gabriel, Juliette, and Cecily. Gabriel formally introduced them and Juliette morphed into a fan girl.

"Hi, Riley St. James!" She was giddy with excitement. "I'm a huge fan. I watch you all the time. The stories you cover are always the best on the American channels."

"Wait—you're *Riley on the Run*?" A flicker of recognition formed in Cecily's eyes. "Oh, em, gee! Was that your fiancé, Jonathan, causing the stir yesterday? Did he catch you with your lover?"

Gabriel grabbed Cecily and pulled her away, hoping that Riley at least saw that she no longer was wearing the engagement ring. But he couldn't be sure.

Juliette hung back and she and Riley walked down the pier together. Gabriel glanced back at the two of them, and saw his future—and his little sister's dream come true.

When they arrived back at the hotel, Gabriel met Donovan in the lobby. His father had agreed to the meeting and was on his way.

Gabriel was distracted by Riley and Juliette, who found an open table at the hotel restaurant and proceeded to order breakfast. Thankfully Cecily had gone back to her villa and wouldn't be a cause for concern, at least not at the moment.

Gabriel, his father and Donovan were seated at a table indoors. They only ordered coffee and got right down to business.

Donovan took the lead and Gabriel was impressed. But he was watching his father and it appeared that he was equally as impressed. As Donovan spoke, his father studied the prospectus, injecting questions into Donovan's presentation. And Donovan was gracious, but assertive. It was a good deal and he knew it. Honestly, Gabriel knew that if his dad walked away from this deal, soon Donovan would be their biggest competitor and pose a serious threat.

Ninety minutes later and after several cups of coffee, they had reached an agreement. The three men shook on it, and Gabriel made plans to travel to Los Angeles to finalize the deal the following week. He was ready to celebrate. He looked over at Riley, who was smiling and laughing with his sister, and she was the only person he wanted to share his news with.

In that moment he remembered his college-roommate-turned-high-powered-broadcast-network-executive that had inquired about Riley's whereabouts. She hadn't mentioned speaking with anyone and guessed maybe that meant the offer fell through.

Opting to not disturb their girl time, he simply stopped their server and told her to charge the meal to his room.

He returned to his villa, called his company's chief of staff and offered his resignation.

He had turned the page on his old life, and hoped that meant he had more time and space for Riley. Whenever she was ready.

CHAPTER FORTY-TWO

Riley

Back in her villa, it was eerily quiet. She couldn't decide which playlist was better for the moment—Brown Liquor or Black Girl Magic. She went with the Black Girl Magic, and Sade's voice filled the space. She was tempted to fast forward to the next song, caught off guard by a pang of sadness at the thought of walking away from Gabriel. But she let it play instead, and thought of him as she dressed for dinner with Jonathan.

She had agreed to a public meal because she thought he'd remain calm and they could get some closure. While she dressed, she let her mind wander back over the nights she'd spent with Gabriel. Not just the way he made her feel physically—which was definitely among the most memorable moments of her trip—but it was how he made her feel as a woman, as a person.

Sharing breakfast with Gabriel's sister had been enlightening. She was a smart, intuitive and delightful young woman with a bright future ahead of her. She was a business and marketing major with plans to take over their family business and launch an empire with a solid commitment to corporate social responsibility. Riley knew those were big dreams—but she was impressed and believed she could do it. But it was her fondness for Gabriel that was most striking. She admired and trusted him, and said she knew him better than anyone else. When she told Riley that she could tell that her brother was crushing on her, Riley was stunned. But she didn't deny that the feeling was mutual. Juliette didn't press Riley for details, because—wait for it—she didn't want to invade her brother's privacy. Plus, she knew he'd eventually spill the full truth, and that was always better than her playing a guessing game.

Lost in her thoughts, her phone vibrating on her nightstand startled her. She answered and it was Octavia. She broke the news in her no-nonsense way—which was a blessing and a curse. The network had bought her out of her contract, and Octavia had protected Jeremy's job, if he still wanted it. She arranged a time for them to meet in New York on Monday following her return, and just like that, she was unceremoniously unemployed.

But not unemployable, she reminded herself. She was a damn good journalist and she'd land on her feet. But she would decide where and with who. She had endured more disappointments and upheaval in the past ten days than she had over the last ten years—and she was two parts exhausted, but one part exhilarated. She stood in the open sliding glass door of her villa, looked out over the opulent waters and cried. She released a tsunami of tears, grieving all that she'd lost and cleansing her heart for all that was to come. It was just a first step, but most necessary.

Beyonce's *Who Run The World* was next in rotation. And it was just the reminder she needed of who she was and what she had proven she was capable of in an industry dominated by men. She had not lost her job. The job had lost her.

She met Jonathan at the restaurant, where he was already seated. He stood when she arrived at the table and pulled out her chair for her. He was a gentleman...especially when people were watching.

Seeing him in this space that she had claimed as her own was surreal. She was still angry with him—for Issy, for ruining their wedding, for his misleading narrative on social media, for making a scene at the restaurant. It felt like she was having dinner with a stranger. And she had changed so much, reconciled so much with herself during this trip, that she guessed she would also feel like a stranger to him.

He had ordered champagne—her favorite—but she asked for sparkling water with lime, feigning remnants of a hangover. She didn't want alcohol dulling her senses. He had also taken the liberty to order appetizers, but at least gave her the option of selecting her entree. She couldn't believe that she actually thought that him taking these liberties was an indication of care. It was just more of his need to control her. But she let it go because tonight would be his last opportunity, so she hoped he enjoyed it.

As they began snacking on their appetizers, Jonathan spoke first.

"Riley, I'm sorry. And not just about Issy, but about showing up here and lashing out like a wounded animal. Please forgive me."

Riley had bit into a shrimp and took her sweet time chewing before responding.

"And what about your statement on social media? Are you sorry for that, too? For accusing me of leaving you for Donovan?"

He cleared his throat and sat up straighter in his chair.

"Yes. I'm sorry for that as well. But I was angry, and you two did look very close. He always had a crush on you. You were the only person that couldn't see it."

This time she chuckled.

"Are you listening to yourself, Jonathan? We were kids in college. Even if that were true, we are grown ass people with full lives. Donovan has a girlfriend that he plans to propose to when he's back home, and he was only here trying to convince one of the hotel's executives to join his company. It was a complete coincidence. But you couldn't be bothered to try to learn the truth…"

He stopped her. "That's not fair, Riley. I called you and texted you multiple times every day. You refused to respond, so I lashed out. I'm sorry. But don't blame it all on me. You pulled the disappearing bride act—I just responded."

"I apologize for not responding. But I don't apologize for leaving. You hurt me. The damage you did to me, to our relationship, is irreparable. And your behavior afterwards reprehensible. Because of you and your self-righteous statement on social media, I've lost my job." She leaned back in her chair, arms folded across her chest with the red-hot heat of anger rising up her neck and across her face. "So, I hope you're happy."

"Baby, don't worry about that. I've always told you, you don't have to work. I can take care of us."

She tapped her fork against the plate and then lowered it back down. She lifted her napkin from her lap and wiped her mouth, signaling the end of the meal and the conversation.

"Baby? Don't worry?" she mocked him. "This is not a scene from *Love Jones*, Jonathan. *I don't have to work? You'll take care of us?* When have I ever given you the impression that I didn't want to work and wanted to be taken care of? Do you even know me, Jonathan? Seriously. Do you? Or even better, do you even like me?"

He took a big gulp of champagne and small beads of sweat began forming across his neat shape up.

She knew he was nervous. "Choose your next words wisely, Jonathan. You're on thin ice."

"Of course I know you, Riley. I've loved you since college. I know you don't want to be taken care of, that you love your career. I just meant that I can take care of you until you find a new job. That's what I meant."

Riley laid her napkin across the plate.

"Jonathan, I appreciate that you want to take care of me. But I know that's code for control me. I'm not interested. I just wanted to give us both a chance to get some closure on this relationship. We are not getting back together. I love you, but I'm not in love with you. And I forgave you the moment I walked away from you more than a week ago. I did that for me. And Jonathan, don't confuse forgiveness with forgetfulness. I will never forget how you treated me and our relationship. But I'm not angry, I don't need revenge, and I'm not looking for your sympathy. All I want from you is a promise to be respectful of me and my profession in public, to keep my name out your mouth, and to not be present when I return to D.C. to collect my things from your house."

Jonathan wiped his forehead with his napkin, his hopes for reconciliation absorbed into a piece of cloth.

"Can you do that, Jonathan? For the woman you proclaim to love?"

He bowed his head and took in a long, deep breath. When he lifted his head again, his beautiful grey eyes were misty, revealing the storm brewing inside him.

"Yes, my love. I can do that. For you, I'll do that."

Riley stood, pushed her chair back and thanked him for the meal. As she prepared to walk away, she paused, bent down, kissed Jonathan's forehead and whispered, "I did love you, the best way I knew how."

She took two steps forward and heard Jonathan's chair scrape the floor. She looked back and he asked, "Can I walk you back to your villa? Not because I expect anything else from you, but just because I don't want you to walk back alone."

She smiled and said, "Sure, man."

As they departed the restaurant, they walked through the lobby and ran into Gabriel, who was toting a small box. She nodded in his direction, but didn't stop, didn't slow her pace. It pained her to see him, and she glanced over her shoulder to catch what might be one last look at the man—against her best judgement—she had fallen for on the other side of the world.

He just stood still, watching her walk away with Jonathan.

CHAPTER FORTY-THREE

Gabriel Riley

Two days later, Gabriel landed in Los Angeles and checked in to one of Donovan's hotels. He was immediately impressed by the decor, the personalized service, the amenities and the vibe. The target market is diverse and the potential for global growth is massive. Duplicating the small footprint, the feature that's become the company's gold standard, across Europe will be easy—finding the right properties and playing the long game will be the challenge. Gabriel followed the hotel and hospitality trends and would protect the company from mere transactional pursuits. They would build an empire of boutique hotels fit for royalty and celebrities, business travelers and honeymooners, the party crowd and the Netflix-and-chill crowd. They would have something for all tastes and price points.

He got settled in, then met Donovan at their corporate headquarters and was immediately invited into a conference room with a celebratory spread complete with the very best French champagne. When they were done with the business of the morning, they spent some time just catching up and replaying the events of the last few days in Bora Bora.

Hesitant, Gabriel asked about Riley and Jonathan.

"I honestly don't know for sure what happened between them once he arrived on the island. But social media has been quiet, and I've left her messages but she hasn't called back yet. She texted to say she'd be in New York for a day meeting with her attorney and then back to D.C. The network bought her out of her contract, so she's back to square one. But she'll land on her feet."

Gabriel was quiet and contemplative. He wanted to know if she was okay—even if that meant she was back with Jonathan. He saw them leaving the restaurant together and they looked friendly, maybe even reconciled. And he wanted to know what happened with Jefferson's offer. He hadn't followed up with him, but it seemed legitimate.

When Gabriel didn't say anything, Donovan continued to fill the void. "I've known her a long time. She's a perfectionist at heart, but that's just because she believes in real happy endings—and she believes you have to work for it. That perfectionism can also be her enemy, but she means well."

"Yeah. You definitely know her," Gabriel tried to lighten the moment. "Really, I just want her to be happy. I'd be lying if I didn't admit that I want to be the man to make her happy, but I'll be okay as long as I know she's good."

"Okay, Frenchman!" Donovan joked. "I told her you had to earn your invite to the cookout, but you'll never get it without her. So, I suggest you figure out how to get your woman back because we're having a bunch of cookouts this summer."

Gabriel's expression was a mix of confusion and contentment. "What's a cookout? And why do I need an invitation? Who's hosting? Is it Riley's friends and that's why I need her to secure an invite?"

Donovan was literally laughing out loud. "I'll explain all of that later. Let's finish our business and we can strategize about #ReturnToRiley."

It was Gabriel's turn to laugh. "Please. No more hashtags!"

Riley checked out of her New York City hotel and headed straight to Octavia's office. When she arrived, she was ushered into a conference room with contemporary furnishings, a flat screen monitor, floor to ceiling windows and the smell of old money, coffee and pastries. Octavia joined her minutes later in a sassy cream pant suit with matching silk blouse and nude Jimmy Choo pumps owning the room. Her signature YSL perfume lingered and Riley was fairly certain she caught a whiff of coconut oil—probably in her hair.

Always efficient with immaculate attention to detail, Octavia had the documents prepared and Riley began signing. She felt like she was giving an ounce of blood with every signature.

When all the pages were signed, Octavia put them in their relevant folders and then slid another folder in front of Riley.

"What's this?"

"It's an offer?"

"What kind of offer?"

"An offer from an international broadcast network. I followed up with Jefferson Saxton, the executive producer that contacted your friend in Tahiti. He's a powerful man and the network is solid. I had my paralegal compile a dossier; it's included in the package. And, I can't believe I'm saying this, but it's impressive. Jefferson is impressive and wealthy and well-respected in the European market."

"Is this a joke, Octavia. I'm really not in the mood," Riley said matter of factly, exhausted from the internal lashing she was taking after signing away her livelihood.

"Do I joke when it comes to handling business, Riley St. James?"

This was true. Octavia Gray did not play games and she did not waste words.

Riley opened the folder and began reading. "Why didn't you mention this before today? With everything else that's been happening, I forgot about this. About him."

"We've had some back and forth and I wanted to be sure it was a good deal for you before presenting it. If it didn't work out, I just would have told you I made contact and it wasn't a good fit. But I did the hard work and you can see the high-level points of the offer on the cover page. I'll give you some time to read through the documents and will return to answer any questions."

"But how is this possible?" Riley really didn't understand how this could happen without her knowledge.

"When I made contact, I suggested he also reach out to you, to officially share his interest with you. He said he left you a message. When you didn't return his call, he assumed it was because you were on holiday, so he circled back to me."

"But, how…"

"Someone name Gabriel Laurent confirmed you were on holiday. Said he was his college roommate or something like that."

Riley smiled and opened the folder. She couldn't think about Gabriel—not yet. She needed to review this offer to see if it was legit. And more importantly, if it met her standards. She had played by all the rules, even when the rules and the goal posts kept changing. Now, she would make her own rules.

As she read, she smiled at her good fortune. Having Octavia on her team—someone who really understood her—was the reason she had a deal worthy of her experience and aligned to her professional vision.

They were offering her a one-hour syndicated program, anchored to her name and with a producer credit. The offer also included two to four special series annually with topics of her choosing, a three-book deal, a flat in the city, sizable stock options and her choice of a new board member. She couldn't have asked for more.

Well, she did have two counter offers: she wanted an executive producer credit and she wanted to bring Jeremy with her as her producer.

When Octavia returned, Riley asked a few questions, added in her changes and instructed Octavia to send in the counter offer and schedule a call. Expecting a response in a couple days, they sat and chatted over coffee while Riley shared all the drama of her trip.

As she sipped her coffee, she felt her stomach rumble slightly and then again with a little more force. Suddenly, the contents of her stomach felt like they were forcing their way up through her throat, and she excused herself to the lady's room.

She made it just in time. She vomited up everything she had eaten in the last 24 hours. It felt like a toxic blend of nerves and the remnants of all the anguish lurking in her conscious and gripping her emotions. Better out than in.

When she returned, Octavia asked if she was okay and gave her a hot cup of mint tea to settle her stomach. As she sipped, Octavia's assistant poked her head in and said you have an email response.

"Already? Are you sure?"

The assistant handed her an envelope and inside the cover page was signed. They had accepted Riley's new terms and they had scheduled a call for the next day. They had offered to talk that afternoon, but Riley wanted time to think about her questions and to review the package one last time.

"So, I have a new job?"

"Seems so, my dear. Once you add your signature to the offer."

They both looked down at the document and back up at each other and giggled like school girls.

As Riley continued shuffling through the pages, Octavia took advantage of the silence.

"Riley, you know I'll always look out for you and your career, right?"

She had Riley's attention. This was her homegirl tone—not her 'kicking ass' attorney voice.

"Of course. You know I trust you implicitly."

"Well, this is me looking out for you."

Octavia slid a business card across the table.

"This is the contact information for my therapist. Whenever you're ready."

Riley took the card, looked at it and slid it in her purse.

"Thanks, Sis. It's been a tough few weeks and I really needed to hear that and now I have someone I can pour all this penned up anguish and frustration on."

"I'll warn her," Octavia joked.

"Nah. Let me surprise her."

They both laughed. Two women owning their livelihoods and their lives.

CHAPTER FORTY-FOUR

Riley

Gabriel

One Year Later

Riley had finally checked out of her hotel and officially moved in to her flat. Though she'd been living in Paris for more than six months now, it had taken some time for the renovations and to finally move her furniture into her new home. Her new network had included a flat in her contract, but she renegotiated for the cash equivalent of the rental matching the length of her contract and used it towards purchasing a flat. She needed to own something—and the tax write-off certainly helped.

While in transition, she stayed at the very posh Élite Paris—in a suite fit for royalty. A spectacular view of Palais Garnier. Culinary treats that kept her in their fitness center daily. And an upscale vibe with charming hospitality. Whenever she walked through the lobby, she glanced around, half expecting and half hoping to catch a glimpse of the man she left behind. But she knew that was as much of a fantasy as the time they'd spent in Bora Bora. He had left this company and was now working with Donovan. According to Donovan, it was going well. That made her happy, but it was a bittersweet ending for them both.

The hotel's five-star treatment was second only to the welcome from her new network. Their plans for her brand—she never imagined she'd be referring to *her brand*—met and exceeded her expectations. And she had full creative control. Her transition was eased by the arrival of her faithful producer, Jeremy—comfort in the familiar. He was worried about the language barriers, which now made her laugh. He had adapted to his new city and was out nearly every evening with his colleagues at some lounge or restaurant or cafe or artistic opening.

She had managed to find a flat not too far from her mother—the closest she's lived to her since she was a girl. The proximity gave them some much-needed time to reconnect and work through their issues. Getting her mother to admit that they had unresolved issues was half the battle. But when she released her resentments and just listened, she understood and found she had more in common with her mother than she wanted to admit. They both had run away from situations that were repressive just to find themselves. It had hurt Riley as a child. But as a woman, she sympathized with her mother and forgave her.

Strangely enough, her mother was spending more time back in the states, being courted by her ex-husband. They called it dating, and it still made her nervous. They seemed genuinely happy and a small part of Riley was grateful that they were the silver lining in her hashtag-trending breakup.

Her routine now included an early afternoon walk along the River Seine—when she could make the time. A couple weeks ago, she had noticed trees blossoming along its edges and was reminded of her home in Washington, D.C. When she ventured closer to capture a few selfies to send to her sorority sisters, she saw a cherry blossom tree in the distance. She changed course to be certain and it was like finding a piece of herself. When she told her mother, she had called it fate. Her dad said it was a connector and all the evidence she needed to know she hadn't lost as much as she thought she had. He also promised to visit before the blossoms disappeared—he was scheduled to arrive next week with her mother. His first visit ever to The City of Love.

Riley found a perfect spot beneath a cherry blossom tree with limbs and blooming florals that bent and stretched, licking the grass and providing ample shade. The sun sat high and bright today, slipping through the branches while small clusters of people passed by walking or on bikes. It was more like summer than spring. She laid out her blanket and popped open her container, releasing the sweet scents of Nutella blanketed inside a warm crepe, drizzled with thin streams of dark chocolate. She rushed to get her first forkful when she heard her name.

Assuming she'd been spotted, she tensed but remembered to plaster on a smile as to not get caught in an unflattering position if someone snapped a photo.

"Mademoiselle St. James."

She turned slowly towards the sound of the voice as the familiarity of the accent began to register. Heart pounding, tummy butterflies fluttering, she was desperate to believe it was really him.

In dark blue jeans, a black t-shirt and thin black bomber jacket, Gabriel Laurent was in Paris, walking in her direction. She quickly stood to her feet and smiled, hoping he could see just how happy she was to see him again.

Gabriel picked up his pace and she put one impatient hand on her hip. When he was right in front of her, time stood still and she threw her arms around his neck, kissing him deeply. When their lips touched, all her nerves stood on edge. And as his tongue found hers, she was desperate to taste every part of him. When they finally pulled back, they both laughed.

"What are you doing here? However did you find me?"

"One word. Donovan."

"I'm not surprised. He's been updating me in small doses and I've been quietly excited that my two favorite men—who aren't my father—

are working together."

"I've never been happier. I'm leading our international offices right here in Paris, but I've been splitting my time between Europe and Los Angeles this first year. And my father has stepped back, as he promised he would."

"I'm so happy for you, Gabriel. You deserve it."

He squeezed both her hands and his eyes softened. He was a man on a mission. "Can we sit?"

"Of course. I'm so sorry. Yes, please join me."

"First, I want to congratulate you on your new show and this big move. I knew you were fierce and a force to be reckoned with, but I was surprised to hear that you were leaving the states to live in Paris."

"Thanks, Gabriel. But you know I have you to thank for this win fall."

"I didn't do much," Gabriel said, not wanting to accept credit for her success.

"I give credit where it's due. You were the spark that lit the flame. You gave Jefferson just enough information and they made me an offer. Once they accepted the terms of my counter-offer, it was a done deal. I left for Europe the following month, shuffling back to the states when needed to wrap up my personal matters."

Gabriel didn't want to push, but he was curious about how things had worked out with Jonathan. Donovan told him that they'd both moved on, but with little details.

"How did you leave things with Jonathan?" That seemed the easiest way to ask.

"Well, now that I've been in therapy for nearly a year, I've not only forgiven Jonathan, but I've asked him to forgive me as well."

"Forgive you? For what?"

She bowed her head slightly and laughed, tracing tiny circles on her thigh. It immediately transported him back to Bora Bora.

"I hadn't been honest with him because I wasn't honest with myself. I should have never agreed to marry him. Hell, I should not have moved in with him. Yes, he betrayed my trust, but I betrayed myself. So, I think we're even."

"Wow," Gabriel whispered. "I didn't expect that."

This time she looked directly at him. "It really shouldn't surprise you. I was at least honest with you when we last spoke. I wasn't whole and you—*we* deserved better."

They sat quiet and motionless, her use of the term *we* lingering between them. She worried he had missed the inflection. He worried that it was a slip of the tongue.

Riley's stared out across the river, head tilted away from him. He reached out and touched her cheek, guiding her gaze towards him.

She smiled, tentatively.

"What about now? Is there a chance for us?"

Her smile grew and her eyes sparkled.

"If you'll have me. I'm not perfect..."

He stopped her. "I'm not looking for perfect, Riley. Just perfect moments with a woman that is her whole self. That's more than enough."

"I just want you to be sure. This therapy thing is real and I believe I'll need my sessions for at least another year."

"Therapy doesn't scare me, Riley. Do whatever you need for you. That's all I've ever wanted for you. But what does scare me is the thought of walking away from you—again. I wanted you from the first moment I laid eyes on you—even though it scared the hell out of me."

He paused, tucked a stray curl behind her ear and leaned in to kiss her, breathing his next words into her. "I still want you."

This time when they kissed, it was a new kind of kiss. Same soft lips and the sweet taste of him, but the melding of their breath was different. The remnants of pretense and anxiety and apprehension slipped away, and she willingly lost herself in him. All the loneliness, the grief, and worry came tumbling down—the barriers between them disappeared.

When he finally pulled back, a beguiling smile and a self-assured grip on her, she was flustered. She had never been flustered.

Gabriel looked pleased.

"Well, that was different," she said, breathless and flushed.

"Good," he said. "Everything from this moment forward should be different. So why don't we finish this cold, but still delicious, crepe. And then maybe you can show me your new flat."

"How do you know I have a new flat?"

"One word…"

She completed the sentence. "Donovan."

They both laughed and talked until sunset.

When they crossed the threshold of her new rooftop flat, Gabriel surrendered his control and lifted Riley off her feet.

"Which way to the bedroom?"

She laughed and pointed to the right. "Still more neanderthal than French."

For the few seconds he was at the entry of the place she now called home, he admired the furnishings, her warm and elegant decor, but mostly her spectacular views. The sun had set and from her floor to ceiling windows on the west wall, the Eiffel Tower sparkled in the distance. A fairly large stone patio was just beyond the windows and he realized they were doors, not windows, and was instantly transported back to the nights they spent alone in Bora Bora.

When they entered her room, a king-sized bed faced the floor-to-ceiling window with another picturesque view. The soft cream bed linens were turned down on a four-poster bed, and sheer golden panels on both sides of the bed hung loose, creating a cloak of pure luxury. He pushed one panel to the side and laid her gently down on her back.

Her cashmere sweater was open and the thin shirt beneath clung to her breast. When she reached to begin unbuttoning her jeans, he stopped her.

He slowly began pealing the layers of clothing from her skin until she was fully nude, never taking his eyes off of her. He expected her to move to cover her delicate parts, but she didn't. She held his gaze and then said, "you next."

Through their long absence, he had dreamed of her voice, her eyes, her scent, her presence—hypnotic and sensual—but even his dreams couldn't contain how she looked against this dark and endless night.

He undressed, quick and purposeful.

Her eyes lingered on him, ravenous and appreciative. But she didn't speak and she didn't move. He was uncertain, but eager to be near her again. He took his time.

"May I kiss you?"

"Oui, Monsieur," her voice quivered in response as she raised her arms above her head.

"I see you still don't play fair," he said, his eyes coveting the places his hands were desperate to touch.

She propped herself up just slightly and sliding one knee up in the same motion, "I didn't know we were playing. Am I winning?"

Her bent leg drifted off to the side, exposing her and the immediate object of his desires.

A crooked smile spread across his face. "For now," he said.

He stepped forward and she reached out an arm to prevent him from getting closer.

"Do you want to wait?" He wanted her, was desperate for her. But he didn't want to rush her.

"No. But there's one thing missing."

His eyebrows furrowed in confusion. From his vantage point, they had all they needed.

She slid to the edge of the bed and grabbed a remote control from her nightstand. With a few taps, the sultry and forlorn melodies of Miles Davis flooded the space. Riley leaned back and their eyes locked, two people shrouded in a moment a year in the making.

Riley's hair was splayed out around her and she took one deep swallow—digesting the choice they were making together. "May I kiss you anywhere I like?" He fought back nervousness and the declarations he wanted to make, forcing himself to just be present.

"You may kiss me anywhere you like if, and only if, I can do the same with you."

"I am here to please you, and if it pleases you to kiss me whenever and wherever you like, your wish is my command."

Satisfied with his response she sat up, her head now level to his abdomen. His muscles flexed when her tongue made contact with his skin. She parted her lips and gently kissed across his stomach, the heat from her breath weakening him and his resolve to be patient. She alternated between licking and sucking the contours of his muscles, easing her hand up and around to his cock. She stroked him, rhythms synced to her tongue and the moans escaping between breaths. His head fell back, thrusting his hips forward and burying his hand in her tangle of curls.

Riley responded with her mouth, wet and ready to receive him. She teased the tip with moist kisses and a searching tongue before having him fully. He gasped as she accepted him fully and slid him in and out, her motions switching from slow and torturous to quick and vigorous. Unable to hold his composure, he cupped her head with both hands and guided her movements, watching her, bewitched by her, lost in her.

He was so close to exploding, but he held back. He slowly pulled her face away and she looked up at him with insatiable eyes.

He saw in her all the passion and intensity that she had bottled up and kept secret. Tonight, he would give her the freedom to explore and he would give himself to her physically. But this time would be different. He wanted to slow down and explore every inch of her.

When Riley laid back, Gabriel knelt down on one knee and took her left foot in his hand, first massaging his fingers against her arch, planting a succession of soft kisses from the top of her foot and over her ankle.

Stretching out her leg, his kisses lingered as he climbed the front of her leg. Tilting his head, his tongue tickled the delicate skin behind her knee and her body arched in response, desperate for him to continue his travel north.

He paused, the intensity of his tongue against her skin heating him from the inside out. He was in a duel with his body, determined to take his time and savor these moments. Gazing over the length of her outstretched body, he fought back the instinct to press his body against hers and find that connection they both craved, and instead moved over to her right leg and released a warm, slow breath against her inner thigh. He watched with a triumphant desire as her eyelashes fluttered and closed while her body tensed and released, relishing the sensation of his tongue against her skin. There was no pretense between them. The air was thick with yearning, their senses synced in anticipation.

In every new place he touched and kissed and teased, her hips swayed and lifted, inviting him in and demanding his attention. He listened as her breath caught and stood to spread both her legs, slowly gliding his hands up her body and then back down again, denying her as she tentatively began to thrust her hips, guiding his hands towards her warm, wet center.

His resolve was fading fast, matching his ragged breaths and his rapidly hardening manhood.

Slowly, she spread her legs, her moans growing louder.

"Slide back," he instructed her, and she obeyed.

Now spread out in full view of him on the bed, he knelt beside her and began kissing and licking the inside of her thighs, while she squirmed and moaned.

"I want you, Gabriel," she said, voice laced with pleading desire.

He was making his way up her right thigh, but this time didn't switch to the left side. He kept going until his lips met her sweet spot and she gasped.

When he was done, he continued up to her naval, kissing around her diamond navel ring and teasing her with his tongue. He continued the climb until he found her lips.

She grabbed him by his hair and pressed her mouth against his, devouring him.

He pulled back, reached for a condom and slid it on. Watching through ravenous eyes, Riley wrapped her warm thighs around his waist, rising just slightly off the bed to guide him inside.

This time, he went slow, figuring out what she liked most and giving those things to her over and over again. She whispered his name between moans and sighs, and he had to fight to control himself.

When he felt her body begin to shiver beneath him, he moved faster and more deliberate. He wanted to feel and watch her release, give in to pleasure and ecstasy. Just as he felt her right on the edge, he gave in and they melted into each other.

After several seconds, he slid off of her.

Both laying on their backs and breathing like they'd just run a marathon, she spoke first.

"So, is it too soon to ask you to spend the night?"

Turning his head towards her he said, "On one condition. And I would like this conversation on the record."

"Name it and I'll be sure to quote you."

"Riley St. James, it would be my pleasure to spend the night with you if we can have breakfast…together…in public…tomorrow morning."

Riley was quiet, then leaned over on her side, head propped up on her arm.

"What if someone recognizes me and takes a photo or video," she said through a smile.

"Not worried at all about any of that," he replied, leaning on his side to face her.

"Really? We might become a hashtag," she teased.

"Or, I might have to rescue you again," he quipped.

"Well, that would be in order. You started out stalking me again today, so I am due for another rescue. So, I guess you have a deal, Monsieur Laurent."

He shook his head. "I'll be your stalker and protector any day.

Gladly."

She reached in for a kiss and whispered, "Perfect."

Riley was ready. She had stopped seeking perfection, and only sought perfect moments—like this one, wrapped in the arms of the man of the dreams she never knew she had, in a city that nurtured him and welcomed her, following her calling and not another job, and secure enough to really fall in love. This was enough…and she was enough.

The End

Acknowledgments

Writing a romance novel in the midst of a pandemic! Mind blown! This novel—the inspiration for it and the motivation to see it through—was a true labor of love and I have so many people to thank who've helped along the way.

First and foremost, I have to thank the women who breathe life into the romance genre, sprinkle gems of wisdom, and leave footprints for aspiring authors joining the community. For every phone call, email, conference connection, webinar invite, recommendation, Facebook group chat and invitations to share my work—mere words cannot express my gratitude. Without you, I may have never known what was possible.

To the women of color in newsrooms all across America—the storytellers of our lives in living color—thank you for showing up and sometimes having to show out, keeping the faith, honoring those who came before you and preparing the way for those on the rise, risking it all, bringing your full authentic selves to the table, and for building tables when you can't get a seat at the tables that are too small for your talent and ambition. We see you.

Rhonda Merwath—you were the first pair of eyes on Riley's story, and your feedback was priceless. Thanks for pushing me to broaden the story and take some chances, for cheering when I got it right, and showing me the places that weren't serving the story. You are a treasure.

To Christine and Nicole, my beta babes—you helped me see the forest beyond trees. For your encouragement, enthusiasm and feedback, I can't thank you enough.

A huge hug of gratitude to the Alexandria Women of Color Writing Group for reading my early drafts, giving me feedback, and being a part of this journey. Having you all on my side means the world to me.

To my visual team—Jacqueline Bisset, the illustrator who bought my vision of Riley and her entanglements to life; Jennifer Stimson, for making the inside as lovely as the outside; and the sister duo at Najla Qamber Designs—Nada and Najla—for a gorgeous book cover design. If in fact a book is judged by its cover, then we have a winner!

To my sisters—birth, sorority and friends—thank you for being my unofficial focus group. You are the squad I always want on my side.

And to all my family and friends from across my life, my career, my education and all the spaces in between, thank you for taking a chance on me, cheering me on, letting me drone on for hours about writing, and filling me with coffee, wine, and fellowship. Eternally grateful for you all.

To my hubby and my stepdaughter, I know it's corny, but you are the wind beneath my wings. Thank you for your patience and for always finding me when I got lost in this world of my imagination. Your love and support are everything to me.

You, Raymond, keep showing me this is how love is supposed to be.

Connect with Leila

On Facebook, join my Lovestruck Lounge reader group
for updates, fun and insider scoop:
https://bit.ly/LeilaLoveFBGroup

Get the *Entangled* playlist on Tidal or Spotify!

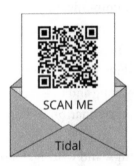

Get a free 60-day Tidal subscription
https://bit.ly/3bUaRqL

Never miss sales, new releases, freebies and exclusive content
when you join my mailing list:
https://www.leilalovebooks.com/newsletter

Facebook: Leila Love
Instagram: @LeilaLoveWrites
Twitter: @LeilaLoveWrites
Goodreads: Author Leila Love
Follow on Amazon
#weareinthislovetogether

About the Author

LEILA LOVE weaves "happily ever afters" featuring women that exist in unexpected spaces and courageously conquering unexpected odds authentically and unapologetically. The heroes of her stories worship, respect and cherish these women who challenge and capture their hearts.

With an award-winning career in communications and magazine publishing credentials, she was lured into creative writing through children's literature, earning an MFA in writing from the Vermont College of Fine Arts. But during a year-long lockdown and nothing but time to explore the possibilities of her writing and to design the creative life she always imagined, she joined a webinar on indie publishing romance novels and the rest is history.

Today, Leila juggles family, friendships, and writing. She combines her love of all things romance with her storytelling spirit to sprinkle a little sweet and spice into the lives of other hopeless romantics.

Entangled is her debut novel and is first in the *In Paradise* Series.

Readers Guide

DISCUSSION QUESTIONS

1. Riley is rebounding, Gabriel is rebelling, and they both know the other is off limits (but that doesn't stop them). What are your feelings about forbidden romantic relationships between two consenting adults?

2. What are your thoughts about Gabriel's friend and colleague, Victor? Is his advice about Gabriel's pursuit of Riley solid and in Gabriel's best interests? Or are men more conditioned to put career above all else?

3. Riley is a woman of color and a high-profile broadcast journalist whose career is easily threatened by a personal setback. What other successful women of color have you seen in the news or on social media in a personal crisis, and where are they now? Were they held to a different standard than men in similar situations?

4. In *Entangled*, Riley is surrounded by men who are successful, financially secure, and in positions of power. She is also successful and financially secure, but the reach of her power is limited. How do you think women in predominantly male industries can continue to put cracks in the glass ceiling?

5. Both Riley and Gabriel are haunted by their college relationships. Is this a universal circumstance or are some people more susceptible to their past associations? And if so, why?

6. Riley catches her fiancé with another woman on the eve of their wedding and chooses to run away. How do you think you would react in the same situation? How do you think Jonathan would have reacted if the roles were reversed?

7. Gabriel and Riley have lunch off the hotel property and she's introduced to authentic Tahitian cuisine. When you travel to other countries, do you immerse yourself in the culture or do you play it safe?

8. Gabriel's father is old school, and his interference in his son's personal life is decidedly European and borderline insane. Or is it? What are some of the cultural norms in America that people from other countries might consider ridiculous?

9. When Riley's misfortune becomes internet fodder and leads to a trending #RileyOnTheRun hashtag and a viral video taken out of context, her career is instantly at-risk. What are your thoughts about social media and its impact on public figures? Should some issues be off-limits or is it all fair game?

10. Riley meets a group of four women on holiday in Tahiti. What did you like most about her new friends? Who was your favorite character and why?